MW01115750

INFLAMED IN HIS LOVE

TAY MO'NAE

STAY UP TO DATE WITH TAY MO'NAE

Want to stay up to date with my work? Be the first to get sneak peeks, release dates, cover reveals, character updates, and more?
Join my Facebook reading group: <u>Tay's Book Baes</u>, and like my like page: Tay Mo'Nae.
Make sure you check my website out for updates as well:
Taymonaewrites.com
Also, join my **mailing list** for exclusive firsts by texting **AuthorTay** to **33777**

© 2024
Published by Tay Mo'Nae Presents
All rights reserved.
No part of this book may be used or reproduced in any form or by any means, electronic
or print, including photocopying, recording, or by information storage retrieval system,
without the written permission from the publisher or writer, except for brief quotes used
in reviews.
This is a work of fiction. Names, characters, businesses, places, events, and incidents are
either the products of the author's imagination or used in a fictitious manner. Any
resemblance to actual persons, living or dead, or events is purely coincidental.
Unauthorized reproduction in any manner is prohibited.

CHAPTER 1

TRIPP CLARK

"Fuck that was a tough one," Leo commented as we pulled into the firehouse.

"Hell yeah. It's been a minute since we had a fire that big." Harlem took his helmet off and ran his hand down his face.

A yawn escaped my mouth, and I rubbed my eyes. I had been at work for the last twenty four hours and couldn't wait to have the next two days off.

Climbing out the truck, I rubbed my eyes again and rolled my neck between my shoulders. All I wanted to do was shower and head home.

"You all did great work tonight. That fire was larger than we expected, but we got everyone out. Good job!" Omiras, our captain, commented.

We had got a call for a warehouse close to The Shore being on fire. Turns out some kids were playing with fireworks and things got out of hand.

"Yeah, I bet they won't do no dumb shit like that again," Journi, one of the EMS's in the house, commented.

"I'm sure he lost a finger, so I hope not," Royce, her partner, mentioned.

"Ay, TJ, we're going for some drinks at Victory. You coming?"

Harlem called out to me, referring to the bar a lot of first responders hung out at. I shook my head.

"Nah, I'm about to go home, pray my daughter is asleep, and take my ass to bed." I yawned again.

Having an infant while working long hours wasn't ideal. Thankfully, next week I started my three twelves on and four days off.

"How is baby girl?" Journi questioned.

I grinned. "Growing too fast."

She snickered. "I remember those days. Appreciate them before the walking and crawling comes."

"Listen to her. My oldest is twelve going on twenty. She stresses me the hell out too," Leo called out.

"Thankfully, I ain't gotta worry about that anytime soon."

"Candidate!" one of my squad mates called out as I headed for the locker room while they all continued to chatter.

Station 112 had become my family away from my family. I had been at this firehouse for the past nine years, since my previous house was shut down.

Once I was showered and changed, I collected my things from my locker when Harlem stepped into the room.

"You good?" he questioned.

I grabbed my phone, checking my notifications and making sure I hadn't missed anything. "Yeah, why wouldn't I be?"

"Things good with Skye? She still—"

"Things are fine. She's better." I shut his line of questioning down and looked around the locker room.

Harlem was like a little brother to me, and he and I had grown close the couple years he had been at Station 112. He knew some of the troubles I dealt with when it came to my daughter's mom, so his question was justified. Still, it wasn't something I wanted to think about right now.

"My bad. You just seem so worn lately."

I chuckled and closed my locker. "Being up for damn near seventy-two hours because of the job and infant will do that." Picking my duffle bag up, I hung it over my shoulders.

"I'm out," I told him.

We slapped hands as I prepared to leave.

I prayed I had a smooth rest of the night when I got home and didn't have to deal with any bullshit.

———

Pulling up to my house in Ridge Valley, I cut my truck off, grabbed my duffle bag, and climb out before heading for my front door.

My body felt heavy, and a headache was building—eyes brimmed with exhaustion.

Unlocking my door, my brows furrowed as my muscles tensed hearing the shrills of my daughter from upstairs.

I hurried inside, dropping my bag at the door, and rushing up the steps. When I entered my five-month-old daughter's room, my blood boiled, seeing her flustered, red, tear stain cheeks. She had just started sitting up, and her glossy big brown eyes stared up at me. By how loud she was crying, I knew it had to have been awhile.

"Scottlynn, Munchkin. What's wrong?" I swooped her up and bounced her, attempting to soothe her. She continued to cry. I felt her butt and clenched my jaw when I felt how soaked her diaper was.

Pushing a heavy breath out, I walked over to the changing table on the wall. "Daddy's got you, Munchkin. It's okay." I kissed the top of her head. Her cries turned into whimpers, and she gripped my t-shirt tightly. "I know, baby."

Quickly, I stripped her out the soaked onesie she had on, realizing she had peed through her diaper, and tossed it in the dirty clothes hamper near the table then worked on her diaper.

Once she was changed, I found her new clothes to put on. "There you go, pretty girl."

She giggled as I kissed on her cheeks. My daughter was my world and came out looking just like me. She was happy baby and hardly cried unless something was wrong. That was why I was so pissed off right now.

"Let me go find Mommy." I laid her back in her crib with her pacifier and looked around her room for the remote to the TV on the wall. I turned *Gracie's Corner* on knowing it would keep her occupied while I found out what the hell was going on.

"I'll be right back, pretty girl." I stepped out of her bedroom, closing the door behind me.

Inhaling a deep breath, I pushed it out heavily and stalked toward my bedroom.

Pushing the door open, I laid eyes on Skye lying face down on her vanity. My body ran hot, and my jaw clenched while my heart pounded loudly in my ears.

"Skye!" I called out, making my way to her.

When she didn't budge, my anger only grew. "Skye! Wake the hell up!" I grabbed her shoulder and shook her roughly.

My head pounded, and my eyes burned. All I wanted to do was come home one night without bullshit so I could sleep.

She grumbled something I couldn't make out and shifted.

"Skye!"

She popped up suddenly, looking around with wild eyes. "What?" Her pupils were dilated, and her face was pale.

"You're shitting me, right? You're high while my fucking daughter is in there crying for God knows how long!" I bellowed.

She flinched. "Scottlynn. Oh my God, Tripp. Is she okay?" Her words were rushed.

I stared at her partly disgusted, partly distraught that this was what she had succumbed to. Skye wiped her nose and looked around our bedroom, avoiding my eye.

I shook my head and brushed my hand over my head. "I can't do this shit anymore."

She blinked rapidly. "What? No, Tripp. I'm sorry. It was an accident." She went to grab me, but I stepped back.

"No, Skye. You need help. I can't keep going through this shit. How long were you in here passed out while our daughter was up crying?"

Tears clouded her eyes. Normally, they would get to me, but this time they didn't. I had been patient with Skye. I knew she was dealing with shit, and the drugs helped. We had done rehab a couple of times, and each time I thought it would get better, it didn't. I thought us having a kid would make her stay sober, but I was wrong. I loved Skye. Outside of my daughter she was the most important person in my life, but I couldn't keep doing this.

"You gotta go back to rehab," I told her, making eye contact with her.

She shook her head quickly and went to speak, but I put my hand up. "No. I can't do this anymore. I've tried for years, but it's obvious I can't help you alone. We have a daughter now, and I can't have her around this shit."

"But... but I can do better, Tripp. I promise." Her bottom lip trembled.

Sighing, I stepped toward her and wrapped my arms around her, pulling her into a hug. I kissed the top of her head and closed my eyes. She clung to me with pleading eyes.

"I love you, Skye. You know I do, but either you go to rehab, get clean, and *stay* clean, or we're done. Scottlynn deserves better than this. *You* are better than this." I released her and stepped back again.

Tears ran down her face, and she hugged herself. "Okay," she whispered. "I'll go."

I knew it wasn't what she wanted to hear, but I was at my limit. There was no way I could go to work every day and run in and out of fires with a clear head knowing my daughter wasn't safe at home with her own mother.

"Ima look into some programs," I told her and headed for the door.

"Where are you going?" she rushed out.

"To put Scottlynn to sleep, then I'm sleeping in the guest room."

I didn't bother to look at her again. It was time to show Skye some tough love. I had been too lenient with her for too long.

———

"You look like shit!" my younger brother Troy said as I set Scottlynn's car seat down and took a seat on his couch. Thankfully, she had fallen asleep on the ride here.

"I feel like it, too." My shoulder's sank.

"Ima grab us some beers." He walked out the living room toward his kitchen.

It didn't take my brother long to come back into the room. He handed me the beer and took a seat across from me on the loveseat.

"Her ass is getting big." He smiled down at my daughter.

I glanced down at her.

"I know. Too big." I cracked the can open, brought it to my mouth, and took a large sip. It pained me to look at my daughter knowing she wasn't getting the best version of her mom. It had been two days since the night I came home and found her high, and since then she'd been avoiding me—leaving out of rooms when I entered and jumpy when I spoke to her. I had been researching rehabs in the area she could go to while trying to take care of Scottlynn and mentally preparing for my next shift.

"Skye's ass, man." I sighed and lowered my beer can. "She's gotta go back to rehab."

I hated the sympathetic look that filled my brother eyes. There were three of us, but me and Troy were the closest since we were only two years apart. Our little brother Terrance was six years younger than me.

"Damn, man. Really? I'm sorry to hear that."

Clenching my jaw, I nodded. "Yeah, me too."

I didn't have to go into detail. My family knew my ups and downs with Skye, mainly because we grew up with her, but Troy knew more since we were closer.

Scottlynn whined in her seat, so I bent down and located her pacifier, sticking it in her mouth.

"You gon' be up to doing this by yourself?" I dragged my tongue across my top teeth. "With your job and all it's not gonna be easy being a single dad."

"Shit… it already feels like I'm one." I chuckled bitterly.

Straightening my back, I took another large drink of my Silver Shadow Beer.

Finding out I was gonna be a dad was the best news of my life. I had longed for so long to start my own family, and when Skye finally got on the same page as me, I couldn't have been happier. I thought it would be a new beginning for us. Now here we were, six months into being parents, and we were right back in the same fucked up cycle as before.

CHAPTER 2

BRYLEE ADKINS

"So, what you're telling me is you can't make it?" I plopped down on my bed, feeling defeated.

"Sorry, babe, but something came up with work," Russell, my boyfriend, stated.

Sighing, I rolled my eyes and kicked my heels off. "What's new?" I muttered.

Russell worked as an insurance risk analyst. I knew there were times he had to put in overtime, but it seemed it happened more frequently than I cared to admit.

"Ima make it up to you, a'right? My boss has been on my ass to get these cases closed. If I could put it off anymore, I would, but—"

"It's fine, Russell. I get it. Just remember you owe me a date night."

"That's why I love you. If I'm not done too late, I'll be over tonight."

I nodded as if he could see me and looked at myself in the mirror across my room attached to my dresser.

"Okay. Love you, too."

We hung up, and I tapped my foot, poking the inside of my cheek with my tongue.

I didn't go out often, and since I was already dressed, I decided not to waste a good outfit. Going to my contacts, I went to my best friend's name and hit the FaceTime button.

"Hey, boo!" she answered. Her background was loud with music and chatter.

I squinted my eyes, checking her surroundings. "Where are you?"

"The Sea Note!"

My brows crinkled. "What the hell is the Sea Note?"

"The new karaoke bar on The Shore. I'm with my cousins. Come join us!"

"Leia, we got a room. C'mon!" I heard someone call out to her.

"I gotta go, Brylee. Come down here!" She hung the phone up before I could answer.

I thought for a second. The Shore was about twenty-five minutes away from my house in Ridge Valley. Since Russell canceled and me, and I had nothing else to do, I decided to go. It was Saturday night, and I refused to be in the house wallowing in my feelings.

———

The Sea Note was on the beach. There was an outside patio with an outdoor bar and dance area where people enjoyed themselves. In the inside there were a bunch of private rooms people could reserve to sing with a private party or alone. The main area had a stage in the front, a bar, and an open area surrounded by chairs and tables for live entertainment.

Leia and her cousins were in one of the private rooms when I arrived.

"Hey!" I called out as two of Leia's cousins huddled around the tablet searching through the list of songs. Leia sat on the couch with a drink in her hand and phone in the other.

Her head popped up, and she grinned. "Hey, boo!"

"Hey!" her cousins Maddisyn and Porsha called out.

I waved and went to where Leia sat, taking a seat.

"I thought you were having date night tonight?" she questioned.

The beat to "These Boots Are Made For Walking" started, and the words popped up on the TV screen.

"Work came up." I rolled my eyes, grabbing a cup and bottle of Crown Apple and cranberry juice.

"You need to leave him."

"And now someone else is getting all your best!" Maddisyn sang along, moving around the room while Porsha laughed and recorded her.

"Not tonight, Leia." I shook my head, already knowing that would be her response. My best friend wasn't Russell's biggest fan, and she never hid it.

She squinted her eyes and pressed her lips together. I took a long drink and got comfortable.

"I'll worry about Russell another night. I wanna enjoy tonight with people my own age for once."

She snickered and nodded. "Fine. I'll let it go for now."

I was thankful. Sundays and one Saturday out the month were the only times I had to enjoy myself. I wasn't going to let Russell ruin that for me.

"Brylee, your turn!" Maddisyn stepped toward us with the microphone held out. Smirking, I nodded and stood before grabbing it from her and walking to the podium with the tablet.

———

"I'm starving and cannot wait to eat," I groaned, rubbing my stomach as we walked into the diner a couple streets over from The Sea Note.

"Me too! I really want some pancakes," Leia said.

"Take a seat at any open table, and I'll be right over," the lady by the entrance told us.

We found a booth toward the back. "My name's Courtney, and I'll be your waitress. Here's some menus. Can I get you guys something to drink?"

"Sweet tea," I told her.

"Same," Leia said.

She nodded and walked off. Picking up the menu, I scanned it over. Once I figured out what I wanted to eat, I laid it down and picked my phone up.

"Okay, bitch. We need to talk," Leia said finally.

"About what?" I continued scrolling through my phone.

"You and Russell. Are you gonna leave him or what?"

I didn't want to lose the small buzz I had, and I knew talking about Russell would do that.

"Leia." I sighed, this time looking up from phone and giving her my attention.

"No, Lee. I'm for real. It's time for you to move on. That nigga doesn't deserve you!"

"I know, Leia, okay? But it's not as easy as it seems. We have history, and that's not easy to throw away because of a few problems."

"*A few?*" Her mouth turned upside down.

Our waitress came back with our drinks and took our food order.

"Look, Leia, I appreciate you, but I'll handle Russell, okay? I know things need to change. I'm not blind to shit. I just need to figure a few things out. That's it."

Leia twisted her lips to the side. I knew my answer didn't satisfy her, but I was serious when I told her I would handle my relationship when I was ready.

"I just hope you leave him sooner rather than later. All he does is drag you down and make you unhappy. You're better when y'all aren't together."

This time I twisted my lips and bit the inside of my cheek. I knew she was right. Today proved that we had run our course. He didn't make me a priority anymore, and looking back, I wasn't sure if he ever did.

———

"Hi, Gran." I leaned down and kissed my grandma's cheek. "Grandad." I went to my grandad doing the same. They looked at me with a smile. My Grandad at the head of the table and Gran sitting at his side. Gran had her salt and pepper hair in tight curls, pinned up, while Grandad kept his hair low in almost a fade.

"Hi, sweetheart. You doing alright?" Gran asked.

I walked around the table and took a seat. Since I was a kid my grandparents always smelled of lavender and vanilla with a hint of oranges. Whenever I came over and the scent hit my nose it always made me feel warm and at home. I felt centered and at ease.

"Of course. Life's life." I shrugged. "What bout you two? Are you okay? Do you need anything?"

The shared a look then a laugh. "You ask the same thing every week, and we tell you the same thing. We're fine."

"Just checking."

I eyed the food on the table.

Every Sunday since I was a kid, my grandma cooked Sunday dinner, and I tried to never miss one. My grandparents were more like my parents, and they sacrificed a lot to raise me and give me a good life. I owed them everything, so if a family dinner was all my grandma asked for, I had no issues with that.

Grandad blessed the food then we dug in. Today we had roast, baked mac n cheese, and candied yams.

"How's work been, Brylee? Those kids working your nerves still?" my Grandad asked.

I snickered. "Every day, but I love those kiddos."

"I knew you would go into some profession that had to do with kids. You always used to play school with your stuffed animals and baby dolls when you were younger."

I shoved some roast into my mouth. "Even though not all the kids are pleasant, I love my job. Working with kids is fun, and there's never a dull moment."

The daycare I worked at was in Ridge Valley, which was not too far from my house, and I had been there for the last five years.

"You must get that patience from your Grandad, because I don't have it," my gran said.

She was right about that. My gran was the greatest woman I knew, but she didn't take any bullshit either.

We continued eating until my gran spoke up. "I talked to your mom the other day."

I lifted my head and gave her a blank look. "Oh. Okay," I told her unenthusiastically.

"She asked about you."

Still, my face stayed blank. My parents were still together, but I barely spoke to them. They were teenagers when they had me but gave me up to my grandparents to raise when I was five. They went to live their lives without me.

"You should talk to her. She wants you two to grow closer—both her and your dad. They also want you to get closer to your siblings," Grandad said.

"They had their chance, and they didn't want it. Our relationship is fine how it is." I shut his suggestion down.

My gran sighed but thankfully let it go. Every once in a while, the two of them brought my parents up and tried to get me to let them into my life. I understood they were young when they had me, but they just said fuck being parents, and now they wanted me to forgive and forget?

"Where's that boyfriend of yours? I noticed you haven't brought him over lately," Grandad asked, changing the subject to something else I didn't want to talk about.

"He's been busy with work." Honestly, I hadn't even spoke to Russell today, but I wasn't going to tell my grandparents that. Ever since our canceled date three days ago, he hadn't made an effort to call, instead just sent half ass text.

"Mhm." My gran huffed. Neither of them was a fan of Russell, but she was more vocal with it.

I always enjoyed spending time with my grandparents. They were a listening ear when I needed it. My support when I felt down. Whenever I felt low, coming over here always picked me up.

CHAPTER 3

TRIPP

My temple throbbed, and my head pounded as Scottlynn's cries grew in the middle of the store. She was running low on formula, and I thought this would be a quick trip in and out, so I didn't bother bringing her car seat in. Turned out I forgot I needed diapers and before I knew it I threw in some wipes. Now I was stuck balancing everything.

I was running on fumes. Between work and her sleepless nights, I was at my breaking point. It had been over two weeks since Skye left for rehab, and I started to feel the pressure of being a single dad. I could feel the stares from people as they passed but chose to ignore them.

"I hear you, Munchkin. We're about to go home." I bounced her in my arms and patted her butt as I scanned the shelves for the right formula.

"Excuse me, do you need some help?" a female's voice sounded next to me.

I glanced over, and my eyes landed on a caramel skin, average height woman. She had brown and black locs that were pulled into a bun on the top of her head. Her heart shaped pink lips curled into a small smile.

"Swaddling usually helps, especially if the baby feels stress or restless. Brings them comfort." I glanced down at her confused. I could barely hear myself think over the cries.

"If I may?" she said again, this time holding her hands out. "I'm a daycare teacher and deal with this often. I promise I'm not on any funny stuff."

I hesitated for a second before handing her a hysterically crying Scottlynn. At this point, I'd accept anything.

"Now, why is a pretty baby like you crying like this?" Her soft voice sounded so soothing and gentle.

I watched as she used Scottlynn's blanket and wrapped it tightly around her, making her a burrito.

"There you go." She grinned, bringing Scottlynn to her shoulder and patting her butt. I was amazed to see my daughter calm down.

I blinked slowly, finally feeling a moment of peace. My ears still rang from the excessive crying.

"Shit." I ran my hand over the top of my head. "Thank you. I'm usually a good multitasker, but I guess I haven't mastered the dad thing yet."

Her naturally upturned chocolate brown eyes beamed down at my daughter.

"She your first?" She glanced up at me.

I nodded. "And only."

Her smile grew wider. "What's her name?"

"Scottlynn."

"That's a pretty name for a pretty little girl," she cooed down at my daughter who was finally dozing off. I gawked at her, surprised by how easily she soothed my kid.

"You must be named the baby whisperer," I joked.

She giggled and shook her head. "Possibly as a nickname. But no, my name is Brylee."

Brylee. I rolled the name around in my head. Her parents did well because the name fit her face. She was dressed comfortably in a midlength black wrap dress covered in red, orange, and white floral patterns. She had a single gold necklace with a cross hanging around her neck, a couple brown stacked beaded bracelets on her wrist that matched the patterns on her dress, and gold hoops in her ears. She gave me a boho feminine chic vibe and wore it well.

"Nice to meet you, Brylee. I'm Tripp. I would shake your hand but…"

"No worries. If that's all you have to get, I can follow you to the register so you can check out."

"Oh yeah, even if I wasn't I'd come back tomorrow. I think it's time to get her home and in bed."

Brylee snickered. "There's nothing a good bottle and swaddle can't help."

Scottlynn's face nuzzled into Brylee's chest; her body turned into her. It sucked to say, but this was the first time I hadn't seen a woman outside of my mom bring comfort to my daughter, and this stranger did it with ease.

Silently, we walked through the department store to the checkout. Thankfully, they had the self check out still open, and I was able to hurry and buy my items.

"Sorry for inconveniencing you," I mentioned once Scottlynn was back in my arms. Thankfully, she was still asleep.

"It's no inconvenience. Like you said, I'm the baby whisperer." Her soft eyes went to Scottlynn, whose head now rested on my shoulders.

"Well… I won't hold you up anymore. Thank you again."

With a small nod, she waved and moved around me, heading further into the store.

I watched her for a minute, feeling gratitude fill me. Peeking down at Scottlynn, I couldn't help but smile. "It's back to me and you, Munchkin," I muttered, heading for the entrance.

———

"Royce, my boy. I think you missed your calling. These lasagna rolls are the shit," Harlem expressed as he bit into his food. Royce was normally the one who took on cooking during a shift, because out of everyone, he was the best cook with Cap coming in close second. The two usually alternated.

I slapped a domino on the table and waited for Leo to make the next move.

"He's right. This shit is good as hell," Journi expressed.

Royce chuckled. "As much as I enjoy the compliments, cooking is just something I do to pass time."

"Your wife is a lucky woman; I'll tell you that."

A tight smile formed on Royce's face that I wasn't sure anyone caught.

"C'mon, TJ, you holding the game up," Leo called out, gaining my attention.

"Shit, my bad." I checked the table to locate his last move.

I was still getting used to working twelve hour shifts instead of my typical twenty-four. Luckily, Omiras accommodated my situation and was willing to temporarily change me shifts. While my parents didn't mind watching my daughter now, I knew I needed to figure out a permeant solution for her. With Skye gone, and my job being so demanding, I didn't have much leeway.

"Hey, Leo, y'all get handle on that bullying situation?" Journi sat down with a bowl of salad in her grasp.

Leo's mouth turned upside. "Nah, my little lady handled the situation herself." He chuckled before laying down a domino. "Turns out she got tired of the girl picking on her and knocked her ass out with a textbook."

My eyes ballooned. "Her brother had to pull her off after that."

Leo had twelve-year-old twins—one girl and one boy. While the two were lovely kids, they made me pray hard every night my daughter didn't turn out like them. They were always giving Leo and their mom hell.

"My girl!" Journi choked a laugh out.

"I know." Leo shook his head. "That girl's got a temper like her mama. Got suspended too, which had Myla going up there and going off because the other girl didn't get in any trouble and been fucking with my baby for days now."

Harlem whistled. "I don't envy you."

"Hell, I don't envy myself."

In the middle of the conversation, the alarm went off.

"Let's load up team!" Omiras commanded while standing up with everyone following behind. For the most part, the shift had been tame. I kind of hoped for some excitement with this call.

———

"You're gonna wear yourself thin, TJ. I don't like this," my mom expressed as I scooped up dirty rice and shoved it in my mouth.

"At the moment, I can't do anything but what I'm doing," I said, wiping my mouth with a paper towel.

"Skye's gonna be gone for what at least three months. You think you're gonna be able to handle a infant along with your job without burning yourself out?"

I looked up at my mom, who watched me with worried eyes. Today was the first day off of my four-day twelve-hour shift run. I went home and got a couple hours of sleep before coming to my parents' house to get Scottlynn.

"I don't have any choice but to make it work. I gotta work."

While I had a nice amount of savings from an inherence, I didn't want to touch it.

"Why not look into getting some help then?" she suggested.

"Help?" My brows dipped in confusion.

"Yes. A nanny. Not that me and your dad have an issue with keeping our sweet grandchild, but you're gonna need more help at home. When's the last time you actually slept peacefully without having to jump up and change a diaper or make a bottle?"

"Your mother is right, son." My dad walked into the room and cosigned. "You're not gonna be good for anyone, especially not your daughter, if you're not taking care of yourself."

I rubbed my eyes, feeling an ache forming behind them. My parents weren't completely wrong. Even when I was off, I still had the duty of parent to maintain. It'd been like this since Scottlynn was first born. Skye might have been there physically, but she wasn't always as helpful as I would have liked.

"I don't know about no random person watching my daughter or being all up in my house." I shook my head. In theory, the idea sounded nice, but it made me uneasy knowing a stranger would be heavily involved in my life.

"You have to do something, Tripp. I can look at you and see you're a sleepless night away from passing out," my mom fussed with concern etched all on her face.

Scottlynn whined.

"Ima go change her," my mom said, turning to walk out of the room.

"I know you're a prideful man, TJ. You're a lot like me in that way, but son, it's okay to need help sometime. You have a lot on your plate. Kids aren't easy, especially an infant. Nothing's wrong with outsourcing some help to lessen the load," my dad assured me.

"She already doesn't have her mom. I don't want to be less present by having some random person come in and raise her."

"It's not raising her. It's helping you. Shit, why do you think babysitters and daycare exist? Like your mom said, we love having Scottlynn here, but either you need to rethink your career choice, or you need to get someone to help for days your off."

"I'll think about it," I said to end the conversation. My dad patted my shoulder and walked out of the room.

I stared down at my food, not even having an appetite anymore. My daughter had already been through a lot and was down a parent. The last thing I wanted to do was leave her down another parent and neglect her.

CHAPTER 4

BRYLEE

"Didn't I tell you I would make it up to you?" Russell moved my locs off my neck and pressed his lips against the nape of my neck before pushing his groin into me.

I rolled my eyes and stayed silent as I stared at the wall in front of me.

Russell's version of making up barely had any thought in it. I regretted even letting him between my legs, but I chalked it up to a lapse of common sense. He came in here with some flowers, and the next thing I knew I was propped on my table, and my legs were over his shoulders. Cumming with Russell was always a hit or miss too, but tonight he must have known I was fed up because he managed to make me cum twice from penetration and once from head.

Nudging him off me, I turned so I faced him. Sitting up, I wrapped the cover around my body and stared down at him. He was now on his back with a proud expression on his face.

"We need to talk, Russell," I started. "I'm not happy."

His brows furrowed. "We just had amazing sex, babe. How the hell aren't you happy after that?"

I rolled my eyes and huffed. "Russell, I'm being serious. I'm not happy. Something in this relationship needs to change."

His frown deepened. He glared at me, his face unmoving for a moment before he pushed a heavy breath out and shook his head.

Tossing the cover off him, he prepared to rise off the bed. "I never met someone so damn miserable," he mumbled, but I heard him.

"Miserable?" I shrieked. "Are you serious?"

Russell moved around my room gathering his clothes and putting them on. "Yeah, man. Every time I talk to you, you're complaining about something. That shit gets tiring as fuck."

I sat there with my mouth gapped in disbelief. "So, because I'm tired of receiving the bare minimum from you, I'm complaining?" My voice hitched as I spoke. Climbing out the bed, I made sure to bring the sheet with me, keeping it wrapped around me.

"You act like I'm not trying!" He shoved his shirt over his head.

"Not enough! I keep getting the bullshit end of the stick. You always put me second. You barely make time for me!" For too long I been pushing how I felt to the side so I wouldn't start an argument, but I couldn't keep it up anymore. Russell no longer made me happy. This relationship was becoming emotionally draining.

Once he was dressed, Russell turned to face me with his face void of any emotions, so I wasn't sure exactly what he was thinking. My stomach flipped and knotted.

"Ima keep it real with you, Brylee. In the beginning, shit was fun with us, but over time, you've become too clingy. Sometimes you just need to let a nigga breath and have some space."

I stumbled back as if he struck me. My mouth gapped but words were unable to form. His confession not only caught me off guard but caused something to twist inside of me.

"Let you breath?" I started slowly, still processing. "So, it's wrong for me to want to spend time with my boyfriend?" My head cocked to the side as I waited for him to respond.

His hand dragged down his face, and he pushed a heavy breath out. "That's not what I'm saying, but you act like we gotta spend twenty-four-seven together. We don't need to be attached at the hip."

Blinking rapidly, I bit the inside of my cheek and swallowed slowly while nodding.

Russell sighed, and his face softened. "Look, I got shit to do. We'll have to finish this later." He stepped closer to me and moved in like he was about to kiss me, but I moved my head. He stared at me as if he was affected before shaking his head. He placed a quick kiss on my cheek then stepped back. "I'll call you later."

I shook my head. "Don't bother. You just said everything you needed to right here. I'll give you the space you need."

"C'mon now. Don't be dramatic," he groaned.

"I'm not forcing you to be with me, Russell. If you think I require too much attention, then we can end this."

His jaw ticked as his eyes narrowed. "Your parents fucked you up, and you try to fill the hole they left inside you with a relationship. I'm not here to heal that shit. I just wanted a normal relationship. Once you deal with your shit, we can talk."

The knot in my stomach grew. My heart felt like someone sent a knife through it.

"Fuck you. Fuck you and get out of my house," I muttered while attempting to keep my voice steady. Russell knew my parents were a soft spot for me, and for him to throw it in my face felt as if he had struck me physically.

"Yeah, I'm out." He stared at me a couple seconds longer before turning to leave. I didn't stop him. Ice crept in my veins. I viciously chewed on the corner of my bottom lip. Seeing how easily Russell walked out showed me how many years I wasted when it came to him. Years I would never be able to get back.

———

"Miss Adkins, do you like my picture?" one of the kids in my daycare class asked.

I glanced at the green, yellow, and red picture, not really sure what I was supposed to be seeing but smiled and nodded anyway.

"Of course, I do. It's so pretty!"

I taught three and four year olds at the daycare I worked at. Right now, we had art class, and I allowed them to freely expressive themselves. I loved kids and working with them. Typically coming to work brought me joy, but my argument with Russell the other day had been hanging heavily on my mind.

"Okay, everyone." I stood up and clapped my hands. There were twelve kids in my class, which made it easier to manage. "Let's finish up paintings up so we can lay them on the drying rack and get ready for circle time," I told the kids. "Lilly, it's your turn to pick a book. Once you finish your painting, go to the book bin."

I turned and went to my desk. While the kids finished up their paintings, I lifted my phone off my desk and checked the screen.

"Miss Adkins, what's that smell?" a kid asked.

Lifting my eyes from the phone, I bunched my brows together. "What smell?"

I inhaled. My frowned deepened.

Locking my phone, I slid it in my pocket and walked around my desk while sniffing the air. My eyes widened, realizing there was a burning scent in the air. I looked around, trying to locate the source.

Suddenly, an alarm blared. The kids screamed, covering their ears. My door pushed open.

"There's a fire. We need to evacuate," one of the other teachers shouted.

"Shit," I gritted. "Kids, listen!" I spoke in haste. Quickly, I gave them instructions, attempting to keep them and myself calm.

"C'mon! C'mon!" I urged them, looking around to make sure everyone was leaving. Thankfully, our class wasn't too far from an emergency exit. Smoke filled the halls, and the smell grew. Some kids coughed and cried. Panic surrounded us.

"Is everyone here?" I questioned, coughing myself and doing a quick count once we were in our destinated areas for situations like this. The sun beamed down on us, the wind lightly blowing. Black and gray smoke could be seen coming from the building filling the air around it.

Once I made sure all my kids were accounted for, I looked around and saw other teachers and kids filling the area too. It was unruly with a lot going on. The kids threw questions left and right. Teachers attempted to keep everyone calm.

When I looked toward the school, I saw black and gray smoke coming from it—flames cackling and growing larger.

I didn't know what the hell was going on, but my heart pounded, and my heart raced.

Sirens blared, growing closer as chaos spread around us.

"Everyone get back on the other side of the turnaround!" the head of the daycare yelled through a blow horn. We were already on the other side in the grassy field.

Fire trucks, ambulances, and police soon filled the turnaround and parking lot.

We all stood and watched as they moved with quickness to get in control of everything.

It took some time, but eventually, we were able to get the kids under control, and the fire department gained control of the situation.

"What the hell happened?" I asked another teacher, feeling the weight of today fall on me.

"I don't know. I just know it started in the staff's kitchen."

My eyes bucked. The staff kitchen was close to where my classroom was.

"Oh wow," I said in disbelief and shifted my eyes back to the building. The firefighters had gotten the fire put out. Paramedics made sure everyone was okay. Police tried to gain order and speak to the director.

"Brylee," I heard a deep voice call out to me.

I spun around. My eyes squinted then widened. "Tripp?"

His helmet rested in the crease of his folded arms against his side.

He said something to the guy next to him then nodded, making his way to me.

I was surprised to see him again. I had thought about him a couple times since helping him with his daughter a couple weeks ago. His bronze skin glistened with sweat. The uniform he wore made his already bulky, toned frame look broader. Sweat glistened on his top heavy, pink lips under his mustache.

"You work here?" he asked.

I nodded still surprised Tripp was here in front of me. Out of everything I wouldn't have thought of him as a firefighter, but the profession looked good on him. "Uh, yeah. I do." Swallowing hard I shifted my eyes behind him. "How is it?" I wondered about the daycare.

He glanced over his shoulder. "We were able to get the fire, but there was a good amount of damage already done. I can't call it until everything is completely cleared, though. Are you okay?" His hooded, warm brown hues searched me over.

Tripp was a handsome man, and the way he looked me over made my stomach flip and fill with heat.

I nodded and swallowed. "Yes, a little shaken up and wondering if this will put me out of a job." I ran my hand over my locs that were crinkled and down from the braids I put in them the night before.

Both of us looked toward the building again.

"Tripp!" one of his collogues called.

"Here I come!" His eyes found me again. "Listen, I gotta go, but..." he tucked his lips for a second and dipped his brows, "take my number. I might have a way to help."

I stared at him curiously and unable to speak. Too many thoughts went through my mind at the moment.

Going into my pocket, I grabbed my phone. He rattled off his number then nodded.

"You stay safe," he called before jogging over to the rest of the firefighters.

"You know him?" one of the other teachers came over and asked. Her eyes locked on him. "He's fine as hell."

I nibbled on the corner of my bottom lip and looked down at the number, shaking my head. "No, not really."

I sighed when the directors voice rang out throwing out directions. Parents had started filling the area in a panic. My head throbbed.

When I woke up this morning, the last thing I expected was for my life to blow up in flames.

———

I sipped on my cookie butter iced latte and looked around wondering if I made the right choice. After the fire, we were informed that the daycare would be closed for a while, so reconstructions and wiring could happen. Apparently, the fire was electrical, so for now, me and all the other staff were out of jobs until further noticed. Knowing I couldn't go jobless, I remembered Tripp told me he might be able to help.

I had only met him that one time at the store, but something told me I could trust him. It took a few days, but I finally reached out, and we agreed to meet here at Love Latte in Ridge Valley to talk. I sat at one of their outside tables feeling antsy. I didn't like not knowing what was next and not having a plan. With my job gone, my anxiety had been through the roof.

My eyes circled the outside, and small flutters filled my stomach when I laid eyes on Tripp. He walked down the sidewalk coming from the parking lot on the side of the building.

"I hope you weren't waiting too long," he spoke once he approached my table.

He wore a sleeveless cut off shirt, putting his cut, thick arms on display.

I shook my head, watching as he took a seat. "You can grab something if you want. I can wait," I assured him.

"I'm good. Ate before I came." His hand went over his Caesar cut. "I 'preciate you reaching out and agreeing to meet with me."

Shrugging, I brought my cup to my mouth and drank from the straw. "Not like I have a job or anything to take up my time." I tried to force a smile, but my shoulders sank forward.

He licked his lips and leaned in. "That's what I wanted to talk to you about. I know the daycare is gonna be outta commission for a while, and I figured you were gonna need a job."

My brows furrowed. "You're right..." I stated slowly.

Tripp looked around briefly, then his eyes fell back on me. "I'm in need of a nanny, and after seeing how you easily calmed my daughter down at the store, I think you would be a perfect fit."

That wasn't what I expected when I reached out.

"It'll be a live in position," he continued. "With my job, I work crazy hours, so it'll be easier if you're in the house at all times. Being that you worked at a daycare, I know you know the basics when it comes to taking care of kids. I'm not sure on your wage there, but I'm willing match or increase it depending on what it is. I know this might be a lot to ask since I'm a stranger, but I'm in a bind and don't have a lot of options. I don't really have the time to try to find a nanny on my own, either."

I didn't respond right away because I was unsure what to say. While the offer caught me off guard, it sounded good, and I couldn't afford to turn it down. At the same time, I didn't know Tripp or anything about him. Moving into his house and living with him was a big deal, even if it was just to be his nanny.

I stared at the condensation running down the clear plastic cup and sank my top teeth into the fat of my bottom lip.

"What about her mom? How does she feel about this?" One thing I didn't want was to gain drama because another woman felt I was stepping on her toes.

When I looked up, he now had a doleful expression his face. "Her mom isn't an issue you need to worry about." He didn't explain further than that, but by the heavy emotions radiating off him, I was sure it wasn't something I wanted to push.

"You don't have to make the decision right now. I know this is a lot to ask and a big step since we're strangers."

"We *are* strangers," I stressed, "so it's odd for you to offer me this position."

His shoulders slightly lifted. "If it's not you it would be someone else. At least with you I know you have the experience, and I've seen you calm my daughter down and care for her, even if for only couple minutes." His eyes shifted to the side. "But okay, tell me about you. How long you been working with kids?"

I studied Tripp's face. Lines of stress and worry embedded in his skin. Exhaustion rested in the pocket of his eyes. His five o'clock shadow had a little more fuzz to it.

"Since I was fourteen. I started babysitting a couple neighborhood kids 'til I was eighteen. I went to college and got a degree in early childhood education. I was a substitute teacher for a couple years and been at the daycare for the past five."

Astonishment covered his face. "That's dope. Why not stay in the education field?"

I shrugged. "I enjoy dealing with smaller kids. I wouldn't mind teaching kindergarten or even first grade if the opportunity was there. I don't think I would go any higher."

He nodded with a small, crooked grin on his face. "Impressive. How old are you now, if you don't mind me asking?"

"Twenty-nine."

His brows shot up. "I would have guessed younger."

I snickered. My lashes fluttered, and I stared at him. "Everyone says that. Thankfully, I have a youthful face. How old are you? I know you're a firefighter. How long have you been on the job?"

"Thirty-one. Been doing this since I was twenty."

That surprised me. "That's a long time."

"Doesn't feel like that when you're doing what you love. I'm sure you can understand that."

Slowly, I nodded and brought my straw to my mouth.

He pulled his phone out and looked at. "I gotta go, but you have my number. Take some time and think it over, and if you're interested, then let me know."

Slight disappointment passed through me knowing he had to leave. I enjoyed our conversation.

"Okay," I agreed softly.

Tripp pushed away from the table and stood to leave. "I look forward from hearing from you, Brylee." He smiled down at me, then turned to leave.

I inhaled a deep breath and slowly pushed it out. Tilting my chin up, I embraced the sun as it beamed down on my skin. Maybe Tripp's offer was the shaking up I needed in my life.

CHAPTER 5

TRIPP

I bobbed my head to the J. Cole track playing through my noise cancelling headphones, while running the sander over the chair I was finishing up in my workshop in my backyard. I had two more days to have it finished for the client who had hired me to restore it. Apparently, it had been in her family for years, and she wasn't ready to part from it.

Woodshop and furniture restoration had been a stress relieving hobby for me for years. It wasn't until recently I started making a profit from it.

I bobbed my head, silently rapping along while periodically checking the baby monitor to make sure Scottlynn was still sleeping.

My music stopping gained my attention and caused me to stop the sander and peek at my phone.

My heart fell from my stomach. Blood rushed through my veins, and my tongue suddenly felt too heavy for my mouth as I saw the rehab flash on the screen. It had been a month since Skye's been in treatment, and I hadn't spoken to her since.

Clearing my throat, I laid the sander down, wiped my hands over my sweats, and swiped the screen.

"Hello?" I answered with an uneasy feeling passing through me.

"Hey, Tripp." Skye's voice rang through the phone, dancing with hesitation.

For a minute, I was rendered speechless. For the first thirty days, Skye wasn't allowed any contact with the outside world while the drugs detoxed from her body. After, they monitored her to see if she was stable enough to talk to people outside the center.

"Wassup, Skye?"

"I miss you."

A small silence passed through us. I sighed and dropped my head, picking my phone up, putting it against my ear, and turning to lean the back of my hip on my worktable.

"I miss you too, Skye. How you doing?"

"Okay, I guess. This week was the first week I felt strong enough to get out of bed and not be sick. It was rough in the beginning, but I stuck it out for you."

Again, I sighed and dropped my head with my eyes closed. "You should stick it out for you *and* our daughter, Skye. Not for me."

She didn't reply right away. "How is Scottlynn?"

The thought of my daughter caused one corner of my mouth to lift. "She's good. Getting bigger. I think she'll be crawling soon."

For the next couple minutes, I talked more about Scottlynn before switching back to her. She told me a little about her therapy sessions, both individual and group. This was the third time Skye had been in rehab, so she was familiar with the process, but this one was more costly and private than the previous ones. It put a little dent in my savings, but if it would help Skye get and stay clean, I didn't mind the sacrifice.

When it came time for Skye to get off the phone I didn't miss the sadness in her voice. "They said I should be able to get visitors soon. Are you gonna come see me?" she questioned.

I pinched the bridge of my nose. A heaviness built in the center of my chest.

"I'll see what I can do, Skye. It's been tight with work and the baby."

"Oh," she murmured. "Right." Guilt hit me hearing the defeat in her tone. "I gotta get ready for group session. I love you, Tripp. I really do."

I swallowed the lump down in my throat. "I love you too, Skye."

We hung up, and a dark cloud now loomed over me. It felt like a pound of rocks had been dropped in my stomach. My muscles felt tighter than before. I was no longer in the mood to finish the chair I had been working on.

Deciding to come back later, I cleaned my work studio up and left the shed, going through my backyard back to my house. I needed to shower before Scottlynn woke up from her nap.

———

"She came back clean," Evie, my best friend handed me the folder.

I took it and opened it up, scanning through the papers.

Evie worked at the police station, and I asked her to run a background check on Brylee. I was able to find her last name by the daycare's website. Although she seemed like a good fit, it would be crazy for me to allow this woman in my house and around my daughter without doing my due diligence.

"Are you gonna tell me who this girl is?" Evie's head cocked to the side, and her eyes peered into me.

"Someone I offered a job to. As much as I hate to admit it, I need help when it comes to Scottlynn. I don't want to keep relying on my family, so I'm hiring a full-time nanny." I glanced down at the paperwork again. Part of me knew Brylee would come back clean. I didn't think a daycare would hire anyone with a criminal background.

"Skye put you in a tough spot, huh?" The distain wasn't hidden from her tone. "I hope this opened your eyes, TJ."

"Evie." I sighed.

"Don't Evie me," she cut me off. Her eyes cut into slits. "For too long you been letting Skye's antics pass, taking on the stress of her addiction and lies. When is enough gonna be enough?"

"She's not just some random girl I can throw away. She's my

daughter's mother, and regardless of what anyone says about her, I *do* love her. I'd be wrong to leave her while she's at her lowest."

"But how many more times are you gonna save her, Tripp? This is wha? The fourth time she's went off the wagon? You keep dishing out money for her to get clean and sacrificing your mental health just for her to relapse. For God's sake, you've had to sneak Narcan home just because you thought she would OD and you would have to bring her back. You have a daughter now, and she couldn't even stay clean for her. When is enough, enough?"

My hands balled into tight fist. "Skye might not be perfect, but she's trying. Her life wasn't easy. You know that, Evie. This time will be different with her. She knows I'm serious about her staying clean, or things with us are over."

Evie shook her head. "Tripp, seriously, sometimes people just don't want to be saved. I know Skye has her demons, but she has to want to overcome them on her own. To me, it doesn't look like that's the case."

Me, Skye, and Evie all grew up in the same neighborhood. We all used to be close until the two starting butting heads when it came to Skye's addiction. A lot of the time I felt like I was playing the middleman with the two. Skye didn't like Evie's judgement, and Evie didn't like the way Skye chose to handle her trauma.

"Regardless, she's Scottlynn's mom, and I owe it to Scottlynn to help her mom. I don't turn my back on the people I love. You know that. While she's getting help, Brylee will be here to help me, if she chooses to accept the job."

Evie gave me a stern look before her shoulders sank forward. "Fine, TJ." She tossed her hands up. "If you believe that this time will be different, then there's nothing else I can say about it. But at some point, you need to put yourself first."

"You don't have anything to worry about, Evie. Scottlynn is my main priority, and if Skye doesn't get it together, then I'll move accordingly."

I heard everything Evie said. It wasn't anything she or any of my family hadn't said to me before. Everyone wanted me to give up on

Skye like we hadn't been in each other's life's all our lives. Like for the past eight years she wasn't the only woman I'd known. As much as she put me through, I knew her battle was worse, and for that, I refused to be another person who gave up on her.

CHAPTER 6

BRYLEE

"How you been holding up?" Leia questioned me as she wiped the sweat from her forehead. We just finished our weekly spin/yoga class. We had been at it for two months now it, and it was getting easier. We did the bikes, strength training, and ended with yoga.

"As good as anyone who became single and unemployed in the same week." I drank from my water bottle and eyed the locker room. It was starting to clear out. There were usually around ten people in each class, which I liked. It took pressure off me.

Leia rolled her eyes and smacked her lips. "You needed to be single. Russell wasn't good for you anyway. He was a dick."

I couldn't deny that, especially after our last encounter. I hadn't seen him since he left my house, but he had reached out to talk. I'd been ignoring him, though. Right now, I had more important things to worry about.

"That's true. It still sucks, though." I grabbed my gym bag and placed it on my shoulder, and Leia did the same. We started for the entrance of the locker room.

"I do possibly have a job offer," I mentioned cautiously.

I still wasn't sold about working for Tripp. Not that I was in the position to turn down a job. I had been looking for a new job and found a couple, but when I looked at the actual places, they didn't meet the standards I had for work. I wanted something that felt more like a family and didn't feel like work. The places I checked out didn't have that warm inviting feeling I was accustomed too.

My main hesitation was moving into Tripp's house. I didn't know him or what he was about. He seemed nice but looks could be deceiving. Not to mention, he was handsome, stocky, with an athletic physique, and he was nice to look at. His voice was smooth as whisky. He spoke in a guttural tone that made my hairs stand at attention. The last thing I needed was to be lusting over my boss.

"Where at?"

I waved to one of the girls in our class who just finished speaking with the instructor then gave Leia back my attention. I told her about Tripp, summarizing our interactions and his offer.

"Why not take it?" she questioned as we walked through the parking lot to our cars.

"Did you not hear me? He wants me to move into his place. I don't know that man." I scrunched my face.

"Yeah, I get that part, but it's not like people won't know where you'll be. Plus, you'll only be dealing with one kid and not a bunch of brats."

"Don't call them that." I frowned at her, making her snicker.

"I'm just saying. It seems easier. You've already met his daughter, right?" She shrugged. "Sounds like a no-brainer to me."

We arrived at our cars and stood at the rear.

"I told him I would think it over. It's a promising offer, and the pay is more than I made at the daycare. I just hope he doesn't turn out to be a damn weirdo. What if I get there and he has some sex dungeon or something." My brows bunched and mouth pinched. After meeting with Tripp we spoke once more to go over specific details of the job and finalizing pay.

Leia laughed. "A sex dungeon? Really? I'm sure if he *did* have one you wouldn't be expected to participate. But maybe you might want to?" She wagged her brows in a suggestive manner.

I flicked my wrist. "Yeah no. Not my thing."

"Mine neither, but I wouldn't be against it." She cheesed.

Rolling my eyes, I dug into my pocket to hit the button for my car so I could throw my bag in it.

"Leia, I'm being serious."

"Hell, me too! Firefighters be sexy as hell. I bet he fits the standard, don't he?"

Slamming my car door closed, I turned to her. I tried to keep my face blank but failed. "Okay, he does, but that's half of the problem. How the hell am I gonna live in this man's house and want to jump on his dick at the same time?" My head cocked to the side.

"I mean, who says you can't do both?"

"That'll be messy."

Leia rolled her eyes. "Only if you make it."

I thought about it but quickly pushed it out my mind.

"Look, even if you don't have sex with him, still take the job. It seems easy enough."

I bit the inside of my cheek. My lease at my place was month to month right now. I wanted to buy a house, so I didn't want to be on a lease in case I found something soon. Moving out wouldn't be an issue for me. I would be doing what I loved, and Leia was right, although I loved working with a bunch of kids, it would be easier dealing with a single one.

"Maybe you're right."

"Don't let your blessings pass you by because you wanna overthink things, bestie." She walked around her car and opened her back door.

I headed for my driver's side. "Now, speaking of work, I need to get home and showered so I can get ready to clock in."

Leia was a clergy down at the courthouse. "Okay, boo. I'll talk to you later." I opened my door. Leia gave me a wave and climbed in her car.

I had a lot to think about and didn't want to make Tripp wait too long. It was important to introduce structure in kids at a young age, and I was sure that was what he wanted.

———

I was surprised when I pulled into my grandparents' house and saw an additional car in the driveway.

Climbing out of my car, I walked to the front door and pushed it open before stepping inside. I stopped as soon as I stepped inside the living room, seeing two people I could have done without.

There sat my grandparents along with my parents. They were in mid conversation, but it died out once they noticed me.

"Brylee. We've been waiting for you," Gran mentioned with a gentle smile on her face. She shifted her eyes to my parents then back at me.

My lips pressed together, and my eyes shuffled around the living room. I didn't see my younger siblings anywhere. My parents now had a four and six-year-old they happily raised together. While I didn't care to have a relationship with our parents, I never took that out on my younger siblings. I saw them frequently and even got them a couple times, through my grandparents, of course.

"I didn't know you were having extra guests," I said tightly, crossing my arms over my chest, refusing to give any attention to my parents.

"We figured it's been awhile since we came to a Sunday dinner, and the kids wanted to see Mom and Dad, so we decided to stop by," My mom, or Breann, as I referred to her, said.

Twisting my neck, I gave her a blank stare. One thing I could admit was she looked good. My gran always said we could pass for sisters since I favored her so much, especially when I was teenager.

"It's good to see you, Bry. You look more beautiful each time I lay eyes on you," my dad, or Corey, referenced.

"Isn't she? I swear she looks just like me." Breann laughed.

My face stayed blank. "My name is Brylee." We weren't close, so they didn't need to give me any nicknames. I had made this known before.

"Brylee—" My Grandad started.

"Second, it's not like you see me a lot, so..." I let my words trail off.

My dad's jaw clenched. "You're still beautiful. Your sister looks like a younger version of you."

"How would you even remember that? Isn't she at the age I was when you two took off?" I cocked my head to the side.

My sister, Brittani, was six—a year older than I was when my parents decided they didn't want the responsibility of raising a kid anymore.

"That's not fair—"

"Please, spare me," I spat and looked at my grandparents. "You guys could have warned me that they would be here. I wouldn't have come." I turned to leave.

"Brylee!" my Grandad called out. "We get you were blindsided, but that doesn't mean you need to leave. It's Sunday, meaning we have dinner as normal."

I clenched my jaw. The last thing I wanted to do was sit and have dinner with the two people who were too selfish to be there for me.

"Lee-Lee, please don't go," my gran pleaded.

I closed my eyes and pushed a heavy breath out. I didn't like upsetting my grandparents. If they wanted me to stay, I would, but that didn't mean I would talk to my parents.

"Fine," I huffed.

A small smile formed on Gran's face. "Thank you."

With a stiff nod, I walked deeper into the living room and took a seat close to my grandparents. The tension in the room was thick. They didn't continue the conversation from before I got here. I already regretted agreeing to stay and counted the minutes until this dinner was over.

———

Normally, I enjoyed coming to my grandparents' house and spending time with them, but today I wasn't feeling it. While everyone around me talked and laughed, I stayed quiet, silently eating my food.

The main people I talked with were my siblings, who were napping but woken up when it was time to sit down and eat. Brittani and our younger brother, Brandon, sat on each side of me. Brittani excitedly told me about kindergarten. I was happy my sister enjoyed school, while Brandon told me about whatever came to his young mind. I genuinely liked being around my siblings. The age gap between us was large, but I didn't care about that. I tried to make sure they still knew me.

"How's the job searching going, Brylee?" Grandad asked after a while. They were aware of the fire. My gran called me that same day after seeing it on the news.

"I thought you worked at a daycare? I was actually looking to get Brandon enrolled in it," Breann interrupted.

"Promising. I got an offer recently. I'm still debating on it, however," I answered ignoring Breann.

"The daycare had a fire, so it's closed right now," my gran told my mom and gave me a stern look, but I paid it no attention.

It was none of her business what was happening in my life. I knew the only reason she or her husband knew anything about my life was because my grandparents insisted on keeping them informed on my life.

"Was anyone hurt?" Corey asked, and like his wife, I ignored him and scooped up some creamed corn before shoving it in my mouth. One of them sighed, and I paid it no mind.

Dinner continued, and as soon as I finished my plate, I cleaned up to leave.

"Brylee," Breann called after me as I walked into the kitchen to ditch my plate.

"I don't want to talk," I told her, not slowing down.

"Well, then just listen." Ignoring her, I walked to the sink and placed my plate and glass in it. "Look, I know me and your dad fucked up, but we were kids ourselves when we had you. Neither of us knew how to raise a kid. We were too unstable as a couple alone. Trying to be parents wouldn't have been good for anyone. We did what we felt was best for you at the time," she explained.

Turning to face her, I stared at her youthful face. Her face was perfectly beat with her hair in box braids that were currently wrapped in a bun.

"Breann, please. If you're gonna tell it, tell it right. You two wanted to live your lives, and having a kid hindered that."

My parents both left for college after giving me to my mom's parents. Periodically, I would see them when they came home for breaks, but even still they didn't make much effort to be around me. By the time they were home for good, I had adjusted to being with my grandparents and wanted nothing to do with them.

"Like I said, we were young and made mistakes. We know that now. Raising Brittani and Brandon showed us how much we fucked up and what we missed out on. You're obviously not a kid anymore, but we *are* trying to right our wrongs and be in your life now."

"Oh, you mean now that I'm old enough to not need you guys?" A pissed off laugh left my mouth. "I'm good, Breann. You two can focus on the two kids you have now, and hopefully you don't fuck them up." I went to walk around her, but she grabbed my upper arm.

"You still need to respect me, Brylee. I'm still your mother."

I snatched away from her. "Don't touch me. *My mother* is the woman sitting at the table out there." I glared at her then stalked off.

I stepped back into the dining room and walked to my gran first. "I'm gonna head out, Gran." I bent down and kissed her cheek then went to my grandad.

"Already? You haven't even eaten dessert. I made peach cobbler," she mentioned.

As much as I would love to stay and eat, I chose against it. "Yeah, I'll come by tomorrow and grab a slice." I kissed my Grandad's cheek.

My mom stood at the entrance with a sour look on her face while watching me.

"What happened?" Corey questioned. His eyes bouncing between me and Breann.

"Your wife doesn't know when to back off," I said and went to my siblings so I could say my goodbyes.

"Brylee is just disrespectful, and I don't care what we did, I'm not tolerating it."

Rolling my eyes, I hugged and kissed my siblings and stood straight. "Anyway, I'm out."

"Brylee, please don't go," Gran pleaded.

This time, however, I wasn't giving in. I had stayed longer than I would have liked. My grandparents knew I didn't care to be around my parents, and usually, they respected it.

"Sorry, Gran." I gave her a small smile.

Neither of my grandparents looked pleased with the fact I was leaving, but they would get over it. I chose to protect my peace, and being around my parents gave the opposite of that.

———

"As you can see, the house isn't too much to handle—not that you'll be required to do anything outside of taking care of Scottlynn," Tripp explained.

I decided to take him up on the job offer, and he suggested I come and see the house I would live in. It was a nice four bedroom, three and a half bath, two leveled home. It had a modern style, with a standard kitchen, living room, and dining room. There was a medium sized fenced in backyard, with an attached two car garage.

"Does it meet your liking?" he asked with a smirk on his face.

Currently, Scottlynn babbled away in Tripp's arms, chewing on a teething toy. I smiled at her before giving her dad my attention.

I grinned softly. "It does. You have a nice house."

"Does that mean you'll take the position?" He looked hopeful. It was clear working and taking care of his daughter took a toll on him.

I nodded. "Yes."

He sighed in relief. "Oh, thank God. Going through the process of trying to find someone else was gonna make me say fuck it and be a stay-at-home dad."

I snickered.

We were in the living room now. My eyes circled the room and stopped on a medium sized picture of Tripp holding a fresh Scottlynn and a woman hugging his waist.

I stepped closer to the photo and studied it. "Is this her mother?" I questioned.

"Yeah. Her name is Skye."

"She's pretty," I admitted. I continued studying the picture, not being able to pinpoint what it was, but something about the woman's smile didn't feel as bright and happy as one would be when taking a family picture. It almost looked forced.

"Yeah, she is." I looked up at Tripp, noting change in his face. He stared at the photo with a hint of sadness.

"If you don't mind me asking, where is she? I'm assuming she's not in Scottlynn's life?"

Tripp didn't answer right away. He turned and walked to a play mat on the ground and sat Scottlynn down. His shoulder's hunch over, and when he turned to face me again, his expression was gloomier than before.

"She's in rehab," he answered, shocking me.

My eyes widened. "Oh," I replied, unsure how to respond.

Tripped glanced back at the picture. "It's been a struggle for her for a while, and I thought after having Scottlynn would make her stay clean, but..." His voice trailed off.

My chest ached, not only for Tripp, but his daughter too. By how he spoke I could hear he still had feelings for the mother of his daughter. It was sad she couldn't be what he expected. Then Scottlynn was missing out on a mother, too. I didn't want to judge Skye since I didn't know her, but knowing who missed out because of her usage pained me.

"So, this position is only temporary, then? Until she gets out?"

When he first suggested it to me, I didn't think it was something I needed to ask, but now I had to make sure. If I was going give my house up and move in here, I needed longer than a couple months of employment to sell me.

He shook his head. "No, not at all. Even when Skye comes home, I still want you here. She was having a hard time with the baby, so having someone to help who knows what they're doing will be good for her."

"How long will she be gone?"

"The program is for three months. If all goes well she has two months left."

I nodded and chewed the inside of my cheek. I eyed the picture again. While Skye wasn't here now, I wondered how things would be once she returned home.

———

"I could have just hired movers," I told Tripp when he stepped back inside my house. It took me two weeks to get my stuff packed and let my landlord know I was moving. I had sold and donated a lot of things, only packing my bedroom and few other belongings up to take with me. What I didn't want to part with I put in storage.

"Why hire movers when you have capable people right here?" he said with a grin on his face.

"Nah, you should have let her hire movers. It's hot as fuck out," his brother, Troy, complained.

"Shut yo' ass up. You ain't have anything else to do today," Tripp said, lifting the box off the ground, causing me to snicker. My eyes locked on the way his muscles bulged in the cut off shirt he wore.

Troy cleared his throat, and I turned to him. He gave me an amused look, showing he caught me checking his brother out. I smiled bashfully then turned to grab a couple of the smaller things.

Tripp surprised me when he offered to help me get moved in. He recruited his brothers and a couple other firefighters to come help. The larger stuff had already been handled, now we were working on the small boxes. I didn't realize how much stuff I had in my bedroom until now. The room I was moving into at Tripp's wasn't as big as my current bedroom, but I would make do. I didn't need much space anyway.

"Brylee!" Leia's voice rang, and soon, she appeared in my bedroom. "I got the pizza you asked for. I put it in the living room."

Since everyone came to help me today, I knew the least I could do was feed them.

"Oh, you ain't said nothing but a word." Troy put the box he had in his hands down and started for the door.

"You could have at least took the box with you," Tripp scolded.

Troy waved him off. "It ain't going anywhere."

Shaking his head, Tripp followed his younger brother.

"Girl, how the hell all three brothers fine as hell like that?" Leia looped her arm through mine.

I snickered. "Leia, don't start your shit."

"Girlllllll, I never wanted to be on train so much in my life."

Again, I laughed, this time causing tears in my eyes. We left my room and headed for my living room. "Listen, if you don't shoot your shot at your boss you're crazy."

"I told you he's still with his child's mom." My mouth turned upside down.

"The crackhead? Girl." She waved me off.

"Leia!" I stopped and looked around, making sure no one was around. "Could you not be so loud? I'm sure I wasn't supposed to tell you that."

She shrugged. "Just saying. I don't see her as much competition."

"There's nothing to compete with because I'm not going there for that. I'm being paid to take care of his daughter and that's it."

"Hmph, we'll see."

We continued for the living room where the guys stood around talking and eating. Tripp had both his brothers, Troy and Terrance with him. Harlem and Lee from his firehouse were also here. They made sure to get the larger stuff to the storage unit a lot faster than I expected.

"Girl, everyone is just fine. I need to visit that fire house and see the whole squad," Leia leaned over and whispered.

"Behave." I snickered, nudging her with my shoulder.

"I hope I got enough for everyone," I called. "I know this is probably the last thing you would want on your day off."

"You're good," Tripp spoke up, stepping forward. "These niggas ain't have shit else to do."

A small smile formed on my face. My eyes circled my living room, watching his friends and brothers talk among themselves. Leia had left my side and grabbed a piece of pizza, joining in the conversation.

"What's going on here?"

I snapped my eyes to my front door. Standing in front of it was Russell. Confusion filled his face as he looked around.

"What are you doing here?" I wondered. I walked toward him.

Russell narrowed his eyes and scanned the room again. "You haven't been answering my calls, so I came to talk to you in person." His brows creased. "You moving or something?"

Tripp was now at my side. Russell's eyes cut tighter as he eyed him.

"Yes, I am." I crossed my arms over my chest. "And I didn't answer because we have nothing to talk about."

"We got a lot to talk about." He stepped closer.

I noticed the chatter in the room seized, and everyone watched us. "No, we don't. Everything was said the day you walked out. You can leave now."

His jaw clenched. "Not until we talk."

"She's made it clear she doesn't want to talk to you," Tripp spoke up, stepping in front of me. His friends gathered close to him, along with his brothers.

I glanced at Leia, and she looked impressed as she chomped on her pizza.

Russell snorted. "What, you got bodyguards now?"

Sighing, I stepped around Tripp so I could see Russell again. "Russell, you need to leave. Me and you are over. You obviously weren't happy with me, so there's no point in prolonging anything. Now, please go."

"You heard what she said. Either you can leave, or we'll toss you out," Terrance told him. Out of the three brothers, he was the bulkier one. While all three had size, he looked like he lived in the gym. I hoped Russell wouldn't allow it to go that far. The last thing I wanted was a scene caused in front of my new boss. I didn't want him thinking I was problematic before I even officially started.

Russell tucked his lips in his mouth and slowly nodded his head. His hand went to his jaw were he rubbed it slowly.

"A'right, you got it. It seems you still need some time to calm down. I'll try to talk to you again another time."

I shook my head, watching him turn and leave.

I sighed in relief once he was gone. I turned to look at Tripp to explain. His eyes were still focused on the door.

"Sorry about that."

He glanced down at me with penetrating eyes. "He won't be an issue, will he? I don't need any more drama appearing on my doorstep."

I shook my head. "No, he won't. Me and him are over."

Stiffly, he nodded then glanced back at the door. Everyone went back to what they were doing before, leaving us to ourselves.

"I thought it was understood that the two of us were done, but it seemed I was wrong. Today, I made that clear. Working for you is giving me a fresh start, and Russell isn't a part of that." Again, he nodded. This time, his body looked less tense. "I appreciate you and your guys stepping up for me too, even though it wasn't needed."

He shrugged. "When a woman tells a man to fuck off, and he doesn't, then that's a problem."

I smiled softly. "You're right."

Pushing a deep breath out, I turned and looked around my living room again with my hands propped on my hips. There was only a little left to clear out, then I would officially be moved out. I was excited to start my new job and the next part of my life.

CHAPTER 7

TRIPP

"Y̶ou settling in okay?"

Brylee jumped and spun around, holding on her chest. "Shit. I'm so used to being in my house alone." She snickered, looking around.

Leaning against the opening of her door, I crossed my arms and scanned her over. Her locs were pulled up in a bun. She was officially moved in. I was picking up my daughter tomorrow from my parents before I had to clock in for my next shift.

"My bad, I didn't mean to startle you. Just wanted to know if you needed anything?"

She had taken the room across from mine but next to Scottlynn's.

Brylee gave me a small smile. "Nope. Just gonna put my things away then shower."

I looked around at the empty bins. She was in the middle of putting the clothes in them away. A few boxes were stacked up on the walls. I noticed she didn't bring a lot of things to the house with her.

"You mind if I come in? I wanna talk to you about something."

She nodded and waved me in. "Of course. It's still your house."

I stepped in the room. "But I still want you to have your privacy. I won't ever enter your room without your permission. I want you to be comfortable here." I walked to the bed and sat on the edge. "Anything you need help with?"

"Nope. Once I put these last few clothes away, I'll be good. The rest can be done later."

I tapped my fingers on the top of my knee. "The guy who popped up at your place earlier. Your ex. You mind telling me the story there?" It shouldn't have, but it had been gnawing at me since he appeared at Brylee's house. "You don't have to if you don't want to, but I'm curious."

She stared at me in confusion before leaning on the dresser behind her. "About what?"

"Why did you break up?"

Her shoulders deflated as her eyes dropped. "Oh. In short because he never had time for me. All he did was work, and apparently, I nagged too much about wanting some time with him." A forced laugh fell from her mouth. "It doesn't matter, though. The relationship should have been over a long time ago. I just kept holding on hoping things would get better."

Her confession caused me to rub my sternum. "Did you love him?"

Her lips twisted to the side. "I thought I did. Now, I don't know if I even know what love truly is." She sighed. "Anyway, I'm closing that chapter of my life and starting another. This job is a new beginning for me." She grinned, making me do the same.

"I'm glad you feel that way. You don't know how much stress you're taking off me by agreeing to this."

Standing, I wiped my hands over my sweats. "If you need anything, let me know. You have free range of the house. Treat it like it's yours."

I headed out of the room. I wanted to go spend a few hours in my workshop before officially calling it a night.

———

Pulling my hat off, I looked at the scene in front of me. There was a house fire we were called to, but it spread like crazy, taking half of the front half with it. We were able to get the family out, although the mom was on her way to the hospital from intense smoke ventilation. The two kids were safe with the neighbor, following behind the ambulance.

"I hope they have insurance. That fire did a number on their house." Lee walked up on me.

It was a shame because the mom was so tired, she fell asleep on her young kids, and they knocked a candle over, which caught fire to the curtains.

The team finished up at the scene and then loaded up in the trucks. This was only our second call on shift, and part of me hoped for more so the night would go by quicker. It was a little after twelve at night. As I sat in my seat, I stared at my phone, fighting the urge to dial up Brylee to check in.

"She's okay, man. Stop looking like you're about to jump out of the truck to run home," Lee joked.

I looked up at him. "What you talking about?"

"The way you looking at your phone. You're worried about Scottlynn, right?"

"Why would you be worried about her? Something happened?" Omiras asked from the captain seat in front of us.

I shook my head.

"He got a new nanny," Harlem spoke up.

"Already? That was quick. Who is she?"

"Remember that daycare that had that fire a couple weeks back? One of the teachers."

I cut my eyes Harlem. "Damn, you gon' let me talk?" He tossed his hands up. "Anyway, yeah. She was one of the daycare workers. I knew they would be out of a job for a while, so I thought we could help each other."

"She fine as fuck too. If I wasn't married—" Lee started.

"But you are." I cut my eyes in his direction.

"Shit... I'm not. She is fine. I don't know how you gon' keep your hands to yourself," Harlem agreed.

"In case y'all forgot, I do have a girl that's the mother of my child. I ain't even looking at her like that."

"Man." Harlem waved him off.

I looked down at my phone. Instead of calling like I wanted, I went to camera app. As much as I wanted to say I trusted Brylee a hundred percent, I didn't. Part of it was because of Skye. She was right under my nose still getting high knowing she had a daughter to take care of. The other half was because as nice and knowing as she seemed to be, Brylee was still a stranger, and I had to make sure my daughter was in good hands.

Brylee was lying on the couch with Scottlynn lying in her swing, feeding herself a bottle. She laughed at something on the TV. Everything seemed to be fine, which caused some worry to leave me.

"Have you heard from Skye?" Omiras questioned.

I cleared my throat. "Once."

"She good?"

"Seems like it."

"Good." He nodded and turned back to the front. I turned and looked out the window. The streets of West Pier were busy.

A call went off on the radio, calling for our station house to respond.

"House 112 in route," Omiras answered. The sirens were flipped on, and the horn went off. I looked down at my phone before locking it and putting it down. I needed to get focused and not worry so much. With this job my head had to be in it, or someone could get hurt or even killed.

———

I crept into my house, yawning and ready to climb in my bed and get some sleep. It was a little after nine in the morning. I wanted to get some sleep in and spend a little time with Scottlynn before I had to go back in at eight tonight. The sounds of my daughter's laughter caught my ears.

I shut the door behind me and walked down the hallway to the kitchen. When I stepped inside, Scottlynn giggled at something on the iPad screen sitting on her highchair table. Shifting my eyes, I watched Brylee dance to the song while stirring something on the stove.

"Baby on the boat. Baby on the boat," she sang along, bouncing her ass.

I bit into my bottom lip.

"This song's the shit, isn't it, Scottlynn?" She glanced over her shoulder at my daughter.

"That it is."

Brylee jumped and spun around. I chuckled and walked over to my daughter. When Scottlynn saw me, she eagerly bounced in her seat and reached for me.

"Hey, Munchkin." I lowered my bag and reached for her. "Whatchu watchin' that's got you so excited?" I glanced at the screen.

"*Gracie's Corner.* She loves dancing along to the songs," Brylee answered.

I peeked at her. "She ain't the only one." I smirked.

Her cheeks reddened. "They're catchy." She whipped around, facing the stove again. I kissed my daughter's cheek.

"Whatchu makin'? Smells good."

"Just some French toast, eggs, and grits. You want some?" She looked over her should at me.

"Hell yeah."

Some good food would put me right to sleep. I ate something light a few hours ago, but I wasn't going to turn down something homecooked.

"Go ahead and take a seat. I'll bring you a plate," she said.

She didn't have to tell me twice. I walked over to the table, grabbing the iPad on the way, and took a seat. I set the iPad up and placed Scottlynn on my lap.

"Were you good for Brylee?" I asked her.

"She was. She's such a sweet, happy baby!" Brylee walked over, placing a plate in front of me.

Scottlynn instantly attempted to reach for it.

"Slow down there. I know it smells good." I laughed, scooping some eggs with my fork and shoving them in my mouth.

After getting us some orange juice and her plate, Brylee took a seat across from us. She lowered her head, and I followed suit while she said a quick prayer.

"Damn, I love a home cooked meal after a long shift." I put the syrup back on the table and dug in.

Brylee cleared her throat and wiped her mouth. "Did her mother…"

"Skye."

She nodded. "Yeah, Skye, did she not cook?"

I chuckled. "Nah, cooking wasn't her strong suit. She was more of a cereal and Roman Noodles kind of girl."

"I grew up with my Gran, and she was old fashioned. She wouldn't hear of me not knowing how to *burn in the kitchen,* as she would say." Her nose scrunched while her face lit up as she laughed.

"Your mom wasn't a cooker?" I wondered, scooping some grits up.

Her smile fell. "My mom wasn't around much. It was just me, my gran, and grandad."

From her voice, I could tell it was a tough subject.

"Sorry to hear that."

Her shoulders lifted. "Thanks, but it's okay. My grandparents were great." Again, she cleared her throat. "Anyway, because of her, I've grown to love to cook."

Scottlynn's hand went to my eggs, and she took a large handful.

"Scottlynn!" Brylee laughed.

"Guess you weren't eating fast enough."

I shook my head and reached for napkin to wipe her hands before she could shove them in her mouth.

"How was work? Any crazy fires?" Brylee asked after a while of silence.

I lifted my head and stared at her in surprise.

"What?" Her brows furrowed.

Blinking a couple times, I shook my head and swallowed. "Oh, nothing. It's just been so long since someone asked me how my day was. It was cool. Nothing too crazy. Long as hell." I yawned. "Speaking of. Ima head off to bed and grab a few hours a sleep. You

54

good with her?" Smiling, she nodded and pushed back from the stable and stood up.

"Of course. That's what I'm here for." She reached for Scottlynn, who didn't hesitate to reach for her.

After handing my daughter off, I stood and picked my plate up to take it to the sink. I picked my duffle bag off the floor and faced the table again.

"If you need me, I'll be upstairs."

She waved me off. "Tell your dad we got this. We're gonna get dress and go run some errands, then maybe go to the park for little bit." She held Scottlynn under the arms and bounced her while taking baby talk.

Scottlynn waved her arms wildly while babbling and laughing.

My heart swelled so large it barely left space inside me as I watched her interact with my daughter. She was a natural with her. It was clear she truly loved kids, and they loved her back.

CHAPTER 8

BRYLEE

"And who is this pretty thing here?" Gran asked, looking over my shoulder at Scottlynn in her car seat. She sucked on her thumb while staring up with wide, curious eyes.

I unhooked Scottlynn and pulled her out of the car seat. "Scottlynn, the baby I'm taking care of."

"She is so precious. Hi, sweet girl." Gran grinned, holding her hand out. Scottlynn happily took ahold of her hand and flashed her a gummy grin.

"Such a happy baby."

I took a seat with Gran following suit. This was the first I'd been back since dinner. I still wasn't over being ambushed with my parents, but I could never hold a grudge with my grandparents.

"I know, thankfully." I reached over and grabbed one of Scottlynn's toys and handed it to her. She happily gnawed on the teething toy.

"So, you're liking your new job I take it?"

"I am. You know working with kids has always been my passion. I can't lie and say although I loved the daycare, I forgot how much easier it is working with just one kid."

Gran gave me a soft smile. "I'm glad to hear that, Lee-Lee, but I'm still a little unsettled with you living in this random man's house. Couldn't you watch the baby without moving into his home?"

I bounced Scottlynn while she continued chewing on her toy without a care in the world. "With the hours he works, this makes it easier. He's a nice guy, Gran. You don't have anything to worry about."

Her lips tucked into her mouth. "Still, I would feel more comfortable if me and your grandad met him."

I groaned. "Gran."

She shook her head. "Don't Gran me. Folks are crazy nowadays. This man could be some serial killer who lures women into his house and buries them in the basement." She frowned, and her forehead creased at the thought.

I laughed and shook my head. "I assure you there are no bodies in the basement. He doesn't even have a basement."

"Then the backyard."

"Okay, lady. No more Lifetime for you." I snickered again.

"What are two of my favorite women in here laughing about?" Grandad made an appearance. He walked to the couch and leaned down, kissing my temple then sat on the other side of my grandma.

"Grandad, you gotta stop letting Gran watch Lifetime. She thinks I'm gonna get chopped up and buried in someone's backyard."

"Walt, tell her we would feel more comfortable if we met the man she currently lives with."

My grandad's face turned serious. "She's right, Lee-Lee. We don't know this man, and if you're going to be living with him, I want to meet him."

"You two act like I'm dating him. He's my boss. It'll be unprofessional to ask him to meet my grandparents."

"No, it's called being cautious. Invite him to Sunday dinner, or just bring him by. Either way, we expect to meet him soon."

"Speaking of Sunday dinner..." Gran said. I felt the headache forming, already knowing what she was about to say.

I looked up and noticed the time on the digital clock on the wall.

"Can you hold her? She's due for a bottle soon." I had been

working for Tripp for a week now, and I was trying to create a routine with Scottlynn. Kids did better when they had balance and structure.

"Of course." Gran took Scottlynn, who didn't put up much fight. "Hello there, pretty girl. You can call me Gran, too," Gran spoke to her in baby talk. "I swear they are the sweetest at this age." Gran sighed with a soft smile.

"Aren't they? I should've popped a few more in you," Grandad mentioned, causing me to frown. The two had three kids altogether— my mom being the middle child.

"Now, I don't know about that. I'm happy with the four we raised, though." She looked at me, and I smiled at her. Even before my parents gave me up, my grandparents had me most of the time, mainly because my mom still lived with them when I was born. My dad's parents were firm on you birth them, you raise them, so they only kept me sometimes. It was always comical to me because my mom's youngest brother grew up like my older brother.

I proceeded to make the bottle while my grandparents played with Scottlynn. When I finished, I handed over the bottle, and she happily dropped her toy in exchange.

"Now, back to you, Brylee. We need to talk about Sunday."

I shook my head and sighed. My shoulders fell forward, and I rubbed my temples. "Gran, please. We really don't have anything to talk about."

"Then just listen to me. I understand your parents hurt you by giving you to me and your grandad to raise. I understand why you don't want to forgive them. That's well within your right, but I do believe you need to sit and have a conversation with them. Walking around angry isn't healthy for you. If you don't want to have a relationship with them or forgive them, that's fine, but at least do it for yourself."

"Your Gran's right, Lee-Lee. We can't force you to do anything you don't want to do but letting go of that resentment will be better for you in the long run."

Lifting my head, I tilted it, pushing my hair out of my face and looking at my grandparents. Not once did I ever hear them complain about stepping up and raising me. They never tried to force me to go back to my parents, even when they were finally ready to be parents. They loved me, not just how grandparents loved their grandchild, but how parents were supposed to love their child.

"I'll think about it, okay? Not right now, though, and I would appreciate not being ambushed by them again either."

Both nodded.

"We can do that."

While I had no issues with spending time with my siblings, my parents would take some time. It hurt at first being around my younger brother and sister, but over time, it got better. They were innocent kids and didn't deserve the resentment I had toward the two that created us.

"And make sure you make plans to bring this little one's dad over soon, too." Gran eyed me with a raised brow.

I snorted and nodded. "I'll talk to him about it, Gran."

I wasn't going to guarantee it, but I would bring it up. I got my grandparents' reservations, but I was sure when they met Tripp, they would see how good of a guy he was.

———

When I stepped inside the house, I was surprised to see Tripp on the couch watching TV.

"Here, let me grab her." He stood from the couch.

I shook my head. "I have her, but you can grab the bags out of my car if you don't mind."

"I gotchu." He nodded and walked around me, stopping to peek down at his daughter, and then heading for the door.

"This is a surprise, huh?" I spoke to Scottlynn, setting her car seat on the couch to take her out. I walked her over to her basinet and laid her down. She had fallen asleep on the way home.

With Scottlynn settled, I turned to help Tripp get the bags out of my car, but I was surprised when he came walking in with all the bags in hand.

"I was coming to help," I mentioned, shutting the door behind him.

"It's all good." He walked down the hall to the kitchen with me behind him.

"You two must have had a busy day."

I went into the bags he set on the island to unload them. He surprised me when he proceeded to help me.

"Yeah, I took her by my grandparents' house, which by the way, you're lucky my Gran even let me bring her back home." I paused and laughed. "Then we went to the grocery store. I also had to go to the mall to return some shoes I couldn't fit. She fell asleep on the way home from there."

"Damn, I was hoping to see her when y'all go back."

"Oh, don't worry. You can wake her up now if you want. It's actually too late for her to be napping, but I needed to put these groceries away and start dinner. I didn't expect you to be here."

"I'm off for the next three days, remember?"

I didn't. I knew Tripp worked four days on and three days off until he switched back to twenty-four-hour shifts, but I didn't realize it was time for his three days off already.

"Whatchu cooking?" he asked, pulling chicken out.

"Chicken fajitas. I have a craving for them."

"Shit. I hear that. You keep cooking like this, and you'll be fired as a nanny and hired as the chef."

I snickered. "Please. I'm not that good. I just don't see the point of eating out when I can make something that'll last days at a time."

"I beg to differ. That smothered chicken with white rice you made last week was good as hell."

I blushed and lowered my head, hoping my hair hid my flushed cheeks. "Thanks. That was one of the first meals my Gran showed me how to cook."

"If you can cook like you do, then I know your Gran throws down."

I attempted to put something in the top cabinet but struggled. It didn't take long for me to learn the kitchen. I inhaled a sharp breath when he pressed into me and grabbed the bottle from me, placing it on the correct shelf. The scent of musk, rosemary, and grapefruit invaded my nose. It was a clean, fresh, citrus smell that caused a tingle in my stomach.

"Thank you," I murmured when he stepped back.

"No problem. I didn't realize how short you are fo'real."

I frowned. "I'm average height. Thank you very much."

He chuckled. "Yeah, you keep telling yourself that. How tall are you? Five one? Five two?"

I rolled my eyes and smacked my lips. "Five three."

Again, he chuckled. "Oh yeah, you're a giant."

I joined in with him before waving him off. "Whatever. I'm tall enough, and that's all that matters." I went back to the island to finish clearing the bags so I could get started cooking. "Since you're here…"

"Uh oh." He leaned on the island and gave me his full attention.

I smirked. "My grandparents want to meet you." I pulled the peppers out and sat them to the side. "They aren't really comfortable with me living with you. They're scared you might chop me up and bury me in your backyard."

His eyes widened before he laughed. It was deep and from the gut. "What the fuck?"

I snickered. "I know, I know, but they won't let up no matter how unprofessional I told them it was." I rolled my eyes.

Once Tripp got his laughing under control, he stood straight and wiped his eyes. "That's wild as hell, but I get it. If it makes them more comfortable, I don't mind." His shoulders lifted.

"Really? You really don't have to. They still treat me like a kid sometimes, not realizing I'm a grown woman."

He shook his head. "Nah, I get where they're coming from. If it was Scottlynn, I would feel the same way. You can't trust people nowadays."

"Thank you. I'm sure they'll be happy to hear that."

It grew quiet between us as I prepared to cook.

"You need help with something?"

"Nope. Go ahead and love on your baby. I got this." I waved him off and took my phone out of my back pocket to turn Pandora on. The first song that came on was "Never Had" by Lady K. She was quickly becoming one of favorite new R&B artists.

"You got it, boss. Let me know if you need me." He tapped the island than turned to leave.

I got lost singing along with Lady K and moving around the kitchen.

CHAPTER 9

TRIPP

"**D**amn, that hit the spot," I complimented, rubbing on my stomach. "I don't remember the last time I had a home cooked meal my mama didn't make."

Brylee's cheeks tinted red, and she lowered her hair slightly, causing a few of her loose locs to fall forward to hide her face. "Thank you."

I shifted my attention to my daughter, who sat happily in her highchair, wobbling her arms and babbling to herself.

"What you over here talking about, Munchkin?" I turned to my daughter. She twisted her neck and picked up some of the baby treats off her tabletop and shoved them in her mouth. "Are they good?" I grinned.

She babbled something else and shoved her hand to my face. I glanced down at the soiled hand and soggy treats, frowning. "Nah, I'll leave those to you."

Brylee laughed next to us. "Don't do her like that. Tell him, pretty girl, he better appreciate your generosity."

I chuckled. "I'll do anything for my baby girl, but eating those soggy ass snacks of hers is where I draw the line." I poked a finger in her chunky cheeks. That brought a laugh from both Brylee and Scottlynn.

"For a first-time dad, you're pretty good at it," Brylee mentioned.

Taking my eyes off Scottlynn for a second, I looked up at Brylee. The hues in her orbs seemed softer and brighter than normal.

"I've always wanted to be a dad. I hoped to have a couple kids by now, but I'm just happy to have at least one." My voice softened, and for a second, I got lost in deep thought. I always had dreams of having house full of kids. Family was important to me. I had always been close to mine, and it made me even more excited to start my own.

"I always wanted kids too," she admitted. Scottlynn still babbled to herself, now playing with my fingers. "For now, I'm satisfied with just working with them."

I cocked my head and examined her. "Your ex didn't want kids?"

She snorted and stared down at Scottlynn. "My ex was too worried about his job to consider kids. I couldn't see myself starting a family with him anyway."

"I think you would make a great mom."

A small smile formed on her face, and her cheeks tinted pink again.

A comfortable silence passed between us. While she watched my daughter, I watched her. I noted the genuine smile towards Scottlynn. The way her face lit up when she interacted with her. A lump formed in my throat. I never saw this with Skye before. I was usually the more hands on one when it came to our daughter.

"I guess I should clean up and get her bathed and ready for bed," Brylee said eventually, setting her phone down. I glanced at the time, noticing it was a little after seven. "I try to have her in bed by eight."

One thing I loved was the routine she created for my daughter. I knew kids strived off structure, and with my schedule, there was no way I could give her that.

She stood, and I reached out, grabbing her wrist. "I'll clean up."

Her brows scrunched. "You sure? I don't mind."

I nodded. "You cooked. It's the least I can do. Matter fact, take the rest of the night off."

"Oh no I—"

I raised my hand and lifted one corner of my mouth. "It's not every day I get to go through her nightly routine and put her to sleep, so Ima take advantage of it."

Understanding filled her face, and she nodded. "Okay, if you insist."

My doorbell going off caught my attention. My brows furrowed, and my mouth pressed together.

"You expecting someone?" I questioned.

Brylee's eyebrows shot up, and she shook her head. "No."

Whoever it was, they were persistent. Frowning, I pushed away from the table and stood up. Making my way out of the kitchen to the living room, I checked out the peephole when I got to the door.

Confusion filled me as I pulled back and unlocked the door for my brother.

"About damn time," Terrance complained, standing straight.

"Given you weren't invited over, you're lucky I opened the door at all." I stepped back and allowed him in. "Whatchu doing here, anyway?" I closed the door behind him.

"Was in the area and decided to stop by before heading home. Where's my niece at?" He lifted his head and sniffed. "And shit, something smells good. Let me get a plate."

I frowned and cut my eyes at him. "Ain't no more," I lied. Oddly, I didn't want to share Brylee's cooking, even if it was just with my brother.

"Hey, I'm gonna go ahead and put her in the bath." Brylee stepped in the room with Scottlynn in her arms. "Oh, hi, Terrance." She stopped next to me.

"There goes my pretty niece," Terrance cooed as he reached forward. Brylee wildly babbled at him. "Wassup, Brylee? That's you in here burning like that?" He grinned at my daughter.

Brylee giggled. "Yeah, I made chicken fajitas. There's more in there if you're hungry."

"Oh, you ain't said nothing but a word." He rubbed his stomach, tossing me a smug smile. "Oh I would *love* a plate of a plate of *your* cooking."

Brylee faced me. "I'm going to go get her washed up. I won't put her sleep, though. You can still do that part."

"Thanks." She smiled softly. "I'll be up in a few." I looked at my daughter. "I'll be up in a little bit, Munchkin. Let me get rid of your worrisome uncle."

Brylee snickered. "No problem." She faced my brother for a second. "Nice to see you again, Terrance."

Brylee turned for the stairs, and my eyes never left her. I licked my lips, and eventually, I dragged my eyes away from her once she reached the top of the stairs and faced my brother. He had an amused expression on his face.

"What?"

He chuckled and brushed passed me. I followed behind him wondering what was so funny. "Nigga, wash your hands first," I complained when he went to get a plate. He redirected himself and went to the sink.

When he finished, he grabbed a plate and turned toward the extra food. "Damn, Brylee be throwing down like this? Shit, she's single now, right? I need a woman who knows how to cook."

I shot him a deadpanned look. "You gone tell me who you know over here?" I crossed my arms over my chest and leaned on the wall near me.

"You gone tell me you fucking the nanny?" He smirked at me as he headed for the microwave.

A frown formed on my face. "You know I'm still with Skye. Plus, she works for me. I wouldn't cross that line."

My brother waved me off. "I don't see you and Skye working out, and when y'all end, you gone need someone else. Brylee's fine as hell, and she cooks. Plus, I saw how you looked at her."

My eyes narrowed. Terrance was always the more carefree one out the three of us. He was the youngest and was babied more than me and Troy. He always found joy in causing mischief, too.

"Brylee's good at her job, and I'm grateful she's good with my daughter. That's it. I don't know what you think you're reading into, but you got it wrong."

The smirk on Terrance's face heightened, and his brows wagged. The microwave went off, and he turned to grab his food.

"Whatever you say, big bro." He sat down.

"You gone tell me what you doing over here now?"

The area I lived in was on the higher end side and more family oriented. I used the money I got from my inheritance from my grandpa to buy it, knowing I wanted a family of my own one day.

He took a large bite of the fajita and swallowed. "This cougar I be messing with from time to time stays over this way."

I pushed off the wall and stepped closer to where he sat. "What the hell you mean cougar? Whatchu got going on?"

He lifted his head, mirth bouncing around in his eyes. "The widow chick I been seeing for a couple months. Her kids all teenagers and don't have time for her. She's lonely and loves young dick." He shrugged. "Who am I to turn her down?"

My brows furrowed as my mouth turned upside. "Yo' ass always into some shit. How old?"

"Forty something, I think. Hell, I don't know."

He went back to his food. I shook my head. I wasn't shocked to learn what my brother had going on. Like I said, he was always into something.

"Just make sure you wrapping yo' shit up. Cougars can get pregnant, too."

He chuckled. "I ain't no fucking newbie. Plus, her tubes tied." That smug grin reappeared.

Sighing, I dropped my head. "Yo' ass is something else." I chuckled. My brother might have his shit, but I loved him, and it was never boring when he was around.

Grinning, he continued eating, and I turned to clean up the kitchen.

By the time he finished, I put the last of the dishes in the dishwasher.

"Shit, that was good." Terrance walked to me, handing me the plate he just finished. I started the dish washer and left the kitchen.

"A'right, you done ate up my food and interrupted my night. Now it's time to take yo' ass home so I can put my daughter to bed."

We headed for the front door.

"And go cuddle up with a certain nanny." He wagged his brows in a suggestive tone.

"Man, take yo' ass on, and get out of my house."

He laughed and opened the door. "Love you, bro."

"Love you, too."

Once Terrance was gone, I locked up and went upstairs straight to my daughter's room.

"I see your eyes getting heavy, but you gotta wait for you daddy, pretty girl," Brylee cooed, leaning over my daughter's crib. My heart swelled seeing how gentle she spoke to Scottlynn. The care was loud in her voice.

Straightening up, I stepped deeper into the room. "Sounds like I came in at the right time." I stepped next to Brylee and peered into the crib. Scottlynn sucked eagerly on the bottle with heavy eyes.

"Sure did, huh, pretty girl? Tell daddy you got a bath and a cereal bottle. Now you're ready for him to finish the job." She brushed her finger over Scottlynn's stomach.

I glanced up at her. In the short amount of time she'd been working here, I could see she already formed an attachment to my daughter.

"I'll leave you to it," she told me and stepped back.

Before she could get too far away, I grabbed her hand. She stared at me under her lashes with a curious expression.

"Thank you for dinner tonight and getting her ready for bed. You've been doing a great job here."

Her face lit up. "Thank you. I love working here. Scottlynn's such an easy baby."

For a second, we held each other's stares. Her eyes glowed. She blinked, causing her lashes to brush against her high cheek bones.

"If you don't need me anymore tonight, I'ma head downstairs to watch some TV," she said, breaking contact first.

Swallowing, I nodded.

Brylee left the room, and I turned back to Scottlynn. I smiled softly and reached in, picking her up. She whined at first but settled in my arms, still sucking her bottle. I took a seat in the chair in her room.

I cherished nights like this. These were times I knew she wouldn't remember, but it still caused heaviness inside me.

"You know daddy loves you, right, Munchkin?" I whispered as her eyes closed. Since Skye was currently out of the picture, I didn't want Scottlynn to miss both parents or to feel like she didn't have love from either of us.

I sighed and leaned down, inhaling the baby wash Brylee used to bath her. A serene feeling covered me. Shit, my life was chaotic, but moments with my daughter quieted all that.

———

Once Scottlynn was asleep, I went into my own room to shower and change. I planned on spending a couple hours in my workshop before calling it a night.

When I got downstairs, I followed the sound of the TV playing. I checked the screen, seeing the show *Once Upon a Ring* playing. I learned she was obsessed with this show. I turned to the couch where Brylee was curled up under a blanket, snoring softly. She looked younger when she slept. Her eyes fluttered under her lids, but she never woke up.

I moved to the couch, grabbing the remote to turn the TV off. I knew after being out and about with Scottlynn all day she had to be exhausted. Instead of waking her up, I pulled the cover off her and leaned down to pick her up bridal style. She stirred before her eyes flickered open.

"What happened?" Panic struck her sleep driven eyes.

"Nothing. You fell asleep on the couch, and I'm taking you upstairs."

Brylee yawned. "Oh, I can walk."

"You're good. I don't mind."

She blinked slowly up at me, and her mouth opened to speak, but then she snapped it closed. Yawning again, she nodded and laid her head on my chest and turned her body into me. Her eyes closed again. The scent of bourbon vanilla, almond, cherries, and some kind of flower radiated off her, filling my nostrils. It was sweet yet alluring.

I ignored how good it felt holding her and walked to the stairs to take her to her room. I sat her down the bed and turned for the door.

"Thank you," Brylee called after me with a slight rasp.

Smiling over my shoulder, I nodded. "Don't mention it."

Sleep was nowhere in my future, I knew that, so I headed for my workshop.

CHAPTER 10

BRYLEE

"Don't leave me in suspense!" Leia pushed, causing me to stare at her curiously. She rolled her eyes and smacked her lips. "Working for Tripp. How is it? Anything sexy happen between you two yet?"

I frowned and scrunched my nose. "Why would there been anything sexy happening with us? And what the hell does that even mean?" My head slightly tilted.

Again, she rolled her eyes and sat straighter. She looked off into the street. She had stopped by the house since we hadn't seen each other since I moved in the house a couple weeks ago. She allowed me to get settled and adjusted before stopping by.

"You know! Tripp is fine as fuck, and he's a firefighter. That makes him double the sexy. Now that you're single and got rid of that baggage, it's time to move on."

I snickered and scooped a couple of the baby snacks from the container in my lap and placed it into the playpen I had set up in front of the house. Thankfully, Tripp had this nice sized tree in the front of his house that applied enough shade so we could sit outside and not have the sun beaming down on us. I made sure to bring some snacks and toys out for Scottlynn.

"Leia, it's not like that. Yes, Tripp is attractive, but he's my boss and *not* single. All I'm here to do is watch this cutie right here, and that's it." I grinned down at Scottlynn.

Leia waved me off. "Whatever. I'm tryna get plugged in with one of his fine firefighter friends, or even one of the brothers."

I couldn't help but laugh. My friend was unapologetically her, and that was one reason I loved her.

"Have you heard from Russell?"

I shook my head and looked out toward the street. "He texted me a couple times. I deleted them, though. We have nothing to talk about. He refused to make me a priority when we were together, so he can keep that energy now that we broke up."

I thought I would be more heartbroken when it came to me and Russell breaking up, but it didn't hit me as hard as expected. Looking back on our relationship, it made me realize I was more invested than he was. The love between us was more superficial than anything. It sucked thinking I wasted two years on it.

I rolled my shoulders back and sighed. "I think he's just feeling some type of way about seeing Tripp and them at my house helping me move, and he knew nothing about it. His ego is more hurt than anything."

"Good! That's exactly what he gets." She got quiet for a second. When she suddenly sat straight and squealed, I looked at her like she was crazy. "I can't believe I forgot to tell you!"

My brows crinkled as my eyes squinted. "What?"

"Kyriq comes home next week," she mentioned, shocking me. A tingle went through my stomach at the name.

"Has it been seven years already?"

She nodded with a grin. "Yep! He's gonna be a parole for two more years, but at least he'll be home."

"Wow," I whispered, tugging on my bottom lip with my teeth.

"He's asked about you."

My hand ran over my locs. "Why would he ask about me?"

Leia smirked. "Don't act like that."

My eyes shifted off to the side. I ignored her suggestive tone.

Kyriq was her older brother who had gotten locked up on a robbery gone wrong. He had been in and out of trouble since I met him. When we were younger, we had messed around here and there. He was older than me, and I had no reason dealing with him at the time, but nobody could tell fifteen-year-old me anything about that man then. Leia knew about me and her brother's past, but once he got locked up, I made her promise to not mention him anymore. I was finally able to detox him out of my life, as well as all the toxicness that came with him.

"You know I'm not checking for your brother like that anymore. That was a long time ago."

She snickered. "Yeah, make sure you keep that energy when he gets here."

Not bothering to respond, I turned my attention back to Scottlynn while picking my bottled water up. When I was a teenager, I went through a rebellion stage. I was angry about my parents and didn't really know how to channel that energy. It made me make some bad choices, one being Kyriq. While I was happy he wouldn't be in prison anymore, I had no desire to reconnect with him.

———

I was currently on the couch catching up on the current season of *Once Upon a Ring* with of glass of strawberry lemonade and my crotchet kit. I was in the process of making a blanket, something I picked up from my Gran, when a knock on the door caught my attention. Leia had left a little over an hour ago, and Scottlynn was down for a nap.

I didn't move right away, shifting my eyes to the door instead. Tripp didn't mention anything about one stopping by. Maybe it was his brother again.

Setting the needle and yarn down, I stood and finally walked to the door, checking the peep hole first. Pulling back, I nibbled on my bottom lip and tapped my fingers on my thigh. The lady on the other side wasn't familiar.

Unlocking the door, I pulled it open and stared at her. "Can I help you?" I questioned.

Her eyes snapped up. She sized me up, pressing her lips together.

"You must be the new nanny my son hired. What was your name again?" she asked.

My eyes widened, realizing who the lady was. "Oh, I'm Brylee."

Again, she sized me up, this time while nodding. "Right, Brylee. I'm Tripp's mother, Rose. I stopped by to see my granddaughter since my son doesn't feel like he needs to bring her by anymore." She rolled her eyes.

"Oh, right. Come in."

I moved to the side, allowing Rose to step inside. We had spoken about his parents before and I knew how close he was with his parents and how much they loved Scottlynn.

Closing the door behind her, I brought my bottom lip into my mouth and shifted on my feet. Since I had only met Tripp's brothers, I wasn't sure what to expect with his mom.

Her eyes wondered around the room before landing on me. "Where's Scottlynn?"

"I put her down for her nap right before you got here. Tripp didn't mention you stopping by, or I would have made sure she stayed up."

Rose waved me off. "My son didn't know I was coming. Normally me and his father watch Scottlynn while he's at work, but since he has an in-house nanny, I guess he has no need for us anymore. I shouldn't have to pop up just to see my grandchild." She muttered the last part to herself.

"Do you want me to text him and ask if she can go with you?"

Rose lifted a brow. "No, I don't want to bother him. I'll call and fuss him out later."

Again, her eyes roamed the room. "I think this is the first time I've been over here since my granddaughter was born, and the house wasn't in total chaos."

I turned and eyed the living room. "Oh, yeah. I try to clean up as much as I can. It's not too hard since Scottlynn isn't mobile yet."

"Mhm, about time someone other than my son steps up and does it," she mumbled then faced me. "You're a pretty girl. Are you single?"

Her bold statement caused my eyes to buck. "Thank you, and yes, I am." I blinked a couple times and scrunched my nose.

Rose tilted her head and pressed her burgundy painted lips together. "And you live here, correct?"

I nodded.

"My youngest son told me you're a good cook as well."

Shyly, I smiled and lifted my shoulders. "I do what I can."

"Interesting."

My brows crinkled while my eyes squinted, trying to decipher what she meant. Before I could question her further, she smiled. "Well, I should go. I'ma call my son and fuss at him about keeping my grand-baby away. You must be doing a good job with her if he hasn't reached out."

The corners of my mouth rose. "Thanks."

Nodding, she stepped toward the door. "It was nice meeting you, Brylee. I'm sure I'll be seeing more of you."

"Nice meeting you."

Rose opened the door and left, leaving me confused. I went over the conversation for a few moments before pushing it to the back of my mind and going back to my place on the couch.

———

"This Sunday, if that boss of yours off, I want you to bring him to dinner," Gran announced as I walked on the porch, putting Scottlynn's stroller next to me.

I dug into my pocket for my keys so I could unlock the door.

"Gran, I'll talk to him, but no guarantee."

Gran had been pestering me about Tripp since I first told her about the job.

"Good. I just worry about you. It'll settle my nerves once we meet him."

I smiled softly, unlocking the door. "I know, Gran. I'll see what I can do."

"There's one more thing I want to talk to you about."

"What?" I glanced down at Scottlynn, who chewed on the teething toy I made sure to bring.

"Your brother's birthday is coming up, and your parents are throwing a party for him. Your mom thought it would be better if I invited you."

I was quiet for a second. My little brother was turning five, and although I didn't want to deal with my parents, I wasn't going to miss my brother's birthday.

"Send me the details. I'll be there."

"Good. I know that'll make him happy."

It made me smile hearing the smile in my grandma's voice.

"I just got home, Gran. I'm going to go in and get Scottlynn settled," I told her.

"Okay, baby. I'll see you this weekend, and try to bring that boss of yours."

I snickered. "Okay. Love you."

"Love you too, sweetheart."

We hung up, and I finally opened the door to the house.

"That was a good walk, huh, pretty girl?" I stepped inside and brought the stroller along with me.

After her nap, and once the sun started set, I put her in her stroller, and we went on a walk. There was a park not too far from the house that had a few trails I wanted to check out. Today, I decided on the shorter one.

"There you two are." I jumped and spun around, shocked to see Tripp. He chuckled and stood with a crooked grin on his face. "My bad. I didn't mean to scare you. I tried calling you after seeing your car but not seeing you guys."

"Sorry, I was on the phone with my Gran and didn't notice you called me." I pulled my Air Pods out and grabbed the case off the top of the stroller to put them back.

"Munchkin, did you miss Daddy?" He stepped closer to the stroller and leaned down to take her out of the stroller.

Scottlynn grew excited and squealed when she saw her dad. She flailed her arms and feet trying to reach him.

"Da-da," she squealed, causing both us to freeze. Tripp's face lit up, and he quickly took her out of the stroller.

"What did you just say?" he asked her.

"Da-da." She grabbed his face.

He looked at me with beaming eyes. "Has she said that before?"

I grinned and shook my head. "Nope. That's the first time."

"Damn." He stared at his daughter again. "My baby's starting to talk. She's growing so fast. Say it again, Scottlynn."

Scottlynn babbled, ignoring his request. I could see the pride written all on his face as he watched her.

"What were you two up to?" he questioned, bouncing Scottlynn in his arms.

"Walked one of the trails at the park." I cleared my throat, taking him in. Tripp towered over me. The cut off tee he sported showed off his large, ripped, muscular arms. I got a glimpse of his stomach and of his toned frame. "Your mom stopped by earlier."

He chuckled and rested his eyes on me. "I know. She called me, letting me know I better bring Scottlynn over soon."

I laughed. "She seems nice. Kind of intense."

"That she is." He paused and chuckled. "Her and my dad have been big help when it comes to Scottlynn though."

I leaned on the stroller. "Did they get along well with her mom?" I glanced at Scottlynn, who played with the chain hanging around his neck.

He coughed out a laugh. "Something like that. They were never flat out disrespectful to her."

I nodded. Since being here, I tried to not overstep and ask too many questions when it came to Skye. All I knew was the minimal information he gave me when I first started.

"You weren't planning on cooking today, were you?"

"No, I was probably gonna order some Chinese or something."

"Good. Let me take you to dinner."

My eyes widened. "Really?"

A crooked grin formed on his face. "Yeah, to celebrate a month of you being here, and to thank you for taking care such good care of my daughter. Also, we gotta celebrate her first words."

My stomach fluttered at his compliment.

"I'm just doing what I'm being paid to do."

He shook his head. "It's more than that." He didn't finish his statement, and I didn't push him. For a moment, something flashed through his eyes.

Scottlynn took it upon herself to start her da-da rant, repeating it over and over while her dad watched her in awe.

"Okay, I'll go wash up, and then we can go."

"Good. I'ma go change too."

I dropped my eyes down, glancing at his solid thighs under his basketball shorts. I needed to keep reminding myself he was my boss when he dressed like this.

"Do you want me to take her?" I stepped forward.

"Nah, I got her." He smiled and kissed Scottlynn's cheek. Every time I saw him interact with his daughter my heart did an erratic dance. Not growing up with my dad made me longed for that daddy-daughter relationship. I loved seeing little girls who got to experience it. I could look at Tripp and see the love he had for his daughter dancing in his eyes.

Suddenly, my heart felt too full for my chest. I rubbed between my breasts and stood straight. Snatching my eyes away from them, I collected my things from the stroller and headed for the steps.

CHAPTER 11

TRIPP

"**E**veryone made it out though, right?" Brylee asked, referring to the car crash I told her about before I left work. The two of us settled on Duchess, a popular restaurant in the city. Before going, I dropped Scottlynn off at my parents' house for the night. I didn't want them feeling like I was taking my daughter from them now that Brylee was here.

"Yeah, although the mom was rushed into surgery since she took the brunt of the impact. As far as I know, she made it out."

"Wow." She set her fork down and wiped her mouth with her napkin.

"Shit, that's a buzz kill, huh? My bad."

She shook her head. "No, I asked you about your day. I just don't know how you do this day in and out. I would be a trainwreck."

I grabbed my knife to cut into my steak. "It could take a toll on you. Not just anyone can do it."

"Do you ever get scared?"

"Hell yeah." I shoved my fork into my mouth and bit into my steak. Swallowing, I continued. "When you're rushing into a raging fire, you have no idea how things are gonna turn out. Your adrenaline's running wild. Your mind is going a mile a minute. There're so many factors you have to account for. Making sure you get everyone out, putting the fire out, keeping yourself and your team outta harm's way. That shit's stressful as fuck."

"And here I am dreading getting spit up on a daily basis." The two of us shared a laugh. "Okay, on a scale one to ten, how nervous were you the first time you dealt with your first fire?"

Grinning, I leaned back in the chair and ran my hand over my head. "Shit, that was a minute ago." I moved my hand to my chin and stroked it. "But probably an eight. That shit was nerve rattling as hell. It wasn't anything too crazy, just a house fire, but at the moment, so much shit rushes through your mind, and your body moves on autopilot. We were able to get everyone out and get the fire maintained before it got out of control."

"I always thought firefighters were cool, but you guys are crazy as hell to willingly run into burning buildings." I chuckled, watching her pick her wine glass up.

"You sound like my mom."

"Did your parents always support you wanting to be a firefighter?" She scooped some of her mac n cheese and shoved the spoon into her mouth.

Again, I stroked my chin. "Nah. My dad wasn't that bad, but I nearly gave my mom a heart attack. For the first year, she demanded I called her after every shift, no matter what time I got home, so she knew I was home safely."

Her eyes twinkled. "That's amazing. It's great that you have such loving parents." Her face slightly fell.

"You mentioned you were raised by your grandparents, right? Do you have a relationship with your parents now?"

She shook her head and took another drink of her wine. "My grandparents told me I should try to forgive them, but it's not easy, especially since they have more kids who they're actually raising now."

"Do you have a relationship with your siblings?"

"Oh, yeah. I love my brother and sister. It's not their fault my parents were shitty to me. I know my grandparents are probably right.

Maybe I do need to let go of my anger toward my parents, but it's easier said than done."

I studied Brylee. It was clear by how her posture changed that talking about her parents wasn't an easy subject, so I switched topics.

"How was your day with Scottlynn?" I asked her.

Brylee's face lit up as she started explaining the day with Scottlynn. Her eyes sparkled and voice became animated the more she spoke. It brought a smile to my face.

The server came back over to check on us, and once we assured her we were good, Brylee gave me her attention again.

"I have a question, but I don't want to feel like I'm overstepping."

"Let me decide on that. Go ahead and ask." I had a feeling the question had something to do with Skye. Brylee shifted in her seat.

"Have you spoken to Scottlynn's mom lately? Is she getting better?"

My eyes went to the table. Skye was a sore spot to me. The rehab center had contacted me and told me she had a set back after speaking with me. I hadn't spoken to her since the first time she called.

"Nah, she's having a rougher time than I thought she would."

"I'm sorry to hear that."

"You know what I hate the most? The fact that my daughter is missing out on time with her mother at the time she's soaking everything up the most." My hand balled on the table.

"I can't imagine how that feels, but just remember your daughter is surrounded by love. Skye is fighting demons, and she's working to overcome them, right? That's a good thing."

"Yeah…" I didn't want to talk about Skye anymore. The situation with her was too much to handle right now. It pained me knowing she had a hard time getting clean, but it also frustrated me because it felt like she wasn't trying to fight for our daughter or our family.

"On a positive note, my gran wants you to come to dinner this Sunday if you're off and up to it."

Now that I had a nanny, I was able to get a more routine schedule. I was off Sunday, so I didn't see any reason I couldn't go to dinner.

"Okay. Let's do it." I nodded.

Her eyes widened. "Really?"

I grinned. "Hell yeah. If you learned to cook from your grandma, then I know she throws down."

Brylee laughed. "You won't have to worry about that. I don't know anyone who cooks better than my gran."

"You two are really close, huh?"

"Oh, yeah. I love my gran. Her and my grandad scarified so much for me. They didn't have to step up and raise me when my parents didn't want to."

"Are they your mom or dad's parents?"

"My mom's. My dad's family was around, but they weren't there like my gran and grandad."

My tongue went across my lips. It was clear Brylee still held onto the hurt her parents caused. It was written all on her face.

"Are Skye's parents in the picture? I notice you never mentioned them."

My body stiffened, and I sat straighter. "No." My voice came out rougher than I meant, but the subject of Skye's family was a tough one.

Brylee nodded. "Sorry for being so nosey. I've been told I need to learn to mind my business."

I waved her off. "You're good. You're involved in my life, so you have questions. It's understandable."

She was quiet for a second, tucking her lips into her mouth. "Still, if I overstep or push too far, just tell me."

The server came back and asked about dessert. I ended up requesting the strawberry cheesecake.

"I don't think I can take another bite," Brylee groaned.

I chuckled. "We're here to celebrate. You can't celebrate with no dessert."

The way she bit back a smile by biting into her bottom lip and lowering her eyes was cute to me. Brylee was someone I enjoyed being around. She was a breath of fresh air, easy to talk to, and genuinely cared about those around her. Her coming into my life couldn't have come at a better time.

———

"Baby, we have a stranger in the house," my mom commented while walking to the couch and taking a seat.

Laughing, I shook my head. "Don't be like that. You know I be busy working."

"Da-da." Scottlynn wiggled in my dad's arms when she laid eyes on me.

I walked to where my dad sat with Scottlynn in his lap and picked her up. "Wassup, Munchkin?" I kissed her cheek. "You have fun with grandma and grandpa?"

"I told you it's Meema," my mom injected.

"Right. My bad." I walked to my mom and took a seat beside her.

"How you been, son? You look better than the last time we saw you," Dad commented.

"I feel better too. Now that I don't have to worry about Scottlynn, I can breathe easier."

My mom frowned at me. She held out a bottle, and Scottlynn happily took it. "You didn't have to worry about her before. You know me and your dad had no issue watching her."

I sighed and looked down at my daughter, who now laid on my chest, sucking on her bottle.

"I know that, Ma. I just don't want you guys to feel like you have to be responsible for my kid. I know you both love your grandchild, and I appreciate all the help I get from y'all, especially because of everything with Skye. I know it hasn't been easy to accept her and our situation. Brylee's good with her, though, and it's easier having her in the house."

"Mhm, speaking of Brylee. She's a pretty girl," Mom commented.

I side-eyed her. "Where that come from?"

She lifted her shoulders. "Just making an observation."

"How are you managing with everything going on?" my dad cut in. He shot my mom a look then faced me.

"Taking it one day at a time. As long as my daughter is happy, I can handle everything else."

"Any word on Skye?"

"They have her on restrictions right now. She hasn't had the best time adjusting, but they said they're hopeful. She seems to be slowly coming around. Hopefully, within the next couple weeks, she can get phone privileges again, then eventually visits."

"I hope you don't plan on taking my granddaughter up there to see her," my mom said.

"No. I don't want her in that environment."

"Good." Her face softened. She reached over and grabbed my arm. "Everything's gonna work out, son. I don't want you out here stressing out about her. You've been making her problems your own damn near your whole life. It's time to live for you."

I stared at my mom, knowing her intentions were right, but they didn't make me feel any better.

"I'm not gonna abandon the mother of my child."

Even before we became intimate and got together, we were best friends. I told her I would always have her back.

"We're not saying that, son," my dad stated. "You're a good man because we raised you to be a good one, but at the same time, you have to put you first at some point. We know you love Skye, and you want your family to work. There's nothing wrong with that. At the same time, sometimes you have to let a person hit rock bottom in order for them to change and get better."

My mom gave my arm a squeeze. "We love you, Tripp, and we don't want you to waste your life trying to save someone who doesn't want to be saved. It's scary seeing you go through the motions with her. Not to mention, you have a child now. You have to do what's best for her, even if that's removing her mother for the time being."

My parents' feelings were valid. Now that I was a parent, I wouldn't want my daughter to go through the shit I'd been through with Skye. At the same time, they didn't know the whole story. Skye had her reasons for being how she was, and I wouldn't betray her trust by telling them, but I wished they gave her more grace.

"I need to get this little girl home and get ready for work," I eventually announced, standing with my sleeping daughter in my arms.

"You better stop keeping my granddaughter away just because you have a nanny now. We can still watch her from time to time."

"I hear you, Mom. I'll do better." I leaned over and kissed her cheek.

My mom owned her own cleaning service, but she rarely did the actual labor anymore since she had a team under her. She worked from home running her business. My dad used to work at a steel factory but was now retired after hurting his back.

"You better. I love you."

I grinned. "Love you too, lady."

My dad came over with Scottlynn's diaper bag. "Stop being a stranger." He pulled me into a side hug.

I chuckled. "I got you."

The last thing I wanted my parents to feel like I was pushing them to the side in me and my daughter's life. That was never the case. My daughter finally had structure and stability in her life, and I just didn't want to disturb that.

CHAPTER 12

BRYLEE

"My thighs are screaming," Leia groaned as we gathered our stuff in the locker room. I wiped my forehead with my towel and nodded.

"I know I'ma feel it later."

We went up to level two in our spin/yoga class, and today was the first time. It was not for the weak, either.

"I'm definitely gonna soak in an Epsom bath tonight." She rolled her neck to the side.

"At least this ass is looking good. That's one good thing about these classes." I grinned, staring behind me in the mirror, examining my ass.

"I know that's right!" Leia slapped my cheeks, making me snicker.

My eyes went around the locker room. "It feels weird not having Scottlynn on my hip. I've grown accustomed to her being with me every day."

Rose kept Scottlynn today, which was fine. It gave me a free day, but it still felt odd. I enjoyed spending time with Scottlynn.

"You sound like a mom who's away from her kid for the first time."

I snorted and bent down to pick my duffle bag up. "Crazy, I kind of feel like that. She's not mine, but I've grown used to having her. It's like I don't even know what to do without her."

We started for the doors.

"I think it's nice that you've attached to Scottlynn, but I want you to be careful, Bry."

"What are you talking about?"

"I mean, at the end of the day, you aren't her mom, and when her mom comes home, you might not be needed anymore. I don't want you to get hurt if that happens. Remember, you're there for a job."

Her words caused a hollow feeling in my chest and stomach. "I know. It's not like I'm trying to replace her mom or anything, but I have grown attached to her."

"Just be careful. I know one day you'll be a great mom. She's lucky to have you in her life right now."

I smiled softly. "Thanks, Lei."

We walked through the parking lot to where our cars were parked.

"We need to have another girl's night out. We haven't had one since we went to the karaoke bar," Leia said.

"Plan it and let me know."

"I will. Now I need to go home and shower. I have a date tonight."

My eyes narrowed. "With who? Heffa, you didn't tell me you were dating!"

She snickered. "Because it's a blind date. Well, kind of. He's friends with Maddisyn's boyfriend and saw me on FaceTime with her. We exchanged numbers, and this is our first date."

"Okay then, bitch. I see you. What's his name?"

"Dustin. He's a contractor. And bitch, he is so fine!"

I couldn't help but laugh. "I hope it works out, and I can't wait to meet him."

We arrived at our cars. We spoke for a little longer before going our separate ways.

I waved to Leia as she drove off, and just as I was about to throw my car in drive, my phone rang.

I checked the screen in my car and bit on the corner of my bottom lip seeing it was Russell. We hadn't spoken since the day at my house.

Sighing, I hit the answer button on my wheel. "Hello?"

"Damn, it's like that?" he asked.

Rolling my eyes, I threw my car in drive and pulled out of the parking lot. "What do you want, Russell?"

"Why you sound like I'm annoying you? I'm just tryna see how you are and make sure you're good."

I pressed my lips together and turned out of the parking lot. "I'm good. Great, actually. How are you?"

"I'm good... I miss you."

I wasn't sure how to respond to that. Russell was someone I had grown comfortable with, and I realized I wasn't in love with him like I thought. Since we hadn't been together, I hadn't missed him or anything, not like I would have in the past.

"Can we meet up?" he asked after he saw I wasn't about to respond.

"What?" I snapped out of my head.

"Can we meet? You busy right now? I got some free time right now."

I checked the clock. I still had some time before Scottlynn was due back at the house.

"Okay," I answered.

"We can meet at that one Italian place you like."

"Sounds good."

"A'right, I'll see you soon then."

We hung up.

I rolled my hand on the steering wheel and changed my original direction. Hopefully this meeting was peaceful. Russell had a temper, and when he didn't get his way, he liked to throw tantrums. The last two times I saw him, things didn't end well with us. I wanted us to have closure so we could move on.

———

I sipped on my strawberry lemonade while looking over the rim of my glass at Russell. The two of us had been here for about ten minutes, and since neither of us were unfamiliar with the menu, we'd ordered our food and were now waiting for it to arrive.

"You look good," Russell admitted. He arrived shortly after me, but I had been waiting for him to start the conversation since he wanted to meet. When he first sat down, I waited for my stomach to flutter or heart to race like it used to, but nothing happened. I felt nothing as I stared into his deep-set brown eyes. He was still as handsome and well put together as he was when I first met him, but the attraction I used to feel was nonexistent.

"Thank you." I set my glass down and adjusted myself in my seat. "What is it that you wanted to talk about?"

His face stilled as his lips thinned. "Straight to the point, huh?" He chuckled and adjusted his tie, sitting straighter. "I don't like how things ended with us. We both were heated, and some things were said in the heat of the moment."

"Oh, you mean how you told me I was getting too clingy?" I chewed the inside of my cheek and lifted a brow. When he first confessed how he had been feeling about me and our relationship, it stung, but I had grown used to disappointment when it came to people, so it wasn't something I dwelled on anymore.

A half smirk formed on his face. "You gotta realize I was stressed out with work and tryna keep you happy. Shit was hectic, but it's starting to slow down, and now I'm ready to work on our relationship."

For a moment, I waited for the cameras to pop out and Russell to laugh, but when I saw he was serious, I couldn't help but laugh myself.

"Russell, you can't be serious." I laughed.

Confusion filled his face. "What's funny?"

I shook my head. "I'm not so desperate that I want a man who doesn't value me. Not anymore."

"What's that's supposed to mean? You act like I was out here disrespecting you."

"No, but at the time we were together, I thought the two of us had a good relationship. Looking back on it, I realize I was always more invested in it than you were. When it came to dates, I planned the majority of them. I never got put before your job. You never made me a priority, and I accepted it, because at the time, I *did* just want someone who wanted me, but I'm not accepting the bare minimum anymore."

Since my breakup with Russell, I noticed I didn't second guess myself like I used too when we were together. Being without him had me seeing things clearer.

"I want a family, Russell," I continued. "Kids and a husband, and I realize I don't see that with you."

By the look on his face, I could tell he wasn't happy by what I said. His face reddened and balled up.

"Excuse me, can you actually pack that in a to-go container?" I asked the server when he came back with our food. He looked surprised by my request but nodded, set Russell's food down, and turned around to leave with mine.

"You think you're better than me?" Russell questioned.

"I didn't say that."

"But that's what you implied. You're so desperate to have a kid to fill that hole your parents left inside you, and you tell me you don't see a family with me."

Russell's ego was always an issue in our relationship. He always tried to act like this great alpha, but in reality, he was a little boy that threw tantrums and was desperately trying to gain validation from those around him. Still, his words felt like daggers pierced in my chest. Part of me did crave a family of my own to help the emptiness not having my parents caused. Russell knew that, and him throwing it in my face showed me I made the right choice.

My lips pressed together, and I turned for my purse to grab my wallet.

"If that's how you feel, then there's no reason for us to even try to get back together."

His eyes narrowed.

The server came back with my food boxed up this time.

"Thank you. This should cover my half of the bill." I grabbed the bag and handed him the cash. I faced Russell. "Thank you for giving me the closure I needed." I stood to leave.

"You're acting like this because the nigga that was at your house when I stopped by. You're already fucking someone else, huh?" Heat flushed my cheeks, and I froze. The server's eyes widened and bounced between us.

"Who and what I'm doing is none of your business anymore. Fuck you." I went to leave but paused again. "Oh, and by the way, that man is ten times the man you'll ever be. While you're trying to throw my issues in my face, maybe you need to heal the broken little boy inside you first!"

I stalked out, not bothering to wait for him to reply. Heat flooded through my body. His words hit a nerve, not because they were true, but because they were disrespectful.

I pushed past the people in front of me until I got outside and inhaled a deep breath. It was time to officially close Russell's chapter in my life.

"Penny for your thoughts?"

I jumped, shooting my eyes over to entrance of the living room. Tripp stood there staring at me in concern in half his uniform. His arms rippled in the navy blue tank top he wore. It was quite a site.

"I didn't hear you come in." I straightened up and cleared my throat, setting my strawberry lemonade down. My heart leaped as my eyes trailed him. I had seen him in his uniform before, but that was when the daycare caught fire, and there was too much going on to truly appreciate it. Now looking at him, I couldn't help but sink my teeth into my bottom lip. Out of all the civil service careers, firefighters always stood out to me. Tripp was no different. Blinking, I shot my eyes back to his face.

"I came through the side door."

My teeth scrapped over the side of my bottom lip. "Did you get off early?"

His brows crinkled. "Nah. Just had some down time and needed to stop by the house." He lifted a bag.

"Oh, if you would have told me, I would I have brought it to you."

He shrugged. "It's all good. I'm more concerned about you. You good?"

My hand went over my locs that were currently in a low ponytail on my neck. "Yeah, sorry. I promise I don't zone out like this when I'm with Scottlynn."

He lowered the bag and walked to the couch, sitting on the arm of it. "I have no doubt my daughter is in good hands. Everything good with you? You looked in deep thought."

Sighing, my shoulders lowered. Tripp's eyes locked on me, bleeding of concern. "Yeah, I'm fine. Just thinking about a meeting I had earlier today."

He pulled his phone out of his uniform pocket and tapped the screen a couple times. "I got a few seconds to spare. Anything you wanna talk about?"

A small smile formed on my face. Tripp was so caring. It was one thing that made him a great father. He was aware of those around him and empathetic to their feelings.

"I met up with my ex." His mouth slowly dropped, turning upside down. "I don't even know why I bothered to meet him. I guess to have closure on our relationship." I rolled my eyes. "Long story short, it was a waste of time and had me doing some self-reflecting. I like to think I'm a good person, but seeing how my ex was has me questioning how I dealt with him as long as I did. Maybe I just wanted to be loved so bad I ignored everything bad about him."

Tripp shook his head. "Nah, don't even do that to yourself. Because you're a good person is probably why you were with him. People come in your life for a reason. Just because it didn't work with you two doesn't mean you should question yourself. Just because someone has flaws doesn't mean they don't deserve love. Being the good person you are, you saw something in him that made you stay around. There's nothing wrong with that. Y'all time just past. Did he say something to you that has you questioning yourself?"

My lips twisted to the side, and I ran the conversation over in my head. "No, not really. I just feel like so much of the relationship was me trying to make it work and him just being there. It's kind a depress-ing." My smile saddened.

"Sometimes we stay with people past our prime because we see potential in the person they can be. Wanting love isn't bad. You're a good person, Brylee, so you want to see the good in those around you. Don't think that's a bad thing. If you feel like the relationship was a waste, then he didn't deserve you. Take it as a lesson learned and use it for your next relationship."

His phone rang.

I watched Tripp answer and put it to his ear.

"Yeah, I'm coming out now." He stood up. "I gotta head back to work, but if you wanna talk later, I'm here, a'right? I want us to be more than just boss and employee. I want us to be friends."

My stomach fluttered. "Thank you, boss man."

He grinned. "We still on for dinner at your grandparents house Sunday, right?"

I nodded.

"Bet. Kiss my baby girl for me. I'll see you tomorrow." He turned to leave.

Maybe Tripp was right. Me and Russell didn't work for a reason. A lot of times they say opposites attract, but the two of us were too differ-ent. Our values never really lined up, and it made me wonder what I stayed around for. Still, I agreed with Tripp. Instead of dwelling on it, I was going to take it as a lesson for the future.

CHAPTER 13

TRIPP

I grunted as I pushed the bar up one last time, feeling the ache in my muscles as I put it on the supporter.

"I thought you was about to hit yo' limit." Harlem laughed as I slowly turned and sat up. Reaching for my towel, I wiped the sweat from my forehead before I reached for my water bottle.

"You know better than that. You don't get arms like this from tapping out." I paused from drinking my water and flexed my arm.

"Nigga, ain't nothing special about yo' damn arms." He waved me off. "Now, move so I can take a turn."

Smirking, I stood so he could get to the machine. He wiped it down then tossed the towel to the side before laying on the bench.

"You want me to take some weights off?" I questioned.

Harlem was about my height, but I had a couple pounds on him in weight, mainly because I took working out more seriously than him.

"Fuck you."

I laughed, setting the water bottle down and positioning myself in front of the bench to spot him.

Our shift had been up and down with emergencies. Most of them had been tame. It had been a couple hours since our last call, and we were basking in the downtime.

Harlem started his reps. We were halfway through our shift, and I planned on trying to get a few hours of sleep after our work out.

"Y'all workout too damn much. The food's done. Come eat!" one of the crew members called said just as Harlem finished his last set. I grabbed the bar, helping him stabilize it.

"Fuck," he gritted, breathing heavier.

"Should have let me take a couple pounds off."

He mugged me as he slowly lifted. His neck rolled between his shoulders. "Food sounds good as hell. I wonder what they made."

"I think Chicken Alfredo."

It paid to have crew members who enjoyed cooking. We all pitched in money to keep the fridge stocked and hardly had to ever eat out or pack lunches.

I went to go get cleaned up but paused to study Harlem, seeing he hadn't moved. "You good?" I asked, seeing him zoned out.

He snapped his eyes to me after a couple seconds. "Yeah, I'm good."

My eyes narrowed. "You still been having issues sleeping?"

He stood, waving me off. "Nah, just letting the adrenaline slow down. I'm good."

I watched him go to his bag on the bench next to us and dig inside, pulling a towel out.

"Harlem, you know if you need to talk, even if not to me or someone here, we have professionals—"

"I don't need to talk to anyone. I told you I'm good," he interrupted, tossing the towel back in the bag and picking it up. "Now, a nigga's starving. I'll see you in the main room."

I didn't believe him and wanted to say more but allowed him to leave. This job could take a toll on us. Some gained more mental scars than physical. I feared Harlem was one of them. He brushed everything off, like it was good, but I made note to keep an eye on him.

Gathering my things, I headed out of the gym to the locker rooms before going to join the others at the table in the main room. My stomach growled at the Italian dish.

"Shit, I didn't realize how hungry I was until now." I rubbed my stomach and walked to the sink.

"You can say that again. I feel like it's been days since I ate," Lee proclaimed, sitting at the table with a full plate.

One thing I always appreciated about this firehouse was the sense of family we had. We spent so much time away from home, and here with each other, it was like a home away from home.

I took a seat next to Harlem, who was already halfway through his plate.

"I swear yo' ass is a human garbage disposal," I noted, watching him scarf his food down. He ignored me, continuing to eat. I lowered my head to say a quick prayer. Just as I opened my eyes and was about to take a bite, the alarm blared.

"Son of a bitch!" Journi exclaimed, throwing her fork down.

"Let's go, y'all!" Omiras said, pushing away from the table and standing.

A few of us grumbled as we stood to follow him.

———

"I apologize in advance for my grandparents, mainly my gran. Sometimes she does the most," Brylee warned.

I glanced at her as I turned on the street her grandparents lived. "I'm sure it's nothing I can't handle. Don't worry. They raised you, so I'm sure they're great people."

I didn't miss the smile creeping on her face.

"Okay, don't say I didn't warn you. It's the house on the right, where the red car is. You can park behind it." She pointed.

Doing as she said, I turned into the driveway and put my truck in park.

Brylee turned to face me. "Thanks again for coming. I know you would probably rather be sleeping right now than this."

"Sleeping over a home cooked meal? I'd be a dummy to turn that down. Ain't no comparison." I winked at her and pushed the button to turn my car off.

"I'll grab Scottlynn if you get her diaper bag," I suggested.

Once I got Scottlynn out of her car seat, I followed Brylee to the door.

"Da-da-da," my daughter babbled, clapping her hands and making me smile. It was bittersweet seeing how fast she grew and knowing her mom was missing it.

"I swear that's all she says nowadays. You truly are her favorite person," Brylee cooed, poking Scottlynn's stomach.

"And she's mine. Ain't that right, Munchkin?" I kissed her cheek.

Brylee opened the door and allowed me in first.

"Well, look what the cat dragged in," an older man said from the chair he sat in.

"Grandad." Brylee's face lit up at the sight of the man. She kicked her slides off and made her way across the living room, bending down and kissing his cheek.

"And how is my beautiful granddaughter?" he asked.

"I'm good. How about you?"

"Still kicking, as you can see." He smiled at her then shifted his eyes to me. "And who is this?"

Brylee stood straight. "My boss, Tripp. Tripp this is Walter, my Grandad."

I stepped out of my shoes and walked further into the room. "Nice to meet you, Mr. Adkins."

"Oh, call me Walt." He stood with his hand out. Brylee took Scottlynn out of my hands as I shook her grandad's.

"My granddaughter tells me you're a firefighter."

"Yessir."

"Hard job. Takes courage to do something like that day in and out."

"It's not for the weak, but I love what I do," I assured him.

His eyes went to Brylee, who had gotten lost playing with Scottlynn. "Beautiful little girl you got there."

Pride swelled in me. "Thank you. She's my greatest accomplishment."

Walt grinned. "As she should be."

"Walt, will you call that grandchild of ours and tell her—" a woman's voice sounded but halted.

"And tell me what, Gran?" Brylee turned toward the lady with a smirk on her face.

"I thought we were still waiting for you. I just took the last of the food out of the oven." She wiped her hands over her pants and walked toward us. "I remember this cutie, but who is this one?" She arched her brows in a playful manor, causing a bashful grin on my face.

"Gran, please don't start. This is Tripp. Tripp, my gran, Susan."

"Nice to meet you, ma'am." I held my hand out.

"Oh, foolishness call me Gran." She caught me off guard when she wrapped her arms around me, pulling me into a hug. "Oh, you're a nice strong man, too. Reminds me of my Walt back in the day."

"Whatchu mean back in the day, woman? I'm still strong," Walt protested.

"Yeah, yeah whatever you say, old man." Gran released me with a smirk and winked at me. "Now, let me see this little angel here. I swear you are the prettiest baby I've seen in a long time."

I loved how she gushed over my daughter who ate the attention up. Gran got lost in my daughter for a few seconds then turned to me. "I hope you brought your appetite. I cooked a good ole fashion soul food platter."

"Oh, you don't have to worry about that. It smells good, too," I assured her, causing her smile to grow.

"Compliments will get you everywhere with me. Lee-Lee, go take Tripp to the half bath so you two can wash your hands."

"Yes, Gran," she said and nodded for me to follow. I checked the living room out as we walked a short path to a closed door.

"They seem like nice people," I noted as she turned the water on while I stood at the archway.

"They are. The best people I know."

"I can tell you're all close."

She snatched a couple paper towels from the holder then moved to let me have a turn.

"We are. They always supported me no matter what and were

INFLAMED IN HIS LOVE

patient with me during my rebellious times. I love my grandparents more than anyone in the world."

After I finished washing my hands, I turned the sink off and grabbed the paper towels Brylee handed me.

"C'mon, they're probably waiting for us in the dining room." Brylee turned to the left with me behind her.

I could hear my daughter's squeals and babbling as we walked the short distance to the dining room. She sat in a seat close to Gran, hitting the table top of the highchair.

"I didn't know you guys still had a highchair."

"Oh yeah, we don't throw away anything like this. Never know when you're gonna need it for future grands," Gran said.

My stomach rumbled as I eyed the spread on the table. Fried chicken, baked mac n cheese, greens, yams, and cornbread.

"Do you want me to grab her?" I started for the seat.

"She's fine. Just take a seat." Gran waved me off. I noticed she had grabbed some of her baby snacks from her bag and scattered them on top of the tabletop.

Doing as she said, I took a seat, wiping my mouth and making sure it wasn't drooling. Everything smelled amazing.

"Now, let's lower our heads, and Walt, bless the food." Walt said a quick prayer, and once he finished, I couldn't wait to dive in. "There's plenty to eat, so don't hold back," Gran encouraged, and she didn't have to tell me twice.

The meal started off quietly, outside of Scottlynn's random babbling and outbursts, and the forks hitting the tray.

I picked up my glass of sweet tea and took a sip. "Brylee, you can cook, but I can see where you got your skills from. Gran, the food was delicious," I complimented after a while. I was working on my second plate and contemplated about a third.

"One thing I didn't play about was my kids knowing how to provide for themselves. All of them were forced in the kitchen at some point. Lee-Lee took to it more than the others." She smiled at her granddaughter.

"How many kids do you have?"

Brylee didn't talk about her family much, outside of her grandparents. I knew she was estranged from her parents, but nothing past that.

"Three. Lee-Lee's mom and her two brothers."

"Do you have siblings?" Walt questioned.

"Yessir. Two little brothers."

"I think I would have lost my mind having all boys. My sons were so rumbustious growing up, Breanna balanced everything out." Gran snickered.

I noticed Brylee didn't comment, and her eyes stayed locked on her plate.

"Those boys did give us a run for our money. Brenna was so spoiled that she was in her own world, and we all lived in it," Walt agreed.

"And we wouldn't have wanted to interrupt that world, huh?" Brylee muttered.

"Brylee, got something to say?" Gran faced her.

"No, ma'am." She shoved some greens in her mouth. Gran stared at Brylee a moment longer then faced me again.

"Anyway, why a firefighter?" she wondered. I kept my eyes trained on Brylee for a second. Her body was more tense then a few minutes ago.

"I'm going to go get Scottlynn cleaned up." She stood abruptly. Halfway through the meal, she was fed baby food and got it all over her.

No one spoke as we watched her collect Scottlynn out of her highchair.

Slowly dragging my eyes back to Gran, I noticed her smile was more forced now. I cleared my throat. "Honestly, a fire happened at a friend's house when I was a kid. Seeing how the firefighters came in and helped stuck with me."

"What you do is honorable. It's a demanding job too, right?" Walt cut in.

I nodded. "Yeah, it is. You sacrifice a lot, mainly time with your family."

"How does your family feel about it?" Gran asked.

"They support me. My mom was more hesitant in the beginning, but I've been doing it so long she's on board with it."

"I can't imagine one of my boys doing what you do. My hair would be white by now."

A crooked grin split on my face. "Trust me, I hear it from her frequently. I'm careful, though. Of course, you never know what can happen when you're out there, but I love what I do."

"And that's all that matters," Walt said.

"Still, it's gotta be hard having a new baby and handling your job."

My attention went to my half-eaten plate. "It's not easy. When Scottlynn was first born, I thought about quitting and finding something more suitable, but it was my parents that talked me out of it, believe it or not."

"And forgive me if I'm prying, but the mother isn't around?"

My chest suddenly felt tight. "At the moment, no. It's a complicated situation.'"

"We'll be praying for all three of you," Gran said. When I looked back at her, she gave me a smile of comfort—the one only a grandmother could give.

"Thank you. Honestly, having Brylee there with me makes it easier. She's great with Scottlynn and keeps my house in order."

Right on cue, Brylee walked back into the room. Instead of putting Scottlynn back in the highchair, she sat her on her lap.

"That's because I'm fabulous." She seemed to be in better spirits.

I chuckled at her and reached over to grab my daughter's hand.

"Da-da." She brought my hand to her mouth.

"I was worried when I first learned Lee-Lee was moving in with you to work. It made us uncomfortable, honestly, but after meeting you, it seems we had nothing to worry about."

"I told you, Gran. Tripp is a good guy. He's been nothing but respectable since I moved in." Brylee stared up at me with sparkling eyes. Her smile grew, taking up most of her face. I liked this version of her better than the upset version earlier.

"You can never be too careful. We're glad it's working out, though," Walt said.

"With having a daughter, I can understand. You have nothing to worry about, though. I'll always be respectful when it comes to Brylee. I wouldn't do anything that could cause me to lose her."

Brylee's cheeks tinted. "I'm not going anywhere," she replied lowly. The bashfulness in her eyes made my stomach leap. Brylee was a soft spirited person, and after meeting her grandparents, I could see why. I didn't know how her parents were, but it was clear her grandparents raised her well.

"Since we got that out the way, I guess it's time for dessert," Gran said after a while. She stood.

"Do you need help?" I asked, preparing to stand.

"Oh, no. You stay there. Walt, come help me."

"I hope it hasn't been too much," Brylee mentioned when we were alone.

"Nah, it's been straight. Your grandparents are cool people. They remind me of mine."

"Are both of your grandparents around?"

I nodded. "Yeah, well my mom's dad isn't alive, but my grandma is. I don't see her or my dad's parents as much as I like because of work. After being around yours, I realize I need to make time to change that."

"Outside of Sunday dinners, I talk to them at least one to two times out of the week. If I don't, I'll hear their mouths." She snickered, making my smile grow. Her laugh was airy and soft. I realized I enjoyed hearing it.

"You have a nice laugh."

Her cheeks flushed. "Oh. Really?" Her mouth snapped shut as her eyes shifted.

The loss of her eyes tempted me to grab her chin and force her attention back on me.

"Okay, here we are. I hope you don't have allergies. I forgot to ask," Gran said, setting a pan on the table.

"No, I don't."

"Good. I made banana pudding and a caramel cake."

"Oh, Gran, you showed out!"

"Go lay that baby down and come back to get you some."

I glanced down and noticed Scottlynn had drifted off to sleep. She still had a hold on my finger but was cuddled against Brylee's chest.

"I'll be right back." She stood.

"Our Brylee's gonna be such a good mom one day. I can't wait to see it," Walt commented.

"I know. It's hard to believe that was the same brace face girl who used to throw tantrums in the middle of the grocery store."

I chuckled.

Brylee came back in the room and took a seat. "What?" she asked with furrowed brows after seeing me eye her.

"Just tryna picture you with braces."

Her eyes bucked and whipped between her grandparents. "Which one of you told him?"

The two shared a look with smiles on their faces.

"Before you leave, I'll show you pictures, Tripp," Gran said.

"Gran, no!"

"I'd love to see them." Brylee turned, mugging me. "I'm sure you were still a cute girl."

Her eyes grew again. I opened my mouth and snapped it closed, realizing what I just said.

"Oh, the cutest."

"Your Gran's right. You were a beautiful young lady."

"Okay, okay." She blushed. "You two can be so embarrassing sometimes."

The evening continued, and once we finished with dessert, Brylee helped her grandma clear the table while me and Walt left for the living room.

"You into sports?" Walt asked me. Being here with made me feel right at home. Her grandparents were welcoming people.

"Somewhat. I don't keep up with them all like that, but I know enough about them. Football, mainly."

"I'm more of a basketball and baseball guy myself, but I'll watch football when it's on."

Walt was an easy-going guy. The conversation with us continued, with him asking small questions to get to know me, which I didn't mind. If getting to know me better put their minds at ease, then I was all for it.

CHAPTER 14

BRYLEE

"You were right. Me and your grandpa have nothing to worry about. He's a nice man," Gran commented as she bagged the leftovers for us to take home.

"He is," I agreed, leaning against the counter. "If I felt any different, I would have quit. You guys didn't raise me to be a fool."

"It was clear the two of you get along well, too."

I side-eyed Gran, hearing a lingering hint in her tone. "Yeah, he's a good boss and is easy to work for."

"Mhm."

When I looked at her, a smirk was on her face, causing my eyes to narrow. "Mhm what? And why are you smiling like that?"

She shook her head and tied the bag of food, sliding it my way. "Nothing. I'm just happy for you is all."

I didn't believe her, but with Gran, she would tell me what was on her mind when she was ready, so I didn't push it. "That little girl is beautiful, too. Such a precious baby."

The corners of my mouth lifted upward. "Isn't she? It sucks her mom is missing out on so many moments with her, but I plan to cherish them while I'm around."

Gran's face softened, her eyes lightening and smile turning toothless. "I know you're just getting out of the situation with that knucklehead, but I pray I'm alive to see you in motherhood. You're gonna make a child so blessed to have you."

Her words caught me off guard. Suddenly, my throat grew thick, and my chest grew tight.

"Gran," I whispered. "Don't talk like that."

I knew death was meant for everyone, but I didn't want to think about my gran being gone any time soon.

She reached over and cuffed my cheek. "I know you have scars from your parents, but you have become such an amazing woman. I'm so proud of the woman you are. Both of them are lucky to have you in their lives. Continue to shower them with your light." Her thumb stroked my cheek before she pulled back. "Now, let's go see what those boys are doing. Your grandad is probably talking that man's ear off." She snickered and walked off.

Pressure built behind my eyes as I watched her. My gran was an amazing woman. I didn't know if she realized how impactful she was to me.

Sucking in a deep breath, I slowly released it and closed my eyes. My hand went to the center of my chest, and I slowly rubbed the tautness out. I hated when she spoke into me then walked away, leaving me to think. It was something she did often.

Clearing my throat, I grabbed the bag and left the kitchen.

"Look what Gran gave u—" My words faltered, and I lowered the bag when I got into the living room. "What's that?" Quickly, I went to the couch Tripp was on and looked over his shoulder. My head whipped in Gran's direction. "Why does he have this?"

Gran gave me a smug grin. "I told him I would show him your old pictures. You were a cute girl. I don't see the problem." She shrugged.

"She's right. You look the same, just younger," Tripp commented. I flicked my eyes down and groaned, seeing the picture of me in an elephant costume. I was ten or eleven in a school play. Moving around the couch, I slumped down.

"I can't believe she's showing you this."

"Be glad you weren't here when he looked at the ones of you in the tub," Grandad mentioned. My eyes bucked and heat flooded my cheeks. I knew my gran would take it too far, I just didn't expect her to bring out the baby book.

"I got so many pictures of Scottlynn on my phone. Looking at this makes me want to do one for her. Something she can have for a lifetime."

"If you print the pictures out, I can help you get it started," Gran stated. "I did one for all three of my kids, in addition to Brylee's."

"I'ma do that. Thank you. The more moments I can save, the better, especially with my job. I don't want Scottlynn to look back and think I missed all this time with her. I want her to know I was around, even with my demanding job."

"She will," I cut in with a small smile on my face. "That little girl loves you. Her whole face lights up whenever she lays on you. You have nothing to worry about. Plus, if there's any moment you miss, I'll make sure to capture it so you can feel like you're a part of it too."

The smile that spread on Tripp's face caused my stomach to flutter

"Keep saying things like that, and I'll never let you leave." He cocked his head and stared at me with a crooked grin on his face. My heart stuttered and swelled with heat.

"I don't see an issue with that."

Even though they weren't, part of me felt like him and Scottlynn were mine, and I didn't want him being down on himself for providing a live for her. She was taken care of and loved by so many. He had nothing to worry about.

"Well, I think that's great for both of you," Gran announced, inter- rupting the moment.

I shot my eyes in her direction. She watched us with a complacent expression. I shifted my attention to Grandad, and he smirked. Sitting straighter, I cleared my throat and tucked my lips into my mouth. The last thing I needed was for them to read more the room wrong.

"Are these your parents?" Tripp asked after a while. I looked down and frowned. My head slightly cocked as I studied the picture. It was my thirteenth birthday. The last one I cared about them being around for. After that, my resentment for them grew quickly.

"Yeah," I finally said.

"Dang, you look just like your mom." He lifted the book to study it closer. Both my parents were behind me while I sat at the table in front of a cake with a one and three candle on it.

I rolled my eyes. "So I've heard."

"Oh, if you see their baby pictures, you would think they were twins," Grandad mentioned.

Again, I rolled my eyes. "Good thing our personalities differ."

Gran cleared her throat. "Speaking of your mom, your brother was excited when I told him you would be at his party."

"Yeah, I need to make time to hang out with him and Brittani." Guilt consumed me thinking about neglecting my siblings. I tried to distance myself from our parents so much that sometimes I felt like a bad sister because they got caught in the mix.

"They'll like that. They both love you so much."

We stayed around my grandparents' house a little long before finally calling it a night. Scottlynn ended up waking up cranky, and I knew it was because it was drawing close to her bedtime.

"Oh, before you go, I forgot I have something for you," Gran said as we prepared to leave, causing me to pause. She turned and walked off. I looked toward my grandad for indication on what it could be, but he shrugged.

A couple minutes later, Gran came back. "Look what I found while I was cleaning out the closet in your old room."

My eyes widened at the sight of the ballerina box. "I thought this got thrown away a while ago." I sat the bag of leftovers down and grabbed the box from her. A nostalgic feeling filled me. It didn't make noise or move anymore; the paint was chipping, but it brought me back to my fifth birthday when my gran first gave it to me.

"What is it?" Tripp questioned.

"A ballerina box. Gran gave it to me when I turned five. I was upset about my parents not being around, and she used this as a bribe."

"It worked, didn't it?" She grinned. "It actually was mine from when I was a kid. I would have given it to her mom, but she had no interest in it, so I saved it for when she had kids. Lee-Lee used to want to dance ballet as a little girl, so it was fitting."

"Why didn't you?"

I snorted. "I went to one lesson and realized it was too much work. I enjoyed watching it but had no desire to be that disciplined." Joy passed through me as I examined the box. My finger brushed over the chipped corner from when it fell.

"I remember this chip from when I accidently knocked it off my dresser."

"Ah, yes. During one of your many tantrums as a child. You were so upset that day, and then the box stopped working, which only made it worse."

A stabbing shot through my chest. That same day I learned my parents went on vacation and didn't bother to take me.

"Take it with you. It might not work anymore, but it still can be useful."

Sighing, I rushed Gran and tossed my arms around her. "Thank you," I choked out, squeezing my eyes shut.

She tapped my back a couple times then rubbed it soothingly. "I love you, Lee-Lee. Always."

"Love you, too."

A few seconds later, I released her then hugged Grandad. "Love you, too," I told him.

Pushing a breath out to gather myself, I pulled back from him and noticed Tripp watching me. A look I couldn't make out was on his face. The smile on his face was soft, and his eyes brimmed with compassion. Embarrassment filled me over my outburst.

"We should go. I'll see you guys next Sunday."

"It was nice meeting you, Tripp. You're welcome to come back any time."

"If meals like today are on the table, I'll take you up on that, Gran." He gave her a one-sided hug since Scottlynn was in his other arm, then moved to shake Grandad's hand.

"My wife's right. Come back any time."

We left the house and headed to the car. It felt good leaving my grandparents' house and knowing they approved of Tripp, which I knew they would, but it still felt good having their approval.

"See, you were worried for no reason," Tripp commented, pulling out of the driveway.

"I wasn't worried about us coming. I just knew Gran was gonna Gran, which she did."

He laughed. "They're proud of you, that's all. Be happy they have those memories for you to look back on. I remember my parents doing stuff with us when I was younger, but they didn't keep a picture trail of it."

I tapped my fingers on the door arm in the car. "Yeah, I guess you're right, but they still didn't have to show me in the tub."

He was quiet for a second. "Do you think you would have had the same experiences if your parents were around?"

I scoffed. "Who knows. They seem like decent parents now, but I don't know them all like that."

"There's bad blood between you and your parents, but your grandparents made sure you were showered with love. It's obvious how much they mean to you."

"Funny thing is I used to resent them because I felt like they enabled my parents not being around and like they were overcompensating, but the older I got, the more I realized they just wanted to make sure I was taken care of, even if it wasn't by my parents." I watched the scenery as Tripp drove, almost getting lost in my head.

I jumped when his hand covered mine.

"Your parents missed out on someone great. You still turned out to be a big-hearted person without them."

I lowered my eyes to his hand, trailing the multiple veins running through it. Goosebumps covered my arms and flutters returned to my stomach.

"Thank you."

He squeezed my hand before releasing it and resting it back in his lap.

The music filled the silence between us. The sun was setting, and the streets were busy but calming. I got lost in my head, thinking about today. Me and Russell never had moments like this. He had been to my grandparents' house for Sunday dinners a handful of times, and it never felt like today did. My grandparents didn't care for him, but they tried to be respectful to him at the same time. He knew they were a big part of my life, but I never felt like he tried to get along with them or cared to. The room always felt tense whenever he was around. It made my heart smile that it wasn't the case when it came to Tripp.

CHAPTER 15

TRIPP

"Hey, Tripp. It's good to see you," Joy, Troy's wife, said as she answered their door.

"Wassup, Joy?" I stepped into the house, already knowing to take my shoes off.

"I'm happy one of you remember. I just got on Terrence's ass about his damn shoes." She closed the door behind her.

"You know my little brother's a little touched in the head."

"A little is an understatement," she muttered, making me laugh.

I followed her as she walked away from the door.

"You should have brought the baby. She could have kicked it up here with me."

"You'd have to fight my mama for her. She called dibs tonight."

"Hmph. Should have known. She doesn't play about her grand-daughter."

Since Scottlynn was the only grandkid at the moment, she got all the attention from my parents. Even before having Brylee at the house, I never had to worry about a sitter.

"At all. That's why you need to hurry and pop one out so I don't have to fight for my baby's time." I grinned, causing her to wave me off.

"We got a few more months before we go that route."

Joy wanted to be married at least a year before her and my brother had kids, which I respected. They dated for two years before my brother popped the question, and her reasoning was wanting to enjoy being newlyweds before kids got involved.

"They downstairs?" I asked, already heading for the basement door.

"Always. Go ahead down." She took a seat on the couch and picked up a tablet. "And tell my husband don't be down there being all loud either."

I chuckled. "I told him to get the room soundproofed. You know how he is when he's watching a game."

While I might not be that serious about sports, Troy was the opposite. He played his whole life and didn't stick to just one. He watched them consistently and got passionate about whichever one was on at the moment. It'd been a few times we almost got into fights with other people at bars because the shit he talked.

"Look who finally found time for his brothers," Terrance joked as I stepped into Troy's basement that he deemed his man cave.

"Get off my dick." I took a seat on the couch and turned to Troy, who sat in his favorite chair, eyes already locked on the TV. A big fight was on tonight, and instead of going out somewhere and watching it, he invited us over. "Yo' wife said don't be down here acting like you ain't got no sense either."

He ignored me and brought his Silver Shadow's beer to his mouth.

"You know that's gonna happen. How much money you got on this fight?" Terrance asked.

"Five hundred," Troy answered, his eyes never leaving the TV. We still had some time until the main event.

"Yeah, Joy gone kick yo' ass. Didn't she tell yo' ass stop betting on this shit?" I stood and walked to the back bar where some buffalo dip and finger sandwiches were. "One thing I appreciate about sis is she always makes sure we have food when we come over." I got a couple sandwiches after scooping some dip and grabbing chips.

"Y'all lucky my wife fucks with y'all because I was gonna let y'all fend for yourselves."

"Because yo' ass ain't shit." I glanced over and noticed Brenden, Terrence's best friend, coming from the bathroom.

"Wassup, Tripp?" He tossed me a head nod, which I silently returned. I wasn't a fan Brenden. I felt like he always had my brother in some shit, but most of the time, I kept my comments to myself. I grabbed a Coke and walked back to the couch.

"Anyone else coming?" I asked, getting comfortable.

"Yeah, Noah and Marshall," Troy replied, referring to his two friends.

I nodded. We fell silent as we watched the fight, Troy talking shit in between. Terrence and Brenden had their own conversation while I ate. Eventually, Noah and Marshall showed up, and things got a little louder. I stayed quiet, commenting here and there on random subjects.

"How's my niece doing?" Troy finally asked once the current fight wrapped up.

I finished the last of my dip and looked up at him. "Growing too fucking fast. It's like every day she's doing something new. She's finally talking." I beamed with pride.

"Word? That's what I'm talking about. I'ma have to come over so we can work on her saying Uncle Terrance."

"Don't count on that anytime soon. She just mastered da-da."

"That's what's up, big bro. I can't wait for Joy to pop me out a few."

"A few? How many you want?" Terrance asked.

"Four, maybe five."

I choked on my drink. "Joy ain't about to give yo' ass that many." I laughed.

A snarky grin formed on his face. "Why y'all be acting like Joy got the final say in everything?"

"Nigga, because she do!" Terrance laughed.

"It's her body," both me and our brother answered at the same time.

"Yeah, don't do it. My two baby mama's give me hell, and I just learned I got another possible on the way," Brenden objected.

I frowned at him but kept my mouth shut.

"The difference between us is I'm married and having kids with my wife, not random ass women."

"Hell, wives give you the blues, too," Marshall mentioned. He just recently separated from his wife.

He waved us off. "I let Joy have this year kid free, but I'm ready for some mini me's running around. I think she's starting to want it too because she been hinting at it." He rubbed his hands together.

"You know what? I ain't even mad at you." I leaned back and gapped my legs. "Scottlynn's the best thing that ever happened to me. When Skye told me she was pregnant, I was ecstatic. I lowkey thought she couldn't have kids fo'real, so it was a shock, but the best news she could have given me."

"Speaking of Skye, how she doing?" Noah asked. He grew up around us, too. Him and Troy been friends since we were in grade school, so he'd been around for my relationship with Skye.

"Managing." I kept it short. It was no secret Skye was an addict and now back in rehab, but at the same time, it wasn't something I discussed with just anyone. Thankfully, Noah nodded in understanding that I didn't want to talk about it.

"What you need to be asking him about is that fine ass nanny he got living with him," Terrance threw out, causing me to shoot him a look.

"Oh yeah, I heard you got a live in babysitter. She looking to take on new clients?" Brenden licked his lips and smirked, causing my frow to deepen.

"No, she's not."

"That nigga ain't gone share her, and if you saw her, you'd understand. She got that girl next door, mixed with seductive schoolgirl going on."

My face balled up. "How the hell you get that out of meeting her twice?"

He shrugged. "It's a gift. I bet she a freak, fo'real, ain't she?"

A deadpanned look formed on my face as my eyes cut to my

brother. I loved him, but he said the dumbest shit at times. "Even if I did know, I wouldn't tell yo' ass."

"Man, you still ain't hit that! You slippin', big bro. Skye's ass ain't around. You better have fun while you can."

Instead of responding to him, I turned back to my more sensible brother. "Anyway, like I was saying, kids are a blessing. If everything goes smooth with Skye, I wanna try for another."

Troy's face fell as his forehead creased. "You really pussy whipped to have another baby with that cra—"

My head whipped over and hardened as I faced Brenden.

"Finish that sentence, and I'ma lay you out on this floor," I warned him, never raising my voice but making sure I locked eyes with him. My pulse picked up as my hands flexed.

"Too far, bro." Terrence nudged him and muttered, but I heard him.

The mood shifted and grew silent. I waited for more bullshit to spill out of Brenden's mouth, but he did the smart thing and stayed silent.

"They need to hurry up with main event so I can make some money," Troy eventually said after a while.

"You got that right. I can't wait to take yours," Marshall commented. The two debated on why each of their guys would win. The room slowly came back to life.

"My bad, big bro. He shouldn't have said that shit," Terrence said as he walked up on me. I was at the bar getting another sandwich.

"Just tell that nigga to keep his mouth shut about my family," I told him, and he nodded. Regardless of Skye's situation, I would never let anyone talk down on her.

"Done."

We walked back to the couch, and I pulled my phone out of my pocket. Evie had hit me up, checking in on the Brylee situation, wondering how it was going. I responded to her then saw I had a text from Brylee too. That slightly brought my mood up.

I clicked on it, and the corner of my mouth slowly lifted.

BRYLEE

Saw these for Scottlynn and couldn't pass them up *heart eyes emoji*

Pictures attached.

Today, she had the day off since I was off, and then Scottlynn went with my parents. I had been in and out all day after catching up on sleep, so I hadn't laid eyes on her longer than two seconds. I swiped through the pictures of the little girl outfits. It warmed my heart that she went out of her way to buy stuff for my daughter. It wasn't a part of her job description, but she still thought of my daughter. It was clear she had love for Scottlynn by the way she treated her. Seeing her show my Scottlynn the maternal love she lacked sent a wave of emotions through me to my chest, causing swelling in my heart.

ME

If I didn't tell you already, I'ma tell you now, I appreciate the fuck outta you. Thank you for loving my daughter like you do.

As if she was waiting for me to respond, she texted back instantly.

No need to thank me. She stole my heart the first time I saw her throwing that tantrum in your arms lol.

I smirked and was about to reply when she sent another message.

I need more friends. Leia had a date, and Scottlynn's gone. I'm here by my lonely self watching my show.

Attached to that was a picture of the TV screen. The lights were off, and she sat in the living room. Suddenly, I had the urge to ditch the rest of the night and go back home. Since Brylee had been around, I'd grown to enjoy spending time with her. I learned she was a simple girl but made herself known. There were plenty of times I'd come home to her dancing in the kitchen while singing and cooking, or her and Scottlynn lost in their own worlds doing something stimulating for her mind. She was big on learning and teaching, saying that at this age Scottlynn's brain was a sponge. She had gotten her a few toys that helped with progress. In some ways, I felt like I was slippin' because I didn't think of it first, but she never made me feel bad and was always eager to show me what they learned that day.

I recently learned she was into crocheting too. I had caught her one day in the middle of working on a blanket and watching TV while Scottlynn slept next to her. Brylee had layers to her, and just when I thought I had her figured out, I learned something new.

"What's got you lost in your head?" Troy asked.

"What?" I snapped out of it, not realizing I had zoned out.

"We were calling you. You cool?"

I nodded. "Yeah, just thinking."

I looked down at my phone. Unlocking it, I quickly replied.

> I'll be home soon.

Locking my phone, I sat it on my lap and zoned back into the conversation. It had been a minute since I spent time with my brothers, so I wasn't about to leave early, but I couldn't deny I was eager to get back home.

———

Stepping into my house, I walked to the over to the couch, and it was like Déjà vu. The TV played, and Brylee was asleep with her crotchet set on her lap. I took the moment to take her in, admiring how even dressed homely she was still beautiful. On the days she technically had off, she always stayed close to home, unless she was running errands or hanging out with her friend. I always appreciated a woman who didn't need to be done up to be attractive.

I looked around until I laid eyes on the remote and grabbed it to turn the TV off. That was when Brylee's eyes snapped open.

"Shoot." She yawned and rubbed her eyes. She looked around in confusion for a second before laying eyes on me. "You just getting home?"

I nodded. "Yeah. I'm starting to think we should put your bedroom in here since you always manage to fall asleep on the couch."

She gave me a sleepy grin. "I always say one more episode, and then I'ma go to sleep, but then one becomes two and so on. I planned on going to my room after the last one, but obviously that didn't work out." She glanced at the TV and squinted. "I think I'm still on the same episode."

I took a seat next to her. "What we watching?"

Turning her head toward me, she blinked and stared at me surprised. "You're gonna watch it with me?"

I shrugged. "Yeah. I'm not tired. Unless you planned on going upstairs."

She shook her head. "I think I'm up now."

"Cool." I licked my lips and got comfortable, taking my phone out of my pocket and setting it next to me. "What we watching?"

"*Lucifer.* You ever watch it?"

I glanced at the screen. "Nah, I think some of the guys at the firehouse used to watch it, though. He's the devil helping the cops, right?"

"Yeah. I never finished the series, so I'm starting it from the beginning. It's a good show." Brylee grabbed the remote and rewound it.

"How was the fight?" Brylee asked after a while.

"It was cool. My brother was happy because he wasn't gon' have to sleep on the couch for losing five hundred dollars. His wife hates him gambling."

"Troy? I didn't know your brother was married."

"Oh yeah, been with her for like four years now."

"Mhm. He's married, you got a kid, what about Terrance?"

I snorted. "That nigga out here living his life carefree being someone's sugar baby."

"Wait." She choked on her drink.

"Shit." I chuckled, leaning over and hitting her back a couple times.

"Please tell me that was a joke." She coughed.

"I wish. My little brother loves him an older woman, especially cougars."

"I would have never guessed." She snickered.

"Terrance is the one that keeps you on your toes, my mom always says."

"I can definitely see that. He funny, though. I bet growing up with him wasn't boring."

"No, it wasn't."

Brylee smiled sleepily at my then turned her attention back to the TV. I studied her side profile. Her facial bones were delicately carved, and her mouth was full. She had a straight and short nose, fitting her oval face. The glow of the TV reflected off her caramel skin.

We got through the rest of the episode, and by the time the next one rolled around, Brylee was dozing off again. I was focused on the TV when her head fell over and landed on my arm, causing me to glance down at her. Her breathing was slow and steadied while her body relaxed. I watched her chest slowly rise and fall. Her small breaths tickled my arm hairs.

Laughing to myself, I gently removed myself from her and rested her head on the couch. Grabbing the remote, I turned the TV off then scooped Brylee up in my arms. Walking through the dark, I made it to the stairs. She muttered something inaudible and shifted slightly, causing me to drop my eyes to her. Brylee weighed next to nothing in my arms and fit perfectly.

"I feel asleep again, didn't I?" she mumbled with her eyes still closed.

With a grin, I answered, "You did. It's all good, though."

Nodding sluggishly, she yawned and sighed.

When I got to her room, I laid her on the bed and stepped back. My eyes traveled around the space, noting how she made it her own. She was officially unpacked and no longer living out of the boxes she brought here. That fact made me happy. I wanted her to feel at home and comfortable.

Something on her dresser caught my eye as I was about to leave. I checked over my shoulder, and Brylee peacefully slept. Bringing my attention back to the dresser, I picked the white and pink ballerina box up and examined it closely. A thought passed through me.

With the box in hand, I left out room and headed for the steps.

———

"I hate when cap agrees to this shit," Harlem complained.

"You act like he's forcing us to go to war. They're just kids," Lee defended.

"Still, I signed up to be a firefighter, not a babysitter."

The two went back and forth while I stuck the rest of my things in my locker, closing it behind me.

Omiras set up a youth group to come tour the firehouse today. We did it often during the active school year, so it wasn't new to us. Cap loved giving back to the community, and especially the youth.

"It's a couple hours. Suck it up," I cut in. Harlem mugged me.

"A couple hours I could be sleeping," he muttered.

My phone rang, gaining my attention. Checking out the screen, my stomach twisted seeing the name displayed.

"Let cap know I'll be out in a second," I told them.

"You good? You just got tensed as fuck," Lee commented.

"Yeah. Just gotta take this." I lifted my phone.

The two nodded and left the locker room. I took a seat on the bench and answered the call.

"Hello?"

"Hey, baby," Skye's voice rang from the other side.

"Skye," I breathed, folding my shoulders forward.

"It feels good to hear your voice. I feel like it's been forever."

I nodded as if she could see me.

Since she had a setback, we hadn't talked. I got updates on her, but it felt good to hear her voice too.

"How you doing? You done giving them people hell, huh?" I joked with a small smile on my face.

She giggled. "Yeah, my head's a lot clearer than when I first got here. I still have my days, but I'm officially past the detox stage."

My smile grew. "I'm glad to hear that, Skye. So fucking glad."

We got lost in conversation. She was only allowed on the phone for fifteen minutes, so it was a quick conversation. I made sure to update her on Scottlynn, letting her know about her recent speaking.

"Before we get off the phone, I wanted to let you know they said I'll be able to get visitors soon. Will you come see me?" Hope bled from her tone.

Skye seemed to be trying which made me hopeful she was serious this time around. "Of course. I can't wait to lay eyes on you again."

"I hope you like what you see. I know I lost a lot of weight and stuff before coming here. It's starting to come back now."

I shook my head. "You still looked good, though. Just focus on continuing to get yourself together and get healthier. I can't wait to see you."

We talked a little longer before hanging up. My chest was tight with my stomach in knots. Talking to Skye gave me a bittersweet feeling. She sounded healthier and like herself, but I knew she still had a long battle to fight. We had been through this before. I just prayed her sobriety lasted.

Needing to focus on something else, I gathered myself and prepared to go into the main room. The kids should be arriving soon.

Just as I was about to leave the locker room, my phone vibrated.

Brylee: *picture attached* *We have a surprise for you when you get home!*

I couldn't stop the smile from forming on my face. Some of the tightness faded from my chest. Scottlynn looked to be in mid-laugh, while Brylee made a funny face in the selfie. The picture was heart-warming.

Instead of replying, I hearted the picture and locked my phone, shoving it back in my pocket. My daughter was happy, and she was growing bigger every day. Bringing Brylee in to take care of her showed to be the best decision I could have made.

CHAPTER 16

BRYLEE

I walked into the kitchen, surprised to see the light on. My brows crinkled, and I looked around, knowing I turned it off before going upstairs. I came down to grab something to drink, but now I was curious about the light. My stomach flipped when I didn't notice anything out of the ordinary.

I moved to the counter where the knives were and grabbed one of them. It was just me and Scottlynn here, and my phone was upstairs, so I wasn't taking any chances.

"Brylee," I heard from behind me, causing me to jump and spin around, gripping the knife.

"Shit," I groaned, holding my chest. Tripp's eyes widened and dropped to the knife. "Tripp. I thought it was just me and Scottlynn here."

"My bad." He slowly stepped closer, moving away from the back door. "I didn't mean to scare you. Today started my new schedule. Three days on, four off and I was too wired to sleep."

My grip on the knife didn't loosen, and I didn't realize it until he cautiously stood in front of me and wrapped his hands around mine. I inhaled a deep breath and stared down at our adjoined hands.

"Oh, sorry." I released the knife.

My eyes shot to his face. He smirked at me and set the knife on the counter. "Nah, I'm glad you're cautious. If something were to happen, at least I know my daughter would be protected. I didn't mean to scare you."

I shook my head. "It's fine." My heart still raced, but I didn't think it was because of Tripp surprising me. He still had his hand wrapped around mine, and neither of us seemed bothered by it.

I cleared my throat and slowly pulled my hand out of his. "What were you doing in the back?" I wondered, looking behind where he just came from.

His tongue swiped across his lips, drawing my attention to them. They were cupid bow shaped, medium size, nude, and fit his face well.

"Oh, I was in my workshop. I just came in to grab a bottle of water."

"Workshop?" I stared at him curiously.

He grinned. "Yeah, c'mon. I'll show you." He turned and went to the fridge. I watched him open it and pull two bottles of water out. He turned and held one out for me.

"Oh, thank you." I stepped toward him, grabbing the bottle.

I'd enjoyed being around and working with Tripp. He was a great boss and man. He was respectful, a wonderful father, close to his family, and hardworking, too. I often wondered how his child's mother could choose drugs over him and their daughter. I would love to have a man like him in my life.

"You coming?" Tripp turned and faced me once at the back door.

"Oh, yeah. Wait, I should go get my phone so I can listen for Scottlynn."

He smiled. "Don't worry about that. I have a monitor in my shop."

"Of course, you do." I grinned softly and followed behind him.

My eyes locked on his wide, muscular back as I opened my water and brought the bottle to my mouth. I had been in the backyard before, but I always thought the shed back here held tools and such. When Tripp opened the door and invited me in, I was surprised to see how spacious it was and the equipment inside.

"What is all this?" I asked in amazement. I walked to the wood rocking horse on the wall and ran my hand over it.

"My workshop. I took a liking to woodshop in high school, and it stuck with me afterward. In my spare time, I do furniture restoration and creation."

"That's so cool. You restored this?" I ran my hand over the horse.

He nodded. "Yeah, I found it at an antique shop not too far from here. I normally find pieces there when I don't have client work to do and restore them, then sell them for a higher profit."

"Wow, it takes some real talent to do something like that." I turned to face him.

A sheepish grin formed on his face, and his shoulders lifted. "I haven't gotten any complaints yet."

"So, not only do you save people, but you're handy, too. What can't you do, boss man?" I walked over to him and eyed the table. Wood chippings were scattered around it.

Tripp chuckled. "Trust me, there's a lot of shit I can't do. Stuff like this just relaxes me."

"I get it. I took to crocheting, and when I get too stressed out or overwhelmed, it helps center me."

"So, I'm not the only one who's good with their hands then."

The back of my neck grew warm when his eyes fell on me. They beamed with interest.

"I mean, I don't know if I can restore a rocking horse, but I can make one hell of a blanket." I snickered.

He licked his lips. "That's dope too." His hand landed on my wrist. "I think any sign of creativity is dope, no matter what it is."

My eyes locked on his hand. They were large, rough, and could wrap around my whole arm.

"What are you working on now?"

I flickered my eyes up, staring at him under my lashes.

"I just finished that rocking horse. I got another one that needs to be restored, but I think I'ma take care of it tomorrow."

"You really are an amazing guy." I spoke before I could think about it. My eyes bucked.

The corners of Tripp mouth rose. "Well, thank you. I try, at least."

"You're succeeding. Scottlynn's a lucky girl to have a dad a like you."

He gave my wrist a squeeze. "I can say the same about you. We're *both* lucky to have you in our lives."

My cheeks flushed. "Oh, I don't know."

"Don't act all shy now. It's the truth. You saved my ass, fo'real. I'm forever indebted to you."

"I guess it was a good thing we ran into each other at that store then."

Again, he chuckled. "Hell yeah, it was. You saved my ass that day, too. I don't know what I would do without you. Scottlynn's usually an easy baby to deal with, but when she has her moments, not just anyone can settle her down. Usually just me and sometimes my mom. I was shocked by how easily she quieted for you."

"I just have the magic touch," I boasted playfully.

"You do. Since you been here things have been so much smoother." His voice softened. "I couldn't have picked a better person to help me with my daughter."

My chest suddenly flooded with warmth at his compliment. Taking care of kids had always been my passion, but this was the first time I felt like this was where I was meant to be. Since being here, I felt welcomed and at home.

I stayed in the workshop a little longer, and Tripp showed me a few pieces he had worked on lately. He didn't just restore furniture, but he also created different pieces, too. He was talented, and by the way he spoke about them, I could tell he took pride in his work. It made me wonder what other things my boss hid about himself.

I moved forward and tapped his shoulder. Tripp stopped sanding and turned to face me. He currently worked on a coffee table. "I should probably head back to bed. That little girl of yours will be up in a couple hours looking to eat," I announced. I wasn't sure how much time had passed, but I'd been back here for a good while.

He removed the googles on his face and stared down at me. "Cool. I'ma take her out with me tomorrow. It's been a while since we had a daddy and daughter day, so you're off the hook." He flashed me a crooked smile.

My heart stuttered as I returned his smile. "Okay. I know she'll like that." My eyes bounced around his face. Without thought, I lifted to brush some dust that was on his cheek away.

"Oh... sorry." Heat crept into my cheek realizing what I just did. His smile grew, and he reached for my wrist, causing the thin hairs on it to rise.

"It gets messy in here. Thanks for looking out."

Staring into Tripp's warm orbs brought me comfort. They glowed like a glassy volcanic rock. Sheen with purpose. I dropped my eyes to his lips that were still pulled into a smile that softened his masculine face.

Before I could think about it, I pushed off my feet, crashing my mouth into his. My eyes closed as my heart raced. An electric current filed through me, sparking my insides. His hold on my wrist tightened.

My eyes snapped open, my stomach filled with a ball of knots.

"Oh, shit," I muttered, slowly pulling back. Blinking slowly, I pushed deep unsteady breaths out as I stepped back. Tripp had a shocked expression on his face. His brows rose, and his eyes wide. An awkward silence loomed between like a heavy mist.

"Brylee," he started, causing me to flinch.

"Sorry!" I squeaked. Snatching my wrist out of his grasp, I turned and rushed out of the workshop and back into the house. I didn't slow down until I was back in my room.

My heart thundered loudly, my stomach clenched tight with anxiety, and my pulse raced erratically. Embarrassment crept through me. I couldn't believe I would boldly kiss Tripp like that. Whenever I was around him, I always felt so calm, and over the weeks, my attraction for him was hard to ignore. Still, I planned to keep those feelings tucked away.

"Fuck!" I balled my fist and slammed them against my forehead. I knew I had crossed a line, and I prayed it didn't cost me my job. I loved working here and being around Scottlynn and Tripp. Inside this house felt like we were in our own private bubble that no one could interrupt. Most of the time, when Tripp was off, he hung out around the house, bonding with Scottlynn and attempting to give me the time off, but it was hard not to be involved. We ate together, and sometimes he would hang around the kitchen while I cooked. It was easy to grow feelings for him.

"No!" I stated out loud, opening my eyes.

I couldn't think of Tripp that way. If he allowed me to keep my job, I would never cross that line again and make sure to keep things professional.

I rubbed the center of my chest, attempting to ease some of the tension still building. Hopefully, we could chalk this up to a lapse of judgement and forget it ever happened.

———

"Are you excited to hang out with your daddy today, pretty girl?" I cooed at Scottlynn, poking her nose making her shriek in laughter and babble. Tripp was still asleep by the time Scottlynn woke up, so it had been just me and her this morning. I was on edge and not sure how things would be once I laid eyes on Tripp. I was still embarrassed by my actions last night.

"I know I'm excited to hang out with her," Tripp announced behind me, causing me to jump. We were on the ground, both on our stomachs, and in our own world.

My stomach twisted as I pushed a slow breath out and sat up.

"Hey." I avoided his eyes. "She's been fed and everything already, so she's good to go whenever you are."

"You're a life saver. Thanks."

"No problem." My hands rested in my lap, and I watched Scottlynn aimlessly play with the toy in front of her.

"Brylee." Tripp calling my name made the hairs on the back of my neck rise.

"Yeah?"

"Are you gonna look at me?"

As much as I didn't want to, I knew I couldn't avoid him. Swallowing hard, I slowly turned my head to face him. My heart pounded like a drum inside me. Tripp had a slight smile on his face.

"We good?"

My brows crinkled then shot up while my mouth turned upside down. Maybe he wasn't going to bring the kiss up. That would be for the best, but part of me was disappointed he didn't acknowledge it.

"Yeah, we're good," I finally answered.

His smile grew. "Good." He cleared his throat. "Now, you texted me and said you two had a surprise for me."

It took me a second to remember before my body lit up. "Oh, yeah. Hold on."

Reaching for the toy in front of Scottlynn, I grabbed it, causing her to grow fussy.

"I know, I know." I scooted back slightly. "I've been doing tummy time with her," I announced, keeping my eyes on Scottlynn.

"C'mon, pretty girl. Show Daddy what we've been working on." I hit one of the buttons on the toy, causing it to make noise.

Scottlynn eyed the toy and kicked her feet. We both waited a moment. It took a little bit, but eventually, she did something in the middle of a crawl and scoot.

"Ah hell!" He gasped behind me. "You done taught my baby to crawl." Emotions dripped thickly from his throat.

Once she was close enough, I sat the toy down then stood up. "Yeah, she had been showing signs of it for a little bit now, so I just been encouraging her. It's not a full crawl yet, but we're getting there."

Tripp stared at his daughter in awe. I could see the mixed emotions on his face, which made my chest taut.

"Damn, she's growing so fast, and I feel like I'm missing it."

I shook my head and went to the couch to grab my phone. "You're not. There's still so many firsts she still has to have, and plus, I recorded it for you."

I moved next to him and ignored the fresh woodsy scent coming off him. Clearing my throat, I unlocked my phone and went to the video.

"Here you go." I handed him the phone.

I watched as his eyes lit up as he watched the video. Her crawl was clumsier than today, but I was happy she got it.

"Damn." He looked up at me. Warmth burned from his orbs.

I yelped when he suddenly pulled me into him, hugging me tightly. My eyes closed, and I inhaled a deep breath, taking in his body wash.

"You're dope as fuck, man. Thank you for this."

Emotions got caught in my throat. Slowly, I lifted my arms and hugged him back when his grip tightened.

"Just doing my job," I muttered into his chest.

"Nah, you doing more than that. You're being exactly what my daughter needs right now. I can never repay you for everything you're doing." His breath was warm against my ear, causing my nerves to tingle.

Scottlynn grew fussy. When he released me, I instantly missed his touch but gave him a smile. "Better not keep her waiting any longer. She's getting antsy."

He stared at me with a curious expression on his face, almost as if he was trying to figure something out. A small chuckle left his mouth. "You're right."

I stood back and watched as he walked to Scottlynn and bent down to pick her up. The *dada's* started instantly. He showered her with kisses, which caused her to grow more excited.

"Whatchu got planned today?"

"Gonna meet Leia for lunch then gotta go find my brother something for his birthday."

"A'right, then I guess we'll see you later. Say bye, Scottlynn."

She clapped her hands and blew spit bubbles.

Laughing, I shook my head and walked to the side of the couch. "I got her diaper bag together for you. She shouldn't get hungry 'til like three."

"Yeah, I'm never letting you go." I knew he didn't mean anything by it, but those words spiked my heartbeat into a frenzy.

Tripp and Scottlynn left, leaving me alone in my thoughts. My eyes circled the living room. Since Tripp didn't feel the need to bring up last night, I figured maybe things were going to be okay between us.

"You're laughing, but I was fucking mortified!" I groaned as I sipped on my mimosa while Leia sat across from me laughing as I told her about last night.

"I'm sorry, friend." She struggled to speak between laughs. She grabbed her chest and took a few breaths. "Okay, okay. It just reminds me of when we were teenagers, and you were such a rebel. I didn't think you had it still."

I rolled my eyes and stabbed the middle of my pasta, shoving it into my mouth.

"I'm glad you find humor in my embarrassment."

"Why are you embarrassed?

"I basically sexually assaulted my boss, and then he didn't even bring it up today."

"Okay, now you're being dramatic." She rolled her eyes. "And maybe he just didn't want to make it a big deal. Obviously, he didn't mind it that much if you still have a job."

"For now," I grumbled, wiping my brow.

She shook her head. "Seriously, though, Lee-lee. I'm sure you're overthinking it. If he doesn't bring it up, just leave it alone. Or hell, maybe even act on it and see how far you can push it." She shrugged.

"He has a girlfriend." Guilt shot through me. I wasn't even thinking about Skye last night when I kissed Tripp. It wasn't until today it hit me; I kissed another woman's man.

Leia rolled her eyes. "I mean, are they really even together? Maybe they just co-parent."

"They're together."

Tripp didn't talk about her, but as far as I knew, they were still together. "Okay, then just let it go. You did it and can't take it back. If he isn't making it a big deal, then you're good."

I knew she was probably right. The more I tried to rationalize my actions last night, the more I would overthink things.

"Right. You're right." I scooped up more of my pasta. "Anyway, tell me about this new boo. I'm guessing things are going well. You've been on a couple dates now, right?"

"Girl!" In true Leia fashion, she animatedly gave me details about her new boo. I was happy for my friend. She dated frequently, but it wasn't often one guy caught her attention. By the way she spoke, it seemed like she really liked this one. It was good to hear. At least one of us had a positive love life going on right now.

CHAPTER 17

TRIPP

"I can't believe how big she's gotten!" Evie gushed over Scottlynn as she bounced her in her lap.

I stared at my daughter happily suck the attention up. "You're telling me. Seems like just yesterday she was born. Now she's starting to talk and trying to crawl."

"She looks just like you, too. At first, I thought she was gonna favor Skye, but your genes fought back."

That caused me to laugh. "I don't know why you had any doubt. That's my baby."

"Let's hope she takes more after you than her mama, too."

"Evie." I cut my eyes at her.

Her shoulders rose. "Just saying. Skye isn't the greatest role model."

I shook my head, not bothering to entertain the conversation. "But she's still Scottlynn's mother, so chill."

She shifted her eyes to my daughter. "Do you plan to be with her when she comes home?"

My head tilted as my eyes brows furrowed. "What made you ask that?"

"Just curious. You know I love Skye, but she's taken advantage of your love for her for too long. I hoped you would take this time to move on from her."

"You act like I'm being held against my will or some shit."

Evie shook her head. "I'm not saying that, but I do feel like Skye knows how manipulate your feelings for her. No matter what she does, you refuse to leave her."

"Because you don't give up on those you love," I defended.

Evie sighed and rolled her eyes. "You can love her and not be with her. Since she's been gone, there's less stress on your face. Don't you want to find someone who's easier to love and deal with?"

For a brief second, Brylee's bright, smiling face popped in my head. My mind went to last night. The kiss caught me off guard, and she ran away before I could even address it. It should have been a deal-breaker for me. She crossed a line she shouldn't have, but I couldn't find it within me to be upset with her. The kiss was over before I could fully realize what she was doing, but I didn't miss how soft her lips were. I didn't bring it up when I saw her because it was clear she was mortified about her actions, and I didn't want to make it worse. It *was* something we needed to discuss eventually. I knew that.

I didn't want there to be any weirdness between us. We meshed well, and she made my life ten times easier. There were no ill feelings toward what she did, and I needed to make that clear to her.

"Evie, I appreciate your concern, but let it go," I told her firmly.

Since we had been friends for so long, she knew not to push further. I respected what she said, but in the end, she needed to respect how *I* felt.

"I'm assuming since you haven't asked me to look anyone else up, things with the nanny still going well?" Evie stated after a few minutes. Scottlynn had settled down and was now resting peacefully in her arms, gnawing on her teething ring.

Brylee's face popped in my head again, making a smile split on my face. "Yeah, things are good."

"Hold on, what's with that smile?"

Keeping the smile on my face, I turned my head in her direction and stared at her in amusement. "What you talkin' about?"

"Don't play with me, Tripp Allen Clark."

"Umph, the full name, huh?" I huffed a laugh out and stroked my chin. "Things are smooth. She's great at what she does and good company."

"And…" Evie stressed.

"And what?"

She rolled her eyes. "And you like her, right?" She lifted her hand and pointed a finger at me. "Don't try to deny it either. Look how big your smile is when discussing her, and your eyes are twinkling."

My eyes cut into slits. "The fuck? My eyes don't twinkle."

"They're definitely twinkling. When am I going to meet this amazing nanny?"

Another chuckle left my mouth. "Chill. You're getting yourself excited for nothing."

Evie smacked her lips. "I swear niggas stress me out. That's why I prefer my own sex."

"Speaking of… what's up with you and Alisha?"

This time it was Evie's face lighting up. "Great. I think she's gonna propose soon."

My eyes brightened. "Fo'real? That's what's up!"

She nodded. "Yep. I caught her looking at rings a few times but haven't said anything, obviously. I hope she plans on doing it soon, because if not, I'ma do it myself."

"You deserve it too, Evie. Alisha's dope, and she's good for you."

"I know." A dreamy expression formed on her face. "And at the wedding, you gotta be my best man."

I grinned. "You don't want one of your sisters?"

She made a sound with her mouth and twisted her lips. "No. I love them. They'll be in the wedding, but you're my best friend and have been there with me through some tough times."

I nodded in understanding. Evie suffered from depression, and when she had her episodes, she liked to completely shut down and block the world out. It was one reason I was glad she had Alisha. They've been together for almost two years, and she understood her and knew how to handle her when she got in one of those moods.

A lot of people didn't trust me and Evie being friends because of how close we were, ignoring the fact that she liked the same thing I did. Even though we all grew up together, it caused a couple arguments with me and Skye, but that was because she was always paranoid that I was going to leave her. It was her insecurities mixed with the drugs. Evie was more than just my friend, though. She was family.

———

Since it was nice out, I took Scottlynn down to The Shore and walked the boardwalk. The beach in front of us was full of people. The water was calm, with slight waves rising here and there. The sun shinned brightly, and the smell of seawater filled my nose.

A couple times women stopped us to gush over Scottlynn. At first she soaked it up, but I think she was growing restless and needed a nap because she was becoming cranky. After leaving Evie's, house I took her with me to run a couple errands. Days like this I cherished, since I didn't have them often.

"Okay, pretty girl, you ready to head home?" I pushed her stroller back and forth as I waited for the guy behind the cart to give me my frozen lemonade. When I realized what I said, I couldn't help but chuckle. Brylee called Scottlynn pretty girl so much, I was starting to, too.

"Here you go." The guy handed me the cup.

"'Preciate it." I turned to walk off. A lot of the shops were full of people from kids to adults, which wasn't uncommon. The boardwalk was always full of hustle and bustle.

"Tripp? Tripp, is that you?" I heard a woman call out to me. Pausing, I looked over, and my mood instantly darkened. Skye's sister, Vee, strutted over to me with a chilled smile on her face. "I thought that was you. It's been ages since I saw you. And is this my niece?" Her eyes went to Scottlynn. I pulled her stroller back protectively and tossed her a deadpanned look.

"What do you want, Vee?"

Flicking her eyes back to my face, her smile turned upside down. "You always been the straight to point kind of guy. Good to know that hasn't changed." She flicked the blonde bundles over her shoulders and looked around. "Where's that sister of mine?" Facing me again, her head cocked to the side.

"She's not here."

Her lips pressed together. "Mhm. I did hear something about her falling off the wagon again. Let me guess, she's in rehab?" She stuck her hand out in front of her and examined her nails. "She's always been troublesome."

My blood ran hot and boiled. Gritting my teeth, I tightened my hold on the stroller handle and stood straighter. "You enjoy the rest of your day, Vee," I stated and went to walk off.

"I'm just saying, she's not worth the trouble you put up with. Any sensible person would have left her."

"Like you did?" I lifted a brow with a sneer on my face. "You were her older sister and did nothing when she needed you."

Vee's arched brows bunched together. "Skye made up lies all the time. She was like the boy who cried wolf. If she didn't have attention, then she was making a scene to receive it. When people stopped listening, she did something dramatic and turned to drugs. What was I to do? Beg her not to?" She waved me off. "You better hope your daughter is more like you and not my troubled sister."

My heart slammed against my ribcage as my jaw ached from how hard I clenched down. "Your troubled sister, as you called her, only ended up like she did because she grew up in a fucked up household with muthafuckas who didn't give a fuck about her and turned a blind eye to her being touched by a grown ass man." My voice grew louder than I wanted, but Skye's family always took me out of character and left a bad taste in my mouth.

"Please. I can't believe she ran to you with those lies. You just proved my point. She made shit up for attention, and she always knew you would believe her because you clung to her like a damn puppy."

Vee was lucky I would never raise my hand to women, but my right one itched to touch her. She was just as delusional and fucked up as her parents were. Skye dealt with a lot in that house and had no one to protect her from the fucked up shit going on. It was one reason I never judged how she chose to cope.

"I was looking for you," a deep voice sounded behind Vee. Vee flinched and put a forced smile on her face.

"Oh, I ran into my sister's boyfriend and her daughter and came over to say hi."

Looking up, I eyed the medium sized man. He was an inch taller than me but smaller in size.

He hardly spared me a glance when he spoke to her again. "Let's go." He turned and walked off without waiting for her to answer.

Vee, like the 'puppy' she just claimed me to be, turned and hurried behind him without another word.

My body was still hot, and my temple throbbed thinking about the conversation with her. Knowing her stance hadn't changed for her sister made my stomach churn.

I checked on Scottlynn, and she thankfully had dozed off. I studied her for a second, forgetting where we were. So much innocence radiated off her, and I knew it was unrealistic, but I hoped it always stayed like that. I would never allow her to be treated or go through any of the shit her mom did.

———

Scottlynn barely budged when we got home. She slept the whole way home and stayed asleep when I put her in her crib.

"Oh, shit. Sorry." Brylee jumped, bumping into me as I stepped out of Scottlynn's room. I grabbed her to steady her.

"Where you in a rush to?"

Her eyes avoided mine. "Actually, to come see Scottlynn. Figured you might want a break."

"I never need a break from my daughter, but you're good. She's asleep."

"Oh, right." She nervously laughed. "Well, then Ima go get dinner started. I was thinking something simple. Taco lasagna?"

I had never had it before, but it made my stomach stir anyway. "Sounds good to me."

The corners of her mouth slightly lifted. "Okay, good."

I still held her, and part of me didn't want to let her go. Brylee was petite. Her waist was slim, which flared into agilely rounded hips.

We needed to talk about last night, and seeing how she wouldn't even look at me proved that point even more. Plus, talking to Brylee always relaxed me because the conversation was always so easy. After my run in with Vee, I was still slightly irritated.

"I'll come keep you company," I told her.

"Oh, you don't have to do that."

"I know I don't *have* to, but I *want* to," I stressed. Slowly, she lifted her eyes to mine and gave me a slight nod.

"Okay."

Finally releasing her, I followed behind her to the steps. My eyes dropped to the roundness of her ass that sat nicely in the biker shorts she sported.

We got to the kitchen, and at first, I stood off the side watching her wash her hands then move around the kitchen, pulling stuff out. When she grabbed the knife and cutting board, I stepped forward.

"I can cut those," I told her, nodding toward the peppers and onions.

"I can—" She stopped when she looked at me. "Fine." She shrugged and stepped back.

"Ima make the cream cheese mix."

Going to the sink, I washed my hands then went to the place she just was. Music played to fill the silence.

"You're not cutting them right," she finally said, peeking around me. I studied the peppers.

"There's a wrong way?" I scrunched my nose with a frown.

She giggled. "Yes. Let me see." I handed her the knife and stepped back. "See, cut like this, then dice them small. Makes it so much easier." Brylee showed me.

"You know, I'm glad I snagged you as a nanny, because if not, I could see you in someone's kitchen or owning your own restaurant." I leaned against the counter and crossed my arms.

Brylee shook her head. "Nah, that's doesn't even sound appeasing to me. I might know how to cook and semi enjoy it, but not enough to make a career out of it. I just like to eat, and it's cheaper to stay inside." She giggled.

"Good for me then, because I know how to do a little something, but I'm nowhere near as good as you. My poor daughter would be living off spaghetti, fried chicken, and tacos messing me with me."

"Good thing you got me, and I'll make sure my pretty girl is well taking care of."

"I know you will. That's why I have no plans on getting rid of you." The amusement left my voice. I stared down at her, noticing how the air froze for a second. Her breathing changed as she pushed a shaky breath out.

Clearing her throat, she sat the knife down. "These should be good. Ima turn the stove on so I can put these in to sauté."

Before she could move, I placed my hand on her shoulder, halting her. "When you finish cooking, we need to talk," I told her.

Her guarded eyes found mine over her shoulder. Slowly, she bobbed her head.

Releasing her, I continued watching her prepare dinner. I pulled my phone out of my pocket, and before I could stop myself, I snapped a couple pictures of her. She got lost in her head as she cooked. When I asked if she needed help, she told me no. Eventually, I decided to get out of her way and headed for the nook and took a seat.

I finished a text when she sat down across from me.

"Now, we just wait for it to bake."

I went to my camera app to check on Scottlynn, seeing she was still asleep. I figured we could knock this conversation out and move on.

"I don't want shit with us to change," I started, causing her fingers on her phone to pause. "I don't want you to start acting different around me or avoid being in the same room as me."

Slowly, Brylee lowered her phone and gave me her attention. Her face was blank from any emotions.

"I kissed you last night." She took the corner of her bottom lip into her mouth and nibbled on it.

Licking my lips, I nodded. "You did."

"And you don't want to fire me?" Confusion passed over her face.

I looked at her. "Fire you? Why the hell would I do that?"

"Because I kissed you! It was unprofessional as fuck and inappropriate."

Chewing the inside of my cheek, I ran my eyes over her. "Maybe." My shoulders rose then fell. "But you don't see me complaining."

Her eyes widened, and her mouth parted. I was tiptoeing on a thin line right now, but I couldn't help myself.

Leaning forward, I rested my forearms on the table and wet my lips again. "Look, Brylee, having you makes my life a hell of a lot easier. What you did might have been unprofessional, but you realized it right away. If I had a major problem with it, I would have spoken up. I don't want you thinking you need to tiptoe around me, because you don't. I enjoy you being here. For the first time in a long time, it felt good coming home. It might be fucked up to say, but you brought so much life back to my house. You easily brighten my day up, especially after a rough shift. My daughter is taken care of, and I know she's always safe with you. I'm a grown man who got a mouth to speak out about anything that's bothering me, or that I don't agree with. You are a one of kind person, Brylee, and I'd be crazy to let you slip through my fingers."

Blinking a couple times, she watched me under her lashes. "You're not upset with me? I've been known to be impulsive at times, mainly when I was younger. It's something I've been working on. Last night, I..." Her voice trailed off, but I clung to her words, wanting to know exactly what she was about to say.

"You what?"

"I felt that maybe we—" Before she could finish her words, a loud cry blared through my phone.

Both our eyes shot down to it. Scottlynn had woken up, ruining the moment. Her cries grew louder.

"I'll get her!" Brylee popped up, hurrying out of the kitchen.

I huffed a chuckled and shook my head, leaning back in my seat. I would let her have this out for now, but the conversation wasn't over. I was curious to know what she was about to say.

CHAPTER 18

BRYLEE

My nerves were jittery as I finished getting Brylee ready. Things in the house were still tense, mainly because of me, and I knew that, but I couldn't help it. Tripp told me not to let the kiss affect things with us, but it was easier said than done. That day in the kitchen a few days ago, I almost confessed I had caught feelings for him. Thankfully, Scottlynn crying was the perfect distraction I needed to get away from the table. The rest of the day, I avoided Tripp. I brought Scottlynn outside in the back and sat her on the patio with me as I ate.

Today was my brother's birthday party, and I planned on taking her with me. The last thing I wanted to do was be bothered with my parents, but I couldn't let my little brother down after telling him I would come.

"You guys about to head out?" Tripp's voiced sounded by the door.

I nodded and adjusted the bow on Scottlynn's head, smiling. It matched the pink and orange dress I put on her. I put some product in her hair to make her curls pop and left it in a fro.

"You cute, pretty girl." Picking her up, I sat her on my hip.

Tripp ran his eyes over both of us. "You both look nice."

I wore a pink crop top and white shorts. My dreads were half up, half down. I had gotten them retwisted yesterday after leaving lunch with Leia.

"What are you gonna do while we're gone?" I wondered.

He shrugged. "Maybe go work on a few pieces in my workshop. I ain't got shit planned fo'real."

Twisting my lips to the side, I hoped I wasn't jumping the gun and wouldn't regret this. "If you want, you can come with us," I suggested. My stomach flipped as the words left my mouth.

A crooked grin formed on his face. "You sure? I'm cool with kickin' it alone."

"Yeah, I'm sure."

He didn't respond for a couple seconds, watching me, but eventually, he nodded. "A'right, cool. Let me go change." He turned to leave.

I pushed a deep breath out and look toward Scottlynn, who was entertained with my hair.

"What am I doing, pretty girl?" I asked her.

She gave me a gummy smile and babbled her baby talk.

"Looks like someone will have teeth soon," I noted, eyeing how visible the white on her bottom gums were. There was a faint imprint on her top gums too.

"Da-da," she babbled.

"Yeah, da-da's coming with us." I tickled her stomach.

Hopefully, today would be a smooth one.

———

"Have you spoke to your parents at all since you agreed to come?" Tripp asked as he pulled into the parking lot of Fun Zone. The ride here had been silent for the most part. I still wasn't exactly sure how to act around him, but right now that wasn't my main concern.

"No." I shook my head, eyeing the building in front of us.

He parked the car and undid his seat belt, turning to face me. "Do I need to prepare myself?" He had a smirk on his face, but I knew he was serious.

"Nope. I came for my brother, and that's it. My parents will probably try to speak to me, but hopefully they'll be too occupied to."

After taking my seatbelt off, I made sure to grab the gift bag off the floor, then climbed out of the car and waited for him to grab Scottlynn. We walked into the building, and the sounds of kids playing and screaming filled my ears. I looked around for the party room my gran told me they would be.

"I think they're over there." I pointed.

As we moved through the crowd, Tripp placed his hand on the small of back, causing me to grow hyperaware of him and release a deep breath.

"Lee-Lee!" a loud, high voice shouted. Soon, my sister came paddling toward us with a couple of other little girls.

A smile instantly graced my face. "Hey, Brit-Brat."

"Hi! Did you just get here?"

I nodded. "Yeah, we're about to go check out the party room."

It was then she looked behind me and noticed Tripp. A goofy smile formed on her face, and I knew she was about to say something out of line.

"Is that your boyfriend?"

Heat rushed to my cheeks. Tripp chuckled behind me.

"No! He's my boss."

She shifted her eyes back to Tripp and eventually shrugged. "C'mon. Bye, Lee-Lee!" She turned and rushed off with the girls behind her.

"My little sister," I said over my shoulder.

I jumped when his breath brushed against my ear. "You two favor."

Licking my lips, I glanced over my shoulder. Our eyes made contact. I inhaled a sharp breath. I could easily get lost whenever I looked into his brown orbs.

"Da," Scottlynn shouted and reached for my face. My eyes shifted to her, and I smiled slightly.

Turning back around, we continued until we got to the party room. I saw my grandparents right away and made my way to them.

"Hey!" I called out.

Both turned toward me. "There's my Lee-Lee. I was wondering when you were gonna arrive." Gran said then shifted her eyes. When they landed on Tripp and Scottlynn, her smile grew. "And you brought extra guests. Nice to see you again, Tripp."

"You too, Gran. Walt." He nodded to my grandad.

I looked around the party room, waving to a couple of family members I knew, I didn't see my brother. "Where's Brandon?"

"Somewhere out there being a menace," Grandad mumbled.

"Walt." Gran hit his arm.

He settled a stare on her. "You know I'm right. I love my grandson, but that little boy is nothing but a ball of energy."

I snickered, because he wasn't lying. I glanced down when someone grabbed my hand. "I'm glad you decided to come." Gran tapped the top of my hand.

"It's for Brandon."

"I know." Her smile was understanding. "And then you brought miss pretty girl here." Gran stood and stepped forward. "May I?" She held her arms out for Scottlynn.

"Oh, yeah. My arms need a break anyway." He chuckled, handing Scottlynn to Gran.

"Don't do my baby," I scolded with a smile on my face.

"Her little behind is starting to get heavy." He focused on Scottlynn, who was now sitting on Gran's lap, soaking in the attention from her and Grandad.

"Kids are so precious at this age." Gran tickled her belly.

A few family members in the room came over to speak, some I hadn't seen in a while.

"I swear I'm not young anymore. Them kids wore me out in that ball pit."

My shoulders tensed at my mom's voice. Soon, she stood next to me.

"Oh, Brylee, I didn't know you were here. Hey!" She went to step toward me with her arms out, but I dodged her, stepping back. Tripp's hand went around me to stable me when I bumped into him.

"Sorry." I tilted my head toward him.

"You good." He studied my face. It was more of a question than a statement.

I nodded slightly, slowly moving my eyes to my mom. A saddened expression formed on her face, but it didn't last long. Lifting her attention up, a smile twitched on her mouth.

"Oh, and who is this?"

Instead of responding, I looked back to my grandparents. "Anyone know where Brandon is?"

"Didn't you hear your mom ask you a question?" Grandad narrowed his eyes at me.

He might not push me to have a relationship with my parents, but neither of my grandparents played that disrespectful shit.

"It's okay, Dad," Breann said.

"No, it's not. We didn't raise her to be like that."

Tripp's hand on me tightened, reminding me he was still holding me. Oddly, neither of us tried to break apart.

"This is Tripp, my boss. Tripp, Breann."

"Her mom." Breann cut her eyes at me then smiled and stepped forward with her hand out.

I scoffed but chose not to answer. "I'm going to put this with the other gifts." Breaking away from Tripp, I walked to the table where the other gifts were. I closed my eyes and pushed a deep breath out. I was here for Brandon. I had to remind myself.

"Mom, Dad's cheating!" My brother finally came rushing in the room with Corey right behind him.

"Your son's just a sore loser. I told you about that cry baby crap."

Brandon hugged my mom's legs and turned to mug our dad.

Breann chuckled. "Look who's here, Brandon." She turned him to face me.

His eyes lit up, and he released her. "Brylee!" He rushed me.

"Hey, bud." I grinned, kneeling so I could hug him.

"I'm five now," he announced, making me snicker.

"I know. You're officially a big boy now."

"Did you bring me a present?" He looked behind me at the table of gifts.

I laughed. "Yes, little boy, I brought you a present." I tickled his stomach. He cheesed at me. Releasing him, I stood, and we walked back to the group.

"Hi, Brylee," Corey said.

"Hi," I answered stiffy. "Brandon, I want you to meet someone." I turned to Tripp so I could introduce him.

"Brittani said you're my sister's boyfriend!" Brandon announced after I introduced them, causing heat to creep into my cheeks. Gran and Grandad snickered.

"Brittani don't know what she's talking about." I cleared my throat. "Anyway, I'm ready to go get some tokens or whatever and play some games."

Brandon's eyes lit up. "C'mon, you gotta get a game card. Can you get me some more tokens too?" He grabbed my hand to pull me. "Oh, and can you take me on the go karts too?"

"Go ahead with them. I got her," Gran encouraged Tripp. The two of us made eye contact, and she had a sly smile on her face. Shaking my head, I turned to Tripp.

"Coming?"

"You sure you don't mind?" he asked Gran, who waved him off.

"Go, go. She's fine."

Not bothering to fight her anymore, he followed behind as Brandon pulled me out of the party room. A couple of my kid cousins rushed us, throwing random sentences and questions at us. I tried to keep up with what they were saying, but eventually, I gave up.

When we got to the counter to get the game cards, Tripp surprised me by having his card out to pay before I could.

"You don't have to."

He shrugged, putting his card back into his wallet after tapping it on the terminal. "Consider it a birthday present for Brandon."

"Thank you!" My brother grinned.

"Brandon, let's go to the basketball game!" a kid called out.

"C'mon!" This time, he grabbed Tripp's hand and pulled him. It made a smile form on my face. I was glad he decided to come, and he was willing to interact with my siblings as well.

———

"Aye, I never played laser tag before, but that shit was fun," Tripp commented as we walked back to the party room.

"I still say y'all cheated." I pouted, making him grin.

"Nah, you just sucked."

"Hey." I pushed his shoulder, causing him to chuckle.

The party was going good, and we just finished our destinated laser tag time for the party. Before laser tag, we ate then sang happy birthday. Turned out since we got the party package, they handled pretty much everything. Now, the only thing left was gifts.

We continued behind the group of kids to the party room when my dad appeared next to us. "You were good in there," he commented to Tripp.

I cut my eyes at him but stayed silent.

"Thanks. My grandpa used to take me to the range when I was younger. I always been a good shot."

That was news to me. I looked at him surprised. "I didn't know that."

"My dad's old man is country as can be. Grew up in the south and never left his ways."

"Nice, and my in laws tell me you're a firefighter."

"Corey," I stated blandly, wondering why he felt the need to come discuss anything.

Corey's eyes found me. "What? Is it a crime to want to know the man my daughter is working for?"

"Actually, it is. What I do isn't any of your business," I spat with a frown.

Tripp's hand landed on the small on my back. I flicked my eyes to his face, and he gave me a soft smile.

"Yes, sir," he answered Corey, causing me roll my eyes.

"That makes me kind of jealous. I thought about being a firefighter at one point, but my wife damn near had a heart attack when I brought it up." Corey laughed.

"It's not for everyone, that's for sure."

My irritation grew as Corey continued to converse with Tripp. When we got into the party room, I grabbed Tripp's arm.

"Excuse us." I pulled him away.

"Hey," Tripp called, planting his feet and prompting me to stop.

"Yeah?" My eyes circled the room for Scottlynn. I narrowed them when I noticed my mom holding her.

"Don't let them bother you like that. I understand there's a lot of bad blood there, but you shouldn't allow that to make you act out of character."

Snatching my eyes from Scottlynn, I faced Tripp, who watched me with concern. My shoulders drooped forward.

"It just annoys me that they try to act like parents now that I'm an adult now. They had my whole life to be involved and interested in what I had going on and choose to care more about being kid-free."

"And that's understandable. You have the right to feel some type a way about them, but at the same time, you shouldn't let them ruin your peace. You're happy with your life, right?"

Chewing the inside of my cheek, I nodded.

"Okay then, that's all that matters. Parents or not, don't give them that kind of power over you. Your grandparents did a great job with you, and I personally love the person you became. Your parents will have to live with not being the reason for that."

My heart tripled in speed, threatening to beat out of my chest. "Thank you," I replied softly, basking in his words. The hairs on the back on my neck rose. I knew Tripp was right. My grandparents had told me something similar multiple times, but their advice was easier said than done. It was hard at times seeing them give their all to my younger siblings when they had nothing for me.

When he reached down to grab my hand, goosebumps flooded my arms. "Let's go get our girl. I'm sure she's hungry now."

Our girl.

I wasn't sure if he realized he referred to Scottlynn as mine too. My stomach exploded in a wild dance, and jitters crept through me. Looking down, I took in the difference in size when it came to our hands. While mine was average size and fit a female, his were larger, and surprisingly, not as rough. His skin was a shade or two darker than mine.

"Oh, I think her bag in still in the car. She's probably due for more of the medicine for her gums too," I noted, remembering I gave it to her early this morning.

"Shit. You go grab her, and I'll run to the car." He released me, causing me to miss the warmth of his hand instantly.

"Can you hand her here?" I asked when I got to my mom. Scottlynn's eyes landed on me, and she whined and wiggled to get to me.

"She is such a cute girl. A busy body too. Reminds me a lot of you at this age."

I tucked my lips in my mouth, biting down the comment I wanted to give, and grabbed Scottlynn. She was fussier than normal, which I was sure had to do with her teething and being around all these people.

A few minutes later, Tripp came back with her bag.

"Ima go to the bathroom to change her. Can you get her bottle ready? I have premade ones already in there. She'll probably go to sleep once she eats."

"Got it, boss."

Tossing him a small smile, I headed for the exit. "I know pretty girl. That woman irritates me, too," I cooed, patting her butt to sooth her.

Once I got to the bathroom and changed Scottlynn, I headed back to the party room and found Tripp sitting down with my sister next to him talking his head off.

"Whatchu doing, Brittani?" I questioned, taking a seat.

"Nothing." She batted her eyes innocently. I narrowed mine, not believing her.

I held my hand out for the bottle, and Tripp didn't protest as he handed it over.

"Can I help?" Brittani shot up and rushed to my side.

"She can hold her own, but she's sleepy and might let you do it," I told her.

My mom called everyone's attention to let us know they were

about to do the gifts. Brandon cheesed wildly and bounced excitedly next to her.

"Guess what, Lee-lee?" Brittani asked.

"Wassup?"

"One of my teeth is loose. Mommy said Ima get money from the tooth fairy."

"Oh snap, you gone give me some when you do?"

She balled her face up and shook her head as she reached over to hold the bottle.

"Damn." Tripp laughed.

"That's messed up, Brittani."

"You got a job." She shrugged, making Tripp laugh harder.

My mouth dropped as I stared at her in disbelief.

"I'll remember that when your birthday comes around."

Obviously, she didn't take me serious because she turned her attention to where our brother was currently snatching the wrapping paper off a gift.

"They're lucky to have you." I jumped when Tripp's warm breath brushed against my ear. "You're a good big sister, and it's clear they love you."

When I twisted my neck to face him, I inhaled sharply, noticing how close our mouths currently were. I stared at his mouth and licked my lips. My chest rose and fell a little quicker.

"Ew! Are you about to kiss?" Brittani called, making me jump.

I snatched back and shot her a glare. "Stay in a kid's place, little girl." I swallowed around the lump in my throat, willing myself not to face Tripp again. I was playing with fire and needed to get a grip. Today was a good day. I had forgotten about the awkwardness between us and had fun with him. He was like a big kid, playing with my brother, cousins, and the other kids. He didn't complain when all the kids wanted him to play a game with them or help them win tickets for a prize. Maybe it was because he was an older brother.

"I guess she had a long day," Tripp spoke after a while. I was confused at what he was talking about until I looked down and saw Scottlynn asleep, the milk spilling out her mouth.

"Oh." I hurried and took the bottle out of Brittani's hand. Tripp handed me a spit rag.

Eventually, I passed Scottlynn over to Tripp because he was right, she was getting heavy, especially when sleeping. The party was drawing to an end, and as much as I enjoyed seeing my siblings and was glad I came, I couldn't wait to head back home.

CHAPTER 19

TRIPP

"I t was nice seeing you again, Tripp. Don't be a stranger." Gran hugged me as best as she could with Scottlynn in my arms, then stepped back.

"I won't."

"Love you guys." Brylee stood at my side, smiling at her grandparents. The party was ending, but we were cutting out a little early to get Scottlynn home.

"You're leaving?" Brandon rushed over with Brittani at his side.

Brylee kneeled so she was eye level with them. "Yeah, we gotta get the baby home. I'll see you guys soon, though." She hugged each of them.

"Can we come over soon?" Brittani asked.

Brylee looked over her shoulder at me, and I gave her a slight nod. I enjoyed her siblings. They reminded me of me and my brothers when we were younger, or more like two Terrance's, but still, I wouldn't mind them coming over to spend time with their sister.

"Sure. We'll set up a time soon before you two are due to go back to school."

"I'm gonna bring the Spiderman gloves and mask you got me too," Brandon told her, making her snicker. The gloves were a water gun but shot out as if they were Spiderman's webs. Apparently, the kid loved everything Spiderman. She got him a whole set of different Spidey things.

"Sounds like a plan." She kissed them each on the cheek.

"Happy birthday again, Brandon. Brittani, it was nice to meet you."

"Bye!" They waved and turned to rushed out of the party room.

"Those two are gonna sleep so good tonight." Walt laughed.

"I'll see you guys Sunday." She hugged her grandparents one last time, then turned to me.

"Ready?" Nodding, I adjusted Scottlynn in my arms, and we started for the door.

"You weren't gonna say anything before you left?" Her mom stopped us as we got to the door.

A blank expression formed on Brylee's face. "Bye." She hardly gave her second glance before continuing for the door. Her mom turned to me with a saddened expression and forced a smile on her face. Giving her a subtle nod, I followed behind her daughter.

The whole time we were here, Brylee barely gave her parents the time of day. They would attempt to interact with her, and she would keep it short every time. She agreed to take pictures with them for her siblings' sake, but besides that, she didn't bother with them. It was odd to see her so cold, because that wasn't the Brylee I had grown to know. She was nurturing, always smiling, and joyous, usually. I didn't like seeing her turn into a different person when she was around her parents.

Neither of us spoke again until we pulled out of the parking lot. Scottlynn made a small fuss when I put her in the car, but after getting her pacifier, she drifted back off to sleep.

"Your brother's party made me remember I got less than four months to plan Scottlynn's first birthday party."

Brylee whipped her head at me. "You do! Do you have any ideas for it?"

Huffing a laugh out, I shook my head. "Nah not anything major. Maybe just cake and ice cream with close family."

Brylee's mouth turned upside. "Cake and ice cream?" She shook her head. "Absolutely not. She needs a party."

I peeked at her before focusing back on the road. "She's turning one. She won't even remember it."

Brylee waved me off with her hand. "That doesn't matter. It's the experience itself. She'll see pictures later and love it. I'm sure you saw pictures of my first birthday in the book Gran showed you." She rolled her eyes. "Every year her and my Grandad made sure I did something and captured the moment so I could see it later."

I flicked my turning single on to prepare to get on the highway. "Then what do you suggest?"

Her hand went to her chin, and she tapped it with her pointer finger, while twisting her lips and squinting her eyes.

"A donut party."

Coughing a laugh out, I looked at her and saw she was serious.

"Donut?"

Grinning, she nodded and picked her phone up. "Yes! I'll show you." She tapped her screen a couple times. Out of the corner of my eyes, I watched her. She smiled at her phone, and excitement beamed from her face. It was clear this was something she felt strongly about, which made me feel good. By the time Scottlynn turned one, I wasn't sure what state her mom would be in or how things would be once she was back home. I didn't want anything to ruin my daughter's first birthday. Thinking about it, I realized Brylee was right. She deserved to be celebrated big.

"See." She flashed the phone toward me.

I reached for it and peeked at the screen, making sure to still watch the road. She had pulled up Pinterest, and the theme did look good for a one year old's birthday.

I held the phone back out for her to take.

"A'right, I think that's a good idea. I'm putting you in charge of it." One corner of my mouth rose.

"Me?" Her brows shot up. "Isn't that something her mom might want to do?"

My tongue swiped across my lips while my hand adjusted on the steering wheel. "Nah. Even if Skye gets out, and she's stable enough for the party, she's never been a planner for things like that. Birthdays and all that never really excited her, so she wouldn't have any interest in it. You're excited for it, so I think you're the perfect person to plan it. Unless I'm overstepping."

"No," she rushed out, shaking her head. "I'm the one who doesn't want to overstep. If you want me to plan it, I don't mind." A shy smile formed on her face. "I think she should have a photoshoot so we can have them blown up. Oh, I think I follow someone on InstaFlik that does custom kid clothes."

Brylee got lost in conversation about the party, her voice growing more excited the more she spoke. Listening to her made me *know* I made the right choice about asking her to plan the party.

———

Once we got home, I put Scottlynn in her crib upstairs, then went to change to do some work in my workshop. It was my last day off before I had to return to work, and I planned on finishing the second rocking horse so I could resell them.

Just as I was about to leave my room, my phone vibrated. I grabbed it off my dresser and saw it was the rehab center. Staring at the screen for a second, I compilated if I wanted to answer. Guilt filled me, lately talking to Skye left me drowning in different emotions.

"Hello?" I walked to the bed and took a seat.

"Hey, baby," Skye's voice rang through.

A tightness I wasn't used too filled my chest. I couldn't explain it, but as soon as her voice sounded, I felt heavy. "Skye. How are you?"

"Good. Really good. I'm sorry for calling so late. I've been in therapy all day, and then we had yoga, too. I'm just getting settled."

"You doing yoga?" I chuckled. "That's something I never thought I would hear."

She giggled. It had been a long time since I heard that laugh. For the first time in a while, Skye sounded like her old self.

"I know, right? I didn't necessarily love it, but it did help center me or whatever."

Slowly, the corners of my mouth rose. "That's good to hear, Skye. It sounds like you're doing well."

She was quiet for a second. "I am." She cleared her throat. "They finally approved me for visits. Do you think you can come see me? I miss you." I didn't want her to see me and get set back again, knowing she wouldn't be able to leave with me. Still it would be wrong to leave her hanging.

My eyes lifted when I heard someone by the door. Brylee stood there, and her eyes went to the phone. "Sorry," she whispered and turned to leave. I held my hand up halting her, then waved her in.

"Sure, Skye. I have recent pictures of Scottlynn too. She's trying to start crawling now," I mentioned, noticing she didn't bother to mention our daughter. It seemed like the only time our daughter was brought up was when I made a point to mention her. I wanted to chalk it to her trying to focus on recovering, and not take it personal, but it *did* bother me that Scottlynn seemed to be an afterthought to her.

I watched a surprised look form on Brylee's face at the name.

"Oh, really?"

"Yeah. Brylee, the nanny I hired, been working with her." One corner of my mouth rose. I ran my eyes over Brylee. She still had on the biker shorts and crop top she wore to the party. Her locs were loose now.

"Mhm, yes, the nanny. How old did you say she was again?"

My brows furrowed. "Why?"

"Just wondering." Someone said something in her background. "My time on the phone is up. Are you gonna come see me soon?"

I rubbed my eyes. "I said I will, Skye."

"Okay, I can't wait to see you." Silence passed through us. Whoever was on the other side spoke again. "Bye, TJ. I love you."

"Love you too, Skye." The phone disconnected, and my head dropped forward along with my shoulders.

"Is everything okay?" Brylee questioned after a while.

"That was Skye," I told her as if she didn't already know.

"Did something happen?" When I looked up at her, I saw hesitation filled her face. "You don't look happy to have heard from her."

I rolled the statement around in my mind, not truly sure how to respond. Telling her that my daughter's mother hardly showed any interest in her, even sober, didn't sit well with me.

"I'm good. Just takes me a minute to get my mind right after talking with her. Wassup? Did you need something?"

"Oh, yeah. I was just letting you know I'm about to go to a spin/yoga class."

"Spin/yoga class?" I couldn't hide my surprise.

She grinned. "Yep, it's a mix of cycling, cardio, and yoga. I try to go two, sometimes three, times a month. If I leave now, I can catch the last class of the day."

I checked the time, noting it was a little after five. My eyes locked on her legs. For the first time, I noticed how toned her thighs were. Not just her thighs, but her legs too. Now that I paid attention, I noticed how in shape she was. I could tell she took care of her body.

"Okay. I'll see you when you get back."

She hesitated again. "Are you sure you're fine? If you need me to stay, I can go to a class later on in the week."

I shook my head. "No, go ahead. I'm fine." I stood, towering over her. She tilted her neck upward to face me. "I'll order pizza for dinner, so don't worry about it."

"Oh, great. Feed me fat and greasy food after I work out." She giggled, making me grin.

"Gotta replenish the body afterward." I reached forward and pushed a couple of her locs out of her face. "I hardly see you wear them down. They look good on you."

Bashfulness filled her face. "As much as I love them, I hate them being in my face, so I hardly wear them down because of that. Thank you."

"Understandable. They look good up, too." I licked my lips as my eyes bounced around her round face. Brylee had a youthful face. It was bright, blemish free, with a faint hint of smile lines near the mouth. Her locs down complimented her beauty well. Her eyes were always vibrant and beaming.

The air in the room intensified. It became warmer. I dropped my attention down to her mouth when she tucked her bottom lip into it. I remembered how they felt against mine. It was quick but not easily forgotten. My blood surged through my veins.

The differences between her and Skye were so loud, and I didn't just mean looks. The way Brylee cared for those close to her was refreshing. Seeing the concern for me written on her face made my heart enlarge inside. Pulling my hand back, I balled it at my side.

Her lashes fluttered, and she cleared her throat. "I should get going," she uttered, stepping back.

Clearing my throat, I nodded, shaking the cloudiness from my head. I shouldn't be envisioning Brylee in any other way other than as my employee. I needed to get a grip. Being around her all the time, seeing her mannerisms, even today seeing her with her family, clouded my judgement. Looking at her in any other way other than being my nanny was wrong, and I had to make sure I kept reminding myself of that.

———

"Everyone ready for the cookout this weekend?" Captain asked, sitting at the table in the upstairs kitchen dining room area of the firehouse.

"Oh, damn. It's that time again? I didn't even realize," Royce mentioned.

"Yep, and I expect everyone to bring something, too." His eyes went around the table.

Omiras always gave back to the community, so every year, right before school, he always held a cookout at the park not too far from the firehouse. We did a bookbag drive, where we gave away a hundred bookbags full of supplies for kids. It was a big event that seemed to grow every year, and the people loved it, not to mention, the free food.

"The bookbags have already been prepared. Leo's on the grill, so everyone else is in charge of the sides and drinks you agreed to bring."

Sometimes, people of the community brought things to eat, too. I scooped up the pasta salad and shoved it in my mouth.

"TJ, your mom making the pound cake and lemon cake again this year, right?" Harlem questioned.

Swallowing, I nodded. Ever since my mom surprised the firehouse one year with a lemon pound cake and regular pound cake, they request one any time an event happened. My mom never minded making it for them, either.

I was almost done with my food and checking my nanny cams when the alarm blared. Everyone hopped up and moved quickly.

"I'm glad I got to finish my food this time," Harlem spoke as we suited up.

"All yo' ass think about is food," I commented.

"I'm a grown man with a big appetite." He pulled his coat on.

"I hope whatever girl you end up with can cook."

"She ain't got no choice, or she gon' have to learn."

"Or you can," Journi cut in as we headed for the trucks.

I climbed in the back of the truck, taking my seat next to the window like normal.

"Where we going, Cap?" Leo asked.

"The Shore," Omiras answered before shutting his door.

The horn blared as we pulled out of the firehouse, warning anyone close that we were pulling out. The team chatted around me, but I had zoned out, turning my head and looking out the window. My last conversation with Skye had been heavy on me. I was due to go see her soon, and not knowing how the visit would go had me uneasy. Seeing how happy and taken care of my daughter was without her mom being around made my chest tight. I didn't want to make it seem like I was giving up on Skye or abandoning her, but I would be lying if I said life hadn't been more peaceful since she'd been away.

———

"Wow, I didn't think the turnout was gonna be this big," Brylee commented as we got closer to the pavilion. She pushed Scottlynn in her stroller while I carried the food. When she found out about the cookout, she offered to make something. I told her she didn't have to, but she insisted on making a fruit salad and pasta salad. "I hope I made enough." She glanced at the containers in my hand.

"You didn't have to make this. Don't worry. This is enough."

She flashed a small smile.

"That doesn't look like cake to me," Harlem noted as he walked up. His eyes went to Brylee, and he grinned.

"I wasn't expecting you to come, but it's good seeing you again."

"Harlem, right? It's good to see you again, too."

We stopped where the food was, and I found two empty spots before setting the two large tin pans on the table. Next, I went to the stroller and reached under where the cakes were and took them up out, moving down to where the desserts were.

"We didn't get to talk much when we were moving your things, but today we got all the time in the world," Harlem suggested. I lifted my head to face him. When he licked his lips and eyed her, a frown formed on my face.

Brylee giggled. "Sure."

My eyes narrowed. "We can leave the stroller over there by the wall. I wanna introduce you to the captain," I interrupted them, stepping closer to Brylee. My arm brushed against hers. She lifted her eyes to meet mine with a warm smile still on her face as she nodded.

"Okay. Guess we'll talk later."

She turned to walk off.

"Aye, she seeing anyone?" Harlem asked when it was just the two of us.

I cut my eyes at him. "Why?"

Again, he licked his lips and ran his hand over his head. "Because if not, I'ma shoot my shot. She fine, and some of them leftovers you be bringing in be smelling good as hell. I told you I need a woman that can cook."

My tongue dragged across my top teeth as my hands balled at my side. I didn't have any right to feel any type of way about Harlem inquiring about Brylee, she *was* single, and he was within his right to try to shoot his shot if that was what he wanted, but still, it left a bad taste in my mouth. While I loved Harlem like a little brother, I didn't see him as the right fit for Brylee.

"Ready." Brylee popped back up on us with Scottlynn in her arms before I could respond.

Scottlynn sucked on her bottle as her eyes bounced around, taking in the busy park.

"Brylee, please tell me you cooked something for today? I be seeing how you hook TJ here up with leftovers, and that shit be looking good as hell."

She snickered. "I did. Nothing special because it was last minute. I made pasta salad and fruit salad."

Harlem rubbed his stomach. "I don't discriminate with food. I keep telling TJ he needs to stop being stingy."

She laughed. "One day I'll have to make something for the firehouse and have him bring it in for everyone, or if you ever want to come over for a plate, as long as it's okay with Tripp, I don't mind."

Harlem's smile grew. "See, I knew I liked you the first time I saw you. TJ act like he can't share the wealth."

She snickered. My eyes narrowed and bounced between the two. My arm went around Brylee, and I pulled her closer to me.

"C'mon, let's go speak to everyone."

She looked up at me shocked but nodded. "See you later, Harlem." She flashed that signature warm smile at him. I knew the gesture was innocent, but my jaw still clenched.

"A'right." He nodded before he looked at me with a smirk on his face.

"He seems nice," Brylee commented when we walked away.

"Yeah, he's a little shit at times, but I see him as a little brother. An annoying ass little brother, that is."

She giggled, causing me to smirk.

"Da-da." Scottlynn threw her bottle on the ground.

"Scottlynn!" I groaned, pausing and removing my arm from Brylee to grab the bottle. Standing back up, I grabbed her from Brylee. "Why you do that?"

She babbled and drooled while grabbing my face.

"This drooling is getting outta hand." I scrunched my face up.

"It's all a part of the teething process. Tell him don't judge you, pretty girl." Brylee poked her stomach.

"Remind me what all this is for again? A back-to-school thing?" Brylee asked while watching a group of kids on one of the playsets.

I nodded. "Yeah. Cap does it every year to help parents who might not be able to afford school supplies and bookbags."

"Oh, that's nice of him. Does he buy it all himself?" She glanced up at me.

I shook my head. "Nah, we all chip in, and we get a lot of donations, too. It seems to grow every year."

Brylee looked around the park. A lot of people from the surrounding neighborhoods had come out. Games were ran on the two basketball courts. One game was for adults, and the other one was for kids. Kids were scattered around, and parents sat at tables under the pavilion watching. This park had a splash pad that was put to use.

"Aye, Cap!" I called out, noticing him near the grill. He stopped speaking to Leo and turned to face me.

"I was wondering when you would show." He slapped hands with me. "And you brought this cutie. Damn, she's gotten big since I last saw her." Omiras reached out to touch Scottlynn's hand, but she shied away. "Damn." He chuckled.

"She's teething, so she hasn't been in the best of moods lately. She's really picky with who she likes right now," Brylee defended instantly. A smile ticked on my face.

Omiras's eyes shifted, and a brow rose. "You must be the nanny?"

I shifted Scottlynn and grabbed Brylee, pulling her closer. "Brylee, my captain, Omiras. Cap, Brylee."

"Hi!" Brylee cheesed.

He nodded. "Good to finally put a face to a name."

"I think it's amazing what you're doing here. We need more people willing to give back to the kids."

A modest expression formed on Omiras's face. He was never one to take praise easily. "'Preciate it. Just doing what I can to make a difference."

"It's commendable. Not only are you saving lives but look at all these kids you're gonna help." Her eyes swept the area.

I stepped away and went to the grill. "Whatchu over here burning?" I joked.

"Don't play with me." Leo looked over his shoulder at me. "Oh, you brought baby girl." He smiled and went to reach for her, but just like with Omiras, she pulled away.

"Dad, can we have some ribs?" Myla, his daughter ran up.

"They're almost done and speak when you see another adult."

She turned to me. "Hi, Mr. Tripp."

"Good to see you again, Myla." She turned and rushed away, and he shook his head.

"I swear I don't know who eats more—her or Harlem. I'm glad she's taken up volleyball."

Laughing, I shifted my attention to where Brylee had reappeared at my side.

"Brylee, right? It's good to see you again."

She waved and glanced at the grills. "Smells good. I can't wait to eat." She rubbed her stomach.

"You hungry? We can eat now," I asked her.

"If you are." She nodded, smiling softly.

"A'right, we're gonna go get some food."

Leo looked between us and nodded. "A'right. The ribs are almost finished if y'all waiting on them."

My hand went to the small of Brylee's back, and I guided her away. A few other members from the house stopped us and spoke, wanting to see Scottlynn, but she wasn't feeling it.

"Maybe she needs a nap," Brylee suggested once we got back to where her stroller was.

"She needs something, because this isn't my munchkin."

Brylee moved to push the stroller, and I led her up to the food. We got to the end of the line and nodded at the few people serving behind the tables. To make sure it was fair and sanitary, a few family members volunteered to serve the food every year.

"What do you want?" I grabbed two plates when it was our turn.

The evening continued after we sat to eat. Eventually, Brylee got Scottlynn to fall asleep. Every time I checked in with her, Brylee assured me she was fine and having a good time. I knew she didn't have to come today, but I was glad she decided to come anyway. When it was time for the bookbag giveaways, I ended up leaving her and Scottlynn at the table with Journi, who she seemed to hit it off with.

"You know this is the first year you didn't come here alone. I was surprised seeing her with you," Leo commented as I stood next to him. I looked off to where Brylee talked and laughed with Journi.

"She insisted, honestly. I told her she could have the day off, and she wanted to come." I shrugged.

"Mhm."

I grabbed one of the bags and smiled at the kid in front of me as I handed it to him.

"Thank you!" he said and bounced away to his awaiting parent.

"Say what's on your mind," I encouraged.

He grabbed one of the pink book bags and handed it to the little girl next in his line.

"Nothing, except it's just interesting."

I side eyed him. "How? She's my nanny and knew at some point I would need someone to keep an eye on my daughter."

Leo chuckled. "If you say so, man. I'm just saying in all the time we've worked together, we never seen Skye in attendance."

Ignoring that comment, I turned my attention back to the kids approaching. Skye never bothered to come to one of these because she didn't care for events. It used to bother me that the other crew's family would show up and she wouldn't, but I understood and didn't push her into being uncomfortable.

Looking in the direction of Brylee again, I noticed Journi wasn't sitting with her anymore. Instead, a guy I didn't recognize grinned all in her face. My eyes narrowed as my stomach hardened when she laughed at whatever he said to her. I bit back on my back molars seeing him pull his phone out.

"You good there?" Leo laughed.

I side eyed him but kept quiet. I didn't know where this sudden feeling came from, but seeing Brylee all smiles with the random guy didn't sit well with me. Maybe it was because I knew how her ex made her feel and didn't want anyone else to hurt her in that way. As much as I wanted to barge over there and interrupt their conversation, I knew I couldn't leave until all these bags were given out.

Time seemed to move slowly as we continued handing out the bags. Cap gave a speech thanking everyone for coming out. Of course, the local paper, the *Daily Pier Gazette,* wanted pictures of us, and then interviewed each of us. Cap made sure we all wore our house shirts for this reason.

By the time we were finished with everything, and I was able to make my way back to Brylee, she sat and talking to Harlem. I knew Harlem enough to know he was probably tryna push up on her. His interview wrapped up before mine. In some ways, he reminded me of Terrance. A pretty face was always his weakness.

When I got to them, I cleared my throat and took a seat next to Brylee. I gave Harlem a deadpanned looked, and he looked at me in amusement.

"I didn't mean to leave you for so long," I told Brylee, still eyeing Harlem. Out of the corner of my eye, I saw Scottlynn was still asleep in her stroller.

"Oh, its fine! I got me some more food and entertained myself on my phone. Then Harlem came over and kept me company."

"I bet he did. I think Cap was looking for you," I told Harlem.

He tilted his head. "For what?"

"I don't know, but you should go find out."

His smile grew. "Right. Ima do that. Brylee, I'm not gon' forget you promised me a meal either."

The corners of her mouth rose. "I gotchu. Next meal I make, I'll send a plate with Tripp for you."

I whipped my head in her direction. "You don't need to feed him," I protested, but she waved me off.

"You see how much I cook. My portion control is horrible."

"Yeah, TJ, don't be stingy!"

Harlem stood. "It was nice talking to you, beautiful." He winked at Brylee, causing her to giggle and push one of her loose locs out of her face. "Oh, and TJ, tell your mom good look on the cake. That shit was hittin'." He gave a wave and turned to walk away.

I shook my head. "Was he bothering you?"

"Of course, not. I like him. He's good company."

I looked in the direction Harlem just went. Dragging my tongue across my teeth, I tightened my eyes.

"No one bothered you while I was gone, right?"

She pulled her phone out and shook her head. "Nope. Today's been good. I even got some pictures of you up there." She turned her phone toward me. I grabbed the phone, swiping through the pictures.

"Oh," I whispered, when I got to her last picture.

"What?" She learned over. "Shit." She snatched the phone back. "You weren't supposed to go that far over." Her cheeks flushed red.

I swiped my tongue over my lips. "You got a new man you sending that to?" I studied her. The picture wasn't anything over the top—just her locs crinkled and down with light makeup on her face. She wore a thin yellow tank top and white shorts that could have been considered underwear, if you asked me. Her legs were bent under her with her hands pressed on the bed, and she pushed her chest forward while smiling.

"Uh, no. I was thinking about signing up for Love Connections and took a couple pictures for my profile." Her cheeks grew redder.

Swallowing hard, I shook my head. "You don't need that shit."

"I know I don't *need* it. I just was considering it." She shrugged and looked off in the distance.

The last thing I wanted was for Brylee to go on an app and hook up with random niggas. "You know you're pretty enough to find guys without online dating, right?"

A shy smile split her face. "Yeah, I know that. I just thought I would broaden my selection, especially since all the good guys around me seem to be taken. It was dumb." Her eyes dropped to the phone, and she stared at the picture that was still on the screen.

Her words sent a flame rushing through my veins, heating my body, and pooling in my stomach.

"I believe you're gonna find the right person when the time is right for you."

We sat in a silent stare off. The chatter around us seemed to be miles away. Scottlynn stirred and whined, finally breaking the stare off.

"Guess it time to call it." A yawn left Brylee's mouth before I could finish my sentence. "I guess that's a yes." I chuckled.

"Don't mind me. If we need to stay longer it's fine."

I shook my head. "Nah, once the bags are given out, I'm good." I stood and held my hand out for Brylee. She softly smiled at me and took it so I could help her up.

"Let's say our goodbyes, and we can head out."

"Sounds good."

"Hey, Tripp," Brylee said after a while. I turned to her. "Thanks for inviting me today. I really did have a good time."

I roped my arm around her and hugged her. "I always have a good time when you're around, so thank you for agreeing to come."

She blushed and nodded, her smile never wavering. I would be lying if I said it didn't feel good to have Brylee here with me and Scottlynn today. She didn't have to spend her off day being here, but she chose to for me. It made me realize how nice it was to have someone in my corner, even for the *small things*.

CHAPTER 20

BRYLEE

"I can't believe I agreed to come to this," I groaned as Leia pulled me through the crowd.

"Don't be like that! You deserve a night out," she shouted behind her.

The club was packed with people having a good time. It was loud, bright, and live. When Leia first suggested I come with her to her brother's coming home party, I shut it down. I meant it when I told her I had moved on from him. Even if he changed his life around, Kyriq wasn't anywhere on my radar. Sadly, my heart was occupied at the moment with unrequited feelings. It was Tripp's last night off before having to return to work, and he was spending it with Scottlynn, giving me the night off.

I tugged on the dress I had on. It was red, off the shoulder, slanted at the bottom, and stopped mid-thigh. It *did* feel good to dress up, since I didn't get to do it often. My locs were braided up into a bun on the top of my head. Leia had just done my eyes enough to make them pop, and I had on red tinted gloss.

We stopped by the bar to grab a drink before moving to the large section toward the back of the club. It was already crowded with people. Bottle girls were inside with sparklers flashing, and everyone turned up.

"Oh, shit. We got baby Robinson in the building," a guy shouted, walking up to us and pulling Leia into a hug.

She released me, hugging the guy back. "I told y'all stop calling me that." She rolled her eyes when he released her and nudged his shoulder.

"You know that's always gonna be your name." He grinned at her then faced me. His eyes ran over me before he tossed me a nod.

"Where's my big-headed brother?" she shouted while looking around.

I sipped silently on my drink and bounced my eye around the second. Tons of half-dressed women were scattered around the section. I would think we were at a strip club instead of a nightclub.

"C'mon." Leia grabbed my arm, pulling me, nearly causing me to spill my drink.

"Shit, slow down," I complained.

Ignoring me, she continued dragging me to the other end of the section. A group of men were huddled up laughing and talking loudly. Even from behind I already knew which one was Kyriq. He lifted the bottle of Clase Azul to his mouth, taking a long drink.

"Big bro!" she shouted.

Kyriq spun around, and a large, grill encrusted grin was on his face. "Baby sis." He pulled her into him, hugging her tightly. Kyriq had been home for a couple days now, and I knew my friend had seen him when he first came home, but she still got emotional about him. The two were close before he got locked up, and I knew it hurt her a lot when he was put away.

"I see I gotta catch up!" she announced when he pulled away. He smirked at her and brought the bottle to his mouth again. His eyes shifted over, landing on me. They filled with heat. Slowly, he lowered the bottle, giving me a crooked grin.

"Damn, you brought me a gift too." He licked his plump pomegranate-colored lips. Kyriq was just as handsome as he was the last time I saw him.

He looked more mature and a tad bit rougher around the edges, but still handsome. His square jaw was covered by a short beard that was barely off his face, and his hair was freshly lined up cut low. Kyriq's body was bulky like he spent all his time locked up lifting weights, but it fit his tall frame. The black and white Amiri shirt he had on hugged his wide chest. His neck held two gold chains around it, and his ears beamed with diamond studs. His skin looked like the color of a gingerbread man cookie.

"Hey, Kyriq. Welcome home." A small grin formed on my face.

"Don't just stand there, come show yo' boy some love." He opened his arms for me.

Huffing a small laugh, I shook my head and handed Leia my drink before stepping closer to her brother. He pulled me into his embrace, tightening his hold on me.

"Damn, you still feel good in my arms," he breathed in my ear.

Swallowing hard, I squirmed slightly. Kyriq smelled good—woody with a slight hint of spice and musk.

Pulling back, I stared into his chocolate brown, almond eyes. They were low, indicating his level of intoxication, but the desire in them couldn't be hidden.

"Okay, Romeo it's not that kind of party." Leia grabbed me, pulling me back. "I told you she ain't checking for you like that."

Heat flooded my cheeks. Kyriq chuckled. "Straight like that, huh, My Lee?" His head slightly cocked while he brought the bottle back to his mouth.

My shoulders lifted. "A lot's changed since you been gone."

He nodded slowly. "Aye, Riq!" Someone tapped his shoulder and leaned in whispering to him. His eyes never left mine. I knew Kyriq. He wasn't going to take my word without a fight. In the past, I was unable to say no to him and mean it. The crush I had on him was almost unhealthy. I was always available to him and always craved the heights he took my body to when he was inside me. However, Kyriq was going to learn I wasn't that same young, simple-minded girl anymore.

"I'ma get back with y'all. The bottles are all taken care of, and whatever y'all order is on me. Go ahead and enjoy y'all selves." He licked his lips at me. "I'ma see you later." Turning, he walked away with the guy who just approached him.

"His cocky ass gets on my nerves sometimes." Leia rolled her eyes and handed me my drink. I downed it, not bothering with the straw. For a second, the way Kyriq's eyes burned into me caused me to have flashbacks of our past together.

"No one is worried about your brother."

"Oh, I know it. You're too stuck on a certain firefighter." She grinned.

"Whatever, hoe. I need another drink, and then I wanna shake my ass."

"That's what I'm talking about." Leia laughed.

It felt good to let my hair down and turn up with my best friend. Maddisyn and Porsha eventually showed up to welcome their cousin home and party with us. The two of them were always a good time.

"You got a man?" A guy approached me, pressing against me and leaned down whispering into my ear. Currently, I was dancing to "Wanna Be."

Before I was able to respond, Kyriq appeared. "Not this one."

A frown formed on my face.

"My bad, big homie." He tossed his hands up and moved on.

"What's that about?" I shouted.

Kyriq gave me a boyish grin and stepped behind me. "Keep dancing."

I inhaled a deep breath when his arm circled around my waist. "I can't believe you come to my party looking this damn good and didn't even try to give a nigga no play." His breath was warm with the liquor he drank and mint mixed.

I tilted my head upward as I arched my back and pressed my ass against his groin. "We were a long time ago, Kyriq."

"What that mean? Don't act like we weren't good together." His head dipped as his face pressed into my neck. His lips lightly pressed against my skin while his hand stroked over my stomach.

"Kyriq," I breathed.

His mouth dragged up to my ear, and he kissed it. "Come home with me tonight," he said with a slight slur in his words.

Squeezing my eyes shut, I ignored how my heart pounded in my chest. He knew the affect he always had on me, but I couldn't fall down that rabbit hole again.

"I can't," I said, pulling away from him. Turning so we were now face to face, I lifted my head so I could look him in the eye. "It's not like that with us anymore, Riq. I'm sure you got plenty of bitches waiting for you, anyway."

He smirked. "I don't want them, though."

"Why me?" I looked around. Leia and me made eye contact, and she lifted a brow. I nodded, giving her reassurance that everything was fine. Thankfully, no one else paid us any attention.

Kyriq stepped into me. His hand went to my chin, and he cuffed it. "Because believe it or not, I know you're the one that got away." Leaning down, his lips pressed into mine. I froze, and for a second, I closed my eyes, accepting his kiss. The butterflies and giddiness that used to fill me when Kyriq's lips touched mine never happened. My heart didn't skip like it did when I sprang the kiss on Tripp.

When he pulled back, he kissed my forehead and stepped back. "Go ahead back to my fam and finish enjoying yourself. I'm glad you came and showed love."

Him easily accepting defeat was new to me. *Maybe he did change.*

Kyriq walked off.

"Aht, aht. What was that?" Leia rushed me.

I stared at Kyriq. He was now laughing with a few friends. Some girls were in the mix too. One pushed up against him and leaned up whispering in his ear.

"Nothing. Just closure, I guess," I told her.

She narrowed her eyes at me and glanced at her brother.

"It's all good." I grabbed her arm. "Now, I need another drink!"

I was glad the night turned out good and things with Kyriq didn't go left. The rest of the night was spent with nothing but good vibes.

———

When I stepped into the house, I attempted to be quiet so I wouldn't wake Tripp and Scottlynn. Kicking my heels off, I made sure they were out of the way and continued further into the house.

Slowly, I made my way to the steps just as Tripp came down.

"Brylee? You just getting back?"

Grinning lazily, I nodded. "Yeah."

He scanned me over. "Did you have a good time?"

I nodded again and leaned on the railing. "I did. It felt good to go out."

His brows snapped together. "You know if you ever need a night off or want to take a night to yourself you just gotta let me know. My parents won't mind keeping Brylee or even Troy and his wife."

I waved him off. "I love being here with Scottlynn. That's my baby."

One corner of his mouth lifted. "I know, but it's okay if you want some days to yourself, too."

Instead of fighting him, I nodded and brushed my forehead with the back of my head. The air was on in the house, but the liquor in my system had my body feeling warmer than normal. Not to mention, having Tripp this close, and the way he looked at me didn't help. I wasn't sure if I was imagining it or not, but the way he stared at me seemed more heated than normal.

"That's what you wore out?" he questioned.

Blinking, I looked down at my dress. "Uh, yeah. What? You don't like it?"

Suddenly, I felt self-conscious. Licking my lips, I brushed the side of my neck and jumped when Trip grabbed my wrist.

"No, I do. You look good. Damn good." He said the last part in a lower throaty tone. My heart leaped at the compliment. Flutters sputtered through my stomach. The liquor already had my head slightly buzzing, but now it seemed to increase.

"Thank you."

Tripp continued down the steps, so he was floor level with me. My breathing became heavier when his darkened stare bore into me. "You —" he started but stopped.

Staring up at him under my lashes, I hung onto his words. "I what?" I questioned softly.

"You look good in red. That dress fits you well. Those spin/yoga classes are paying off," he confessed. Now I knew I wasn't confused. He hungrily eyed me. A flame expanded in my chest.

I inhaled sharply. "Tripp." My chest rose and fell slowly. I stepped closer to him, closing the small gap between us. I stared at his mouth, longing to feel his lips on mine again. The heart pounding I missed with Kyriq earlier was now present.

The room felt smaller suddenly. The hair on my arms rose when I stepped closer to him.

He reached out and place his hand on my side. A jolt of electricity shot from my arms to my heart, making it increase in speed. I knew I wasn't imagining it. He felt what I felt. The pull to each other was stronger than anything I'd felt before. His hand tightened on my side. Desire burned in his stare.

"You should go lay down and sleep the liquor off," he uttered. Like a bucket of ice water was poured on me, I snapped back into reality.

"What?" I blinked a couple times roughly.

Clearing his throat, Tripp stepped back. "You'll have to get Scottlynn early tomorrow, so you should go sleep the liquor off."

Disappointment filled me, but I tried to hide it. "You're right." I forced a smile on my face, my stomach heavy with dread.

"Goodnight."

Tripp stepped around me, leaving me alone in my thoughts. I knew I wasn't imagining it. The same desire I felt for him I saw in his eyes, but he held back. I closed my eyes, feeling dumber by the moment. Tripp was my boss. No matter what I felt or thought he felt, it wasn't appropriate for anything to happen with us. Not to mention, as far as I knew, he was still taken.

My chest ached at the thought. I rubbed between my breasts, attempting to ease the tension building.

I knew I needed to stop pushing my feelings on Tripp before it made my job more complicated. Being here and working for Tripp and with Scottlynn had been one of the best things that could have happened to me. I was happy here and didn't want to mess it up. If pushing my feeling back for Tripp until they disappeared was what I needed to do, then so be it.

———

"I hear you, pretty girl. We'll be home in no time," I commented, glancing in my rearview mirror to look at the mirror that faced Scottlynn. "Drink your bottle."

We were on our way home from the aquarium. Her bottom teeth were at the point where I could faintly feel them when I touched her gums, and the white of the top two were starting to show as well, causing her to be fussy and cutting our day out short. I didn't mind it since I was becoming more of a homebody anyway.

My phone rang through the speakers on the car. I checked my screen and hit the button on my steering wheel when I saw it was Stacy, the director of my daycare.

"Hey, Stacy." I stopped at the light and brought my eyes back to the rearview mirror. Scottlynn was now gnawing on the nipple of her bottle, finally quieting down.

"Brylee, hey, how are you?"

"I'm good. Wassup?"

"The insurance company finally stopped dragging their feet, and the building is getting repaired and rewired as we speak. I'm reaching out to previous teachers to let you know we're aiming to be back in business next month and to see if you're still interested in the job."

My eyes shifted back to the road. The offer was tempting but not something I was interested in.

"Sorry, Stacy. As much as I miss my kiddos, I'm happy with the new job I have."

She sighed. "I was afraid you would say that. I couldn't expect everyone to stay available until we were ready to open."

"Sorry," I said again.

"No need to apologize. Just know if things change just give me a call."

"Will do. Bye."

The light changed just as I hit the end button.

Halfway through the intersection, a horn blared. My head whipped to the side, and my eyes widened. The loud sound of metal crashing into each other filled my ears. My body jerked as my head bounced off the window. The last thing I heard were the shrills of Scottlynn's wails before darkness found me.

CHAPTER 21

TRIPP

I scrolled through the pictures Brylee sent of her and Scottlynn at the aquarium with a smile on my face. My chest tightened as I saw the smiles on both their faces. Seeing Brylee giving my daughter these experiences showed me she was meant to come into our lives.

I didn't get to see Brylee before coming into work. Last night was too tempting for me to take her in my arms and upstairs to my room. I could tell she wanted more, and if I hadn't walked away, she would have acted on it. As much as I wanted that, I found myself torn. She was beautifully done up. The sluggish, drunken grin on her face as she stared at me with drooped eyes indicated she was partly intoxicated. Her breasts sat up high in the dress with her cleavage clear as day. The results from her spin/yoga class were obvious in the dress she wore.

I closed my eyes, pushing a deep breath out. It was getting hard to fight the urges I grew for her. There were times I felt like the three of us were a family, one I didn't have when Skye was home. Then I thought of how Skye was fighting to get better, and it caused knots to grow in my stomach, forcing me to push that thought out of my head.

The alarm blared, knocking me out of my thoughts. I popped up off the bed I laid in and ran my hands down my face.

Pushing a heavy breath out again, I stood and hurried out of the room we used for sleep to my gear. Quickly, I joined in with the rest of the crew suiting up.

———

"A'right, they've blocked off the intersection. Journi and Tripp, you're with me with the silver car. Harlem, grab the jaws. Leo and Royce, check the red car," Omiras called out.

"Got it, Cap." We filed out of the truck and rushed to our destinated areas. My brows furrowed when I got closer to the car. Dread pooled in my stomach, and I sped up the pace.

When Journi and Cap reached the car, they froze and glanced back at me, causing the sinking feeling in my gut to grow. My palms grew sweaty. My chest so tight it made it hard to breath. "Victim, female, unconscious and bleeding from left temple," Journi noted, kneeling and sticking her hand into the car. "She's got a pulse."

Finally reaching the car, bile rose in my throat when I laid eyes on Brylee keeled over. Her driver's side was caved in with the air bag deployed. Smoke came from the front hood that was also caved in. Blood ran down the front of her face.

"Tripp," Cap called, out but he felt far away. My chest felt like someone squeezed my heart.

"My daughter," I choked out. Panic rushed through my veins, filling my body. "My daughter!" My eyes shot to the back seat seeing the empty car seat. I felt paralyzed and unable to think and move.

Omiras called me again, but I had zoned him out. I snatched my helmet off, and my breathing picked up. Pressure built behind my eyes as my heart slammed into my ribcage. It felt like all the training I got for situations like this suddenly flew out the window.

Time moved slow until I heard a crying baby.

"Tripp, she's right here, man. She's fine," Cap's voice rang out and dissipated the panicked haze I was in. Blinking a couple times, I inhaled a sharp breath when I laid eyes on Scottlynn. I snatched her from Omiras and clung to her, probably hugging her too hard but not caring. I felt like my world was about to explode and a weight was lifted.

"Oh, fuck," I cried, kissing the top of her head.

"She's fine. The paramedics said she's just a little shaken up, but everything checks out with her."

Swallowing hard, I nodded. Shaky breaths left my mouth.

"Ssshhh, Daddy's here," I whispered to her, bouncing her.

My eyes darted back to the car, and the weight returned. My heart fell into my stomach watching Harlem use the jaws to pry Brylee's door off. They had put a neck collar on her now. "Is… is she breathing?" I called out in a tight voice.

"It's labored, but yeah."

I knew I needed to do something, but I was terrified to let Scottlynn out of my hands out right now. Staring at the car and seeing the damage scared me more than I ever had been in my life. Knowing I could have lost Scottlynn made my throat clog with anxiety. I couldn't breathe easily yet, not until I knew Brylee would be okay. I couldn't lose her. She was the best thing that'd happened to me and my daughter.

My eyes stayed locked on the car, watching them remove Brylee. I was still bouncing my daughter to sooth her. She laid on me, still slightly fussy.

"Cap I—" I choked out, unable to get my words out. My eyes stayed locked on Brylee.

"We got her, Tripp. Don't worry."

Swallowing the lump in my throat, I swiped my tongue over my lips. "I need her," I whispered. Seeing how banged up Brylee was made my stomach churn. When she whimpered and groaned, I felt my heart beat harder. Her eyes fluttered under her closed eyes.

"Scottlynn!" she groaned, attempting to move.

"Brylee, its Journi. You were in an accident. Can you hear me?" Journi took her light out and opened her lids to examine her.

"Slow pupil response. We need to get her to the hospital now. She could have some damage to the brain."

The news caused my stomach to roll and head to spin.

"I'm going with her. Cap I… I have to." My voice sounded rough and strained.

"Go. We got this." He nodded at me. I clung to Scottlynn and jogged after Journi and Royce. He rushed to the driver's door once they got Brylee into the back of the ambulance, and I climbed in after Journi.

"She's gonna be okay, right? Please tell me she's gonna be okay?"

"We're gonna take care of her, TJ. Don't worry." She did a couple things then hit the back wall of the ambulance, indicating we could go.

My pulse raced at an unbearable rate. I pulled Scottlynn, who had cried herself to sleep away from me and examined her again. Her cheeks were red and tear stained. Whimpers left her mouth every so often.

"Fuck," I gritted, lifting her and kissing her cheek again. My eyes squeezed shut as I inhaled the baby lotion on her. Tremors shot through my body.

"Mhmm, Scottlynn," Brylee groaned and fidgeted. Shooting my attention to her, I reached out and grabbed her hand.

"Brylee. It's Tripp. We gotchu. I got Scottlynn. She's fine."

"Tripp." My name fell from her mouth in a pained whisper. Slowly, her eyes fluttered open.

"Her vitals are stable. Brylee, can you hear me? It's Journi."

I flickered my eyes to the machine she was connected to.

Instead of responding, she groaned, and tears fell from her eyes. My heart tugged as I squeezed her hand.

"Brylee, it's okay. You're okay," I assured her, keeping my voice low. "You got a rag back here?"

Journi located one and handed it to me. I used it to wipe her face of the dried blood as much as I could, along with her tears.

I felt like it was taking forever to get to the hospital. The longer we were on the road the heavier the weight on my chest grew.

———

"Tripp, you don't have to stay here. My grandparents are on the way," Brylee let me know. "Go back to work."

I shook my head and squeezed her hand. "It's cool. I got it worked out. I'm not leaving you," I assured her.

As soon as we got to the hospital, they rushed her up for a CT scan to check for any brain bleeds or other head injuries. Thankfully, she only had a concussion, and everything else was ruled out. While she got her scans, I had Scottlynn get checked out just to ease my mind. I ended up calling my parents to come get her while I waited on Brylee.

She swallowed hard and looked off to the side. Her right side was slightly swollen and bruised. She had stitches tracing along her right brow.

"Hey, what's wrong? Is it your head? You feel nauseous again?"

She had thrown up twice since being here. The lights were currently off in the room to help keep some of her pain away.

"I just..." Brylee went to shake her head then winced.

"Don't push yourself." My thumb stroked over the top of her head.

"I'm sorry. The last thing I would ever want to do it put Scottlynn in harm's way."

My brows furrow, and my mouth turned upside down.

Standing up, I moved so I sat on the edge of her bed. "Look at me, Brylee."

Slowly, she turned her head and stared at me with tears pooling at the bottom of her lids.

"I don't blame you for this shit. That idiot that blew that fucking light is it blame, not you."

"But she was in my care. I should have been paying more attention."

"No. This isn't on you. You couldn't have known that shit was gonna happen." I inhaled and deep breath. My stomach rolled. I closed my eyes, attempting to gather myself.

"When we pulled up to the scene, and I noticed the car we were helping was similar to yours, I fucking froze. I felt like I couldn't breathe the closer I got. When I saw you slumped over in that seat... fuck, Brylee, I nearly lost it." Closing my eyes again, I exhaled a shaky breath. Lifting my hand, I brushed it over her forehead right above her stitches. Opening my eyes, I gazed down at her. "Do you know the last time I was this damn scared? It was years ago when I learned Skye had OD'd. That was the last time I felt true panic. Today, knowing I could have lost you and Scottlynn put so much shit into perspective for me."

"Like what?" Her voice sounded low and raspy.

My eyes ran over her face and down her body. The thickness returned to my throat.

"That I need you. That you make it feel like my house is a real home. You're such a fucking blessing in my life, and I never knew how drained and empty I felt until you came in and restored something inside me."

A small gasped left her mouth as her eyes ballooned. "Tripp," she whispered.

"You love my kid like she's yours, and you take care of her as if you pushed her out yourself. Anyone with eyes can see the bond you two have. That is so attractive to me. I don't take shit you do for us for granted, and today...today that could have been snatched away." I licked my lips and leaned in closer to her face. "I don't want to fight it anymore. I can't. Knowing you're at my fingertips but fighting to touch you every day is torture. Today was an eye opener for me. I never want to feel like I'ma lose you again." I didn't give her a chance to respond before my lips were on hers. Her body tensed at first, and her lips froze. It didn't take long for her to fall in line. I kept it light, not wanting to hurt her, but I made sure to put all the emotions I had trouble bringing out into that kiss. My heart surged inside me. Blood pumped heavier in my veins.

"Oh, looks like we're not needed."

I pulled away from her. A dazed expression formed on her face. She blinked a couple times and wet her lips with her tongue. Shifting her eyes to the door, they ballooned.

"Gran!" she squeaked.

"Oh, Lee-Lee." Gran rushed to the bed with Walt right behind her.

I cleared my throat and moved back to the chair, giving them room to get closer to her. Walt and I made eye contact, but I couldn't make out the expression on his face.

"Are you okay? What did the doctors say? Does anything hurt?" Gran fussed.

"Gran, slow down." She lifted her hand. "I'm fine. Sore, a little beat up, and I have a concussion, but besides that, I'm fine."

"I wouldn't say a concussion is fine, but if you're in here locking lips then maybe you're right," Walt said.

"Grandad!"

"Just saying." He leaned down and kissed her forehead. "You scared the shit outta us when we got the call you were in an accident. We didn't know what to expect," Gran commented.

Brylee's eyes softened. "I'm sorry to worry you both."

Walt waved her off. "Nonsense. That's our job. We're just glad you're okay."

Gran moved her attention to me. "Tripp. Thank you for sitting with our girl."

"Of course. There isn't anywhere else I would be," I admitted.

"I told him he could go back to work, but he refused."

Both her grandparents looked surprised. "You were on the clock."

I nodded. "My house got the call."

Walt held his hand out for me. "Thank you."

I shook my head, because honestly, it wasn't me. It was my team. "The thanks should go to my team."

"Still, you made sure she wasn't alone."

Understanding passed through me, and I gave him a nod.

"Your daughter's, okay?" Gran asked.

I nodded. "Yeah, my parents just left with her a couple minutes ago."

"Oh, thank God. So, you two…"

I made eyes contact with Brylee, and she stared at me with a bashful smile.

We were saved by a knock on the door and the doctor coming in to talk. I didn't know what to say about me and Brylee now, just that I felt compelled to feel her lips, for real this time. I didn't want to think the worst of what could have happened today. What I knew was there was no way I could continue to fight the feelings I had brewing for her.

———

"You know you don't have to wait around on me. I can always go to grandparents' house for a few days. They won't mind," Brylee stressed to me as she laid on her bed and watched me with low eyes.

I shook my head and turned to face her. "Tell me your name," I demanded, causing a small smile to tick on her face.

"Brylee."

"Full name?"

"Brylee Nicole Adkins."

"And my name?" I rose a brow. My eyes ran down her frame. I tried to make sure she was as comfortable as possible while she recovered.

"Tripp Clark."

"And what month is it?"

She blinked a couple times. Her eyes focused but were still a little unsettled. "Uh, August?" she said hesitantly.

A smile lifted on my face, and I nodded. "Good." Softening my eyes, I walked over to the bed and sat on the edge of it. "And how's your head?" I stroked her cheek lightly.

"Still cloudy. My ears are ringing, but not as loudly."

It had been a couple days since the accident. Her concussion was minor, but the doctors wanted her to rest for the next week or two until it passed. My parents were keeping Scottlynn while Brylee recovered, and her grandparents suggested she come to their house to recover, but I shut them down. I took the week off work to take care of her. Maybe I should have let her go to her grandparents, but I felt obligated to take care of her. Omiras didn't give me a hard time either. I had some personal time built up to spare.

For the first two days, all she did was sleep. She told me things were still unclear and hazy for her.

"Maybe you should call it a day. You been up for a few hours now and still need to rest."

A small yawn escaped her mouth. "I'm tired of sleeping." Her eyes slowly closed.

Licking my lips, I eyed the stitches across the top of her brow. It wasn't anything dire and didn't take away from her beauty. The doctors said it would heal easily enough, but it still bothered me seeing her harmed. It took until I got her home for the tightness in my chest to go away and for me to breathe easier.

"You need your rest," I told her.

She fluttered her eyes back open, staring at me tiredly. "Thank you for taking care of me. I hate to be a bother."

I inhaled a deep breath and shook my head. I wasn't sure if Brylee remembered my confession to her at the hospital. She was still out of it and full of pain killers. Since she was recovering, I didn't bring it up because I didn't want to stress her out anymore. Once she recovered fully, I planned to bring it back up. It was a risky move, to get involved with someone that worked for me, but I was done being cautious and fighting my feelings for her.

"As much as you've done for me these past three months, it's a no-brainer."

"But it's my job." Her voice sounded low and slightly raspy.

I shook my head. "There's so much more than that, Brylee. So much more. You've been the glue that's been keeping me together these past few months. I didn't realize it until your accident. Let me nurse you back to health. Stop fighting me."

Her mouth parted then snapped closed. "Fine."

"You feeling nauseous or need help to the bathroom?"

Her cheeks flushed. "No, I'm fine."

I nodded. Her eyes grew heavy, getting lower with each second.

"Don't fight your sleep. It's good for you." I leaned over and pressed my lips on her forehead. A small gasp left her mouth. I kept my lips on her a minute longer. Her forehead felt warm. The small breaths she released tickled my nose. "I'll be back to check on you in a couple hours. Gran will be over later to wash you up."

One thing she refused was to let me wash her, so Gran agreed to come help when it was time to wash her up.

I pulled back from her. She watched me with wary yet curious eyes, her cheeks still flushed. "Okay," she finally whispered. Her eyes closed, and she released a small, deep breath.

For a second longer, I stood in place watching her. My eyes shifted to the empty bowl of broth, causing me to grin. She fought me to eat at first, but I stressed how she needed it.

I cleaned up the bowl and then turned to leave the room. While she slept, I planned on finishing up the surprise I had for her.

CHAPTER 22

BRYLEE

"How does it feel getting princess treatment from your prince?" Leia asked, lying next to me on the bed with a goofy grin on her face.

Rolling my eyes, I adjusted my body, so I was more comfortable. "Leia, what are you saying?"

"Just what I said." A deadpanned look formed on her face. "You're injured, and he's waiting on you hand and foot, right? Just like a prince would do for a princess."

"It's not even like that," I defended. But it was, wasn't it? I was still out of it at the hospital, but I thought I remembered Tripp admitting to having feeling for me and then kissing me. Part of me wondered if I dreamed it since he hadn't brought it up again, until the past couple nights when he made sure to kiss my forehead before leaving the room. Whenever he looked at me, his eyes were warmer than before and more intense.

When I first came home, my head felt like someone smacked it constantly with a sludge hammer. My vision was fuzzy, and at times it even hurt to blink. Tripp stood to his word to look after me, though. He brought me water almost every two hours and some kind of broth when he noticed I had no desire to eat any solid food. He never complained either. Outside of my grandparents, I never had someone take care of me when I wasn't feeling well. I was trying not to overthink things, but it felt good to be catered to.

"Hello, Lee-Lee, are you okay?" Leia snapped her fingers in front of my face. "Do I need to get charming?"

I smacked her hand away. "I'm fine. Just thinking." I nibbled on the corner of my bottom lip. "I think Tripp told me he had feelings for me." My eyes squinted as I tried to recall the conversation at the hospital.

"You think?"

Slowly, I bobbed my head. "Yeah. At the hospital. Things were still hazy, and my head was throbbing, so I was in and out of it, but I'm sure he said something about us before the meds took over."

"Okay, so why don't you sound happier about it? You were nervous you fucked up when you kissed him, and now he's saying he feels the same way! That's a good thing, right?"

"I mean, yeah, but what if it fucks shit up between us?" Sighing, I rubbed my temples. I got headaches randomly. It had only been a few days since my accident, and the doctors warned me it would happen. "I love this job. I love living here and taking care of Scottlynn. The last thing I want to do it mess this up. Tripp's a great guy and father. He's a laidback boss, and he makes working for him easy. He loves his family and is big on making time for those who matter. If we were to take things further and things don't work out, then all that will be tarnished, and the last thing I want to do is give him or Scottlynn up."

Leia didn't respond right away. She turned on her side, so she faced me. "I get it, and you're right. It can be a risky move mixing business with pleasure, but if Tripp is all the things you say, then isn't it worth the risk? From what you've told me about him, it seems like you two have a lot in common when it comes to what you're looking for in life and in a partner."

I rubbed my forehead and closed my eyes. Thankfully, the ringing in my ears had gone away. Now I just had to push through these headaches.

"You need to rest, so I won't push the subject right now, but don't shut it down, either. I don't know why you became this timid girl when it comes to him, but bitch, dig inside and get the real Brylee out! The one that wasn't afraid to go for what she wanted and made herself known. Stop this scary shit." She scrunched her nose up, causing me to snicker.

"That's easy to say when it's not your boss you want."

Leia waved me off. "Anyway, I need to go meet my brother at my parents' house." She yawned and sat up.

"Everything okay?"

Kicking her legs off the bed, she stood up and stretched. "Oh, yeah. My mom wants us both to come back to talk about getting family pictures done or something." She shrugged. "I'll stop back again tomorrow when I get off work. Do you need anything?"

I shook my head. Everyone made such a fuss over me, and while I appreciated it, I just wanted everyone to relax.

Leia left me alone to my thoughts. Just as I was preparing to get up to go find Tripp, my phone vibrated. At first, Tripp refused to give it to me because of my concussion, but earlier today, he finally gave it back.

When I checked it, I squinted and had to turn down the brightness. Smacking my lips, I bit down on my back teeth and rolled my eyes.

BREANN

Mom told me you were in an accident. She says you're okay, but I wanted to reach out for myself. Are you okay? Do you need anything? Your dad is worried too.

I stared at the screen unblinking, feeling annoyance fill me. It made me mad that my parents attempted to give a damn about me now when they had twenty-four years to beforehand. Instead of responding, I locked the phone and tossed it to the side.

Slowly, I climbed out of the bed, waiting to see if a dizzy spell hit me.

I walked out of my bedroom and bumped into a solid frame.

"Whoa, what are you doing?" Tripp grabbed me, steading me.

Goosebumps covered my arms at the touch of his hands on me. My stomach swirled.

Tilting my head up, I got lost in his dark brown orbs. They reminded me a of a calm lake of the smoothest whiskey.

"I was tired of lying down and wanted to move around."

His mouth turned upside down. "You should be resting."

"I've rested enough." It came out as a whine, but I didn't care. I had been in bed for the past five days, and now I needed to move around, even if it was for a little bit.

Tripp narrowed his eyes. His grip on me tightened. My bottom lip tucked into my mouth. Tripp pulled my body closer into him, causing heat to flood my stomach. His arm wrapped securely around my waist.

"Do you feel dizzy still?"

Slowly, I shook my head. My heart sounded like a drummer at concert as it pounded in my chest at its own erratic beat.

"A'right, but as soon as you start not to feel well, you're lying back down."

A smile played on my face at his concern. Tripp acted as if I was on death's door, but I wasn't complaining. If I was honest, I ate up the extra attention I received from him.

He held on to me as we headed downstairs and to the living room. "Gran left some beef stew she made. Do you want me to heat you some up?"

Tucking my feet under me, I looked up at him and bobbed my head.

"I'll be right back."

When I looked at my phone again, I saw Breann had texted me again, noting that she saw I read her message. Still, I didn't respond. I was sure Gran and Grandad kept her updated on my condition. There was no reason I had to, too.

Closing my eyes, I laid my head back on the couch. I had a mild headache still, but it wasn't overbearing like the past couple days. I complained about being in bed all week, but I was thankful for both Tripp and Gran for taking care of me. Grandad had come by to keep my company when I was awake, while Gran took over the kitchen.

While I enjoyed being catered to, I couldn't wait to get back to work and have Scottlynn back home.

"Here you go." Tripp's voice grabbed my attention, causing me to open my eyes. He placed a tray on my lap then the bowl. "I grabbed one of those strawberry lemonades you like too." He sat the bottle on the table next to me.

"Thank you." I gave him a small smile.

Tripp turned and walked off and returned a couple seconds later with his own food, taking a seat next to me.

At first, we ate silently. I had turned the TV on so we could resume watching *Lucifer*, which he made me promise not to watch without him since he was now invested in the show.

"Tripp," I uttered, tired of the tightness that gripped my chest. Leia was right. I'd never been one to hold back, and I shouldn't start now. We were both adults and should be able to have a conversation like this. I just hoped this wouldn't change anything or cost me my job.

His eyes left the screen and focused on me. One thing I loved about Tripp was that he always gave me his full attention when we talked.

Clearing my throat, I moved the tray and now empty bowl off my lap and sat it on the end table then turned to face him.

"I know I was still kind of out of it at the hospital, but you mentioned you had feelings for me, right?"

"I wasn't sure you would remember because of your concussion." A crooked smile formed on his face. Tripp moved his bowl off his lap, the turned to me again. He leaned in and reached up, cupping my chin. "I've been fighting my feelings for you for a while now. Battling within myself not to act on taking our relationship past a professional level."

My chest rose as I inhaled a deep breath. My mouth parted as my tongue slowly dragged across my bottom lip.

"So, you *do* want me?" My voice sounded low and uncertain. My stomach filled with butterflies. I didn't want to jump the gun. Twice I had pushed myself on Tripp, and he hadn't bit, so now I tried to play it cool and let him lead.

He huffed and breath out. That crooked grin appeared on his face again. Adrenaline pushed through my veins. The hairs on the back of my neck rose. It had been so long since someone caused my heart to race like this. When Tripp leaned down, I thought he was going to kiss my forehead again. Instead, his lips pressed into mine. His head slanted slightly while his hand went to the back of my head. My eyes fluttered then closed as his mouth dominated mine. His tongue traced my lips then pushed its way inside.

I sighed against his lips. My heart threatened to escape my chest. Tripp's kiss filled my body with hot passion and desire. I leaned into his kiss. My breasts pushed his against his hard chest. He tightened his hold on the back of my head, causing me to wince.

"I'm sorry." He pulled away, panting heavily.

Licking my lips, I shook my head and moved in to kiss him again. I could deal with a small headache if it meant having him.

Pulling back, I bit on his bottom lip, causing him to groan.

"You're so beautiful," he said against my mouth, pressing his lips into mine again. His tongue dragged over them before he pulled back and gazed at me with a heated stare. "From the day I saw you in the grocery store, I felt attracted you. You kept getting put in my life for a reason, and I'm not denying that anymore."

I swallowed around my heart that was now lodged in throat. "I feel the same way," I whispered. "You're the vision of the man I see a future with." My eyes shifted to the side. "I'm just scared that this might ruin things. I don't want to lose my job or you and Scottlynn."

Tripp grabbed my chin, forcing my attention back to him. "It won't. I've thought about this long before I acted. For one, I'd be a fool to let you go. For two, don't you get how much of a gem you are to me? I don't half ass anything I do, Brylee. If you're for me, you're *for me*."

"You can promise me that my job won't ever be in jeopardy?"

"You love my daughter just as much as I do. I would never take that away from her or you. If you don't want to take things further, I can respect that. We can forget all this and keep moving as we have, but if you're willing to give us a shot, then I can promise to do everything in my power to keep you happy and love you how you're meant to be. Your heart is so big and deserves someone to take care of it properly. Let *me* be that someone."

My heart swelled in my throat, making it hard to breath. Blood rushed through my temples, prickling my scalp and sending a tingle down to my toes. His orbs overfilled with sincerity. I licked my lips. My hand rested on his thigh.

"What about Skye?" I asked, feeling my tongue grow heavy in my mouth. As much as I wanted to eat up and accept what Tripp said, I couldn't ignore the biggest obstacle in front of us.

For a moment, he didn't respond. He continued peering into me unblinking. "Skye will always have a special place in my life. She's Scottlynn's mother and one of my oldest friends. While I still love her, I have to be honest with myself. I'm not in love with her anymore, and as much as I don't want to admit it, I haven't been for a long time."

"How do I know you're not just saying that now, and when she comes home, you won't change your mind?"

Tripp shifted his hand from the back of my head down my jaw, and he caressed it softly. As much as I would love to believe him, I was scared too. Maybe it was my insecurities talking, but with the history they shared there was no guarantee I wouldn't be hurt once she came home clean and sober. I wasn't foolish enough to take that risk without some kind of reassurance.

"I want her to get clean and come out being better than she was before she went to rehab, but even if you decide this isn't what you want, I would feel the same way." He pushed a deep breath out. "Me and Skye hadn't been on the same page for long time—way before she went to rehab. I didn't want to see it or admit it, especially because she just had my daughter, but since she's been gone, I've had to realize our time has passed."

My stomach did a strange dance as my nerves became jittery. His words made my insides light up as if a lighter had been lit and fireworks exploded.

Reaching up, I cuffed his face and leaned up. "You're gonna tell her?" I wondered.

I had been in a situation before where I unknowingly played the other woman and refused to do it again. If me and Tripp were going to do this, I wanted it to only be us.

"I will. When I go see her, I'll let her know."

The corner of mouth slowly lifted. Moving in, I kissed him, still cuffing his face, this time tighter.

"Okay. I believe you," I murmured against his mouth. It was a risk, but I was willing to take it. Tripp hadn't done anything that showed I should question him or believe he would lead me on. Since working for him, he's always been straight forward and able to back up his actions. "I trust you."

"I have something I wanna give you too," he told me, pulling back. He pecked my nose then smiled and stood up. My brows furrowed in curiosity. I watched him leave the living room, wondering what he had up his sleeve.

My hands brushed over my thighs in anticipation.

Tripp returned shortly. My eyes bucked when they dropped to his hand. He held the box, lifted the lid, and fiddled with it until music played.

"Tripp," I gasped. Tears built in the back of my eyes.

"I know how much it meant to you, so I figured I'd try to restore it. It took a little bit of work, but…" He handed it to me once he was closer.

I examined the ballerina box, noting the fresh paint on it. "It looks brand new." Blinking slowly, I swallowed hard, feeling pressure build behind my eyes. No one had ever done something like this for me. Him knowing what this box meant to me made it even more meaningful.

"Thank you." I tilted my head up so I could face him. His hands went to either side of me with his body curled over.

"I just wanted to do something to make you smile."

Stretching my neck, I couldn't fight the desire to kiss him again. The music from the box played between us. An overwhelming rush of emotions shot through me.

"We should get you back to bed," he spoke after a while, lifting and bouncing his eyes around my face.

Instead of fighting him, I nodded. "Will you lay with me?"

Currently, I felt needy and wanted him to hold me. My skin tingled.

"I can do that."

"And we can FaceTime your parents so we can see Scottlynn? I miss my girl."

He grinned. "We can do that too."

Happiness spread through me like a wildfire. The last thing I expect was Tripp to admit he shared the same feelings as me. It currently had me on a high I didn't want to escape.

CHAPTER 23

TRIPP

"Are you sure you're good enough to go tonight?" I asked Brylee, who was on the ground with Scottlynn. A week and a half had passed since her accident, and while I felt she needed to rest at least another week, she assured me she was fine enough to move around. Scottlynn came back home yesterday, and to my surprise, she was crawling better than before. I was shocked when she got on the ground and started moving like a pro.

"I'm fine. I haven't had a headache in two days," she insisted, smiling at Scottlynn who sat in front of her, babbling to herself.

"A'right, but soon as you start feeling sick, we're leaving." I narrowed my eyes at her. There was a carnival on the pier down on the Shore for the week, and since I was off the next two days, I wanted to take Scottlynn. Brylee insisted on coming with us when I told her.

Brylee pushed off the floor and waltzed over to me with an easy smile on her face. Her eyes shined brightly as she wrapped her arms around me and lifted her chin upward.

"I will. I haven't seen Scottlynn in almost two weeks. I wanna spend time with her too. With *both* of you."

While she recovered over the past week, we had become closer on a more intimate level. I had to go back to work, so her grandparents made sure to come and look after her, but when I was home, I couldn't help but be at her beck and call. She fussed about us making a big deal over her, but I couldn't help but want to take care of her. It wasn't often I was able to slow down, yet I enjoyed being able to lay next to her and just be. She still slept a good amount of time, but I wasn't bothered. Most of the time she tucked herself into my side, and her breathing calmed me.

Need slammed into me as I gazed down into her sparkling orbs. I hadn't touched her past holding her at night. Since she was still recovering, and we just established taking our relationship further, I didn't want to push her, but I ached to touch her. Whenever our kisses grew too heated, I always had to remind myself of her accident. Her stitches had dissolved, but she still got headaches up until a few days ago. Control when it came to sex wasn't an issue for me, but wanting to pleasure Brylee and *finally* see all of her clawed at me every time I laid next to her in the thin night gown she wore.

Dipping my head, I pressed my lips into hers. She eagerly accepted my kiss, pressing her body into mine, and opening her mouth to receive my tongue. Her hand slipped between us and brushed over my bulge in my joggers. I groaned and squeezed my eyes shut, gripping her hip tightly. I wasn't the only one who wanted to take things further. Brylee hadn't been subtle with her desires, always brushing her ass against me at night and rubbing on my dick. It was like once we agreed to be together, a new side of her I'd never seen before was unlocked. She cuffed my now semi bulge and ran her tongue over mine before sucking it in her mouth. She didn't know how hard she made it to continue being a gentleman.

"Da-da-da!" Scottlynn shrieked.

Brylee pulled away from me, and I rested my forehead on hers. She sighed and huffed out a laugh.

"Soon," I told her, pecking her lips and moving along her jawline with feather like kisses.

"Not soon enough," she muttered, making me laugh.

"No!" Scottlynn yelled, causing my eyes to widen. I pulled back and looked down to where she now sat next to us. I looked at Brylee, and she looked just as shocked.

"Did she just?" Brylee started.

I nodded, lifting my mouth into a grin.

Bending down, I scooped Scottlynn off the floor. "Say it again, Munchkin," I encouraged.

"No." Scottlynn grabbed my face with her slobbered filled hands, causing me to grimace.

"You gotta get this slobbering under control."

Brylee laughed, and Scottlynn yelled. "No!"

For so long it felt like I lived life on edge. Like I couldn't breathe comfortably without the other shoe dropping. It felt good not having to be on guard. For once, life seemed to be on my side.

———

"I don't remember the last time I had a funnel cake! I forgot how good they were," Brylee gushed, ripping the fried dough apart and shoving it into her mouth. Powdered sugar covered her fingers.

"You must really enjoy them because it's almost gone, and you just got it," I noted.

She grinned and ripped another piece off. "I do! They were my favorite growing up. Here, have some." She stopped walking, prompting me to do the same, and lifted her hand to my mouth. Keeping my eyes on her, I leaned in and took the funnel cake into my mouth, along with the tip of her fingers.

She inhaled sharply as her eyes heated. My tongue swiped across the pad of her fingers, collecting the powdered sugar and nipping her tips with my teeth before pulling back.

"That is good." I licked my lips and winked at her. Her nose flared while her teeth sank into her bottom lip.

Someone bumped into her, causing her to jerk closer to me. I grabbed her to stabilize her.

"Sorry! Kyle, you have to say excuse me." A woman flashed us an apologetic look before rushing behind her son.

"Kids." Brylee smiled up at me, shaking her head.

The carnival was packed with people. Stands were lined up of food and games leading to the end where a few rides were set up. The sound of the water could faintly be heard over the loudness of the people and attractions.

"Where you wanna go next?"

I looked around, still holding on to her with one hand while my other held Scottlynn's stroller.

"Let's play a game." She pulled back and looked around. One corner of her mouth rose. "Let's see how strong you really are!" Brylee let me go and turned, darting off with me behind her. She stopped in front of the game you hit the metal with a sludge hammer for a prize.

"How high does he have to hit for the monkey?" Brylee pointed.

"Gotta hit in the yellow or above," the guy said. I checked the meter. It started in red, then went yellow, then green, and then the bell.

"That shouldn't be too hard." I rolled my neck between my shoulders. "How much?"

He told the price, and I reached in my back pocket for my wallet. After handing him the cash, Brylee stood next to the stroller while I grabbed the mallet.

"Oh, this got a little weight to it." I chuckled.

It wasn't as heavy as the gear I lugged around daily at work, but it still wasn't light either. I knew it was because most of these games were rigged for people to lose.

Lifting the mallet, I held it above my head before slamming it down on the metal plate. The lights shot up. At first, I thought it would land in the yellow, but I crept up and barely hit the green.

"Good job," the man said and went behind the booth to grab the monkey.

"Nah, I'm running this back," I told him, lowering the mallet and grabbing my wallet again. I wasn't satisfied with my results.

Brylee snickered as she grabbed the monkey, and I prepared to hit the plate again.

The second time I did better and was more satisfied with the results.

"That shit was rigged," I muttered when we walked away. This time, I got an elephant I planned to give to Scottlynn. Brylee wrapped her arms around mine and leaned into me. I noticed she had become more comfortable with touching me since our talk.

"You got the stuffed animals, so that's all that matters." Her lashes fluttered, sweeping lightly over her cheek bones.

"I know I could've hit that bell, though. I'm sure it's set up for most people to fail."

She giggled. "Well, I love my monkey, and Scottlynn seems to love the elephant."

I peeked down at my daughter, who nibbled on the elephant's trunk. "I think she just likes whatever she can chew on." I scrunched my nose up. "Your head okay with all these lights?"

The pier was brightly lit, and I knew that could trigger side effects of a concussion.

"I'm fine, swear." She hugged my arm tighter.

A bittersweet feeling passed through me. So many times I imagined times like this with Skye, and they never happened. Most of the time I had to force her out of the house to do things, yet Brylee was eager and insisted on coming out. By the look on her face, I could tell she was genuinely having a good time. Part of me wondered if enjoying this moment with Brylee and our daughter was wrong, but the other part of me was happy to finally be able to experience what a family outing would feel like.

My heart grew heavy in my chest, swelling until there was barely any room left. There were a lot of things Brylee brought to the table that I didn't realize I was missing.

We continued through the pier, stopping to get food after a while and for Brylee to play a couple games.

"You into rides?" I asked her while we sat at one of the tables. I finished feeding Scottlynn, who had grown heavy eyed.

She scrunched her face and shook her head. "Not really." Her eyes shifted. "I should have known she couldn't hang."

"It's because that schedule you got her on. My baby doesn't stand a chance once it hits eight."

Brylee grinned. "You got that right. I'm glad your parents seemed to stick with it too because it took some time for her body to adjust to it."

"Your kids are gonna be lucky as hell to have you as their mom," I commented before I could think.

Brylee's eyes widened, and her cheeks flushed. "Thanks, but I'm not doing anything special."

"You need to give yourself more credit. You're a natural caregiver. A lot of women don't instantly have that maternal instinct." A tight feeling passed through my chest that I ignored as I continued. "You have it, even without having kids. You're gonna kill the role." The thought of Brylee not being around and leaving to start her own family caused knots to grow in my stomach. Now that we were together, I didn't want to think about her with anyone else or starting her own family that didn't involve me and Scottlynn. She fit with us like the final piece of a complicated jigsaw puzzle. It was still new, but I had no plans to let her go as my nanny or girl.

Brylee smiled down at my daughter, who was now asleep, tucked into my arm. I removed the bottle that fell from her mouth and sat it on the table.

"She won't have any reason to be jealous. I would never push her to the side, even if I have kids later down the line. If you allow me in her and your life, I'll be there." She wet her lips and finished the last of the ice cream she was eating. "And since we're together now, how do you know that..." Her words trailed off as her eyes drifted off to the side. Her cheeks tinted pink again, and she cleared her throat.

Even if she didn't finish her sentence, I could tell where she was heading with it. The thought of Brylee carrying my kid caused excitement to shoot through my body. Blood ran down to my dick, and my balls tightened.

"Is that something you might want?" I started slowly. "I know you said you always wanted kids, and my shit is just finally starting to straighten out, but in the future, you want that?" *With me,* I left hanging in the wind.

"I wouldn't be against it." A smile ruffled her mouth.

"A'right, keep that in mind. I'm thinking when Scottlynn turns two."

This time, Brylee faced me, her eyes clear and gleaming with interest. It wasn't hidden from me that I was hinting that we would be together that long, or I was basically telling her I wanted her to have my kid. I wasn't getting any younger, and so much of my life had passed making sure others were comfortable. When I pictured my future, a clear picture of Brylee was in plain sight.

CHAPTER 24

BRYLEE

My stomach fluttered wildly as my heart tripled in speed while my blood seared as it rushed through my veins. The last thing I expected was for Tripp to hint about the two of us having kids in the future. Honestly, I was still wrapping my head around the fact that he was mine.

"I need to use the bathroom," I stated, pushing up from the table. Too many emotions ran through me right now. I needed a second to take a breath. Making my way across the pier, I went to the bathrooms. A couple other women were inside, but I was happy to see it mostly empty.

After emptying my bladder and washing my hands, I didn't leave the bathroom right away. I gripped the sink and stared into the mirror. My eyes went to the faint scar over my right brow from my stitches. Life for me had changed so much in the last few months. Just when I thought I was catching up to it, I got another curve ball thrown at me.

Pushing a couple deep breaths out, I gathered myself and went into my purse to reapply some lip gloss to my lips before leaving the bathroom.

"My Lee!" I heard as I headed back for the table Tripp and Scottlynn were at.

Only one person called me that. Pausing, I turned and saw Kyriq walking toward me holding a little girl's hand.

"Riq, hey." I smiled at him.

He licked his lips and gave me a once over. "I'm glad I ran into you. My sister told me you were in an accident. I'm glad to see you're okay."

"Thanks. My car was the only thing that didn't make it out unscathed." Subconsciously, I ran my hand over the scar my brow.

"I'm glad to hear that. I wanted to hit you up, but I didn't have your number, and my hatin' ass sister refused to give it to me."

That made me snicker. "Don't talk about TT like that." The little girl lifted her head and mugged him.

My eyes widened as I stared at little girl. "This your daughter?"

One corner of Kyriq's mouth rose. "Yeah. This her little bad ass."

"I ain't bad." She rolled her neck and propped her hands on her hips.

Last time I heard about her she was two years old, and her mom had moved them out of state once Kyriq got locked up. I knew Leia spoke to her frequently as well as their parents.

"I thought she didn't live here anymore."

"She didn't, but her mama had me fucked up. I made her ass move back with my daughter."

I snickered and shook my head. My eyes went back to the girl. She looked like a blend of Kyriq and Leia. She was a pretty little girl.

"How you know my daddy?" the little girl asked.

"Myla, watch yo' damn mouth. I done told you about that shit," Kyriq scolded her.

She rolled her eyes.

"I swear her mama got her acting too fucking grown." He shifted his eyes back to me. "You here alone? You can come kick it with us if you want. It'll be like old times." A mischievous look passed through his orbs. A couple times when we were younger, we would come to some of the things they had on the pier together. I had forgotten about those times. He licked his lips and gave me a crooked grin.

"I'm actually here with someone." I lifted my eyes and noticed Tripp making his way over.

"I was wondering what was taking you so long." He stood next to me, holding on to Scottlynn's stroller. I peeked down noticing Scottlynn peacefully sleeping.

Kyriq furrowed his brows. His eyes bounced between me and Tripp then dropped down to Scottlynn. I could see the questions bouncing around his orbs.

"Leia ain't tell me you had a baby." He cocked his head. "This why you turned me down, huh?" He smirked.

My chest tightened, and I cleared my throat. "Oh, no this isn't—"

Tripp wrapped his arm around me, pulling me into his side. "When was this?"

I sighed. "Tripp, this is Kyriq, Leia's older brother. Kyriq, Tripp."

Neither of them spoke right away.

Kyriq smirked. "Damn. I guess I really did miss my chance." He shook his head. "You always wanted to have a family of your own. I knew you'd turn out to be a great mom one day." He dropped his eyes back to Scottlynn. "Cute baby."

"Daddy, can we go now? I'm hungry," Myla complained.

"Yeah, we can." He kept his eyes on me. "It was good seeing you again, My Lee."

Heat crept up the back up of my neck. "You too."

Kyriq walked off with Myla, and Tripp made no attempt to untuck me from his side.

"That was fun." I pulled away with an awkward smile on my face. It wasn't like I was caught doing anything wrong, but for some reason, the interaction seemed odd to me.

"What's the story there?" he asked, nodding in the direction Kyriq just went.

"Can we start walking? We should probably get Scottlynn home."

Tripp didn't protest as we headed for the beginning of the pier.

"We messed around when I was younger for a few years on and off until he got locked up, and I finally decided to leave him alone and move on."

"And you've been around him since he's been home?"

I peeked up at Tripp. A smile trembled on my face. "Tripp." I paused. "Are you jealous?"

He stopped with me. His jaw clenched. "Nah, ain't no reason to be jealous over someone I know is mine. I just don't like how he was looking at you."

I batted my lashes, feeling my heart increase. "And how was he looking at me?"

"Like he wanted that old thing back." His voice sounded flat along with his stare.

Stepping into him, I leaned up and brushed the bottom of his face with my hand. "Good thing I'm not worried about him anymore. I outgrew that situation, and I made sure he knew it. I'm on to bigger and better things." I bit down on my bottom lip and pushed into him.

Heat flashed through his eyes. He shifted his hand down to my ass and cuffed it. "Tonight, just so we're clear, when I get you home, I plan on tasting every inch of you since you're completely healed. I've held back long enough."

Blood rushed to my center, causing my pussy to throb. Fireworks exploded in my stomach and spread through my body.

Pushing up, I pressed my lips into his, swiping my tongue over his lips. Inside, my chest grew taunt by my swelled heart. My head spun. Desire swirled through my veins. Closing my eyes, I moaned against his lips.

"Aye, there's kids here!" a deep voice interrupted us.

Pulling away, my lashes fluttered. It took me a couple seconds to remember we were in public. I peeked over and noticed Troy and a woman walking toward us.

"You two need to get a room." He smirked at me then darted his eyes to his brother.

"Fuck you. We're headed home." He stepped around the stroller and slapped hands with his brother. "Wassup, sis?" He hugged the woman then stepped back.

"Don't be rude, TJ. Introduce us," she encouraged him when he came back to my side.

"Oh, shit. That's right. You two never met. Brylee, this is Joy, my sister-in-law. Joy, Brylee, my...woman."

My insides jangled with excitement at his confession.

"Your woman, huh? What happened to just your nanny?" Troy taunted.

"Stop it." Joy hit his arm. "Brylee, I've heard nothing but good things about you. It's nice to meet you." She stepped forward with her hand out. I reached out to shake it with a smile on my face. "We'll have to get together sometime."

"I would like that." I nodded.

Stepping back, Joy glanced at Scottlynn. "Aw, she is getting so big," she gushed.

I couldn't stop the smile on my face. "I know, right? It makes me kind of upset." The words slipped through my mouth before I could stop them. The couple looked at me, both with mirth.

"Let us take her off your hands tonight," Joy spoke up.

"Huh?" Troy faced her.

"Yeah. We were headed home anyway, and from what we just saw, I'm sure you two could use the night alone. We'll drop her off in the morning."

I looked at Tripp, who looked at me and shrugged. "You won't hear me complain."

"Good." Joy walked over to grab the stroller. Reaching down, I made sure to grab my monkey that was tucked into the bottom.

"Her bag is in the bottom of the stroller. She should be asleep until around four. She wakes for a bottle then goes back to sleep," I told Joy.

She gave me a soft smile. "I gotchu."

We had just gotten Scottlynn back, so part of me didn't want her to leave again, but the other part was excited for what tonight had planned for Tripp and me.

Tripp and Troy stepped away, talking quietly amongst themselves for a while. I couldn't tell what they were talking about, but I had an idea when they glanced over at me. When they came back, Troy gave his goodbye along with Joy, and the two walked off with Scottlynn.

"I want to do one thing before we leave," I noted. Tripp gave me his attention. "The Ferris wheel." I pointed. "We couldn't get on with Scottlynn here, but now we have time."

He turned toward it and watched the lights as they spun.

Reaching down, he grabbed my hand. "Let's go."

I grinned and moved closer into him, nuzzling into his side.

"You enjoyed yourself tonight?" He asked after a while.

"I did. I'm glad I forced myself into the plans." I cheesed, making him chuckle.

We got to the Ferris wheel, and the wait wasn't too long.

"This was always my favorite things to do at any carnival or fair," I admitted, looking out the glass window as we headed for the top. It was dark out, but the water looked pretty as the lights from the carnival reflected on it.

"My grandparents always used to bring me here when I was younger. Back then, there weren't as many booths and stuff, but I still always had a good time." I sighed and hugged my monkey into my chest. It was something simple, but also something I would always cherish. "Have you seen anything more beautiful?" The question was rhetorical, but Tripp answered anyway.

"I have." His tone caused me to turn and face him. I inhaled a sharp breath at the intense passion burning in his darkened eyes. My heart drummed against my ribcage. We were now at the top of the wheel, hanging. The cart suddenly felt smaller.

Tripp grabbed me and pulled me closer into him. My breathing picked up.

"*You're way* more beautiful than any scenery, Brylee. It might have taken me a while to take my head out of my ass, but now that my eyes are open, and I have you, I plan to make you feel just how much I want you every day." His lips crashed into mine. The kiss started off slow. Quickly, it heated up. His lips seared a path down my neck. My lips parted, releasing heavy pants. His large hand went to my thigh, gripping it tightly. A spiral of ecstasy shot through me.

"I can't wait to see you laid out in my bed when we get home. I've imagined too many times how you would look under me while I'm buried inside you." Tripp's voice sounded sultry and throaty, causing my insides to explode with want.

"Yes." A whimper left my mouth when he slid his hand between my legs and pressed against my pussy. My eyes squeezed shut.

Tripp lifted his head, finding my lips again. It had been so long since someone touched me like this. Usually, I played it cool with Tripp, not wanting to push or show him the real me. Now, that was out the window. He was about to see a whole new side awaken inside me.

———

Every atom in my body felt electrified as I laid back on Tripp's bed in nothing but my bra and panties. Propped up on my elbows with my feet planted on the bed and spread open, my pulse jumped. Tripp stood in front of the bed staring down at me with a lustful, captivating expression on his face. His dark orbs tugged at my heart. My tongue swiped over my dry lips. Between my legs was soaked and throbbing.

As soon as we got off the Ferris wheel, we wasted no time leaving the carnival. Things got heated in the cart. Both of us no longer wanted to hold back when it came to our desires.

Dropping my eyes to his center, I inhaled a sharp breath. His dick stood at attention in his boxers. The head peeked out the slit, dripping of pre cum. Raking my eyes up, I swallowed hard. Tripp's body was sculpted to perfection. I could tell he worked out frequently. With his job, it made sense. There wasn't an ounce of fat on his bulky frame. I could count the six abs against his stomach, his chest broad and tight, while his arms were thick and ripped.

"Like what you see?"

Snapping my attention to his face, my heart skirted at his crooked grin. One of his brows lifted.

"*Love* what I see," I breathed. Pushing myself off the bed, I crawled to the edge where he stood. Reaching out, I grabbed the rim of his boxers, keeping my eyes locked on him and slowly dragging them down. His dick popped out, bouncing against his stomach, the same bronzed shade as the rest of his body. He was average in girth but long with a medium-sized head. Ripples shot through my stomach as I brushed his precum my thumb. He jerked against my touch, causing my mouth to turn upward.

"I wanna taste," I whispered, stroking him a couple times then leaning in to swipe his tip with my tongue. I circled the head, keeping my eyes on his face. His stare became darker with his brows drew together and mouth pinched. Wrapping my lips around his tip, I teased it at first, loving how it twitched in my mouth.

"Don't be shy with it," he groaned. A light lit in my chest.

Taking more of him into my mouth, my eyes fluttered at the weight on my tongue. My mouth grew wetter as I bobbed my head, taking him deeper each time I went down. Breathing through my nose and relaxing my throat, I took him until my nose was pressed against his groomed pubic hairs.

"Shit!" he moaned. His hand went to the back of my head. My cheeks hollowed, and I moved back then forward again. Finding my rhythm, I slurped him down as if he was a popsicle on hot summer day. His hand gripped my hair. Looking up at him, I saw the intense stare on his face. As much as I could, I bobbed my head, circling his shaft with my tongue. My hand went to his hip, and I forced him forward. Catching my request, he thrusted into my mouth. His dick hit the back of my throat, and my pussy leaked more.

Tripp soon let go, fucking my face with a heavy grip on my hair. My eyes closed. His grunts and groans fed the fire growing in my stomach. Drool dripped down his pole and out the corner of my mouth. My hand went between his legs, caressing his heavy balls, causing his body to jerk.

"Fuck. Fuck!" he gritted. His thrust grew faster.

I knew Tripp wouldn't last too much longer. Pulling back, I grabbed his base, rotating my grip as I stroked him. He soon exploded in my mouth. My eyes rolled to the back of my head as I swallowed his semen. My tongue lapped over his dick, catching every drop. With a large slurp, I pulled back and swiped my tongue over my lips.

"That's how you coming, huh?" he asked thickly.

I stared up at him with a lazy grin. "I been curious for a while now." My voice came out raspy.

My juices leaked out, soaking my panties and dripping down my thighs. My nipples felt hard and strained against my bra. Biting on my bottom lip, I reached behind me to undo my bra. Tossing it to the side, I went to remove my panties, but Tripp stopped me. He hovered over me, planted his arms on either side of me, his face right in front of mine. Leaning in, I kissed him with burning desire and aching need. His hands went to my panties, and he tugged them down. My legs spread wider. Moving his hand between my legs, he pressed on my clit, causing me to moan against his lips. One of his thick fingers entered me, while his thumb teased my clit. I ground against his touch. My heart raced in my chest.

His other hand wrapped around my waist. He roughly yanked me closer to him. His finger moved faster inside me, and our kiss became harder. I humped his hand as another finger pushed into me.

"Tripp," I whimpered against his lips. My eyes squeezed shut. My pussy clenched around his digits.

"Can't wait to feel you wrapped around me," Tripp grumbled, pushing his thumb into my clit and curling his fingers forward. My legs trembled as my toes curled. My lips parted as ecstasy shot through me, and my tunnel flooded his hands with my essence.

"Need you in me," I begged. A smothering need shot through me. My hand went to his arm, and I gripped it tightly, pulling him closer into me.

Tripp moved his hand on my waist to my breast, and his mouth dropped down to my hardened nipples. His hot tongue went across the buds and pulled into his mouth. His fingers still stroked my insides. He cuffed my breast roughly and covered them with his mouth, sucking and licking as jolts of pleasure shot through me. I moaned, tossing my head back.

"Please!" I pleaded, clenching my walls around him again. His fingers felt good, but I wanted more. *Needed more.*

"I told you I wanted to taste all of you," he growled against my skin before moving to my other breast.

I shook my head quickly. "Later. Need you inside me."

Giving my breast one final lick, he finally obliged my request and lifted. His fingers left my pussy. He brought them to his mouth, licking my juice off. I moaned from the motion alone.

With shaky hands, I reached between us and grabbed his length. It was hard again. I pulled it, guiding it to my entrance. We made eye contact as my heart skyrocket. A gasp left my lips when I pulled him inside me. His dick stretched me wider than his fingers did. He thrusted forward, working his way inside me. My hands wrapped around his toned back. My eyes fluttered then rolled to the back of my head when he pushed all the way in.

God, I knew he would feel amazing inside of me. Tripp was a naturally passionate person, so I had no doubt he would be a great lover. He lowered his body down on me, forcing me back and capturing my lips with his. One of his arms went to my leg, lifting and hooking it under the knee. He fucked me skillfully. Each time he pushed inside me, his long length pushed against that hot spot inside me. My skin prickled with pleasure.

Our tongues wrestled, entangling together in burning need. His lips felt warm and sweet against mine.

I cried out against his lips and arched my back into him. My breasts pressed against the hardness of his chest. Pulling back, he dropped his head into the crook of my neck.

"This what you wanted?" he rasped. His warm breathing tickled my lobe.

"Yes!" I whimpered when his hips shifted, and his strokes sped up. I didn't remember the last time sex felt like this. Tripp moved in and out of me like a man on a mission, his strokes hitting their mark every time he pushed into me. He kept his rhythm, switching between fast and slow, rolling his hips, and hitting my spot every time.

A tremor shot through me. My legs quaked as my nails dug into his back while I tightened my walls around him.

"That's right. Give it to me. Don't hold back," he grunted, pulling up. Tripp grabbed my other leg and pushed them both up. He looked like an Adonis God covered in sweat above me. His jaw clenched and unclenched along with his stomach. His eyes narrowed and focused on himself moving in and out of me.

I gripped his sheets tightly and thrusted my chest upward. "Right there. Right there," I cried as an orgasm rippled through me. He didn't stop. Tripp sped his strokes up, widening my legs and gaining more access to my walls.

Tripp had stamina, even after cumming off head, he made me cum twice on his dick before he finally released inside me. When we started, I wasn't thinking about us not bothering to use a condom. It wasn't until his release coated my insides that it hit me.

My eyes were closed as I breathed heavily. The way my heart raced I would have thought I just ran a marathon. Slowly, I opened my eyes to mention the condom, but my words became lodged in my throat when I eyed him heatedly staring between my legs. He flicked his eyes up to meet mine. I thought he might mention it, but instead, he leaned over and kissed me deeply.

I knew the responsible thing would be to mention it myself, but I pushed that to the back of my mind for now. I wanted to ride the high I was on and worry about the consequences later.

CHAPTER 25

TRIPP

Clenching and unclenching my hands, I stood outside of Skye's room mentally preparing myself for what was on the other side of the door. Today was the first time I was seeing her in over three months. She was due to come home soon, and I was excited to see her progress.

Licking my lips, I pushed a deep breath out as my heart beat wildly inside me. I knocked on her door before grabbing the handle and pushing it open.

When I stepped in the room, Skye sat on her bed, eyes locked on the door. They instantly lit up when she saw it was me. She tossed the book that was on her lap to the side and hopped up, rushing to me. Her body crashed into me, causing me to chuckle and wrap my arms around her.

"I take it you're happy to see me."

She gripped me tighter. "I didn't think you would come." Her voice sounded shaky and muffled.

My chest ached because I had pushed back the last couple times I was supposed to come see her, but it wasn't on purpose. The first time, I just wasn't ready, and the second was Brylee's accident. Still, I didn't want Skye to think I abandoned her. Even if I didn't want to continue our relationship, I still cared about her and wanted what was best for her.

"I told you I would, didn't I?"

Skye lifted her head and tilted her chin, so she faced me with an easy smile on her while her eyes beamed brightly. I could see the difference instantly from when she first got admitted. Her eyes held life in them again, the dark circles gone.

"Let me look at you," I insisted, releasing her.

Bashfully, she nodded and stepped back. I took her in, instantly noticing she had gained the weight she lost back. The sweats she had on hugged her lower frame nicely. Her cheeks no longer looked sunken in.

"You look good, Skye." I licked my lips and lifted my attention to her face.

"I feel good." She swiped her hands through her hair. "C'mon, let's sit down." Stepping forward, she grabbed my hand and dragged me to her bed, taking a seat with me following behind her.

Neither of us spoke right away. Skye watched me shyly, running her hands up and down her thighs. Her foot tapped rapidly.

"You nervous?" I tilted my head and took her in. She chewed on her bottom lip so hard I thought she would chew a hole through it.

A nervous giggle left her mouth, and she shrugged. "A little. I'm just happy you're here. I've missed you a lot."

"I missed you too, Skye," I confessed, because I did. Things were gray with us, but I still considered her one of my best friends. Before the drugs took control of her, we had some good times. While she kept a lot of things close to her chest, we still managed to create a bond that I valued.

"Then why did it take you so long to come see me?" Her brows furrowed.

I sighed and curled my shoulders forward, resting my elbows on my knees. "Life, Skye. With work and Scottlynn, I barely have any spare time."

"I thought you got the nanny to take care of her?"

"Yeah, while I'm working, but I try to spend as much time with her as I can when I'm off."

Her eyes shifted forward. "Oh, yeah. I guess that makes sense."

"She's getting big, you know? Finally crawling and saying words. Not a lot, but she learned how to say no." I chuckled. "I got some updated pictures of her too."

Digging in my pocket, I pulled out my phone and unlocked it. Going to my photo's, I clicked on my most recent one and held it out to her. She glanced at the phone and slowly reached for it.

I watched as she studied the picture for a second. Her mouth ticked before she swiped the screen.

"She looks more like you the older she gets," Skye noted.

"Yeah, I said the same thing." The corners of my mouth rose.

For a couple minutes, we were quiet as she swiped through the pictures. I watched her reaction, waiting to see some excitement fill her face. My chest squeezed when the deadpanned expression stayed instead.

"Who is this?" Her brows pulled together as her mouth turned upside down. Skye flipped the phone toward me. I eyed the screen. It was a picture of me, Scottlynn, and Brylee. Brylee had taken it one day while we all sat on the couch. Scottlynn was asleep in her arms. I sat behind them with my arm on the back of the couch.

"That's Brylee," I said slowly. My eyes darted to her confused face.

"Brylee?"

Nodding, I grabbed my phone and looked at it closer. Both me and Brylee were smiling in the camera, and she held up the peace sign.

"The nanny."

A blank expression covered Skye's face. She blinked slowly. Her lips pressed into a straight line.

"I didn't realize she looked like that." Skye shifted and brushed her fingers through her hair.

"Like what?"

"Young and pretty. When you said you had a nanny, I imagined some older woman. She's..." Her words faded off.

"She's?"

"Not what I expected. Are you two close?"

"It's kind of hard not to grow close to someone that lives in your house and you see almost every day."

Her lips twisted to the side as her foot tapped rapidly again.

I licked my lips and tried to decide how I wanted to approach the conversation. I needed to tell Skye about Brylee. She deserved to know that the two of us were together now. Fear held me back, though. I didn't want her to be set back when she was so close to coming home.

"Tell me how things are here, Do you feel like it helped coming here this time?"

Skye stared at me silently for a long minute before finally pushing out an exasperated breath and filling me in on her time here.

"When I come home, I'm gonna do better, Tripp," Skye said. "I know this has been a long battle, but I swear I plan on staying clean this time. Everyone gave up on me, but not you. Knowing you were home waiting for me pushed me to get clean and take this seriously. When I come home, I know its gonna take some time, but I plan on earning your trust back and becoming the woman you fell in love with again."

My tongue dragged over my top teeth while my hands clenched in my lap. Hopefulness beamed from Skye's eyes, and the last thing I wanted to do was pop her bubble. At the same time, I didn't want to give her false hope.

"You need to come home and focus on you, Skye. I told you before I don't want you to get clean for me. I want it to be *for you*. You're better than the drugs. I want you to come home and get to know our daughter and make her a priority too."

"And what about us?"

"Skye." I sighed.

Some of the light left her eyes, but she tried to keep the smile on her face. "Okay, I get it. You're right. I have to show you I'm serious this time. I will, Tripp. When I come home it'll be like I never touched drugs. I want to love you, Tripp. You've always been my rock, and I can never thank you enough for that."

I hated that Skye didn't see our daughter as a reason to be better. One thing I always wanted was for her to see being a mother as a reason to get her life on track and stop the drugs.

Skye's demon's ran deep. This was her third time in rehab, and just like the first two times, she promised to come home and stay clean. In the beginning, I stayed by her side because I loved her and had faith she would change. Skye had overcome a lot in her past, so I knew she was strong enough to fight the drugs, but she had to want it herself.

———

"Now this is a sight I could get used to." I crawled into my bed and laid on top of Brylee, nuzzling my face into her neck and feathering kisses on her skin. Since the night of the carnival, she'd been in my bed, making it her own, and I had no complaints.

"Tripp." She giggled. The needles from her crocheting pressed into my stomach, but I didn't care.

"What? I'm just letting you know I like you in my bed." Lifting up, I pecked her lips then rolled over, so I laid on my back. "What you making, anyway?"

Brylee moved whatever she was working on and leaned over, laying it on the ground. "It's a surprise." She leaned back and turned to her side so she faced me. "So, how was it?"

I didn't want to talk about Skye. Even though the visit had gone good, I still felt heavy leaving. I didn't end up telling her about me and Brylee. I wanted to wait until she was home. She was so happy while I was there that I couldn't bring myself to ruin that.

"It was good. She looks healthy and seems to be mentally better than when she went in."

Brylee smiled softly. "That's good. I'm glad to hear that." She grew quiet for a second. "And about us. How did she take it?"

Twisting my neck so I looked at her, I ran my eyes over her face. Looking at Brylee always made me feel lighter.

"I didn't tell her." She went to get up, but I quickly maneuvered so I hovered over her, forcing her on her back. "Hold up. Just listen."

Her lips tucked into her mouth as her eyes squinted. "You said you would tell her."

"And I am. I meant that. Just not now. She's almost done with the program, and she's doing good. I didn't want to tell her and then she has a setback. Although I have no plans to be with her when she comes home, I still don't want to hurt her. She's still Scottlynn's mom, and I still consider her to be one of my best friends. I owe it to her to at least let her finish her recovery."

Brylee swallowed hard and averted her eyes. Her body tensed under me.

"Brylee, I'm gonna tell her when she comes home, a'right? You don't have anything to worry about." Reaching up, I grabbed her chin, forcing her to face me. Her face still held indifference, but her eyes were softer. I brushed my hand over her jaw. "I never told you about Skye's past. I won't go into too many details, because that's not my story to tell, but maybe knowing a little of her past will make things easier to understand."

I shifted, and she widened her legs, allowing me more access between them.

"Skye grew up in a fucked up house. Her parents barely paid her any attention. Her mom was too busy chasing after her cheating daddy. Her older sister used to bully her. Eventually, her mom's younger brother moved in when he got out of prison and used to touch on her when she was eleven." Brylee's eyes widened. "She told her parents, but they both called her a liar and claimed she only wanted attention. It went on for two years. He never penetrated her, but the damage was already there. It wasn't until he was locked up again for assaulting the ten-year-old daughter of some girl he was seeing that she was finally at ease. Apparently, he told Skye she was getting too old or some sick shit.

The sick nigga might have been gone physically, but mentally, he had already done damage. The drugs helped Skye escape because her house was so fucked up. No one was ever there for her but me, so the last thing I want to do is make her feel like I'm abandoning her now." I didn't want to betray Skye's trust, but I hoped Brylee saw where I came from.

Brylee didn't reply right away. Eventually, she turned to face me. "I'm not heartless. What she went through was fucked up. I couldn't imagine how she felt all those years suffering in silence. I understand what you're saying, but I don't want to be made a fool of, Tripp. If she comes home, and you change your mind…"

I shook my head before I leaned down to peck her lips. "I'm not. You're safe with me, Brylee. When she comes home, I'll let her know what's up."

"And if she doesn't accept it?"

"She has no choice but to. We'll figure out co-parenting, and that's it." I made sure to keep my eyes locked on hers so she could see the sincerity in them. I knew Brylee's past with relationships. She didn't have the best track record with guys, and I refused to be added to that list of men who hurt her.

"Promise me if she comes home, and you feel different, then you'll tell me. Don't lead me on just to make me look like a fool in the end."

"I'm not going to, baby." I pecked her lips. "I like this space we're in. I enjoy you in my bed. I love the peace I feel with you. You have nothing to worry about." Taking her mouth again, I slowly kissed her this time. Her legs lifted and wrapped around me, locking behind my back and pulling me down.

"You make me happy, Tripp. Happier than I've been in a long time. I like this space we're in, too," she mumbled against my lips. Her hands went to the bottom of my shirt. "We have some time before Scottlynn wakes up from her nap."

She nipped my bottom lip with her teeth. My pulse thumped in throat. Blood rushed to my dick. I couldn't get enough of Brylee, and it wasn't just because of the sex, either. She was alluring. When I first met her, she came off shy, but the more I got to know her, the more I learned she was anything but that.

"Roll over," she muttered, attempting to push me.

Not arguing with her, I rolled to my back, bringing her with me, so she was now on top. I lifted to help her pull my shirt off, then she did the same with hers. I licked my lips, eyeing her breasts. She wasn't wearing a bra, so her hardened nipples greeted me.

"You're already so hard," she moaned, reaching behind her and digging in my basketball shorts before grabbing my dick.

My jaw clenched. She watched me as she stroked me. My stomach rolled with a tingling sensation. "What you gone do about it?"

A mischievous look appeared on her face. "First things first." She climbed off me. I was about to complain until she stripped out of her panties and tossed them to the side. Her small hands went to my boxers, and she pulled on them. Catching her hint, I lifted, allowing her to remove them.

This time when she climbed on me, she faced my dick, and her ass pointed at my face. Looking lustfully over her shoulders at me, she grinned. "You game?"

My eyes dropped to her pussy from behind. Her lips were soaked and glistening.

"Oh, that's what you on?" My arms went around her thighs, and I pulled her back so her pussy hovered over my mouth. I inhaled her fresh scent, causing my mouth to water. Sticking my tongue out, I swiped her pussy lips before sucking them into my mouth. She moaned as she stroked my dick and ran her tongue along the tip. My tongue flickered back and forth, circling her clit and licking down, collecting her juices.

Her legs jerked. "Oh, fuck."

It took a couple seconds, but Brylee eventually took me in her mouth. It felt like heaven as she used the right amount of suction and spit. Her lack of gag reflexes almost had me cumming instantly.

I spread her lips and fucked her with my tongue. She moaned and rolled her hips into my mouth. Her sweet essence coated my tongue, feeding the hunger inside me. Brylee was confident in the bedroom, it was clear. She was vocal with what she wanted and liked to engage physically instead of just lying there. Looking at her, I wouldn't think she was as sexually liberated as she was. As she expertly sucked me, I fought not to cum. Not wanting to be out done, I wrapped my lips around her clit. She jerked and cried around my dick.

Her pussy leaked, running down my chin. Using my middle finger, I pushed it inside her, moving it in and out.

I was able to hold my nut back until Brylee moaned and came. Her body tensed then shook on top of me. I held on to her tighter, sucking and licking her pussy. Fire shot up my spine, and I felt drugged off her juices.

I was hardly ever done after the first round. Brylee stroked my semi-hard dick back to life after I released in her mouth. Her tongue circled around it, and she sucked the tip back into her mouth. Once standing back at attention, she pulled out of my grasp, crawling up. I watched as she held my length and lowered herself onto it with her back facing me.

My mouth parted as my eyes rolled to the back of my head while her tight warm walls welcomed me. She didn't ease me in, either. Once the tip was in, Brylee slammed her ass down and bounced off my pelvis.

My breath picked up. I gripped her hips as she bounced up and down, holding on to my thighs.

"Oh, God!" she cried, clenching her walls around me. "Your dick feels even longer when I'm on top," she whimpered, leaning forward and fluttering her ass cheeks.

I couldn't speak because I was partly surprised and partly caught up in how good she felt. Blinking a couple times, I gathered myself and thrusted up. She moaned, digging her nails into my thighs.

"You're just a bag of tricks, huh?" I grunted.

Inaudible words left her mouth. Tremors shot through her body as she came. My stomach pooled with heat and desire while my pulse raced through my body as if it was in a race.

Pushing myself up, I wrapped my arms around Brylee and turned us, so my legs were now off the bed. I held her tightly and thrusted into her. She bounced on my dick, holding on to my knees. Her moans grew louder, overcoming the sound of our skin slapping together.

I pushed her locs to the side and pressed my lips against the nape of her neck. Our bodies moved in sync as if we'd been doing this for years. Grabbing her breasts, I fiddled her nipples between my fingers, causing her to cum again.

I stood up and turned so she faced the bed. Placing her on her feet, I pressed into her, speeding my strokes up. My hand dug into her hip. Her back arched as her face dug into the bed. Her pussy felt sloppy wet, sounding off every time I pushed inside her.

Her sex pulsated around me. She quivered and cried out when I switched my angle, grabbed her shoulders, and pushed myself deeper inside her.

I gritted my teeth, barely able to still hold on. Keeping my stroke steady, I buried myself deeply inside her and exploded in ecstasy. My head went back, and my eyes closed as my balls released.

Wanting to feel closer to her, I leaned forward, pressing my chest against her back and kissing on the top of her shoulder, making my way to her neck. My heart raced, and her breathing was heavy.

Brylee turned her head and met my lips. The kiss was unrushed yet needy. Another tremor went through her body, and she clenched around me. My dick twitched.

She sighed a moan out and closed her eyes. A softness was on her face. I made sure to capture the moment and save it in my mental rolodex. That serene look on her face was one I wanted to keep close.

———

"Where you going?" I reached down and snatched Scottlynn back before she could reach the end of the bed. She squealed in laughter, clapping her hands and yelling out to me. Brylee laid next to us laughing while working on her crocheting. "You're such a busy body now." I tickled her stomach.

"I know. I sat her down on the floor and ran into the kitchen. When I came back, she was trying to climb the steps." Brylee shook her head. "Once she learns those, we're in trouble."

I knew she was right. Scottlynn was a curious kid, and the older she got, the more her curiosity increased.

My phone vibrated, gaining my attention. Tucking Scottlynn into my arm, I reached over and grabbed it. Noticing it was Evie, I answered, and soon, her face appeared on the screen.

"Evie, wassup?" I positioned the phone in front of me.

"Look at her. She's gets prettier each time I see her. Hi, Scottlynn!" she gushed into the phone. Scottlynn flailed her arms and legs attempting reach for the phone.

I reached for one of her toys. "Here, take this instead." I handed her the keys. She yanked them from me and shook them. "Wassup, Evie?" I asked again.

"I have news!" She flashed her hand in front of the camera. "Issa a fiancée!"

The corners of my mouth lifted when I saw the ring on her finger.

"Oh, shit, congrats! I see Alisha's finally gonna make an honest woman out of you, huh?"

Her smile grew. "She knows I'm a catch, and her life would be nothing without me. I told you she didn't just plan a trip to Cancun for nothing!"

I chuckled and settled back. "I'm happy for you, Evie. You two look good together."

"We do, don't we?" Her eyes beamed with happiness. "I plan on having an engagement party, so make sure you get off work for it!"

"Just let me know when it is. You know I gotchu."

Evie's face suddenly got closer to the phone, and she squinted her eyes. "Is that someone's arm? Are you in bed? Who's next to you?"

Huffing a laugh, I shifted my eyes to Brylee, who had a confused expression on her face. My tongue went across my lips. I nodded my head for Brylee to come over. Her eyes went to the phone then back to me. Pushing a breath out, she shifted closer to me, setting her crocheting on the bed.

"Hey!" She leaned against me, and Scottlynn crawled into her lap.

"Evie, Brylee. Brylee, my best friend, Evie."

Evie's brows rose to her hairline as her eyes widened. "So, *you're* Brylee," Evie stated.

Brylee's looked at her confused before smiling softly. "Yeah. Hey."

Evie pressed her lips together. Her eyes grew tight again. "A lot has changed since the last time we talked, huh? She looks mighty comfy in your bed."

"Yeah, things have. Don't start your shit, either." My eyes narrowed.

A smile suddenly split on Evie's face. "I'm not complaining. It was about time you moved on to someone who deserves you."

"Evie," I warned. Not only was Scottlynn here, but I didn't need the same lecture from her.

"I'm just being honest. Brylee, I hope you know what great guy Tripp is."

Brylee lifted her head and gazed at me dreamily. "Trust me, I do. He's amazing."

A voice sounded in the background. "I need to get ready for this snorkeling thing Alisha got planned, but I have questions! Bring her to the engagement party. Matter fact, let's try to get together before then. Love you, best friend. Bye!"

Before I could get another word in, she hung up.

"So, that's Evie," I said after setting my phone down.

"She seems fun."

I chuckled. "Yeah, if that's what you want to call her. Evie's solid, though. One of the best people I've ever met."

Hesitancy casted over Brylee's face. "And you two are just friends? You've never messed around?"

My brows dipped. "Nah. Me, Skye, and Evie all grew up together. We always been friends, even before me and Skye got together. She's more of a sister to me than anything. Plus, you'd have a better chance with her than I would."

That made her cough a laugh out and grin. Leaning over, I knocked my forehead on hers. "You have nothing to worry about with her or anyone else."

She tilted her head up slightly "Sorry," she muttered.

"You don't gotta apologize. It's my job to reassure you anytime you need it."

A shy smile split on her mouth.

"No!" Scottlynn pushed her hands against my face.

"Damn." I laughed. "Let me find out she likes you more than me.

"Tell him us girls gotta stick together, right, pretty girl?"

Times like this were rare, but I appreciated them. Brylee fit in so perfectly in my life that it made me wonder how anyone would be crazy enough to let her slip out of their grasp in the first place.

CHAPTER 26

BRYLEE

"Have you heard anything about your car?" Grandad questioned.

I shook my head. "Last I heard the adjuster had just totaled it out. Now I'm waiting for it to be paid off."

"I hate dealing the insurance companies. They always drag their asses."

He wasn't lying, I felt like it took forever for them to even go look at my car. For the first two weeks after I was able to drive again, the person's insurance who hit me paid for a rental. Tripp surprised me when it was time to send it back with Skye's car. At first, I fought him when he suggested I drive it. It didn't feel right to me, but he insisted since it was just sitting in the garage anyway.

"Hopefully they'll have everything settled soon. For the time being, Tripp let me use the spare car at his house."

Grandad stared at me with question bouncing around his eyes. I fidgeted and ran my hand over my lap. "What?"

"Just wondering how things are going with him. You said you're going to his parents' house when you leave here, right?"

I nodded. "Yeah, they invited me over for dinner. As for me and Tripp, we're together." A bashful smile formed on my face.

His eyes narrowed. "Since you brought it up, I wanted to talk to you about him."

"What's wrong?"

Grandad didn't respond right away. He brushed his hand down his small beard. "Do you believe it's wise?" My brows knitted together, so he continued. "I mean, he's your boss. You don't want to get in a situation that could get messy. This is your lively hood. He seems like a fine young man, don't get me wrong, but I worry with you two blurring the lines."

My mouth twisted, and I bit the inside of my cheek as I kneaded over his words. They weren't anything I hadn't thought about before. In fact, when we first made it official, I panicked thinking about things going wrong and me being forced to quit and leave him and Scottlynn.

I shook my head. "You don't have to worry, Grandad. I trust Tripp. He's not the kind of guy who would abuse his power or use my job against me. I've made a lot of bad choices when it comes to men, I can admit, but Tripp isn't included in that. He's thoughtful, caring, kind, nurturing, hardworking, protective, and providing. Even before I met him, he's who I pictured when I thought about starting a family." My mouth snapped shut at my confession.

An understanding smile formed on my Grandad's face. His eyes softened. "You care for him a lot, don't you?"

I nodded. "Yeah, I do."

He sighed. "I saw how worried he was when we came to the hospital to see you, and then back at his house during your recovery. There's no doubt in my mind you're in good hands. I do plan on having a talk with him, though."

I snickered. "I wouldn't have it any other way."

The front door opened, and a couple seconds later, Gran appeared in the living room. Just as my smile from seeing her appeared, it quickly vanished seeing she wasn't alone.

"Hi, Lee-Lee baby," Gran said. "I didn't know you were stopping by."

She walked over to me. I stood to hug her. "I'm not staying long. Just planned on saying hi."

She kissed my cheek. "I'm always happy to see you." She released me and took a seat.

"Hi, Daddy," Breann said, then her eyes fell on me. "Hey, baby."

I blinked blankly at her. "Breann."

"How'd it go?" Grandad asked.

"Oh, I…" Breann's words faded as she continued to stare at me. Her bottom lip tucked into her mouth, and she rested her hand over stomach. "I'm seven weeks, and everything looked good."

Something twisted in my chest. My stomach felt as if quicksand quickly filled it. I was sure I was close to drawing blood by how hard I bit the inside of my cheek.

"You're pregnant… *again*." It was a statement. My hands balled at my side.

"Lee-Lee I—"

"Brylee. My name is Brylee," I cut her off. She didn't have the right to call me any nicknames. I was sick of her always trying to act so familiar with me when we were around each other.

Breann sighed, and her shoulders fell forward. "Yeah, I am."

I snorted out a laugh and shook my head. "Unbelievable," I uttered flicking some locs from in front of my face.

"Lee-Lee," Grandad started.

"You gave me up when I was five years old and went to continue to live your life. Then years later, once I'm finally grown, you and your husband decide you want to be parents. Now here you are having another kid like you didn't say fuck the first one!"

"Brylee, watch your mouth!" Gran chastised.

My vision swung between my grandparents. "And you two are okay with this? She forced you to raise me, and now she's having her fourth kid, and you two have nothing to say."

"She's an adult, Brylee, what do you want us to say?" Gran asked.

"Get her tubes tied maybe!"

"Brylee, when I had you, me and your dad were so young. We were careless and selfish back then, and I can't apologize enough for that. My main regret is not growing up and taking care of my responsibilities." Breann's voice wobbled, and she stepped closer.

My eye tightened. "I don't care about your regrets, Breann. Your regrets didn't make you want to be a mother to me. Thankfully Gran stepped up and always loved me like a mother should."

Breann sucked in a deep breath. "I always loved you, Brylee. I might not have always showed it, but I did. I'm so proud of the woman you've become. You're one of the most important people in my life."

I scoffed. "You don't even know me." Now my body was hot as if boiling water poured through my veins. My once happy mood had completely done a one eighty. The last thing I wanted to do was sit here and entertain Breann and her lies.

"I gotta go meet, Tripp," I said, turning to grab my purse off the couch. "Gran, Grandad, I'll seeing you two later. Love you."

I didn't bother to wait for anyone to answer. Maybe some might say I needed to face my issues with Breann, but it wouldn't be today. Knowing she was about to bring another child into the world left a bad taste in my mouth and was like a punch to the gut.

I stormed out of the living room to the front door. If my grandparents didn't see anything wrong with their daughter's actions, then so be it, but I refused to accept it.

———

"Hey, sorry I'm late." I leaned up and kissed Tripp quickly. I took a quick intake of him, seeing he wore a navy-blue shirt that hugged his broad chest with the firehouse crest and station number over his right peck in white.

"You okay? You seem… upset?" His brows knitted, and he studied my face.

I licked my lips and shook my head. "I don't want to talk about it right now. I'm fine."

Today was the first time I was meeting Tripp's parents as more than his nanny. The last thing I wanted was for what happened at my grandparents to ruin it.

He stared at me a little longer before giving me a slight nod. "Later then." He wrapped his arm around me and led me up the driveway. "I know this was supposed to be a simple dinner, but my mom invited my brothers, and my dad decided to light the grill up. I hope you don't mind."

"Of course, not. I like your brothers. They're cool."

He pushed the gate open that led to the backyard. Music played, and Terrance animatedly talked over it as Troy looked at him with a bored expression. Tripp led me to the rectangle glass table where his mom and sister-in-law were. Scottlynn laid eyes on us first and struggled to get out of her grandma's arms.

"What in the—" Rose started but stopped when she noticed us.

We got closer, and Scottlynn damn near jumped out of her grandma's arms to get to me.

"I missed you too, pretty girl." I snickered, kissing her cheek. She had stayed with Tripp's parents last night. It always warmed my heart at the excited greeting she gave me whenever she saw me.

"Brylee, it's nice to see you again," Rose spoke.

I turned my eyes to her. "You too. Hey, Joy."

"Hey, girl. Good to see you again!" She lifted her wine cooler.

Rose's eyes bounced between me and Tripp. "So, you and my son, huh?"

My cheeks flushed, and I nodded. "Uhm, yeah."

"Mhm." Mirth covered her face.

"Go easy on her, Mama." Tripp chuckled, wrapping his arm around me.

"I'm not upset about it or shocked." She rose a brow and hiked one corner of her mouth up.

I was curious what she meant by that but was interrupted by Terrance. "Wassup, sis-in-law? You're looking good as usual." He grinned at me.

"Charming." Tripp gave him a deadpanned look.

"Thank you, Terrance. It's nice to see you, too."

Troy took a seat next to his wife.

"The burgers and hot dogs are finished. We're just waiting on the ribs," Tripp said as he walked over. "Oh, Brylee, I didn't know were here. How are you, sweetheart?" He sat next to his wife.

"I'm good, thanks."

He looked between me and his son. "Good to hear it."

"You two sit down. Terrance, go to the cooler and grab me a Pepsi," His mom demanded.

Walking to the empty seats next to each other, we took a seat.

"I'm just gonna jump into this, so we can get it all out of the way and enjoy the evening," Rose started.

"Ah shit," Troy muttered with a laugh.

"Now, I might not be a fan of her, but I hope you handled things properly with Skye before the two of you decided to be together. Me and your father didn't raise you to be a cheater, TJ, and Brylee, you don't seem like the girl who would play the other woman."

I tensed and gripped Scottlynn tighter. She had grabbed her bottle off the table next to us and was currently drinking it, unknowing to the tension around her. Technically, Tripp didn't end things with Skye. Not in the way he should, at least. I tried to believe he would handle it when she came home.

"I got everything handled. Skye knows when she comes home, she needs to focus on herself and being a better mother."

"But does she know about you and Brylee? I'm assuming she still believes she's just your nanny?"

Terrance walked over and sat the Pepsi in front of his mom then sat next to his dad and across from me. "Uh oh, she started the hot seat, huh?" He chuckled.

Ignoring his brother, Tripp spoke again. "Right now, the most important thing is for Skye to be sober and complete her program. She's almost done, and I didn't want to set her back. When she comes home, I plan on laying everything on the table."

"And Brylee, how do you feel about this? Because at the end of the day, this will affect my granddaughter, too."

I cleared my throat. As if she knew I needed it, Scottlynn nuzzled herself closer into my chest. "I'm trusting Tripp. You're right. I would never willingly play the other woman, but your son has assured me I have nothing to worry about. As for Scottlynn, I love her as if she was my own. I would never do anything to hurt her." I nibbled on my bottom lip. Tripp's hand landed on my thigh, and he gave me a reassuring squeeze. Facing him, I gave him a small smile.

"And that's what we love to hear. Honey, leave them alone. TJ is grown and can manage his own household. The two seemed to have discuss things and have an understanding," Tripp senior said.

Rose looked between us then focused on me. "I don't want you to think I'm being rude, Brylee. I like you. I know you love my granddaughter, and I'm glad she has you in your life. I just want what's best for her and my son."

I gave her a stiff nod. "I understand. No harm done."

Rose's questioning didn't bother me and was valid. As a woman, if I had a son, I would have the same reservations. Things with me and Tripp weren't as simple as I would have liked, but I believed it would smooth out in the end.

"Let me go check these ribs," Tripp senior said as he stood.

"I should go get the sides and start bringing them out. Ladies, care to join me?" Rose stood as well. I turned to hand Scottlynn to Tripp. He stared at me with concern, but I smiled, so he knew I was fine.

Joy and I followed behind Rose toward the patio doors.

"You got off easy. She interrogated me for an hour before Troy stepped in," Joy whispered to me. My eyes widened.

They said moms didn't play about their sons, and I guess Rose proved that fact.

On my way back out of the house after checking on Scottlynn, who was currently sleeping in one of the bedrooms, I paused, seeing Tripp looking like he was headed in the same direction I just came.

"Everything okay?" I asked, approaching him.

The cookout had been going well. I spent most of my time with Joy getting to know her. We had exchanged numbers and agreed to meet up after this. I had watched Tripp with his brothers and could see the trio were close by how the bantered with each other. His parents were welcoming after the mini interrogation his mom gave me. The cookout had been a great distraction from the ill feelings that had been sitting on me since leaving my grandparents' house.

"I just wanted to check in with you." His hand rested on my hip. His left brow rose a fraction. He raked me over with his eyes, causing heat to expand in my chest. "When you came here, you were upset about something, right? You seem to be in better spirits now, but I wanted to make sure."

My tongue dragged over my bottom lip. "Yeah, just a small hiccup at my grandparents' house."

His brows knitted. "What happened?"

Sighing, I rolled my eyes and shifted my weight to one leg. "Breann's pregnant again." The words were heavy as they left my mouth. I hated how it made my chest twist and ache. I was too old to be holding on to this kind of trauma, but it was hard to shake off.

"And that hurt you?" His questioning wasn't teasing but dripped of concern. His voice filled with understanding.

Again, I sighed. "It shouldn't. I know it shouldn't. I'm too old to be throwing tantrums because my parents decided I wasn't good enough to raise but continue having kids who they kept." Shaking my head, I tucked my bottom lip into my mouth and sank my teeth into it. The weight on my chest seemed to be growing larger.

"You're entitled to feel angry or sad. No one can take that away or make you feel wrong. What your parents did hurt you, and you have yet to deal with. Maybe it's time you talk to them so you can move on."

Sad to say, Tripp wasn't saying anything I didn't know already. My grandparents had been telling me this for years.

"Yeah, I know. I just get so mad every time I'm in the same room as them, you know? And then learning they're having another kid and seeing how happy my siblings are with them, it shows me what I missed out on. I loved growing up with Gran and Grandad, and they gave me a good life, but it's still hard seeing what I could have had."

Tripp tightened his hold on me, pulling me closer into his body. I closed my eyes and inhaled him, loving the fresh, clean scent bouncing off him. He must have showered after his shift before coming here.

"I know it might not seem like it, but in a way, your parents did you a favor. You said they were what, fourteen when they had you? They were kids themselves. What could they have given a baby when they couldn't even take care of themselves? Giving you to your grandparents might be the only way they were able to show you how much they love you, knowing you would be taken care of properly."

Swallowing hard, I leaned forward, resting my forehead on Tripp's chest, listening to the soothing sound of heartbeat. "Yeah, maybe," I said quietly.

Tripp must have known the conversation was starting to take a toll on me, because instead of speaking again, he wrapped his arms around me and hugged me tightly into him. His forehead rested on the top of my head.

"You don't have to rush it. Whenever you're ready to talk to them, I'll be by your side if you need the support. I gotchu however you need me. You know that, right?" I nodded. "If you're ready to go, we can dip out. Just tell me what you need right now," he said with quiet emphasis.

Pulling my head back, I tilted my chin up to face him. "No, I'm fine. I'm having a good time with your family. I just need a second, and we can go back out there."

"You sure? My people won't care."

With a small toothless grin, I pushed up and kissed him hard. "I swear I'm fine, but thank you."

I loved that Tripp never hesitated to put my feelings first. He was so caring, and the deep, soothing octave of his voice always made me feel save and warm all over.

"A'right, just say word, and we can go."

My smile heightened, and I nodded.

Tripp and I shared another quick kiss before he released me and grabbed my hand, leading me toward the door. I was good at shaking off my feelings whenever I felt down, and right now would be no different.

CHAPTER 27

TRIPP

"Fuck!" I gritted, moving throughout the smoky room I was in. The fire was growing more intense, making it harder to see and breath. "Top half clear!" I said into the radio before heading for the exit to make my way back downstairs. It was only a matter of time before the fire claimed the upper level too.

Me and the guys inside cleared out as the others worked on putting the fire out. The street was filled with by standers standing around watching. The air around us was smoky and toxic.

"Wait, where are the twins?" a girl shouted through coughs. "No, move!" She pushed off the paramedic attempting to give her oxygen.

"Twins?" Cap questioned.

"My brother and sister." Her eyes widened with freight and shot to the house. "They're still inside."

"Wait, it wasn't just you and the baby? Fuck!" Cap gritted. "Where would they be?"

She shook her head. "I don't know! They were playing hide and seek. I... I upstairs, maybe? In their bedrooms in the closet?"

"What are their names?"

"Anna and Austin."

"A'right, Clark, Rogers, and Davidson, back inside. Be on the lookout for two kids."

Car wheels squealed, and in the background of rushing into the house, I heard screaming.

"Morgan, what happened!" a woman yelled.

Rushing into the house, me, Leo, and Harlem split up inside.

"Front room all clear," Leo spoke in the radio.

"Next room all clear."

My heart fumbled inside me. Adrenaline ran through my veins as my eyes darted around. The smoke was still thick, although they had contained the fire.

"Anna! Austin! Can you hear me?" I called out.

"Tripp, be careful. The hall floor looks like it could give any minute," Harlem called into the mic.

Ignoring him, I continued searching through the room. I got to the closet and snatched the clothes out of the way. Relief hit me seeing two small bodies cowering in the corner. My chest ached seeing the boy crying silently holding his sister who could barely keep her eyes open.

"Found them. Coming out," I said. I swallowed hard and held my hand out. "It's okay. You two are safe now. Come with me. Your mom and sister are outside waiting for you."

Hesitantly, he pushed his sister forward. I grabbed her, and her body weakly collapsed into me. Who knew how much smoke these two had taken being trapped in this small space.

Once both were out of the closet, I held them both in my arms. Both clung to my neck. Making sure I was cautious of my movements, I got them out of the house as quickly as I could. The smoke was thick. I made sure to keep their faces pressed into me.

"Oh, my babies!" a middle aged woman bellowed, rushing toward me once we were outside. "Anna! Is she okay?"

"She's breathing," I expressed.

The same younger woman came up to us this time holding a baby just as the paramedics rushed me, taking both kids from my arms.

"Her breathing is shallow!" one of them stated.

The boy coughed wildly.

I snatched my helmet off and watched as they attempted to stabilize the kids. As much as I loved my job, I hated when kids became the victim in casualties.

"Good work, TJ!" Omiras approached me, patting my shoulder.

It didn't feel good seeing the family in distress and the two younger kids barely hanging on. Times like this always made me think of my own daughter. On the job, I saw so much, and half the time kids were involved. The thought caused a knot in my stomach.

Closing my eyes, I pushed a couple breaths out to ease the tension building in my chest. One of the most important things I'd learned being on the job was to learn to disconnect from the job once I took the uniform off.

———

"Brandon, be careful!" Brylee shouted as we sat on the bench watching her brother and sister on the jungle gym. Since I was off today, I decided to join her when she mentioned picking her siblings up from her grandparents' house and spending some time with them. It was a shock to me that she mentioned getting her siblings since she felt some type of way about her mom being pregnant again, but then again, I knew how Brylee felt about her siblings. She loved them more than she distained her parents.

My eyes went to Scottlynn, who babbled to herself. She was happily sitting in her stroller eating the yogurt melts in front of her.

"I don't think I could handle having a boy. They're so rough."

I chuckled as I watched Brandon flip on the monkey bars. "He'll be a'right. Getting some bumps and bruises will build character."

She smacked her lips. "Just like a guy to say that."

I flashed her a lazy smile. "Tripp, can you push me?" Brittani shouted, kicking her small legs.

"I think my sister has a crush on you," Brylee mentioned, squinting in her sister's direction.

Chuckling, I stood. "Don't sound so upset." I walked over to the swing where Brandon now sat near his sister.

"Can you push me, too?" he begged.

"Me first!" Brittani complained.

"I got both y'all," I assured them, stepping behind them.

I spent the next few minutes pushing each of them until they were able to kick their feet enough to keep going themselves.

Brylee ended up coming over and putting Scottlynn in the baby swing. "Don't go too high. I don't want one of you guys to fall off," she called out to her siblings.

It made me smile hearing the concern in her voice. "You're a natural mom, you know that?"

"I've been told."

My eyes dropped to her stomach. For a second, I pictured her swollen with my kid. She took on the role so naturally. I knew it shouldn't be something I should even think about, but it was hard not to. Each day I found my feelings for Brylee growing.

"What?" Brylee questioned. A small smile crept on her face, and she cocked her head slightly while watching me. "Why are you looking at me like that?"

Licking my lips, I grinned as I stepped closer to her. "I'm just thinking how lucky I am to have you in my life."

Turning to face me, she reached up and wrapped her arms around me. "I can say the same thing."

Our lips met, and my hand traveled down to her ass.

"Ew!" her brother and sister yelled, giggling and running off.

Brylee's grin grew, and she kissed me again.

"I knew you would eventually get tired of being the shining knight to a junkie."

Pulling back, I turned my head with a frown on my face. Distain filled me as I laid eyes on Vee.

"Go play, and don't get dirty." She waved the kids off at her side and turned back to us.

"Looks like you left little sis in the dust, huh?" She smirked in front of the swing.

Instantly, my eyes dropped down to my daughter. I grabbed the swing, stopping it and pulling Scottlynn out.

"What do you want, Vee?"

She examined her nails and shrugged. "Just brought the kids to play and saw you and my niece. Thought I'd come say hi." Her eyes went to Brylee.

Biting down on my back molars, I moved in front of Brylee. The last thing I wanted was Vee trying anything funny.

"What? Can't I meet your new girlfriend, brother-in-law?" A smug grin appeared on her face.

"I'm not your brother-in-law. Skye didn't even fuck with you."

She rolled her eyes. "Is baby sis still pushing that shit up her nose?" She clicked her tongue. "You know it's a good thing you moved on. She was only holding you back."

The void of emotion in Vee's eyes caused my blood to boil. Knowing she could easily talk down on Skye like that caused heat to rush up the back of my neck.

Turning around, I handed Scottlynn to Brylee. I could tell by the look on her face she had questions. She looked around me at Vee, narrowing her eyes.

"Go get your siblings so we can go," I told her. Vee was evil spirited, and the last thing I wanted to do was be anywhere near her.

Brylee looked toward me and gave me a slight nod. Once she had Scottlynn in her stroller and walked to the jungle gym, I turned back to Vee.

"I don't know why you hate Skye as much as you do, but all she ever wanted was for her big sister to be there for her. Your whole family is so hateful. I'm glad I got Skye away from y'all when I did."

Vee scoffed and flicked her hair behind her shoulders. "And look how good that turned out."

My nose flared as my jaw ached from how hard I clenched it. With my hands balled at my sides, I walked a couple steps forward, so I stood closer you her. A nervous expression ghosted across her face, and she stepped back.

"You know, I don't know if whoever gave you that black eye you're trying to hide knocked some screws lose or what, but at least Skye knows she has some genuine love surrounding her now and isn't forced to turn tricks for her child's father." Vee's mouth dropped, and she shakily lifted her hand to brush it over her eye.

I walked around her, not seeing the point in wasting any more time with her. I didn't even want to bring up the rumors about her child's father pimping her out, but even if I was with someone else, I wouldn't let her disrespect Skye.

"You guys ready?" I said when I got closer to Brylee. She looked around me at Vee and slowly bobbed her head. My hand went to the small of her back, and I guided her away from the jungle gym. "How about we grab something to eat before dropping y'all off?" I asked her siblings as we walked off.

They both talked in high voices, excitedly voicing their food choices.

Once in the car, I pulled Scottlynn out of the stroller to put her in the car seat while they climbed in the other side of the car.

"Hey, is everything okay? That woman was Skye's sister?" Brylee grabbed my arm.

Dragging my tongue over my top teeth, I gave her a curt nod. "Yeah, and everything is good. She's just a miserable bitch."

Brylee's eyes widened. I didn't like to disrespect woman. In fact, my mom would pop me in the mouth to this day if she heard me, but I had to call a spade a spade. Reaching around Brylee, I opened the passenger door for her to get in the car.

After shutting it behind her and walking around to my side, I paused and took a second to get my self together. My body was still riled up from Vee's words. For a second, guilt filled me knowing that was where Skye came from. It was one reason I fought so hard to give her a real family.

Pushing a deep breath out, I opened my door and climbed inside.

"Are you sure you're okay?" Brylee stared at me worriedly.

Reaching for the hand closest to me, I lifted it and brought it to my mouth, kissing her knuckles. "I promise, baby. I'm good."

———

"It's ready," Brylee said with a smile on her face. I glanced up from my phone and stared at her curiously. We sat on the couch with *Lucifer* playing on the screen.

She reached over, grabbing the remote, and paused the TV. Setting the needles to the side, she lifted the medium sized pink and white blanket. A wave of emotions passed through me, and tremors shot through my heart seeing my daughter's name in the middle and her birthday right under both in pink.

"It took me a little more time than I liked because I couldn't get the name and numbers right, since I never did either before, but once I got that, it was easy. It's a few months late, but I thought Scottlynn should have a baby blanket. What do you think?" She nibbled nervously on her bottom lip.

I couldn't find the words to express how I felt at the moment. Brylee always thought of my daughter and went out of her way to show how she loved her.

I reached out and ran my hands over it. "It's perfect, baby." Flicking my eyes to her, I met her smile. "You did an amazing job. She's gonna love it."

Tossing my phone to the side, I reached for her. She got the hint and set the blanket down then moved closer to me. I wrapped her in my arms, hugging her, maybe too tight, but I couldn't help it. Brylee always considered my daughter and was doing little things for her that went above and beyond what she was here for.

"Thank you," I said, getting choked up.

She pulled back and stared at me with a smile on her face.

"I can't wait to give it to her."

"Me neither." I kissed her, deepening it as soon as my mouth touched hers. I didn't know what I did to deserve a woman like Brylee in my life, but I thanked God every day for sending her my way.

CHAPTER 28

BRYLEE

Shifting my weight to the side and fidgeting my hands, I waited for the door to open as my nerves ran wild. My stomach was a ball of knots, and my heart hammered inside me. Part of me wasn't sure being here was even a good idea, but I was ready to be at peace.

The door opened, and my eyes lifted, laying eyes on my dad with a smile plastered on his face.

"Brylee, I'm glad you decided to come." He moved back, opening the door wider.

Silently, I stepped inside the house. This was the first time I time I had stepped foot in my parents' house, and I felt indifferent about it. We were in the kitchen and dining room, but directly behind it was the living room.

"C'mon, your mom is finishing up a call." He nodded for me to follow him. We walked a couple steps into the room. I looked around the living room, noting how cozy it looked, decorated in navy blue, gold, and white. A navy blue sectional faced the large TV mounted on the wall. The TV stand under it held a few of pictures on it. I walked closer to it to examine it. It shocked me seeing pictures of myself.

"This is my favorite picture of you," Corey said, stepping up behind me and reaching for the photo. It was a picture of me with cake covering my face. I cheesed into the camera. I wasn't sure how old I was in it.

"You had been eyeing your cake the whole party, and instead of waiting for it to get cut after singing happy birthday, you shoved your whole face in it, shocking us all. You had just turned five."

I bit the inside of my cheek, noting that was the same age they left me with my grandparents.

Not bothering to respond, I turned and looked around once more. On the wall that led to the hallway there were some more pictures, but this time, I didn't go get a closer look. My chest grew taut as I took a seat.

"Sorry about that. That call took longer than I expected," Breann said, coming into the living room.

"Where's Brandon and Brittani?" I asked. It was too quiet for them to be here.

"Summer camp," Corey said, setting the picture down and walking to take a seat with Breann following behind him. They sat on the other side of the sectional, thankfully giving us space.

An awkward silence filled the room. My legs bounced rapidly. The whole point of me agreeing to come here today was to clear the air so I could finally gain closure. It had been a couple weeks since learning about Breann's pregnancy, and since then, it had been weighing heavily on my mind.

"We're glad you agreed to come and talk to us. Your dad and I hate the tension between us," Breann started. "Hopefully, once you leave here, we'll have the air clean and can work on building our relationship."

I wasn't as optimistic, so I ignored that part.

"Why now?" I asked, finding my voice. The sooner the conversation started, the sooner I could leave.

"What do you mean?" Corey asked.

"I mean, why are you trying to have a relationship with me now. I'm twenty-nine and no longer the little girl who wishes her parents gave a shit about her enough to be a part of her life. So, why now?"

They shared a look as if they were having their own conversation. When they looked back at me, I could see regret and remorse on their faces.

"I got pregnant with you at fourteen, Brylee. I had no business having sex, let alone getting pregnant. When our parents found out they all were furious. They wanted me to get rid of you, but back then, I thought I knew it all and fought against them. Both me and your dad wanted to prove our parents wrong and show we could be good parents. Eventually, our parents accepted that we were going to have you and got on board. They helped during my pregnancy. Neither of us were old enough to work, but you never lacked any of the necessities you needed to survive.

"Once you got here, reality set in. Trying to go to school, raise a colic newborn, and still be a teenager was hard. Your dad would stay over to try to help, but even then, it got to be too much." Breann paused and ran her hand through her hair. Corey reached over, grabbing her hand. She gave him a shaky smile.

"After my freshmen year, I dropped out of school and got my GED. I was sixteen. I never really cared for school, anyway. My grades were good enough for me to pass, but your mom was always so smart. I knew I needed to step up and do more." Corey took over. "Even with getting a job and bringing in money to help, I was still young minded and childish. Both of us were. Things with me and your mom got shaky because the pressure of being a parent and growing up was setting in. I started caring more about partying and fucking around than my family. Your mom and I would fight and argue. Shit just got toxic as fuck.

"You were about three then, and by that time, you were with your grandparents more than us. While my parents helped, they also didn't pick my slack up so I could just bullshit around, but Breann's parents were never like that. They always spoiled your mom, and you were no different. Instead of being home with you, we would be out running the streets."

My hands balled on my lap, but I stayed quiet, listening to them. My lips tucked in my mouth, and my leg bounced again.

"By the time graduation came, we made a deal with Mom and Dad," Breann said. "They would keep you while we went to college. It was their one stipulation that we had to graduate with a degree, so that's what we did. You stayed with my parents, and we went to college. I'm not gonna lie, it felt good to be a normal college kid. You were taken care of, so we saw no need to hold back and dived right into the experience. Me and your dad had been shaky since my junior year of high school, always breaking up but too jealous to fully move from each other. It didn't stop in college."

Breanna swallowed hard. "I was so up Corey's ass back then that I was more worried about keeping eyes on him instead of being a mother. I'm not proud of it, but it's the truth. After college, we decided we weren't ever gonna leave each other alone and decided to make it work. You were doing good with my parents, so we didn't see the point in disrupting your life."

"Instead, you went about your lives as if I didn't exist?" Distain dripped from my voice. My chest felt heavy with sorrow. It took a long time for me to get over feeling unwanted. I put my grandparents through a lot acting out because of my parents. They would never understand the emotional rollercoaster they put me through.

"We did," Corey replied somberly. "It wasn't until we got older that we realized just how fucked up our choices were."

"We wanted to make it right, but by then, you were older and wanted nothing to do with us."

"Do you blame me? I hardly even heard from you two when you went away from school. Gran and Grandad were the ones who took care of me and made sure I had clothes and food on the table. Gran was there when I had my period for the first time. Grandad was the one who offered to kick the ass of the first guy who broke my heart. They never gave up on me, even during my rebellious stage, and where were you two? Nowhere to be found. Creating a brand-new family."

The tears that clouded my mom's eyes did nothing to me. It might be wrong, but it brought me satisfaction that she was so upset.

"We're sorry you feel that way, Brylee. You'll never imagine how guilty I felt when I was pregnant with Brittani. Knowing I was about to bring another kid into the world when I abandoned my first one weighed heavily on me. It still does. You're right. We missed so much, even with Mom and Dad keeping us updated, and there's nothing we can do to make up for it, but we want to try." The tears in Breann's eyes fell.

I blinked blankly at her, bouncing my eyes between the two. Dropping my head, I closed my eyes and gnawed on the inside of my jaw. My grandparents and Tripp's words played over in my head. I wasn't doing this for them. It was time I officially came to peace with our relationship so I could move on.

"I'm not saying things with us are gonna be sunshine and rainbows." Lifting my head, I stared at then. "As much as I would like to forget the past, I can't, but I don't want to hang on to it either. I'm willing to try to at least be cordial with you two." Their faces brightened. "This is for me, though. I'm in a good place in my life, and the last thing I wanna do is continue carrying baggage from my childhood. We can start slow and see how things go."

Feeling emotionally drained, I knew it was time for me to put some distance between us. I cleared my throat. "I should head out." I stood up.

"Oh, so soon? I was about to start cooking and—" Breanna started.

"No," I shut Breann down. "I just need some space right now, okay?"

She looked like she wanted to object, but Corey placed his hand on her leg. She turned to face him, and he shook his head. Her shoulders deflated in defeat.

"Can I at least get a hug before you leave?" Breann begged, her eyes pleading.

Exhaling a deep breath, I nodded stiffly.

Wiping her eyes, she stood and walked over to me, not wasting any time throwing her arms around me and hugging me tightly. At first, I stood still but, that didn't deter her. Her hold on me tightened. Closing my eyes, I slowly lifted my arms and hugged her back.

"Thank you, Brylee," she whispered in a shaky tone. Her eyes were still pooled with tears when we pulled apart.

"Got some love for your old man?" Corey asked.

Nodding, I stepped into his arms, accepting his hug as well. It felt odd. I didn't remember the last time I was hugged by my parents. I tried not to think about it.

"I want you to come back over soon for dinner. Maybe you can bring that pretty baby you watch and her daddy. Mom said you two are an item now, right?" Breanna smirked.

"Gran talks too much," I mumbled.

"We'll see." A nagging voice told me I needed to keep my guard up and protect myself from them, but I tried to ignore it. I wasn't sure how things would be going forward with me and my parents, but I was willing to give them a chance to right their wrongs.

———

"Trust me, Tripp. The Brylee you see today isn't the same one from when we were younger. Our girl has come a long way," Leia exclaimed, causing me to shoot daggers in her direction.

"I was not that bad!" I protested.

She waved me off while Tripp chuckled.

"For some reason, I find that easy to believe." His eyes leveled on me, and his mouth hiked into a smirk.

Gasping, I grabbed my chest. "I'm offended."

Again, he chuckled. "Tell me, Leia, what was teenage Brylee like?"

"Wellllll—"

"Leia!" I warned. "And don't act like you didn't used to be right at my side doing the dumb shit."

She shrugged. "Had to keep things exciting. Like remember that time we egged that guy's house you caught cheating on you?"

Tripp's eyes widened, and my head dropped.

Leia continued telling stories from when we were teenagers. I put up a small gripe, but honestly, I didn't mind Tripp knowing more about me. It was nice having two people I cared about in the same room getting along.

"So, this innocent act you put on in the beginning was all for show?" Tripp's eyes bored into me with intensity.

"Of course, not. I was being professional." An innocent grin split on my face. Finally, things in my life fell in line, and I couldn't be more thankful.

Leia hung around a little longer before announcing her goodbye.

"We're on for class Saturday, right?" she asked over her shoulder.

"Yep! I'll meet you there," I confirmed.

"Good! Hey, Tripp, if you're free, you should come check our spin/yoga class out. You don't know a real work out until you do."

"I might take you up on that one day."

She grinned, then looked at me, winked, then left out the door.

Shaking my head, I walked back to the couch and collapsed on Tripp's lap. His arms instantly went around me, and I melted against him.

"I see why you're friends with her. She's cool people."

I smiled and closed my eyes. "That's my sister. Always has been."

"You're feeling better then?" He was referring to my visit with my parents. I came home and told him all about it. It left me feeling drained and emotionally exhausted.

"Yeah, I'm fine now. Even better now."

He rubbed my arms soothingly. Peace covered me like a weighted blanket.

"I was thinking chicken Alfredo for dinner. What you think?" I opened one eye and peeked up at him.

"Works for me."

A knock on the door caused my eyes to open. "I wonder if Leia forgot something."

"I'll get it," I groaned when Tripp moved me to the side.

I leaned back on the couch and laid my head back closing my eyes again.

"Baby!" My eyes snapped opened just in time to see a woman jump on to Tripp and slam her mouth into his.

My stomach churned as my blood ran cold. My throat grew dry, and jealousy crept inside me. Standing, I slowly made my way over to the door.

Finally, Tripp seemed to snap back into reality and pull the girl off him. "Skye? What are you doing here?"

My stomach dropped while my heart squeezed hearing *that* name. My eyes locked on her. Dread shot up my spine. Blood rushed through my head.

I took her in, and the way she smiled up at Tripp as if he was her whole world caused my stomach to recoil.

"Surprise!" Skye grinned. "I finished the program. Aren't you happy to see me? I missed you so much." She threw her body back into him and hugged him tightly.

I swallowed hard around the lump that formed in my throat. My heartbeat slowed, barely containing its rhythm. It felt as if I was having an outer body experience, unable to find my words. Neither of them seemed to notice me, and I felt as if I was interrupting an intimate moment. The air around us suddenly felt stifling.

Tripp hadn't mention Skye coming home. In fact, I thought she had a couple more weeks before she came home. I wasn't sure what this meant for the two of us, but I didn't like how unsettled it made me feel inside.

Slowly, I crept toward the steps and up to my room. Closing the door, I went to my bed as pressure built behind my eyes. My chest was heavy.

I stared forward at nothing in particular until my eyes focused on my music box. Rising, I slowly moved to my dresser and brushed my hand over the box. My heart swelled thinking of Tripp restoring something that meant so much to me.

I didn't know what Skye being home meant. I wanted to believe nothing would change between me and Tripp, but the way my luck typically played out, I knew that was too good to be true.

CHAPTER 29

TRIPP

I t took me a minute to snap back into reality and realize that Skye stood in front of me, healthy and smiling. Confusion filled me as I eyed her. As far as I knew, she had a couple more weeks left in her program before she came home, so if she was here, then did that mean she left early?

"You didn't leave the program early, did you? You only had a couple more weeks left, and I know you could have made it," I spoke.

She snickered and shook her head. "Of course, not. I lied about my release date to surprise you. Are you happy?" Her smile grew.

Slowly, I bobbed my head. "Yeah, of course, I am. I'm just surprised is all." Reaching back, I gripped the back of my neck and exhaled a sharp breath. A whirlwind of emotions passed through me at the thought of Skye being home for good. While I was happy she was back, I was still on edge not knowing if her sobriety would last.

She rushed me again, throwing her arms around me. "Now that I'm home, I can prove to you that you can trust me and don't have to worry about me relapsing. I can't wait to rebuild our relationship. I missed you so much." She nuzzled her face into my chest.

A weight sat on my chest. Now that she was home, I knew I had to come clean with Skye about me and Brylee. Speaking of Brylee…

I pulled Skye away from me and turned toward the living room searching for Brylee. When I didn't see her, an uneasiness passed through me.

"Where are your things?" I asked thickly, shifting my eyes back to Skye.

"On the porch."

Stepping around Skye I walked outside to grab her bags, bringing them in the house, and setting them near the door.

Skye walked further and the house and looked around. "It feels good being in a familiar place. I was counting the days down until I came home." She spun around beaming at me.

I needed to go talk to Brylee and check in on her. I could only imagine the thoughts pondering through her head. Thankfully, Scottlynn was with my mom and wouldn't be back until later this evening.

"I'll be back, a'right?" I told her and started for the steps.

"Yeah, okay. I'm gonna grab something to drink."

Making my way upstairs, I headed for Brylee's room. The door was closed, and I didn't even bother knocking before pushing it open.

Brylee sat on her bed, staring at the ballerina box I had restored. It wasn't even playing, but she had it open, staring at the small black figure inside.

"You disappeared on me," I said, causing her eyes to snap up.

"I didn't hear you come in." She blinked slowly. I hated the guarded look in her eyes and uncertainty in her voice.

Slowly, I made my way to the bed and took a seat next to her. "Why'd you come up here?"

Her shoulders lifted. "Felt like I was imposing." She looked down at the box again.

Frowning, I reached out, gently tugging the box out of her hands and leaning over to set it on her pillow. "Why would you feel like that?"

Again, she lifted her shoulders. I hated how tense and unsettled the air around us was. Even before we made it official, things weren't this bad.

"I didn't know she was coming home. You know that, right? I was just as shocked to see her."

"I'm not upset about her being home. I mean, it's a good thing, right? It means she's clean and completed her program."

My brows grew tighter. Her words didn't match her tone. It was clear that Skye's sudden appearance had shaken her up.

"What now?" she followed up.

"What do you mean?"

"Skye's home now. Does that mean I'm out a job?"

My eyes squinted. "Why would you be out a job?"

"Because Scottlynn's mom is home. She can take over now, right?"

I bit the inside of my cheek. The last thing I wanted to admit out loud was that I wasn't comfortable with Skye being alone with our daughter. At least not right away. Truthfully, Scottlynn didn't know her mom, and I wasn't sure how she would even respond to Skye being back around.

Turning so my body faced her, I reached out and grabbed her hands. "Just because Skye is home doesn't mean *anything* is changing." I made sure to emphasize anything because I didn't want Skye coming home to mess things up with me and Brylee. Over the past weeks, we had grown closer, and I had fallen for her. The last thing I wanted was for her to shy away from us.

Her teeth scrapped over her bottom lip before her tongue swiped across it. Her eyes still looked guarded, but some of the brightness I was used to crept to the surface.

"Are you gonna tell her about us?" Brylee asked with her head cocked to the side.

That was the million-dollar question. While I would have loved to ease the changes in my life on to Skye, I knew that wouldn't be possible.

I nodded. "Yeah, I am. I haven't hidden us this far, and I don't plan on doing it now. When it comes to Scottlynn, nothing changes there either. *You're* her caregiver, and I'm not gonna take that away from you." I grew quiet for a second. My stomach flipped thinking about my next words. "There is one thing, though."

Brylee's brows crinkled as her eyes narrowed. "What's wrong?"

Inhaling a sharp breath, I pushed it out and ran my hand over my head. "It won't be permanent, but Skye's gonna have to stay here temporarily." Brylee's face went blank, and her lips pressed together. "She doesn't have anywhere else to go, and we might not be together anymore, but she's still Scottlynn's mother. I can't just put her out on her ass. We'll tell her about us and let her get adjusted. In that time, I'll work on finding her a place. I don't want you to be uncomfortable, though."

Her face was still blank. I waited to see how she would respond. Her lashes lightly brushed over the top of her cheeks as she blinked slowly.

"It's your home. You can have whoever you want live here."

I shook my head. "This has become your home too. Before you came to live here, this was more like a house but having you here has brought life in this house. Like I said, I don't want you to be uncomfortable. If having her here will be too much for you then—"

"It's fine, Tripp," she cut me off. I was about to speak, but she reached over and grabbed my hand. "I mean it. It's fine. I'm not so heartless that I want you to turn your back on her. As long as she understands that you two are over and boundaries are set, then I'm fine."

The corners of my mouth lifted. I gripped her hand and pulled her body closer to mine. "You're one of kind. You know that, right?"

A smile ticked on her face. "I do, and it's best you always remember that."

Chortling, I reached behind her and grabbed the back of her neck. Pressure built inside my chest as my heart expanded, slamming against my ribcage. Wetting my lips, I moved in, pressing my lips into hers. The kiss was slow, full of emotions, and yearning. Heat flooded my body. Slanting my mouth, I took it further. My tongue forced its way into her mouth, causing a sigh like moan to come from Brylee. Blood shot down to my dick, causing me to groan.

Regretfully, I pulled back. "As much as I want to take you right now, I need to go handle the situation downstairs." She pouted, poking her bottom lip out. "I want you to come down with me."

The pout turned into a frown. Grinning, I pecked her nose, then her lips. "C'mon, it's about time you two meet."

Brylee didn't look excited about my request, but she also didn't fight me when I stood and pulled her up with me.

"I hope she has manners, Tripp. I'll be respectful, but I know how a woman scorned and jealously can make a person. I don't want any drama."

I tossed a look over my shoulder as I led her out the door. As much as I would like to assure her that she had nothing to worry about, I couldn't promise it. Skye had been on the defense her whole life, so she wasn't the easiest egg to crack. I hoped she wouldn't fight this, though.

Instead of answering, I continued leading her out of her room and downstairs. Her hand tightened around mine when we got to the living room. Skye sat on the couch, looking at home, scrolling on the TV.

"Skye," I called out.

With a smile on her face, she turned to face me. Her eyes dropped to mine and Brylee's attached hands, and it slowly faded. She knitted her brows and set the remote down, standing up.

"Hey, I was wondering what was taking you so long." Wariness passed through her eyes as they bounced between me and Brylee.

"I had to handle something."

We stopped in front of Skye.

"You're the nanny, right? Bailey?" Skye asked slowly, her voice upbeat but mixed with confusion.

"Brylee," Brylee corrected with a forced smile.

"Brylee, this is Skye, Scottlynn's mom. Skye, Brylee. She is the nanny but also my girl." There was no point to ease into it. It was easier to rip the Band-Aid off.

It took a moment, but Skye must have realized what I said. Her face dropped, and her mouth turned upside down. Her eyes tightened as her nose scrunched. "Your girl?"

"Yeah."

Skye crossed her arms over her chest. "When did this happen?" She didn't try to hide the attitude from her voice.

"A little while back."

Skye cut her eyes into slits and pinched her lips together. "And you never thought to tell me?" Realization covered her face. "Wait... is this why you always brushed me off when I mentioned us still being together?"

Sighing, I released Brylee's hand and brushed my hand down my face. "I should have said something when I came to visit you, but I didn't want to do anything that would set back your recovery or progress, so I thought it would be best to wait until you came home. I wasn't lying to you when I said you should come home and continue working on yourself and rebuilding your bond with *Scottlynn*." I emphasized Scottlynn since she hadn't mentioned her once.

Skye's eyes shot to Brylee. Fire burned behind them, enough to burn Brylee to a crisp. "So, what now?" Her attention came back to me. "You and the nanny are together, so I'm left alone to just figure shit out?"

I shook my head. Over the years, I had learned to have high patience with Skye. There were times she was irrational and stubborn. She acted on impulse and was always in fight mode. It was the last thing I wanted to deal with right now.

"That's not what's happening. Just because me and you have run its course doesn't mean I'ma just leave you out to dry. I plan on helping you get settled and readjusted to being home. You can stay here for the time being. I want you to get comfortable with Scottlynn again, and her with you. Focus on getting a job and—"

"Getting a job? Tripp, you know I'm not the best worker. My anxiety—"

"I know, Skye, but we can figure it out. There's work from home jobs, so you don't have to worry about going into a job."

Skye puffed her cheeks out still looking unhappy about the situation.

"Look, I don't want to cause any problems," Brylee said, stepping up. "All I want you to do is respect me and what me and Tripp are building. I won't interfere with you and your daughter, but I want you to understand I love her and have a relationship with her too. As long as you don't try to come between either, then I have no issue with you."

Skye started at Brylee with a bored expression. "You do know me and Tripp have known each other damn near our own lives? We have a bond that can't be broken or replaced. I don't have to interfere with anything because things between us come naturally."

While I thought Brylee would get upset by Skye's words, she seemed unbothered and completely different from how she was upstairs.

Brylee smirked. "You two might have *had* a bond, but we've built something solid, and it's still growing. I'm not worried about old flings." Brylee batted her lashes innocently.

"Okay!" I stepped between them. "If we're all gonna co-exist together, then everyone needs to get along. Skye, let's go take you to the other guestroom so you can get settled."

"The other guestroom?" Her face balled up. "I want to sleep in *my* room. The same room I was in before I left."

"Skye." I sighed. "C'mon, man. I'm tryna make this easy for everyone. My parent will be dropping Scottlynn off in a couple hours, and I want you settled before that happens."

By the look on her face, I could see Skye wanted to fight me, but she must have saw I wasn't with the bullshit because her body relaxed, and her face fell.

"Fine. This is going to be an adjustment. I'm not used to seeing you with someone else, and you're all I know." Her voice grew quiet. "But I get it. I fucked up, and I have to deal with the consequences. Show me which room is still open. I appreciate you still letting me stay here for the time being."

Releasing a heavy breath, I nodded with a slight smile. "A'right. I'ma grab your bags. Your stuff is still in my room, but I'll make sure to put it in the one you'll be staying in."

"Okay."

Brylee cleared her throat. "I planned on starting dinner soon. I'm making chicken alfredo. Is that okay with you?" she asked Skye. The fact that she was trying made me grin. Brylee was a good person. I knew I could count on her being cordial.

"That's fine." Stepping around Skye, I went for her few bags. "C'mon." I nodded for her to follow me when I got to the stairs.

I knew most would think this situation was crazy. I already felt like it was too much, but I hoped everyone could be mature about the situation and get along.

———

"Are you sure this is gonna work out?" my mom asked, looking at Skye warily. Her and my dad had just dropped off Scottlynn, who was in the living room with both Skye and Brylee. It was no surprise she instantly went to Brylee, not even paying the woman who birthed her any attention. I paid close attention to Skye to see if it bothered her any, but it was hard to tell. She watched Brylee and Scottlynn with her face balled up, but she hadn't made an attempt get Scottlynn.

"No, but I'm hopeful." Rocks sat on my stomach now that all four of us were here. There was no telling if things would go left or not.

"I don't pity you, son." Dad laughed and patted my shoulder.

"Yeah. Brylee's better than me because this shit wouldn't have flew with me." Mom narrowed her eyes. "You need to get this under control because it's a disaster waiting to happen."

"I know." Me and Brylee made eye contact, and she gave me a small smile.

"We should get going if we're gonna make dinner," my dad announced. "You have fun, son." He chuckled again. "I'll see you ladies later. Skye, I'm happy you're home."

"Thank you." Skye smiled at him. Brylee waved.

"Don't y'all be over stressing my son out," Mom told them, making Brylee laugh.

They said their final goodbyes. Once I closed the door, I exhaled a deep breath and silently prayed we made it through the night at least.

Walking into the living room, I walked to Brylee. Scottlynn instantly reached for me and called out to me.

I swooped her out of Brylee's arms and showered her with kisses. "You missed Daddy, Munchkin?"

"Da-da!" she exclaimed, clinging to my face.

Chuckling, I turned to face Skye. She watched us with a pinched expression.

I walked over to her and took sat next to her on the couch. "You wanna hold her?"

Her eyes locked on Scottlynn. "Sure."

Pulling Scottlynn away, I held her out for Skye to take. The moment Scottlynn was in her arms, she grew fussy. Her body was still facing mine, and her arms reached for me.

Skye balled her face up. "Here. Maybe it's too soon." She thrust Scottlynn back to me. I grabbed her, and she laid her head on my chest.

"She's probably just tired. It's close to her bedtime." Brylee attempted to ease the tension that built around us. "How about I get her bathed and ready for a bed, then you can take over?" she suggested.

Scottlynn went to Brylee easily, rubbing her eyes right on cue.

"Yeah, sure," Skye said.

Brylee walked off, and Skye released a deep breath. It looked like a weight was lifted off her. "She hates me." She huffed a laugh out.

I shook my head. "She doesn't hate you. She just gotta relearn you. She's getting to the point where she's learning people and gaining her own personality. Once she gets to know you again, she'll be more at ease."

Skye still looked defeated. Moving closer to her, I wrapped my arm around her to attempt to comfort her. "It's your first night home. Don't be too hard on yourself."

Her body relaxed into me.

I went back to work tomorrow, and it would ease my mind to know that there was peace while I was gone.

CHAPTER 30

BRYLEE

"You really got a sister-wife situation going on over there, huh?" Leia joked, snickering.

Rolling my eyes, I used my napkin to wipe Scottlynn's mouth before picking the baby food back up to continue feeding her.

"Don't play with me."

It'd been a week since Skye had been back, and it'd taken some getting used to. We stayed out of each other's way for the most part. She mostly stayed in her room, so it didn't make it hard. When she decided to make herself known, she made sure to walk around like she owned the place in little ass clothes and made no attempt to bond with her daughter. Her attention always seemed to focus on Tripp when he was home.

"For real, though. You're okay with your man's ex living with you guys?"

I swallowed hard and focused on Scottlynn and the mess that had appeared on her mouth again from her food. Before leaving, I asked Skye if she wanted me to leave her there so they could spend time together, and she told me no before rolling back over in bed and going back to sleep. Truthfully, it pissed me off that she never felt the need to spend time with her child. She acted as if Scottlynn didn't exist, and I was sure Tripp had to notice it.

Sighing, my chest deflated. I sat the food and spoon on the table in next to me and shook my head.

"No, but there isn't much I can do. It's not my house, and Tripp isn't gonna just toss her out."

"He needs to do something. It's not fair to you having her there."

"It hasn't been all bad. She pretty much ignores us, besides the couple times she tried to act like I was her maid or something." My nose scrunched thinking about her calling me and asking to clean up a spill she had made. I stared at her like she was crazy and went back to what I was doing.

Leia shook his head. "You got more patience than me. Ain't no way I would be that mature. You're not scared Tripp is gonna want her back?"

"It hasn't been easy, but no, I'm not. Tripp seems to genuinely want to help her, and that's it. He's found a few at home jobs for her, and hopefully she's been applying for them so she can work on getting her own place."

As patient as I'd been, it wasn't easy living with another grown woman, especially when she was my man's ex-girlfriend.

"Hmph, I suppose that's good then. Are things with Tripp okay?"

Another sigh fell from my mouth. "As good as they can be."

Truth was, me and Tripp hadn't had sex since Skye came back. It was already hard with the hours he worked, but it felt weird that his baby mama was now in the house. Normally I would sleep in his room, but knowing it used to be Skye's, and having her down the hall had me back in mine.

"Sis, you better not let her fuck with your relationship. Don't change how you and your man interact because her ass showed up uninvited."

I snickered and picked Scottlynn up before kissing her on the cheek and tucking her in my arms. She had dozed off while we were talking.

"I told Tripp as long as she doesn't step outta line, I'm good. Anyway, how are you and your boo?"

The last thing I wanted was to keep talking about was Skye being back. I wanted a few hours where she didn't exist in my world.

"Girl, I had to block him." She rolled her eyes.

My mouth dropped as I huffed a laugh out. "Again? What the hell for this time?"

I still hadn't met this guy Leia was dating, but it seemed like she blocked him every other day.

"Girl…" she started before going into the explanation. Leia was one of the most dramatic people I knew, so just like I expected, the reason wasn't that serious. "I'll unblock him later today." She waved her hand in front of her.

Laughing, I shook my head and rocked Scottlynn gently. She was getting so big, but I couldn't help but still treat her like that little bundle she was when I first started.

"What's going on with your parents?" She picked up her food and opened the container. Instantly, my nose scrunched as my stomach turned at the scent.

"What the hell are you eating?"

"Fried catfish with baked mac n cheese and potato salad."

My mouth turned up as bile grew in the back of my throat. "That potato salad stinks."

Leia looked at me confused and lifted her container to sniff it. "No, it doesn't."

I side-eyed her then the container. "If you say so." I shrugged. "Anyway, things with my parents are coming along. We've texted here and there. They want me to come to dinner one day soon."

I still was on guard with my parents, but I tried to put the effort in I promised them I would.

———

My eyes fluttered open, feeling my bed dip and a body climb in behind me. Tripp's arms wrapped around me, and he pulled me into his hard body while kissing on the back of my neck.

"What are you doing?" I asked sleepily.

"Enough of this sleeping apart shit. It's been almost two weeks since I've held you in my arms or been inside you. Since you refuse to sleep in my bed, I had to come to you."

His length pressed against my ass. My sex throbbed. Wetness grew between my legs.

"But—" I twisted my neck to try to face him. Instead of letting me finish my sentence, he crashed his lips into mine.

"But nothing. I appreciate you trying to be mindful of Skye, but that don't mean you gotta neglect yo' man." His hand went from my stomach down between my legs. Inhaling a sharp breath, I opened for him, allowing him to sneak his hand under the big t-shirt I wore and rub on my lower lips.

My eyes closed when he went back to kissing me while thumbing my clit. A moan left my mouth. I felt Tripp moving behind me, but I was too lost in the kiss to realize he had stripped out of his boxers and pushed his dick at my entrance.

"Open up for me," he mumbled against my lips.

Lifting my legs, I sighed when his tip rubbed against my lips then pushed inside.

"Wet and warm just like I remember," he groaned, pumping in and out of me. His one hand was still on my clit, and the other had wrapped around me again and caressed my breast.

A whimper fell from my mouth before I bit down on my bottom lip, nearly drawing blood. It had only been a couple weeks, but it felt like forever since I felt Tripp inside me. My stomach fluttered like a wild bird's wings. My chest exploded with fireworks.

Tripp's strokes were steady but also patient like he tried to take his time and savor this. Arching my back more into him, I dropped my chin to my chest and squeezed my pussy around his dick. He pinched my nipples that were sensitive to the touch, causing me to moan loudly. His teeth nipped the top of my ear.

My pussy gushed as he moved in and out of me quicker. I tried to keep my moans down, but it was hard. Tripp shifted his hips, finding that sensitive spot inside of me and abusing it repeatedly with no remorse. A ball of passion knotted inside me as my eyes rolled to the back of my head while I came.

"Gon' ahead and wet me up, baby." He nipped my ear again.

Attempting to speak, I failed, releasing a loud moan instead. Tripp trailed open-mouthed kisses down from my ear to my neck. The way my heart slammed against my chest; I was surprised I didn't have a heart attack. Sex with Tripp was always passionate. He fucked like he was being paid for it.

"Yes, right there!" I cried out. My body trembled. Tripp pinched my clit and pounded me roughly. I grabbed his wrist and dug my nails into him. My pussy soaked his dick, leaking between my legs.

"Oh, fuck," he gritted, digging his face into my neck.

My body jerked again when I felt his warm release fill my walls, causing a chain reaction for me to cum *again.*

Tripp didn't remove himself from within me right away. His face rested in my nape of my neck as he panted. His breaths tickled my skin, causing the hairs to raise. My heart hammered violently inside me. Blood rushed through my veins.

A whimper left my mouth when he finally pulled out of me. I winced then sighed, closing my eyes.

Tripp turned me around, so I was on my back. Creeping my eyes open, I stared up at him lazily.

"From now on, you sleep in my bed, or me in yours when I'm not at work. No more sleeping apart." His voice sounded final, leaving no room for objection, not that I was planning to anyway. Fuck trying to be polite. I wasn't about to neglect my man to make any female comfortable again.

Making my way downstairs, I headed for the kitchen to get break-fast started. I slept a little later than normal. After waking up alone and seeing Scottlynn's room empty, I figured they were downstairs waiting for me. Normally when Tripp was off, if he was up to it, we would put

Scottlynn in her highchair, and he would help me with breakfast. It was one thing I looked forward to.

My brows scrunched seeing the living room empty and hearing low murmurs coming from the kitchen. When I stepped into the kitchen, I paused at the scene in front of me. Tripp, Skye, and Scottlynn were all sitting the around the breakfast nook, eating. Scottlynn chewed on a teething ring. My stomach twisted as I registered what I saw. Jealously flooded my veins. They looked like a family.

My tongue swiped across my lips, and I bit on my back molars when Skye laughed lightly and brushed her hand over Tripp's shoulder. It looked innocent enough. Tripp sat where he always did, and she sat in *my seat.* He wore a regular black t-shirt and basketball shorts and seemed to enjoy her company. The two had history, so it was a given, but I hated how twisted it caused my insides to feel.

Swallowing hard, I stepped further into the kitchen. Tripp was the first person to notice me. "You're finally up." He grinned at me.

I met his eyes and nodded then shifted my attention to the table that was covered in empty to-go containers. Out the corner of my eyes, I noticed Skye's face fall, and her lips pinched together as she observed me.

"You guys already ate," I mentioned.

Tripp looked down at the table. "Oh, yeah. Skye was craving one of her favorite breakfast spots, so she ordered us some."

"I forgot to order you some, though. I'm so used to it being just me and Tripp."

I cut my eyes at her. She batted her lashes but had a fake smile on her face.

"Wait, I thought you got enough for everyone?" Tripp frowned at her.

"It didn't cross my mind to order for her, and she was asleep. I didn't want it getting cold."

"It's all good. *I* cook, so I can make *my own* food." I tossed her a smirk of my own. The last thing I was about to do was let her get under my skin. "And how's my pretty girl this morning?" I leaned down and cooed at Scottlynn, who reached out and whined for me.

I picked her up and kissed her cheek. "Let me make something to eat, then I'll give you all the attention you want, pretty girl." I kissed her cheek again before sitting her back in her highchair, causing her to whine. Skye barely batted an eye at her, causing me to smack my lips and shake my head. I turned to go to the fridge. I was craving French toast with extra cinnamon sugar.

I pulled my phone out of my back pocket and went to my music app, putting it on shuffle so I could get started. To say I was irritated was an understatement, but I tried to push it down. It didn't take me long to get lost in my own world as I prepared the French toast mixture.

"My bad about breakfast." I jumped, cracking an egg all over my hand.

"Shit," I hissed and reached over to grab the dry towel when my nose scrunched at the smell of raw egg, and my stomach churned. Pushing past Tripp, I hurried to the trash can, hit the button with my foot, and emptied acid inside of it. My eyes watered as my throat burned while I threw up nothing. Tripp was at my side instantly, rubbing my back.

"You okay, baby? You getting sick?" I grabbed the paper towels he held out for me, wiping my mouth, then tossing them as well.

"No. Those eggs must be old or something because the smell is killing me." My nose twitched.

I pulled out of Tripp's touch and went to the sink to wash my hands. My throat felt raw, and my stomach was even more empty.

"The eggs are still good," Tripp mentioned. I turned and saw him examining the carton.

"Mhm. Maybe it's whatever I ate yesterday then." I shrugged, wiping my forehead with the back of my hand. Feeling eyes on me, I shifted my gaze to Skye. She stared at me with a look I couldn't make out. I frowned finally seeing her full outfit. She looked to be in pajamas still. Her shorts might as well be panties, and she wasn't wearing a bra. Whatever weight she lost when she was on drugs seemed to all come back in rehab. She was slim yet curvy and healthy looking.

"Don't you think you should put some clothes on that are more appropriate?" Distain dripped from my mouth.

One corner of her mouth lifted. "This is what I always used to wear around the house. Something wrong with my pajamas?"

I crossed my arms over my chest. "Besides the fact that your pussy is damn near hanging out."

She snickered. "Girl, my pussy is covered." She waved me off then looked at Tripp. "Are you still taking me by the mall?"

I whipped my head in his direction.

"Yeah. Go ahead and get dressed, then we'll head out. I wanna make sure Brylee's cool." His eyes were locked on me, so he didn't see Skye roll her eyes and stalk off.

Tripp stepped toward me and went to touch me, but I moved out of his grasp.

"Something you need to say?" His brows furrowed.

"You think it's okay that your baby mama's walking around here half naked like that?"

His frown deepened. "Huh?"

"Don't huh me, Tripp. You heard me. The way she walks around here is disrespectful as hell. Then why are you taking her to the mall?" The little tolerance I had for the situation was slowly dwindling.

Tripp seemed genuinely confused before running his hand down his face. "Honestly, I didn't even notice it. I'm so used to seeing her walk around like that, I didn't think about it. I'll talk to her about it and make sure she's covered up if she's gonna be out of her room. I'm sorry." The tension slightly faded from within me. "And she needs more clothes. She doesn't fit a lot of the stuff she had before rehab, so I told her I would take her to get a few things.' He licked his lips, and he gazed at me with a penetrating stare. "You wanna come with me?"

I shook my head. "Hard no. Plus, I'm meeting Leia for our spin/yoga class in couple hours. When is she leaving?"

It was starting to be clear what type of time Skye was on, and I knew I wouldn't be able to tolerate her being here too much longer.

"I'ma take her to go view some apartments while we're out."

Nodding, I went to walk around Tripp, but he grabbed my wrist before I could pass by. Electric jolts shot up my arm.

"Are you sure you're, okay? You don't normally throw up out of nowhere. You sure you not getting sick?"

I shook my head. "I'm fine. I told you." I went to pull my arm out of his hold, but he held on tighter.

"Thank you for dealing with all this. Not everyone would accept their man's ex living with them, regardless of the situation, but you're a real one. I'm working on getting her out of here, though, okay? Just bear with me a little longer."

My body relaxed. "Just know you owe me for this."

He lifted the corners of his mouth. "I know I do. You name it. I got you." He dipped his head, pressing his lips into mine. My heart tripled in speed. I stood on my tiptoes to kiss him harder.

He pulled at me looked at me with so much passion it was smothering. "I love you."

My eyes bucked at his confession. He grinned and winked before turning away and heading back to where Scottlynn was in her seat. My words caught in my throat as I watched him leave out of the room.

I love you. While I felt the same way, it caught me off guard that he said it first. The music on my phone stopped playing, and it vibrated on the countertop, gaining my attention. I shifted my eyes to it see it was Gran.

Blinking a few times, it took a moment for my body to catch up with my brain. Moving to the counter, I grabbed my phone, answering it, and pressing it to my ear.

"Hey, Gran," I said into the phone.

My stomach still felt unsettled, but I didn't think it was because the eggs. The idea of Tripp taking Skye shopping made my skin feel tight and prickly like ants crawled under it. I tried to focus on what Gran said and not what could happen while they were out, spending time like a family.

CHAPTER 31

TRIPP

"T hank you for all this, Tripp. You always take such good care of me." Skye grinned up at me as we walked through the mall.

"It's all good. I just want to make sure you didn't think I was saying fuck you when you got out. You need anything else before we get out of here?" I didn't tell her about the apartments I had lined up, wanting to surprise her. I look down at my hands that were full of bags. While I didn't let her go too crazy, I did let her get enough things to hold her over for a bit. She pushed Scottlynn's stroller and looked around.

"How about in there." She stopped and pointed at the lingerie store.

My face balled up. "Why you need to go in there?"

Skye looked up at me innocently and gave a small smile. "Can't a woman just want to feel sexy?"

I narrowed my eyes and slid my gaze to the store again. "Nah, we gon' skip that."

When I looked back at Skye, her face fell. "But I'll be in and out."

I shook my head. "Nah, my girl wouldn't be cool with me buying you lingerie. She didn't trip about the clothes, but that's pushing it."

She scoffed and rolled her eyes. "I didn't realize she controlled how you spend your money."

My mouth turned upside down. "She don't, but I'm also not about to disrespect her or our relationship either. Just like if I was still with you, I wouldn't be buying any other woman lingerie."

"It's not like I'm some random female. I'm your child's mother."

"That still doesn't make it okay. No, Skye."

I could tell she wasn't happy, but I wasn't worried. Sometimes talking to Skye felt like I was talking to a child. She hated when she didn't get her way, and it was clear that hadn't changed. I knew it was partly my fault since I always gave in most times.

"Oh, and no more wearing those skippy ass pajamas around the house, either. That shit ain't cool."

A dull look appeared on her face. "Let me guess. *You're girlfriend* had an issue with it."

I stared down at her, and I noticed her eyes were full of defiance.

"It's just not cool. You need to be covered up. I'm letting you stay there because you have nowhere else to go, but you need to respect that it isn't your house anymore."

Her eyes flashed as her nose flared. "Wow."

Sighing, I dropped my head, closing my eyes and counted to ten. I wasn't trying to be mean or hurt her feelings, but I had to be direct with Skye for her to get the picture.

"Anywhere else?"

"No, I'm good." Attitude radiated off her.

Ignoring her, I peeked down at Scottlynn, seeing she had fallen asleep. She was up pretty early this morning, so I wasn't shocked.

"A'right. Let's head for the car then."

Silently, we walked through mall. She pushed the stroller, walking a few steps ahead of me. It was the first time she offered to take the lead with anything involving Scottlynn. That was one thing I wanted to talk to her about while it was just us two.

Skye didn't say anything else, seeming to be lost in her head, which concerned me, but I tried not to think too much on it. The month she'd been home she hadn't given any indication that she was planning on relapsing. I knew one of the things I was told from one of the people at rehab was that an addict would always be an addict. I just hoped Skye didn't let me down this time and fought the urges, because I didn't have anymore chances to give.

———

"What do you think of this one?" I ended up taking Scottlynn to my parents' house before going to the first apartment, figuring it would be easier to check the apartments out without her.

Skye had been quiet since the mall. This was the third apartment we looked at. All three were a decent size, two bedrooms, and this one had two bathrooms. They were all about ten to fifteen minutes from where I lived and reasonably priced, closer to downtown.

I turned to look at her. She looked around with an unenthusiastic look on her face.

"It's nice," she expressed blandly.

Sighing, I clenched my jaw and straightened my back. "Skye, you gotta give me something. I'm trying to make sure you're good and help you get on your feet, but you gotta meet me half way."

Her eyes slid to me. Her eyes burned with anger. "Sorry if I'm not happy about coming home and finding out I've been dumped and also kicked out of my house!"

"Look, I fucked up by not telling you sooner about me and Brylee. I thought I was doing the right thing, but I should have been honest. You know how much I pride myself on the truth, so I'll own that. As for kicking you out of your house..." My words trailed off. I ran my hand over my head, not sure what to say. Maybe it did come off like that, but that was one reason I tried to help her find a new place. I didn't want her ass out and feeling abandoned.

"I don't get why I gotta move out. That place is just as much mine as it is yours. In the time I was gone, you moved on and replaced me." Her voice cracked. "Now I'm forced to live alone... without you. I don't want to do that, Tripp."

Her tears caused an ache in my chest. One thing I always hated was seeing her cry.

"Skye, man," I said soothingly, stepping closet to her. I pulled her into my embrace and hugged her. "Stop crying. You know I'ma always be here for you, right? We might not be in a relationship anymore, but you're still my daughter's mother and my best friend."

"Until your girlfriend forces you to choose."

My body tensed briefly. "Brylee isn't like that. She understands the position you have in my life, but at the same time, you need to know hers and respect it. We had our time, and it ran its course. There's nothing wrong with that. You're home, sober, and it's time for you start your life the right way."

She sniffled and dug her face further into my chest. "I just don't want you to give up on me."

I tightened my hold. "I won't. As long as you're trying, then I got you, but Skye," I pulled her away from me and stared at her redden eyes, "I need you to try harder with Scottlynn. I get you're getting readjusted, and before you went to rehab, you had a hard time handling her, but I need you to put in the effort with her. She's your daughter, and the two of you need to bond. Once you're more comfortable with her and vice versa, I want her to be able to come stay the night with you and all that, but I gotta see an effort. It's been a month, and I've barely seen you hold her."

She didn't reply right away, pulling away from me and wiping her eyes. "I'm just scared Ima fail." Her words sounded throaty. She cleared her throat. "I don't want to let you down by not being a good mom. I've missed most of her life because I was getting high and then getting clean."

"Do you have the urge to get high now?"

She choked a strained laugh out. "I feel like it's always there, but no. I don't."

My shoulders fell in relief. "Parents fuck up, Skye, but we learn and figure it out. I'm here for you. My parents, too. I'm sure even Brylee would help if you asked. No one wants to see you fail. Scottlynn is still young. You have time to reintroduce yourself to her and let her get to know you. Her birthday is in a few months, and I want you around for it. Don't let your doubts and insecurities stop you from being the mother I know you can be."

She noticeably swallowed hard and shifted her eyes to the side. "Do you really think so?"

I grabbed her chin, so she faced me again. "I do. You've overcome so much shit, Skye. Shit most people would have folded over. You're stronger than you give yourself credit for. I just wish you believed that."

A small shaky smile graced her lips. "Okay. If you think I can do it, I'll try harder."

That caused me to grin. "That's all I ask." I nudged her. "Now c'mon on so you can look around."

Hopefully, Skye believed my words and found faith in herself. I could speak as much life into her as I wanted, but it meant nothing if she didn't believe it herself.

CHAPTER 32

BRYLEE

"**O**kay, hopefully your Daddy isn't busy," I said, taking Scottlynn out of her car seat and putting her in her stroller. I had just finished running errands and decided to stop by Tripp's job since I was close. Her cheerful babbling caused me to grin.

"Yeah, let's go see Daddy." I handed her the toy phone, and she started pressing it, causing music to play.

Spinning her stroller around, I headed for the entrance of the firehouse. I had never been here before, and hopefully it wouldn't be too much of a bother. We stepped inside, and few members I hadn't met walked around and tinkered with the trucks.

"Can I help you?" someone asked.

I spun around to face them. "Yeah, I'm looking for—"

"Yo, Brylee!" a deep voice called out to me.

I whipped my head around and smiled seeing Harlem heading my way.

"Hey." I waved.

A crooked grin spread on his face. His eyes flickered down to Scottlynn then back at me. "I'm assuming you're here for TJ?"

I nodded.

"He's in the gym. Hold up." He turned. "Aye, candidate! Go grab TJ and tell him to bring his ass to the main floor."

I snickered as some younger looking boy hopped up and did as he said.

"What you doing in our neck of the woods anyway?"

I shrugged. "Was in the area and realized I never been here before, so I decided to drop by."

He licked his lips and eyed me. "You're looking good."

I blushed. "Thank you."

"Get yo' ass away from my girl, nigga," Tripp called out, approaching us.

My smile grew so large my cheeks hurt when I laid eyes on him. He had laser vision on me. He stopped in front of me and put his arms around me before giving me a kiss.

"What do I owe this pleasure?" he asked after a few seconds, pulling away and staring at me with glittering eyes.

"Me and pretty girl were out running errands and wanted to stop by and say hi."

Tripp released me and grinned down at the stroller. Scottlynn was going wild in the stroller trying to get at him.

"Hold up. When this happen?" Harlem asked as Tripp bent down to take his daughter out of the stroller. His eyes bounced between me and Tripp.

"Don't worry about that. Just know she's mine, so all that flirting shit is over with."

Harlem smirked. "Unless I take her from you."

I snickered as Tripp grabbed my hand and pulled me away.

"Set her stroller by the wall," he told Harlem, ignoring his last statement.

I followed behind him and up some steps until we got to a dining room looking area with a small kitchen behind it. It looked over the main floor.

"I hope it's okay we stopped by," I mentioned once we sat down.

"Hell yeah. I'm always happy to see you two." He kissed Scottlynn's cheek. "What y'all been up to today?"

"Nothing much. Ran by the mall, then to the grocery store to grab a few things. Oh, I got the cutest dresses for Scottlynn. I was on my way out and saw them on display in the window and had to stop and grab them."

Tripp looked at me with mirth on his face. "You keep buying her clothes like she ain't got a closet full of shit with tags on it that she'll probably grow out of soon."

My shoulders lifted. "I can't help it. Little girl clothes are too cute to pass up. Oh, and I grabbed some more decorations for her birthday party from the party store out in West Valley."

Since Tripp asked me to be in charge of her party, I'd been buying things here and there as I saw them.

"I put the order in with Sugar Bliss because she books up fast, and we only have a few months left. I showed her the cake I showed you the other day, and she said she can do it." I stopped the rambling about my day seeing the serine expression on Tripp's face. "What? Why are you looking at me like that?"

A soft smile played on his handsome face. "I just love how hard you go for my daughter. The excitement you have about her birthday… it just feels good, man." He shook his head. "I really lucked up running into you at the store that day."

My cheeks heated. "Oh." I pushed a loc out of my face. "She deserves to be celebrated in a big way. You only get one first birthday."

"The way you love my daughter is one reason I love you."

My heart leaped. I felt warm all over, and a giddy rush went through me. This was the second time he made the declaration, and just like the first time, I was caught off guard. Staring into his dark eyes showed me he was being true about his words. They glittered with passion, stealing my breath away.

"I love you, too." I confessed, feeling my pulse beat in my throat.

The corner of his mouth lifted in a panty wetting grin.

Scottlynn and I stayed around until the alarm went off, scaring her and calling for Tripp to get back to work.

"I'll see you tomorrow," he said, kissing me and handing Scottlynn over.

"TJ, c'mon!" his captain called out.

Tripp winked at me then turned and hurried off. I stood there watching everyone prepare to leave. It felt good knowing my man was about to rush off to save lives.

———

"I'm glad this could happen. It's long overdue," Gran spoke.

Me, her, and Breann currently sat in her backyard watching Brittani and Brandon play on the jungle gym set. Scottlynn was inside taking a nap. We had stopped by after leaving the firehouse, and my mom and siblings just so happened to be here.

"What?" I asked.

"You two finally getting along. I've prayed for this." Gran looked at ease as she looked from me to my mom. Breann stared at me happily as well.

"Yeah, well. Can't go into my thirties holding a grudge like that." I shrugged.

"Me and her dad still have a lot to make up for, but we're willing to put the work in. We're just glad she's giving us a chance."

"Life's too short to be so angry. I'm proud of you, Lee-Lee." Gran reached over and placed her hand on my knee.

"Thanks, Gran." She tapped my knee a couple times, then turned her head slightly to the side. "Also, when were you gonna tell us?"

My brows furrowed, and I stared at her in confusion. "Tell you what?"

She removed her hand and sat straight. Her eyes scanned me over, and she squinted. "That you're pregnant."

I choked on air and grabbed my chest. "What? Gran, I'm not pregnant."

She continued staring at me, shifting her eyes down to my stomach.

"Gran, stop." I covered my stomach. "I'm not pregnant."

"I wouldn't doubt her. She told me when I was pregnant with you, Brandon, and this baby, before I even knew. She probably would have done Brittani too, but I learned that when I went to the hospital because I wasn't feeling well," Breann commented.

My stomach twisted. I opened my mouth to speak but quickly snapped it shut, crushing my brows together. Shaking my head, I tried to speak, but suddenly, my tongue felt too large for my mouth.

"Have you gotten your period? Been sick?" Gran asked.

I thought back to the eggs the other morning. "I mean, I'm sure it was because the food was bad. I smelled it," I tried to justify.

Gran smirked. "You need to take a test and talk to Tripp."

Still lost for words, I turned my eyes to the yard, staring out into it aimlessly. My mind ran wild trying to process Gran's determination. I wasn't pregnant. I couldn't be pregnant. Not this soon.

"If you keep thinking hard, you'll get wrinkles. Just stop by the store and take a test on your way home," Gran mentioned. "You and yo' mama pregnant together. Lawd."

I cut my eyes in her direction. She talked about this so casually, like her words wouldn't blow my world up if they were true. My stomach fluttered as my hands rested on it. Could I be carrying another life inside me?

CHAPTER 33

TRIPP

"How's it having your girl and your baby mama in the same house?" Troy asked, drinking his beer. I leaned back on his couch and gapped my legs.

"Like I'm waiting for a tornado to land," I expressed truthfully.

"You brave as fuck for that. Joy would've tried to beat my ass if I asked some shit like that." He chuckled.

"Man, if my baby mama and girl was cool with living together, I'd be busting them both down," Terrence commented.

"Shut yo' stupid ass up," Troy said.

Ignoring Terrence, I focused on Troy. "Trust me. There's a couple times I had to play referee between the two, but thankfully, Brylee does a good job ignoring Skye for the most part. It's all good, though, because I just paid the security deposit and first month rent at a place Skye was approved for. She'll get the keys next week, then she'll be out of the house."

"Why the hell you paying for her again? You acting like a sucka," Terrance cut in.

"Because she's still my daughter's mom."

"That you've done too much for. You already paid for her to go to rehab for what, the third or fourth time? Now you about to get her a crib and probably gonna furnish it for her. You doing too much, bro."

"As much as I hate to agree with his ass, I have to. That is a lot for someone you don't want to be with anymore," Troy agreed.

"Just because I'm not with Skye anymore doesn't mean I don't still have love for her or want to see her down bad. Y'all know she doesn't fuck with her family, and I'm all she's got foreal. She knows she's gotta get a job and maintain things once we get her settled in her place."

Terrance shook his head, finishing rolling his blunt. "She be taking advantage of you, and you let her."

I ignored him.

"And how yo' girl feel about all this?"

I bit the inside of my cheek. Brylee was trying to be supportive, but I could tell she was getting to the end of the rope with everything. "She's good. She gets the situation. The most important thing is Skye being stable enough to have a relationship with Scottlynn. Brylee gets that."

Terrance shook his head and went in his pocket. "You light that shit, and Joy's gonna fuck you up," Troy warned.

Terrance stopped just as he was about to light his blunt. "Fuck. I forgot." He stood. "I'll be back."

"Look, big bro, I'ma just say this, then I'll leave it alone." Troy gave me a serious look. "I always looked up to you and how you handled your relationship. You know that. You never cared about the backlash you got when it came to Skye and stood ten toes down behind her, which I respect, but at some point, you gotta let her fall on her ass. She's never gonna do better if you're always there to save her. Skye's always been your Achilles heel. That's why when I learned you and Brylee were together, I was happy because *finally* you were with something you didn't have to keep saving and could be happy with. Just by looking at Brylee, I knew she had feelings for you. I'm not telling you to say fuck Skye, but at the same time, don't do anything that's gonna mess up the future you're tryna build with Brylee, either."

Troy stood and turned to head for his bar behind the couch.

I bit the inside of my cheek and stared at the TV, but currently, I wasn't hearing anything coming from it. I thought about the last couple times Brylee and Skye were in the same room and how Brylee would make the habit of leaving. She was back to sleeping in my room like before, but something was still off with her. Skye had made an attempt with Scottlynn. It was a slow start, but a start.

Maybe Troy was right. I had put a lot on Brylee. She already had doubts before about me and Skye, and I didn't want her to gain any more. Skye was due to move out next week. I told her the first couple months I would handle her rent, but after that, she was on her own. She would have supervised visits with Scottlynn until I felt comfortable enough for her to be alone with her. After that, she wouldn't be my problem anymore. I just hoped Brylee had a little more patience left.

————

"She should be here any minute," I told the leasing manager of the apartment building. We were currently waiting for Skye to meet us to get her keys.

"I have other things I need to take care of. I can't wait all day," she said with an impatient look on her face.

"I'ma call her again." I stepped away, pulling my phone out of my pocket. I checked my messages first, seeing Skye hadn't responded to my text. Next, I went to my call log and hit Brylee's name.

"Hey. You on your way home? I'm starting dinner."

I couldn't stop the smile from forming on my face. "Nah, I'm still at the apartment. Is Skye still at the house?"

She was quiet for a second. "No, she left like an hour or two ago."

Skye had her car back. Thankfully, Brylee was able to get another rental through the insurance company until she found a new car.

Sighing, I pulled the phone back and checked the time. "Okay. I'll be back home in a few."

"See you soon... love you."

My smile grew. It was the first time she had said it first. I knew the first time I told her, it caught it off guard, but I couldn't let another day go past without confessing it to her.

"Love you too, baby." Hanging the phone up, I pushed a frustrated breath out and went to Skye's name. Clicking it, I listened to it ring before her voicemail come through.

Irritation filled me. I felt a headache forming as my temples throbbed.

Locking my phone, I turned and slid it in my pocket. "Can we reschedule? Something must have come up."

She didn't look happy. "I hope this isn't a reflection on how she's gonna be going forward." Her eyes narrowed before she turned and walked off.

I leaned against the wall. I dropped my head forward. Skye wasn't starting off on a good note. I hoped after the talk we had she would show she was serious about doing better. Her flaky behavior was already looking too familiar.

Pushing my frustration down, I pushed off the wall, heading for the steps. Skye better have had a good reason as to why she didn't show up today. Her days of having multiple chances with me were over.

———

"You still haven't heard from her?" Brylee questioned as she loaded the last of the dishes into the dishwasher.

"Nah. I don't know what her ass on, but if it's some bullshit, then that's it." My jaw clenched. I had been trying to get ahold of Skye since leaving the apartment, but eventually, her phone went straight to voicemail.

"You don't think something happened to her, do you?"

I thought about that. Even with her issues, Skye didn't just disappear without a word.

I leaned on the counter and crossed my arms over my chest. "I don't know. She doesn't have any friends."

I had called the two hospitals in the city to see if Skye had been admitted and was told she hadn't. It eased some of my worry but didn't stop the sinking feeling in my stomach.

"Do you think she's somewhere getting high?"

The thought crossed my mind, and as much as I would like to say no with certainty, I couldn't. "I hope not."

Brylee turned the dishwasher on then stepped in my space. She leaned up and wrapped her arms around my neck. "Don't stress yourself out too much. Skye is a grown woman. I'm sure she's fine."

Wrapping my arms around her waist, I rested my hands on her ass. Instead of responding, I lowered my head, resting my forehead against hers. I didn't want to think about Skye relapsing or the money I wasted again with rehab and then the apartment. I tried not to think about my brother's words from earlier.

"Does it make you upset that I'm trying to help her as much as I am?"

Brylee pulled back, and her eyes bounced around my face curiously. "Tripp, you are the most caring man I ever met. If you would have just said fuck her, I would have been shocked, because that's not in your character. I knew about Skye and the situation surrounding her from the beginning. You're an honorable man, and it's one of the things I love about you." She moved her hand to my cheek and cuffed it gently, grinning softly.

In my heart, I knew I would never meet someone like Brylee again. Her heart was genuine and full of so much love for those around her.

Our moment was cut short when Scottlynn cried on the baby monitor.

"C'mon. let's go check on our girl," she said, pecking my lips then pulling away.

Brylee easily fit when it came to me and Scottlynn. She stepped up in the motherly role for Scottlynn without meaning to. Although she was originally hired to be just the nanny, she was so much more than that. My daughter was more attached to her than she was her own mother. I knew if anyone ever hurt Scottlynn, Brylee would fight for her. The last thing I wanted to do was feel like I was pushing Skye out of the picture, but when it came to family, Brylee's face shined brightly in the forefront.

CHAPTER 34

BRYLEE

I was just putting my shoes on when the doorbell rang. Grabbing my purse, I left the living room to the front door.

"Grandad, you could have called me to come out." My mouth snapped shut and confusion filled me.

"Cor... Dad," I corrected. I was trying to get better with calling them Mom and Dad. There were times I had to catch myself, but I slowly got more comfortable with the titles. "What are you doing here?"

"Dad told me he was supposed to go with you to the car lot, and I asked him to let me take you. Hopefully that's cool."

"Uh, sure, but do you even know about cars?"

His shoulders slightly lifted. "I'm no mechanic, but I know a lil something. Plus, I figured it'll be a good opportunity for us to spend some time together."

Chewing on the inside of my cheek, a small smile crept on my face, and I slowly nodded. "Yeah, sure."

"Cool. You ready now?"

Nodding again, I made sure to lock the bottom lock before stepping outside.

"Do you know what kind of car you want?" Corey asked as we walked to his car.

"I think I want a small SUV. Nothing over the top but still spacious enough."

We got in the car, and I put my seatbelt on.

"And you want to buy or want payments?"

"I got a decent amount from the insurance company after my car was totaled out, so I guess it just depends."

"Any particular lot?"

I shook my head.

"That's cool. One of my dudes owns a car lot. If you want, we can try there first."

I side-eyed him. "He's legit, right? I'm not gone get no lemon, am I?"

Corey chuckled and threw his car in reverse and started down the driveway. "Hell nah. He's legit. I wouldn't even bother taking you there if he wasn't."

Nodding, I got more comfortable in my seat and played with my phone. The radio played, filling the silence.

"Your mom told me the news."

My nose scrunched, and I turned to face him. "What news?"

For a second, he took his eyes off the road and peeked down at my stomach. I tensed and pressed my lips together. I still hadn't taken a test.

"Don't listen to her or Gran."

He faced the road again. "You and him are serious then if there's a potential you could be pregnant? Last I knew, he was just your boss."

My teeth scrapped over my bottom lip as my eyes shifted forward. It felt weird even having this conversation with Corey. We never talked about me dating or anything personal or intimate before.

"Yeah, I mean... this is kind of weird." I rubbed the back of my neck. "We're together, and things have happened, but Gran is just talking."

"You two use condoms then?"

My eyes bucked as my cheeks flushed. "That's personal, don't you think?" My nose scrunched.

Corey chuckled. "My bad. I guess I just hate that this is the first time I'm having this kind of talk with you. I got a few years until Brittani is at the age where boys steal her attention, but in reality, you should have been my first go ahead. Guess I'm tryna make up for lost time."

I tucked my lips into my mouth, not replying right away, and looking down at my phone. "Tripp just makes sense to me, I guess. I always wanted to grow up, fall in love, have kids, and have a family. He fits the vision I had and treats me good. It just happened over time."

"I know I might not have the right to speak on things like this, but at the end of the day, you're my first kid. My first daughter, and I always wanted what was best for you. I never wanted to see you settling for less. Your grandparents mentioned your ex and how they weren't a fan of him, but they don't have those same reservations about Tripp. I'm glad you found someone who values you and treats you like a man is supposed to treat his woman. He does do that, right?" He glanced at me, causing me to smile shyly.

"Yeah, he does."

"Good. You deserve that."

A giddy feeling filled my stomach as I sat straighter. It felt good to no longer hold on to so much anger when it came to my parents.

———

With shaky hands, I placed the test on the sink, then preceded to wash my hands. After a long internal battle with myself, I finally decided to take a test to put my mind at ease. Today had been a good day. Surprisingly, things went well with Corey, and I was able to find a small SUV to my liking and leave with it today. On my way home, I stopped by the store to grab a test. Scottlynn wouldn't back until tomorrow morning, and Tripp was at work, so now was the perfect time.

I dried my hands and sat down on the toilet, putting my head down and resting it in my hands. As much as I wanted to be in denial, I couldn't deny the small things changing with my body—mainly the sickness I randomly got.

Me and Tripp had danced around the thought of having kids in the future, but not right now. In reality, I would love to be a mother right now. Over the past couple months, I'd come to think of Scottlynn as my own child. It got harder not to cross boundaries when it came to our relationship. Tripp never seemed to mind, and even allowed me to make decisions when it came to her. That only caused me to long for my own child even more. I would love to give Scottlynn a sibling she could grow up with.

I wasn't sure how much time passed, but finally, I stood and walked over to the sink, picking the test up. I stared into the mirror examining myself at first. Nothing in my physical appearance gave I could be pregnant—not that I could see. Closing my eyes, I pushed a deep breath out then lifted the test.

I had to blink a couple times to make sure I saw things correctly. Before I was able to process everything, someone started obnoxiously ringing the doorbell. Frowning, I sat the test down and walked out of the bathroom and out of my room, then to the steps and to the front door. The person on the other side wasn't letting up and was now rapidly knocking on the door, too. Standing on my tiptoes, I checked the peephole, surprised to see Skye on the other side.

"Tripp! Tripp!" she yelled, pounding on the door.

My tongue dragged across my top teeth. It had been three days since we had seen or heard from her, and now here she was acting a fool.

Instead of answering right away, I went into the living room where I had left my phone. Unlocking it, I went to my call log and hit Tripp's name. Hopefully, he wasn't busy or in the field.

"Wassup, baby?" he answered.

"Your baby mama is here acting a fool on the porch, yelling, and banging on the door," I said, walking back to the door to unlock it.

I snatched the door open and balled my face seeing how out of it she looked. Her hair was in a messy bun. Her eyes were glossy with bags and dark circles under them, and her cheeks looked flushed. Her clothes were winkled.

"What the hell is wrong with you?" I spat.

She sized me up and smacked her lips. "Where is Tripp?" She attempted to walk into the house, but I blocked her.

"Not here. What are you doing here?"

Tripp spoke in my ear, but I wasn't paying anything he said any attention.

Skye let out an obnoxious laugh. "Little girl, just because you call yourself playing house with *my* baby daddy doesn't mean anything. This was *my* house long before he moved you in."

I didn't miss how her words slurred the more she talked.

"You can come back when Tripp's here. Until then…" I shrugged. Noticing the phone had gone silent, I pulled it from my ear and saw Tripp had hung up. Not bothering to call back, I slid it in my back pocket.

Skye laughed. "Don't you get it? Tripp loves me. He will *always* love me. We grew up together, and I had his child. He would never abandon me."

My eyes narrowed. "Good for you, but do you think he's gonna feel the same way knowing you're high right now?"

That knocked the smile off her face.

"You don't know what you're talking about!" Her eyes turned wild.

"I know you would rather disappear and go get your next fix instead of being here with your child, but you wanna scream about giving this man his first kid. The month you've been home, I've barely seen you interact with Scottlynn. You don't even give a fuck about her."

Skye flicked her wrist. "You're the help, right? Isn't that why you were hired? To take care of her."

My face balled in disgust listening to her. "You're pathetic, and Scottlynn's actually better off not having you in her life." My hand went to my stomach. I just found out I was expecting, and I already felt attached. It was mind boggling to me how Skye had no maternal connection with Scottlynn and how Tripp never picked up on it.

Skye grinned a snarky smile. Slowly, she clapped her hands. "Is that supposed to make me upset? I never even wanted kids!" She wiped her nose with the back of her hands. "Now, move so I can come in." Again, she attempted to push past me, but this time, I shoved her back, causing her to fall on her ass.

"I told you, you're not coming inside. You can wait out here like the trash you are until Tripp comes home." I turned and walked back into the house. Just as I was closing the door, Skye scrambled to get up and toward the door. I shut the door and locked it, then pressed my back against it.

Skye went back to yelling, pounding on the door, and ringing the doorbell. She had truly lost her mind. If this was ten minutes ago, before I took that test, I would have dragged her off the porch.

I wasn't sure how much time passed, but eventually, the knocking and yelling stopped. I turned and checked the peephole again. Seeing Tripp was now outside, I quickly unlocked and snatched the door open.

"You need to go, Skye! The fuck you come here showing your ass like this? What if your daughter was here? Do you even give a fuck about that? Not to mention, you're fucking high! I can't keep doing this shit with you!" Tripp's voice rose each time he spoke.

He was still in uniform, and his car was running. His face was bright red with his hands balled.

"Tripp, I'm sorry!" Skye cried. "I didn't mean to. I just got scared. You were kicking me out and replacing me. You know I don't do well by myself. Please. I won't do it anymore."

My eyes widened at her theatrics that seemed to come out of nowhere.

Tripp clenched his jaw. "No," he said tightly. "I'm done, Skye. Done! Do you know how much fucking money I spent to put you in rehab and then to get you that apartment that you never even showed up at! Too fucking much. I'm not doing it anymore."

"It's because of her!" Another switch flipped, and Skye was suddenly angry. She shot her eyes to me and pointed. "You send me away then move on with the nanny! Just fuck me and everything we've been through! I thought you loved me, and you just tossed me to the side. I can't do this without you, Tripp," she cried, and I felt like I got whiplash from how her mood kept changing.

"This has nothing to do with Brylee. In fact, you should be thanking her for being the mother you never were to your daughter!"

"That's her fucking job!"

I stood there frozen and in shock. Never had I seen Tripp this mad before. His body practically shook.

"You know what…" His nose flared, then he pushed a heavy breath out. "You need to leave, Skye. I been doing this shit with you for too long, and I can't do it anymore. I got a daughter I need to worry about. Not to mention myself. The more you keep taking, the less I got to give. I'll pack your shit up and go drop it off at your apartment."

"But where am I supposed to go? Tripp, you know I don't have anyone else."

I could tell he was struggling to keep it together. Tripp shook his head. "That's not my problem. The apartment is paid up for three months. You can stay there, but after that, you gotta figure it out. Don't come around here anymore, though."

Skye looked heartbroken, and a small part of me felt bad for her. She flicked her eyes toward me then back to Tripp.

"You lied to me just like everyone else in my life. You told me you would always be there for me, but you lied. Fuck you!"

Skye turned and stormed off going to her car.

Swallowing hard, I made my way off the porch to where Tripp stood. "Do you think she should be driving?"

Slowly, he turned to face me. His eyes looked blank, and his face was long. A shaky breath left his mouth, and he closed his eyes for a few seconds then blinked them open. "She's an adult."

I bit the inside of my cheek. I didn't know what to do. I knew that wasn't easy for Tripp to do. He still loved Skye and wanted her to do better. Knowing that she went right back to her old ways had to be a heavy pill to swallow.

"I'm sorry," I said.

His brows knitted. "For what?" His voice sounded raspy.

"I don't know. I just feel like the right thing to say."

While I would have loved to tell him about the test I took, now wasn't the time.

Tripp shook his head. "You don't have anything to be sorry about. Skye's made her choices, and now she has to live with them." He looked off in the direction of the driveway. Skye was gone now. I would have loved to know what was going through his head.

"She didn't do anything to you, did she? I know she can be irrational, especially when she's high."

I shook my head. That seemed to put him at ease some. He looked at me, but it didn't seem like he saw me.

"I gotta get back to work," he admitted.

My stomach flipped as I nodded. "Okay."

I thought he would head straight to his car, but he caught me off guard when he grabbed me and pulled me into him, hugging me tightly. I melted in his arms, loving how warm and secure I felt.

Tripp pulled back and grabbed my chin, forcing my face up. He stared at me for a long while then lowered his mouth to mine. I closed my eyes, drinking in his kiss.

"If she comes back, call the cops."

My eyes widened, but I nodded. It hurt my heart because I knew that wasn't easy for him to say.

"I love you," he declared. His eyes beamed with passion.

"Love you, too."

With one last kiss, Tripp released me and walked to his car. I stood there fumbling with my hands. Hopefully Skye would take the hint and stay away. The last thing I wanted was for her to come back and hurt Tripp even more.

CHAPTER 35

TRIPP

"T ripp!" Leo called out to me, gaining my attention. "You good, man? You been zoned out since we left the station."

We were currently on a call at one of the warehouses on The Shore. More than likely, it was a bunch of kids goofing around. We got calls like this all the time. I only had a few more hours left of my shift, and I would be lying if I said my mind wasn't elsewhere. As unbothered as I tried to be during the moment, I was more upset about Skye relapsing than I'd like to admit. I wanted to have faith in Skye and believe this time would be different from the others, but a small part of me knew she wouldn't stay clean. It was a punch to the gut that she didn't even last ninety days.

As soon as I pulled up to my house and looked at her, I knew she was high. I had seen the distorted, glassy, look in her eyes way too many times. The only difference between this time and the others was the anger I felt. For so long, I made excuses for Skye and tried to have empathy for her, but I couldn't do it anymore. I had my daughter to think about, and I couldn't subject her to that.

"I'm good," I finally said, grabbing my hat and placing it on my head as we pulled up to the warehouse. I had been so into my head that I didn't realize we had arrived at the scene. A few cops were already on scene, playing crowd control. People gathered in a crowd, some with their phones out recording. A couple teens were being held in handcuffs near one of the cars. Just like I figured, they were out here causing trouble.

"A'right, men, get focused. Lives are on the line," Omiras called, climbing out of the truck. The next few minutes, my mind was on autopilot as me and the rest of the team moved to put the fire out that was on the top, left hand side of the building.

"I need some Narcan over here!" I heard one of the crew shout. Apparently, this was one of the abandoned warehouses where junkies came to get high.

We moved through the warehouse checking for more bodies. Cap called for more ambulances over his mic. There were a couple bodies against the wall, some nodding off, not even realizing they were just saved from being burned alive.

"Oh, shit," I heard a mumble. "Aye, Cap," Leo called out.

I turned to look and saw him eying a body on the ground.

"I got a can here," I said, making my way over.

"Nah, I got it," Leo rushed out.

I frowned when he stepped forward. "Why not go check over there?"

"What's wrong with you?" I tried to look around him.

"Tripp, let me talk to you," Omiras started, grabbing my arm. My eyes caught sight of a familiar body.

I snatched away and hurried around Leo. "Skye?" My eyes widened.

I dropped to my knees and picked up her head. "Skye!" I shouted. My heart squeezed inside me. She had dried up vomit on her face and clothes. I checked her over, and my stomach dropped seeing the needle next her and mark on her arm. Skye never did anything that hardcore before.

"I got her." Royce dropped down. He placed the Narcan in her nose.

Skye's body twitched before she coughed, her eyes wild. When they finally landed on me, and lazy smile formed on her face.

"Tripp!" She strained to get up, slowly reaching up to touch my face. "I knew you'd save me."

Her body suddenly shook in my arms.

"She's seizing. Watch out, Tripp! I need a cart over here." Royce pushed me out of the way and went to work.

It felt like I was having an out of body experience as he and Journi worked to stabilize her.

"Aye, TJ, man." Leo grabbed my shoulder, but I shook him off. It was hard to breath as my throat tightened with anxiety. My nerves rattling as blood raced through me. I had only seen Skye OD one time before, and it wasn't this bad.

Guilt crept inside me. Was it me telling her I was done that drove her to the edge? Skye had always been codependent on me, and I ignored it for a long time. I hoped me no longer enabling her would push her to do better, but I guess I had put too much faith in her.

"We got her stable, and we're about to load her up. You riding?" Royce asked.

It felt like Déjà vu, except last time it was Brylee on the stretcher.

"Go ahead. We got it from here," Omiras assured me.

I looked over my shoulder at him. I was having an internal battle with myself on if I should even go, but he made the choice for me.

Nodding, I followed behind Journi and Royce, feeling like the knot in my stomach was growing and not knowing the outcome of this recent event.

———

I had been at hospital for over two hours, waiting for Skye to finally come to. On her way here, she had crashed, and they had to resuscitate her. Now, she had been asleep. They got her stable, and I'd been sitting here with my mind racing and chest feeling like it was about to cave in. I had spoken to Brylee and let her know what was going on, and just like I knew she would be, she was sympathetic.

I stared down at Skye, watching as her chest rose and fell slowly.

Her skin looked pale. Beeping sounds from the machines she was connected to sounded like nails to a chalkboard as I listened to them.

Eventually, Skye stirred and groaned. Her eyes fluttered under her lids before finally coming visible.

"Tripp," she uttered in a raspy tone.

My jaw clenched, and my body hardened.

A small smile formed on her chapped lips. "What happened?" She coughed a couple times as her eyes bounced around the room. So many things swirled through my mind, I didn't know where to begin. For too long I handled Skye with kid gloves, and it was time to rip the Band-Aid off.

"You overdosed and almost died in a warehouse. What the fuck were you doing in that warehouse, Skye? Since when do you even do heroin?"

She winced at my harsh tone, but I didn't care. Fire boiled inside me, fueling the brewing anger I had.

Skye swallowed hard. "I didn't mean to," she murmured, almost kidlike. "I was just so upset, and one of my friends offered... I didn't think it would go that far."

"Do you realize you died, Skye? They had to shock your heart back to beating all because you were upset? Do you know how selfish you sound?"

"It's your fault! All I wanted was to come home and for us be together, but you replaced me."

I shook my head and pushed a heavy breath out of my nose. "You gotta stop blaming everyone else for your shit, Skye! Take some damn accountability!"

The tears started, but I couldn't find it in me to be fazed by them. "I know. I know, but you're here, so that means you still love me? I'll go back to rehab, and this time, stay longer. I know I can fight the urges. I just can't do it alone." She reached for me, but I stepped back.

"I can't, Skye." I swallowed around the knot in my throat. "This is it for me. You don't give a damn about yourself, so I can't either. I just wanted to make sure you made it and let you know I'm heading to the courthouse first thing in the morning to file for full custody of Scottlynn. I don't want you around either of us until you get your shit together. I can't be the anchor holding you together anymore. You gotta find a reason to fight for yourself." I turned to leave.

"Tripp, wait!" she called out. "I'm sorry! I'll do better, I promise!" Her machines went haywire. "Tripp, don't leave me, please! I need you!" she cried.

It hurt to ignore her cries and walk away, but Skye needed tough love. She wouldn't get better without it.

Nurses came rushing in, attempting to calm her belligerent rant. My heart was heavy in my chest, but at the same time, relief filled me. For too long I had put so much energy into Skye and her wellbeing. Each step I took away from the room I felt like I shed a piece of dead weight that had been attached to me for too long.

Knowing Scottlynn and Brylee were at home waiting for me caused some light to shed down on me. The family we had formed over the last few months meant more to me than anything I'd felt before. I felt peace when I thought about them and what lied in the future for us.

———

"Are you sure you're okay?" Brylee asked as we laid in bed. She faced me with a worried expression on her face. She had been checking in on me since I came home.

One corner of my mouth rose, and I ran a hand down her arm. "I told you I'm fine, baby. Just taking in how beautiful you are."

Her cheeks flushed. "I'm glad. I didn't know what to expect when you came home."

I pulled her more into me. "Coming home to you and Scottlynn makes everything okay. You two are what's important to me now. The family we're building is my focus." I held Scottlynn for over an hour when I first got home, just taking the pure innocence babies possessed. My daughter was the best thing that ever happened to me. I would do whatever I had to do to protect her.

Brylee's eyes bounced around my face, and she licked her lips. Her face had gone from calm to nervous.

"What's wrong?"

"I'm glad you mentioned something about building a family because I have something to tell you."

My brows furrowed. "What?"

A shaky smile spread on her face, and she grabbed my hand, moving it to her stomach. Her eyes were glued on my face, watching me. It took me a second to comprehend her gesture. My eyes darted down to where my hand was and then back to her face.

"Wait you're…" My words got caught in my throat.

Tears clouded her eyes, and she nodded. "Yeah, I am."

Excitement slammed into me. I grabbed Brylee, yanking her into me and crashing my mouth into hers, kissing her intensely. Passion gushed up my spine, filing through my body. My heart hammered wildly. The love I felt for Brylee, and now our unborn child, couldn't be expressed into words even if I tried. This felt like a new beginning. A redo at my shot for a real family.

I pulled back and gazed into her orbs.

Since the day I met her, Brylee had been the definition of what I wanted when it came to a mother and wife. I tried to fight it at first, but looking back on everything, I knew our paths were meant to eventually come together and form one.

EPILOGUE
THREE MONTHS LATER...

Brylee
"What happened to my baby?" I asked, making my way over to where Tripp currently held a crying Scottlynn. She looked so pretty, even red faced with tears in her eyes. She wore a white t-shirt that I got custom made. It had birthday girl with donuts printed inside the letters and a big one on the back with the same printing. She wore a pink, blue, and white tutu.

"Mama," she whined reaching for me.

My heart still swelled every time she called me that. It happened out of nowhere at first, with her just calling out the name, but eventually, it started happening when she saw me. I didn't know if I should correct it, but Tripp told me to leave it alone since I was a mother to her and the only one she knew.

"She was trying to walk and fell. She's fine," Tripp said rubbing her back.

"Aw, my big girl." I kissed her tear-stained cheeks.

"It's her birthday. She can cry if she wants." Gran walked over.

The party was coming to an end and had been a success. The small hall was decorated to perfection, and I knew she wouldn't remember it, but I got enough pictures to show Scottlynn when she got older. A lot of the family that was here had already started to leave, and I knew Scottlynn was due for a nap.

"Tripp, I have something for you," she said, handing him a gift bag. "I know it's Scottlynn's day, but it's okay to gift dad, too." Gran winked at him.

Tripp looked toward me, and I shrugged. He looked inside and reached in the bag, pulling out a square book.

I grinned seeing him open it, and his eyes lit up as he flipped through it. "Now you have your first official baby book for your baby." He turned and threw his arms around Gran.

"Thank you for this," I heard him mutter.

She smiled and patted his back. "You're welcome. We'll make sure she has one for every year too."

I loved how close Tripp had grown to my grandparents. They had adopted both him and Scottlynn into the family with ease.

"We're about to get going, Lee-Lee." I looked over and saw my mom waddling over. It was kind a strange knowing we were both pregnant at the same time. She was two months ahead of me but showing more than I was. My small stomach had just started officially forming at five months.

Things with my parents were better than I could have expected. They were trying hard to repair our relationship, and my mom was ecstatic to be a part of my first pregnancy.

"Okay. Thank you for coming, y'all."

My siblings rushed to hug me. My mom attempted to touch Scottlynn, but she whined and shielded away from her.

"She used to be so nice." Her face balled.

"Don't do my baby. She's just sleepy." I kissed the top of Scottlynn's head. On cue, she laid her head on my shoulder.

My dad came over and hugged me the best he could with Scottlynn laying on me. "You guys still coming for dinner next Wednesday, right?" he asked.

"Like clockwork."

While we still did Sunday dinners at my grandparents' house, my parents started their own thing when I came over on Wednesdays. Sometimes Tripp was able to join us, depending on his work schedule.

"Bye, y'all. Thanks for coming," Tripp said to my family.

Grandad ended up coming over, and he and Gran said their good-byes eventually as well.

"All the gifts are in your car, nigga. Ima start charging y'all," Terrance complained.

"Shut up." Tripp shoved him, causing me to grin.

I had grown close to his brothers, seeing them as my own. They treated me like a little sister they said they never wanted.

"Let me see her before we leave." Rose approached and reached for Scottlynn, but she wasn't having it.

"You know she don't pay anyone any attention when her mom's around," Tripp senior said.

I thought his family would have something to say about Scottlynn and the mom thing, but they embraced it like it was natural. No one said anything against it, which made me happy.

We had some issues with Skye at first popping up, high and showing her ass. Turned out she was on drugs worse than before. I was worried Tripp might backtrack and try to save her but he stood strong. He had full custody of Scottlynn, which wasn't hard for him to obtain, and we'd talked about me adopting her too.

"You guys still okay to keep her tomorrow night?" Tripp asked his parents.

Evie was throwing a party for her fiancée's birthday, and although I couldn't drink, we were still attending. She was another one who had embraced me right away, happy to see Skye out of the picture.

"Of course," Rose spoke.

I yawned and adjusted Scottlynn.

"Here, let me take her. You don't need to be holding her anyway." Tripp grabbed Scottlynn, who was now asleep. She whined at first until she was against his body and nuzzled her face into his shoulder.

"You act like I'm so fragile." I playfully rolled my eyes.

"Girl, he sounds like Troy!" Joy walked up. She had recently announced her pregnancy. She was a month behind me, and Troy had been over the moon.

"You're carrying precious cargo. That's why." Troy hugged her from behind and rubbed her stomach.

Tripp had wrapped an arm around me, and I laid my head on him, smiling at the happy couple.

"Terrence, you see your brothers settling down and starting families? You need to follow behind them. You're not getting any younger," Rose fussed.

"But Ma, you and Dad always told me to be a leader, not a follower."

I snickered. Terrence was always stressing everyone out. He kept things entertaining, I could say that.

"Looks like everyone is gone, and we're done cleaning up. You ready to get home?" Tripp looked down at me and asked.

I nodded. "Yeah. I wanna lay down and you to rub my feet."

He grinned. Pregnancy had been easy so far. At first, I was always sick, but once that sizzled out, I had no complaints. Tripp had been the perfect daddy bear, always there when I needed him, no matter the craving or growing pain I was experiencing.

"When do you guys find out the sex again?" Tripp senior asked.

"In a week. I can't wait." I placed my hand on my stomach. I wanted a boy, but Tripp surprisingly wanted another girl. It was beautiful seeing him as a girl dad, though, so I wouldn't be upset.

We all started out of the hall. I was glad the day went off without a hitch.

"Ima follow y'all so I can drop these gifts off," Terrence said.

We drove my truck, but apparently, there still wasn't enough room. I loved how loved Scottlynn was.

Tripp opened the passenger door for me and helped me in the car, then went to the driver's side.

Before he started the car, he reached over and grabbed my hand. "Thank you for today. Because of you, our baby had a perfect party." He lifted my hand and kissed it.

One thing I loved was how affection Tripp was. It didn't matter where we were or who was around.

"It was no problem." I downplayed it, fighting back a smile.

For so long, I was looking for love in the wrong places, but now, I found someone to love me correctly and out loud. I didn't realize how much I craved it until Tripp. Even with our tricky beginning, I wouldn't trade our outcome for anything in the world.

The end!

CHAPTER 36

MORE TAY MO'NAE

STANDALONES:

4 Ever Down With Him
He Ain't Your Ordinary Bae
Overdosed off a Hood Boys Love
These H*es Ain't Loyal
These H*es Doin' Too Much
These H*es Actin' Up
When Love Becomes A Need
When Love Becomes A Reason
When Love Becomes A Purpose
This Heart Plays No Games
This Heart Still Holds You Down
Riskin' It All For A Bad Boy
Rescued By His Love
Tempted Off His Love
DND: Caught Up In His Love
Imperfect Love
Got It Bad For An Atlanta Boss

NOVELLAS:

Let Me Be Your Motivation
Xmas With A Real One
Valentine's Day With A Real One
Switch'd Up
Please Me
Still 4 Ever Down With Him
The Way You Make Me Feel
Who I Used To Be

SERIES:

His Love Got Me On Lock
My Love Is Still On Lock
Addicted To My Hitta
Serenity and Jax: A Houston Hood Tale
A Houston Love Ain't Never Been So Good: Yung & Parker
A Bad Boy Captured My Heart
Down To Ride For An ATL Goon
Still Down To Ride For An ATL Goon
In Love With A Heartless Menace
Turned A Good Girl Savage
Finessed His Love
She Got A Thing For A Dope Boy
& Then There Was You 1-2

MAPLE HILLS:

The Sweet Spot
Strokin' The Flame Within' Her Heart
A Blind Encounter

BUTTER RIDGE FALLS:

Remember The Time
Can't Help But Love You
Chocolate Kisses
Tattoo Your Name On My Heart
Capture My Love
Aisha & Gage: Wedding Special
It's Always Been You
Trust Me With You
A Girl Like Me

NEW HAVEN:

Drunk in Love
All He Ever Needed
All He Ever Wanted

PIKEMOORE FALLS:

When A Bad Boy Steals Your Heart series
Ariah & Lucian: A Pikemoore Novel

WEST PIER:

Wrapped Up In His Ruggish Ways
Love In The Studio

THE PARKER SISTERS:

The Parker Sisters: Gianna
The Parker Sisters: Aurora
The Parker Sisters: Sloane

DARK ROMANCE:

Captured Beauty